PALACE ROGUE

WILLIAM COLES

Legend Press Ltd, 51 Gower Street, London, WC1E 6HJ
info@legendpress.co.uk | www.legendpress.co.uk

Contents © William Coles 2023
The right of the above author to be identified as the author of this work has
been asserted in accordance with the Copyright, Designs and Patents Act
1988. British Library Cataloguing in Publication Data available.

Print ISBN 9781915643810
Ebook ISBN 9781915643827
Set in Times.
Cover design by Kari Brownlie | www.karibrownlie.co.uk

William Coles has been a journalist for 30 years and has worked for a number of papers including *The Sun*, *The Express*, *The Mail* and *The Wall Street Journal*.

Visit William at
wcoles.com

and follow him
@WilliamColes1

For Dexter. How's this for a 21st birthday present? X

FOREWORD

Some years ago, a staff reporter on a London tabloid managed to insert himself right into the very heart of Buckingham Palace. Using some made-up references and a lorry-load of chutzpah, this Palace Rogue blagged his way through the interviews to land a full-time job as a royal footman. He held down the post for two months before spectacularly blowing the gaff. The ensuing security scandal was immense.

Though this story of the Palace Rogue is a novel, most of the events are genuine. The general rule of thumb is that the more eye-popping an incident, the greater the likelihood that it actually occurred. And as for that grand romance that was first kindled on the corridors of Buckingham Palace, well... the palace is, as it's always been, an absolute hot bed of sex.

Names have generally been changed to protect the guilty. Some genuine royals' names do, however, appear; I was not going to start inventing new monikers for the royal family. Their conversations have, for the most part, been made up. But these conversations are nevertheless very much in keeping with the relevant royal's character. For instance, Palace staff universally described the queen as being an absolute model of courtesy and polite good manners. Prince Andrew, meanwhile, invariably comes across as a heartless and utterly revolting toad.

CHAPTER 1

As Buckingham Palace readies itself for bed, the queen kneels by her bedside and, just as she's done since childhood, clasps her hands in front of her chest and says her prayers; the teetotal Prince Andrew continues to celebrate his new-found marital freedom by canoodling with another starry-eyed beauty; Prince Edward mumps back from a West End musical, still conjuring with the impossible fantasy of one day becoming a theatre impresario; and in the servants' quarters on the top floor, there is, just as there usually is on a Friday night, the most riotous party.

Never mind that the footmen's and maids' corridors are both supposed to be strictly single sex. The staff have taken a leaf out of the royals' handbook and are not so much corridor-creeping as corridor-swaggering, corridor-caterwauling. Dancing to the sound of a massive boom box as they mooch in and out of the maids' rooms, some of the staff are sneaking kisses, and others are clowning in their fanciest palace frockcoats. All of this royal mayhem is being fuelled by gallons and gallons of gin. Once the property of Her Majesty, it was recently purloined from the royal decanters and smuggled upstairs in the deep pockets of the footmen's tailcoats.

Campion, a maid at the palace for over a year now, loves the party – and so she should. These historic corridor parties, which have been taking place on the upper floors of Buckingham Palace for well over a century, are such a blessed release from the formal day-to-day life that sometimes the snoots, nobs and even the young princes unbend themselves to go upstairs and join the staff at play.

And though history does not relate whether any royal Prince ever trysted with a maid, it's a cast-iron certainty that they did. Though perhaps the more interesting question is whether any of these trystings ever turned into something more meaningful? Are these upstairs-downstairs romances always doomed to disaster, or can they ever turn into a full-fledged relationship with, who knows, marriage and children and a love that lasts for ever? Unlikely, of course, but still nevertheless the slimmest, the very slimmest, of possibilities...

Campion warbles to the hit of the year, Meat Loaf's 'I'd Do Anything for Love'. She has already developed quite a taste for the queen's favourite tipple of gin and Dubonnet, which powers her through to midnight, but – such a sage head on such young shoulders – she retreats to her bedroom at the stroke of twelve. In the early days, when she'd started out at the palace, Campion had often been the last woman standing, but the next day's household chores had proved so problematic (an ancient Sèvres vase smashed, a decrepit corgi doughtily shouldering the blame) that Campion is now always abed by midnight. Tonight, this night of nights, the night when the points will click and when Campion's life will be set on an entirely different course, she just disappears from the party. One moment she's dancing, and the next, she has slipped away so very quietly that her party-mates do not even realise she's gone.

Her room, when she'd inherited it, had been brutally spartan, just a bed, desk and chair, and also a vast black Victorian wardrobe perched up just a little too high on thin spindly legs. In the past year, she has prettified it with rugs and prints so that with the little heater, and the small posy of gardenias in a wineglass by her bedside, the room is positively cosy. She takes a peek from her window, drinking in this stupendous view of London that she never tires of.

Campion brushes and flosses her teeth at the sink in the corner and washes her face with soap and water, idly looking at herself in the mirror. Not bad – could be worse. She unpins her hair, and out springs a thick lion's mane of corkscrew hair, long and dark, dark brown. Her skin is spot and make-up free, though she does like lipstick, which accentuates what she considers to be her finest feature, her superb teeth. What Campion does not realise is that her teeth are only a part of her finest feature, which is her astonishingly brilliant smile; it's even better when she laughs.

Cheeks moisturized, lips Vaselined, she slips on a white T-shirt and some blue cotton shorts and takes herself to her table, where she writes up the short story of the day.

In bed, she curls up with a copy of *Company* magazine, which had most likely been discarded by one of the queen's ladies-in-waiting. *Company* was a downmarket version of *Vogue*, but in 1993, when this story is set, the magazine has considerable clout, containing the usual mix of fashion and beautiful people – and, of course, sex.

The magazine is well-thumbed, and the small freebie bottle of perfume has been taken, though a trace of Givenchy still lingers. Campion flicks past the pictures of all the lovely ladies and lets out a snort of derision, for next month will see a bumper issue of *Company* magazine, when they'll be revealing the year's hundred most eligible people on the planet – fifty men and fifty women. There will be a party for them all as well, where, Campion imagines, the richest male will pair off with the most beautiful female. She smirks at the thought, perhaps a little cynical, though almost certainly, spot on.

In five minutes, the magazine has all but sent her to sleep. She inserts two earplugs to block out the racket that continues outside her room, and in under a minute, she is fast asleep.

Woken by a thin streak of light as the door cracks open, she can't tell how long she's been asleep, but it feels like hours.

'Who's that?'

'Sorry, Campion,' comes the whispered reply. 'We're hiding from the housekeeper.'

She can't see him, but she knows it is the new footman,

Lawrence – barely a week at the palace and already up to no good.

Lawrence slinks into the room, followed by another footman and another, at least four or five; it's difficult to tell.

'Hi, Campion,' says one of them, probably Jono. 'Sorry about this.'

They all start squirming underneath her bed – as if that is going to do them any good if the housekeeper comes in.

The door opens again. Another damn footman slips into the room. 'Sorry!' he slurs. 'She's on... on the warpath!' He peers under the bed. 'Room for one more?'

'Not a chance.'

'May I use y... your wardrobe?'

'Be my guest.'

Campion can't really see his face, but she can certainly see that he's tall and wearing what appears to be a riding hat. In fact, he's wearing a footman's full state livery, the gaudiest of the gaudy, scarlet with gold brocade and puffs and ruffs.

'What the hell are you wearing?'

'I like it very much indeed,' he says in the ponderous manner of the completely pissed.

The wardrobe door shuts to be followed but a moment later by a brisk rat-a-tat on Campion's door. The door opens, and into Campion's room enters the housekeeper, the formidable Mrs Boyd – perhaps not the queen of the palace, but certainly the maids' matriarch.

She flashes a torch straight into Campion's face.

'Campion.'

'Hello?' Campion mumbles. She stretches and yawns as if awaking from the deepest of slumbers.

'Are you alone?'

'Guess I'd have noticed if someone was in my bed.'

The torchlight plays over the bed, the floor, the wardrobe and comes to rest on Campion again.

'Do you have to dazzle me?'

'Is there a man in this room?'

'I can promise you, Mrs Boyd, that there is not a man in the room.'

Mrs Boyd flashes the torch over the bed again. 'They're certainly somewhere on this floor. Half the footmen's rooms are empty.'

'Good luck finding them.'

'Good night.'

The door is all but closed as Mrs Boyd continues her hunt for rogue footmen when a distinctive titter squeaks from underneath the bed.

This time when Mrs Boyd enters the room, she doesn't bother with the torch but switches on the light. She taps the torch in the palm of her hand. 'Out you all come.'

One by one, out they all come. There are five footmen, Campion sees, not four.

Mrs Boyd jerks her head towards the door. 'Get back to your rooms. I'll have words with you in the morning.'

The footmen troop out in silence, Lawrence mouthing the word 'Sorry', and Campion is left alone with the housekeeper. The silence stretches on. Right down to her black dress and her general air of gloomy displeasure, Mrs Boyd seems to style herself on Queen Victoria. She has worked at the palace for over forty years, and though there has been much speculation about Mr Boyd – is he dead? Did he cut and run? – no one knows what happened to him. What they do know is that having clawed her way up the staff ladder, Mrs Boyd now prides herself on being the palace killjoy. There is no party that she does not delight in wrecking; no unseemly laughter that should not be stifled at the first snicker; and as for maids being courted by footmen, that is not only illegal but immoral and has to be snuffed out at the very first flicker of romance. (Though intriguingly, if two footmen start stepping out with each other, quite a common occurrence at the palace, Mrs Boyd turns an indulgent blind eye.)

Campion, readying herself for the storm, removes her ear plugs and places them next to the gardenias on the bedside table. Mrs Boyd prowls from the window to the wardrobe and back to the desk.

'The queen enjoys gardenias,' she says. 'Where did you get these flowers?'

'I was given them.' Campion feels slightly passive lying back on her pillow, so she pulls herself up against the headrest.

'By whom?'

'By an admirer.'

'And what was his name?'

'Why do you assume it was a man?' Given the circumstances, attack seems the best form of defence. Campion herself had liberated the flowers from the queen's private dining room. They had been slightly past their best, and instead of throwing the gardenias away, Campion had taken them up to her bedroom.

Mrs Boyd sighs. She knows perfectly well where the gardenias had come from, but why bother pursuing the matter when she has just caught this girl with five footmen in her room?

'As you know, Campion, your room is strictly off limits to men—'

'I didn't, actually.'

'It would have been almost the first thing I told you when you started working as a maid the summer before last.'

'I must have forgotten,' Campion says. 'I thought we were living in the 20th century.'

'What does that mean?'

'I didn't think it was illegal for an adult woman to invite a man, or indeed several men, into her room. I could understand why a monkey might be off limits—'

'I am not here to talk about chimpanzees.'

Campion sucks her teeth and squints up at Mrs Boyd. 'I might be wrong, but I don't think a chimpanzee is a monkey. It doesn't have a tail for one thing and—'

'Shut up!'

'I'm so sorry, Mrs Boyd, I thought you'd just asked me

what it was to be living in the 20th century.' Campion wipes her mouth. Rather surprisingly, she is enjoying herself. 'And in my inelegant fashion, I was trying to say that having a man, or even five men, in my room was not that heinous an offence considering we are now living in the late 20th century. A monkey, I could understand – or, as you suggested, a chimpanzee, or indeed any other kind of ape. Though I guess men are apes too, so maybe you should simply ban all apes from the bedroom, most particularly the higher form of apes—'

'Did you invite those footmen into your room?'

Campion leans her head and inhales the gardenias. Such a beautiful smell, creamy peach fuzz; they had been her mother's favourite – and how nice to learn that they were the queen's favourite, too. 'No, I did not invite those footmen into my room,' she says, pausing only a heartbeat before adding, 'I insisted on it.'

Mrs Boyd feels nothing but the most extreme vexation. By rights, by all the rules of what is right, dignified and proper, it should be Campion who is squirming, but not a bit of it, for it is she, the Buckingham Palace housekeeper, who is being bested.

'You lied to me. You promised there were no men in this room.'

'I don't lie – ever,' Campion says. 'You asked if there was a man in the room, and I said, in fact, I promised that there was not a man here – and as I'm sure you'll remember, there wasn't a man. There were five of them.' She admires her fingernails, trim and clean, though there is a hangnail that is just asking to be bitten off. Her thumbnail strays towards her teeth before she has another thought. 'I was amazed they all managed to fit under the bed – three or four, maybe, but five!'

'Yes, five men under your bed, after midnight.'

'I've only just realised, Mrs Boyd, it might even be a record.'

'What were they doing here?'

Campion chews at the rogue dag and inspects her thumbnail.

It was a pleasingly clean break. 'I'm not sure,' Campion says. 'I believe they were playing hide and seek. Thinking about it, sardines seems more likely. That explains why five of them were under my bed. Thank goodness they weren't in my bed – that really would have taken some explaining!'

Mrs Boyd's lips pucker as if about to primly spit out a pip. 'You are the most flippant palace maid I have ever come across.'

'Thank you, Mrs Boyd.'

'And we shall see if you are as flippant at noon tomorrow when I have decided how you will be disciplined.'

Campion smiles. 'I look forward to it.'

'We shall see.' If it had been a few years back, in the seventies, or even the good old sixties, Mrs Boyd would have taken two smart steps across the room and slapped Campion as hard as she could across the cheek. As it is, corporal punishment has shamefully been banned at the palace, and now all she and her fellow officers can do to the minions is dock their salaries, fire them, or just do their damnedest to make their lives a misery. But if there is one thing of which Mrs Boyd is certain, it is that she'll be reporting this incident to the master of the household first thing in the morning, not over breakfast, but after he's had his porridge and toast and after he has retired to his office with his third cup of coffee.

Without another word, Mrs Boyd turns on her heel and switches off the light. She has not quite shut the door before Campion has the last word. 'Good night, Mrs Boyd.'

Campion is left to ponder on whether she'll be demoted, put on light duties, or whether, indeed, her palace career is about to be brought to an abrupt close. If worst comes to worst, she'll have no problem finding another job, but it'd be a shame. She'd miss the whole giddy palace family. She'd miss her friends, the other maids, the footmen, the cooks, the grooms, the protection officers, and the chauffeurs; she'd miss the glorious routine. She'd miss the stories that she'd no longer be able to tell her grandparents. The previous Christmas, just after they'd taken Campion out for lunch in Ballater, near Balmoral, they'd walked past the queen. Campion's pop-eyed grandparents, Paul and Mary, had been utterly tongue-tied. Her Majesty had been charm itself.

She'd miss the art. It's Campion's daily thrill to view some of the greatest pictures on Earth. Very often, when she starts her shift at 7 a.m., she has the whole of the Palace Picture Gallery to herself. It is the very largest room in the palace, and though she does indeed dust the pictures most diligently, she can also spend hours drinking them in. There are a few pictures that she never tires of. Rubens' *Assumption of the Virgin*, with various chubby cherubs aiding the Virgin Mary on her way to heaven. Hals' *Portrait of a Man*, of some now long forgotten gentleman, with a white ruff so realistic you could all but touch it. Agatha Bas, painted by Rembrandt when he was at the very height of his power. Then, of course, there was the Vermeer, a woman playing at a keyboard as a man stands next to her.

There was one other thing that Campion would miss about her life at the palace. She would no longer be the queen's storyteller. As far as she knows, she is the only person in the whole palace, the whole world, who tells stories to the queen.

It started a year ago.

Campion had been cleaning in the Picture Gallery, a little dusting here, some vacuuming there, when she had been waylaid by the Vermeer. She'd been staring at the picture for so long that she'd lost track of time.

The queen had broken into Campion's reverie. 'I like it too.'

Campion quickly recovered and gave the queen a full elegant curtsy. 'Your Majesty.'

The difference between the two women could not have been more stark – Campion in her maid's outfit, a simple white dress, duster in her hand, and the queen in her most formal Robes of State. Intriguingly she was wearing not shoes but fluffy pink slippers. They poked out from underneath her gown as she walked through the gallery.

'Good morning, Campion.' Campion was surprised that the queen knew her name – and utterly astonished when the queen came to join her in front of the Vermeer. 'What do you like about the picture?'

And so, it began. Campion told her a story about the couple in the picture, a good story. Though Campion had not expected it, a week later, the queen found her again in the Picture Gallery. She had obviously enjoyed herself because every few days after that, she would seek Campion out, and Campion would talk about art and about artists, and the queen, who had not been spun a story since she was a little girl, would stand mesmerised as Campion conjured with words and made up stories about the palace pictures. Once, when the queen was down with flu, Campion was requested to keep her company in her bedroom, where for two hours she sat by the queen's bedside and told her a story about Guercino's *Libyan Sibyl* – and the queen, though a bit under the weather, had lapped it up.

Campion sighs as she turns in her bed. So yes, if it does end badly tomorrow, she'd miss her friends, and she'd miss the art, but she'd also very much miss being the queen's storyteller. For, who else in the world has the unbelievable privilege of having the monarch of England, Scotland, and all of the United Kingdom hanging upon her every word?

A shifting creak from the edge of her room is followed, not a second later, by a crack of splintering wood. Campion has a brief glimpse of massive blackness toppling towards her and then the most deafening explosion of noise. Her bed jumps clean off the floorboards.

And after that – nothing.

Campion lies back on the pillow, eyes staring at the ceiling. Those damn footmen. As if five of them hiding under her bed wasn't bad enough, it now seems that the sixth one, the idiot in the gold livery, has smashed her wardrobe.

CHAPTER 2

Into this royal idyll has been inserted a parasite, a bottom feeder, a scum-sucking low-life – by that, I mean myself, Kim. An upstanding (and indeed *outstanding*) member of Her Majesty's Press.

My palace career had been launched six weeks earlier.

It was just another blissful day in *The Sun* newsroom, with me, your humble narrator, being screamed at by Spike, the certifiable deputy editor. As ever and as always, Spike was unhappy about a *Mirror* exclusive that we had missed. More specifically, perhaps, a *Mirror* exclusive that *I* had missed.

So, on that day of days, I arrived at the News International complex early.

Fort Wapping was home to not just Murdoch's newsrooms but also his printworks. *The Sunday Times'* staff were based in an old rum warehouse, but *The Sun* and its sister paper, the *News of the World*, were both on the sixth floor of a vast grey monolith, which looked like a shoebox on its side. The building had originally been a warehouse, which explained why there were so few windows. In *The Sun* newsroom, the only natural light came from a few skylights that had been punched into the ceiling. Most of the time, you couldn't tell if it was three in the morning or three in the afternoon.

In the canteen, I scanned the day's papers and quickly realised the size of the impending storm. It had been some piffling story about Prince Andrew being the captain of a minesweeper, *HMS Cottesmore*, which had come under attack from an Exocet missile. We'd given the story three paragraphs. *The Mirror* had given it the full treatment, world exclusive splash, plus more of Bain's interminable screed on pages four and five.

Bain was effectively my opposite at *The Mirror*. Bain by name and Bane by nature. The pair of us duelled daily over the same stories, flamming and exaggerating and seeing just how far we could stretch a story without turning it into outright fiction. In general, I could stretch with the best of them, but Bain was a wholesale story-stretcher.

Coffee in hand, I sauntered upstairs and once again admired *The Sun's* life-enhancing motto. This legend had been sited above the main entrance to the newsroom, and even cynical world-weary hacks such as myself tended to square our shoulders just a little when we walked underneath. For most other businesses, if they were to have the same motto, it would seem utterly laughable. It's a motto which wouldn't work for a bank, school, or shop, but somehow, above *The Sun's* security doors, it worked – "Walk tall. You're entering *Sun* country!". It was a call to arms, for it perfectly summed up the characteristics that were required of a *Sun* staff reporter: impishness, chutzpah, and ocean-going cheek.

I had hoped to mildly make my way over to my desk to read the boring broadsheets and sip my coffee. That was not to be. Spike was already doing what he loved to do, standing by the news desk, giving the full hair-drier treatment to the four news editors – who, in their turn, were doing what they so loved to do, which was to suck it up like sponges. (One news editor was famously lampooned as a "Human Sponge" in a half-page *Sun* article. Readers were even invited to call up his direct line to abuse him, which they did. In vast numbers.)

I have never been very sponge-like – it blights my soul to have to suck it up, especially from such abrasive toads as the deputy editor.

'Morning, team. Morning, Spike,' I said, the jaunty general greeting his troops.

Spike goggled at me before wiping some of the spittle off his chin. 'What did you say?'

'Morning, Spike. How's it going?'

'What? You!' Spike, small, spiky – I think I'd have preferred a wolf on acid – was so irked he could hardly string a word together. 'You've got a nerve!'

'It's been said.'

'What the hell is this?' He picked up a copy of *The Mirror* with Bain's baloney on the front page. 'They're splashing with it – and you thought fit to give it three paragraphs!' He rolled up the paper and started poking me in the stomach.

'Don't do that,' I said.

'Why not, you piece of shit.'

He gave me another poke.

'Because I am quite close to losing my temper, and if I do, I might lay you out.'

'What?' he said. 'Are you threatening me?'

'I'd claim self-defence, and I reckon I've got quite a few witnesses who'd back me up.'

Over the last few months, I had spent some time pondering who would win in a fight between Spike and me. I was bigger, younger, and probably stronger, but Spike was definitely dirtier. If he got me to the ground, he'd have no problem at all in sinking his teeth into my more tender parts. Still – such idle daydreams would have to wait. 'Before you go off on another one, I thought *The Sun* printed hard news, as opposed to made-up bollocks.'

'And?'

'I checked out this story with the MoD yesterday. No missile came within twenty miles of *HMS Cottesmore*. Got it on tape if you want to listen. I mean, of course, I could have flammed it up like Bain did if that's what you want me to start doing, but this *Mirror* story has been made up. It did not happen.'

[Just a point of note, Your Honour, this was all largely true – except for the bit about having it on tape. I had indeed called up the Ministry of Defence the previous day, but I certainly hadn't bothered to tape the conversation. Who on Earth taped MoD spokesmen? If they ever had anything worth saying, it'd already have been leaked by a thrusting junior minister.]

For a moment, Spike deflated. Only for a moment. 'Don't give me that holier-than-thou shit,' he said. 'You make up more stories than anyone else in the newsroom. I trust you about as much as a wet fart after twelve pints and a cheap curry.'

'That is an image I won't be able to unsee,' I said. Stella, the prettiest of the news desk secretaries, appeared to gag. 'I'm straight as a die, Spike. My stories are so rock solid you could run them on *Reuters*. The Press Association would be happy to have them. Why, the *Financial Times* was on at me only last week, begging me to come join them. And I can tell you something, Spike, I was sorely tempted.'

Spike had the good grace to laugh. 'All right, all right – shut up and bring me some stories.' He wandered off in search of fresh meat while Robert, the news editor, tapped his hands together in silent applause.

I gave the team a modest bow and skulked to my desk.

The newsroom was simply vast, a full acre of grey walls and grey desks, fifty yards across and maybe a hundred long. On the walls were huge copies of some of *The Sun's* greatest splashes: 'Gotcha!', 'Freddy Starr Ate My Hamster', and my favourite, and the front page that was said to have won the 1992 election for John Major, a picture of Neil Kinnock's head in a light bulb, alongside the headline 'If Kinnock Wins Today Will The Last Person to Leave Britain Please Turn Out The Lights'.

Over by the entrance were the news and picture desks, with the news reporters within easy shouting distance. Towards the far end were the sports hacks and the features luvvies, and bang in the centre of this thrumming febrile newsroom were the subs' desks and the real power, the back bench. They got none of the glory. They never had bylines or picture bylines, and they never got to claim lavish lunches at the Caprice on their expenses, but they decided the headlines, the layouts, and the daily bill of fare.

Not my cup of tea at all – reporters, though mere cannon fodder in the general pecking order, were still the guys who brought in the actual exclusives. They also had most of the fun because they were out on the road hunting down stories, not to mention racking up astronomical expenses.

Reporters had begun to drift in, and Grubby, a photographer, blundered over. The rest of the monkeys (technical term for a photographer, as opposed to the reporters who are known as 'blunts') were out on the road, so I was the next best bet for a chat and a sympathetic word. Like the news reporters, he wore a suit, though somehow on Grubby, it always hung like a smock. His un-ironed grey shirt was half in and half out of his trousers, his tie was askew, and his black slip-ons were, as usual, scuffed and dirty. Hence why he was called Grubby. I never knew his first name.

'Saw an amazing thing coming down The Mall.' He lounged on the desk next to me, casually slopping coffee onto the keyboard.

'Good morning, Grubby.' I looked up from my pile of papers. 'What did you see?'

'This royal coach, four horses, groom, and a couple of footmen all in red. It was on its way to Buckingham Palace. Hell of a jam behind it. Who do you think was in it?'

'Probably a middle-aged guy in a top hat, while sitting opposite him was a glamorous younger woman dressed as if she were going to one of Her Majesty's garden parties.'

'Were you there?'

'It'll be some new ambassador to the UK,' I said. 'One of the perks of the job is they get presented to Her Majesty. Though rather than sending out a royal limo to pick 'em up, she sends them one of her coaches, complete with flunkies.'

Grubby belched. 'Sorry – had a fry-up. So what do the flunkies do?'

'The flunkies do what flunkies have done since the first syllable of recorded time. They open doors. They close doors. They bow. They scrape. They lick so many boots their tongues are permanently stained black with boot polish. They do whatever they can to make the boss man—'

'Or boss woman.'

'The boss women love it more than anyone. It is the job of the flunky to make the boss feel like a boss. The more flunkies you've got, the more of a boss you are.'

'Bowing? Scraping? Opening doors?' Grubby ticked them off on his fingers. 'Not to mention boot licking? It's got your name written all over it.'

I snickered as I hurled a mouldy apple core at his head. Preposterous. The very thought of it. As if a serious muck-raking reporter would ever demean himself in such a way… That said, I did once have to dress up as a chicken for a story, but royal boot licking? Never!

Finding news stories is a skill that takes years to acquire. Route one is to start by reading all the daily papers. I usually start off with the populars, particularly *The Sun's* main rivals, *The Mirror* and *The Mail* (perhaps surprisingly, *Sun* reporters rarely spend much time reading their own paper, which, from the very moment it is printed, have become yesterday's news). Then, sufficiently lubed up, I move onto the broadsheets, or, as they are known on Fleet Street, the unpopulars.

Of course, there were hundreds and hundreds of journalists doing the exact same thing every day – reading all the papers and sifting through all the news, just sniffing for anything at all that was just a little out of the ordinary. Some tiny thing that set your news antennae quivering as you realised that with just a slight tweak and a small change of perspective, this workaday stick of a story could be transformed into a splash. (A stick is a thin column-wide story, no more than ten paragraphs, which usually runs down the side of a page).I'd seen it happen not a year earlier. An agency report had come over about a house fire where the only thing to have survived the blaze was a picture above the mantelpiece of a crying boy. The agency story ended with a throwaway line that there was talk of the picture being cursed. One of the back bench had happened to spot the story and went berserk because they'd twigged what none of the rest of us had spotted, that these *Crying Boy* pictures were immensely popular with *Sun* readers. The story was slapped on the front page with the headline, 'Curse of the Crying Boy', and within the week, *The Sun's* army of readers were clamouring for their favourite newspaper to help dispose of all their cursed pictures. It took three immense juggernauts to cart all the thousands of *Crying Boy* pictures to the dump, where they were then ceremonially incinerated.

A great story that ran for weeks – and all because one hack had had the quivering news sense to find it. That was the theory, anyway. Most of the time, though, when you were leafing through the unpopulars, you needed matchsticks to keep your eyes open.

That day, I turned to my least favourite unpopular, the *Daily Telegraph* – all huffing and puffing from the great 'Disgruntleds of Tunbridge Wells' – and turned the page onto the small ads. I blearily scanned the page, just wanting to get this chore over with, when there was a sudden ping in my brain, as clear and piercing as a bell. It might have been down to the conversation I'd just had with Grubby – more likely, it was down to sheer blind luck – but in seconds, I could see the whole thing in its beautiful entirety.

Normally you pitched your ideas to the news editor, who was the middleman between the reporters and the editors, but I knew that if this thing was going to work, then it would have to be top secret. And since newsrooms were as leaky as the *Titanic*, that'd mean sharing the idea with just one person – our deputy editor, Spike.

Spike was editing *The Sun* that day, so he had taken over the editor's office. Walking into the executive suites was like going from an East London street market straight into the gracious grandeur of the Reform Club. In the anteroom, there was a fragrant secretary, pot plants, and a simmering pot of coffee. The room even had windows. For the first time that day, I realised it was raining.

Maria looked up from her computer. 'Don't see you in here very often, Kim.'

'I tend to avoid the editor's office if I possibly can,' I said. 'Could I have a brief word with Spike if he's free?'

'He's just in with one of the advertising execs. Can I tell him what it's about?'

'I'll wait.'

'Like some coffee then?'

'Love one.'

I stared out at the rain and, like hacks the world over, started to wonder if my brilliant idea was, in fact, plain crazy. It was bonkers! It would never work – couldn't possibly work. Spike would just laugh me out of the office, and I would be packed on my way with a volley of insults pinging at my ears.

The editor's door opened, and the advertising executive, clutching at some ofthe next day's proofs, scurried out and left. After a brief query from Maria, I continued to gaze at the rain.

'Spike will see you now.'

With just a slight feeling of trepidation, I walked in. Spike had his feet on the desk, which some might have taken as a sign of disrespect, though I preferred to see those tasselled loafers as an act of comradeship – nothing's too good for the workers! Maria brought him a coffee; sugar and cream were added, the coffee was stirred, and then the door closed.

'Come to tender your resignation?' Beetling eyebrows watched me over the top of his coffee cup.

'No,' I said. 'But I am thinking of applying for another job.'

'Going back to the *Wilts and Glos Standard*? I hear they're in need of a sub.'

'You've been doing your homework.'

'Got your file right here.' He waved it at me. I was surprised at how thick it was. 'It's even got your rotten CV.' He sniffed as he inspected it. 'Only the two spelling mistakes. Surprised we even gave you a shift.'

'Would you like to hear what job I'm thinking of going for?'

'Amaze me. The world's worst [*The Guardian*] is looking for an editor.'

'How about this?' I placed the *Daily Telegraph* in front of him and circled the advert. It wasn't much to look at, barely two inches square.

"Applications are invited for the appointment of a trainee footman based at Buckingham Palace. The successful candidate should have good communication skills, be able to work unsupervised and within a team, and possess a friendly, polite disposition."

Spike put down his coffee and took his feet off the desk. Then, after looking at the ad, he swivelled his chair to gaze out of the window. I usually knew the drill in these circumstances. If the boss didn't want to say anything, you then sweated it out and didn't say anything either. But after a minute, I was a bit unnerved, and I cracked.

'So, what do you think?'

'Shut up and let me think.'

I kept my mouth shut. I could have joined Spike in staring meditatively out of the window – What did it all mean, this rain, these scudding clouds, this brief span that we had on earth? – but instead I wandered over to a picture on the oak-panelled wall. I had briefly seen the picture before, but never had the time to study it up close. It was a Beryl Cook, and, like most of Beryl's paintings, it was of some fat ladies.

That was what Beryl was famous for – fat lady pictures. They have a very distinctive feel – see one, and you'd recognise her style anywhere.

Those particular fat ladies were out shopping in a market. I quite liked it. It was worth an absolute fortune, but more interesting by far than the picture itself was the story behind it.

A year or two earlier, *The Sun* had caught a fading pop star cheating on his wife with the nanny. (My innate discretion naturally forbids me from actually naming this pint-size star.) *The Sun* ran the story for two or three days before the nation's outraged attention moved on to something else. As for the fading rock star, he reacted in a most unusual way. He did not rant about the iniquities of the press. He did not sue. Instead, he rewarded *The Sun's* editor with the very costly Beryl Cook picture that I was currently inspecting. I guess the fading pop star had hoped that, after the gift-giving, he and the editor were the best of pals and that in the future, *The Sun* would kindly desist from sniffing around his private affairs. In this, he was sorely mistaken. Not a year later, the fading pop star had once again taken up with the same nanny, and once again, it ended up all over the front page of *The Sun*. (All right – seeing as you're so insistent, I'll tell you the pop star's name. It was Chris de Burgh, an on-the-small-side crooner who had a massive hit with 'Lady in Red'. He also, as it happens, bore an uncanny resemblance to our vulpine deputy editor. *The Sun's* splash headline was, as I remember, 'Lady in Bed'.)

Spike wheeled back to the desk and made a call. A minute later, the news editor, Robert, came into the office. He was a little surprised to see his most congenial reporter already in the room.

'What's up?' he said. He was in his young thirties, bald, with a little trim of hair above his ears, and always exceedingly polite. If you met him, you would never have believed that he worked on *The Sun*, let alone that he was one of its key executives.

'Robert, you're going to find this very hard to believe, but Kim has had a good idea.'

'Capital!' Robert said.

'Yes, he's going to be applying for another job.'

'Oh,' Robert said. I could have kissed the guy because he looked genuinely crestfallen.

'You will be relieved to hear that Kim will still remain on *The Sun* staff.'

'So, what job's he after?'

All was quickly explained, and then Maria was called for more coffees, and when she came in, she saw the three of us sitting cosily on the editor's armchairs. I don't know what she made of it, but it was certainly the first time I'd ever had coffee in the editor's office.

Spike was ecstatic. 'You'll get all the gen from the palace, all the gossip, and we'll dress it up as an outrageous security scandal!' he gloated.

'What are you going to do about Kim's references?' Robert said.

'I used to work in a hotel,' I said. 'That'll do for one.'

'And one of your toff pals will provide the second,' Spike said with what seemed to me rather misplaced confidence. 'There's only one thing that worries me. You're too damn cocky.'

'Cocky?' I said. 'Moi?'

'You, Kim, put the cock into cocking things up.'

CHAPTER 3

All in all, it has been a rather testing night for Campion.
Getting that damn footman out of the wardrobe had been a
tough one. The wardrobe was too heavy to lift, so in the end,
she'd had to smash the back with a fire extinguisher. When
he finally left the room, the bleary footman had promised to
make it up to her. With what she can't imagine. Probably a
pint of gin that'd been swiped from the royal decanters.

A palace maid's uniform is not at all flattering. Campion
wears a stiff, unlined white dress made of polycotton.
Underneath is a pair of white knickers which, as per palace
regulations, won't show through her dress – though if you
look close enough, you can see that her knickers are, in fact,
decorated with little red roses. Her maid's uniform is topped
off with a cream cardigan. A year ago, this cardigan had been
a good fit, but it has been hand-washed so often that it has
long since stretched out of shape.

She's already put in a couple of hours of dusting – though
not vacuuming, as that is not allowed until after 9 a.m., in
order to avoid disturbing the royals' beauty sleep – and after
breakfast, it'll be up to the nursery corridor to clean up various
royal bedrooms. The one suite of rooms she particularly
detests is Prince Andrew's. Campion is one of two maids who
look after Prince Andrew's apartment. Though she doesn't see
much of him, as he spends most of his time on board *HMS
Cottesmore*, she's already made up her mind that he is – how
to put this charitably? – a total tosser.

For the moment, at least, she wants to have her breakfast in the staff canteen and not give another second of her time to Prince Andrew. She loads up her tray with coffee and two slices of toast and finds a small table in the corner so that she can just – please! – have a few minutes to herself. She buries her nose into her old copy of *Company* magazine – and if that doesn't give people the message that she wants to be left alone, then nothing will. She turns another page. This particular article seems to have been particularly well-thumbed. 'Get the most out of your sex life!' Campion snorts – well, finding a boyfriend would be a start.

A row has kicked off on one of the nearby tables. The queen's two most senior footmen, Gavin and the neurotic Jono, are squabbling. Gavin hits Jono over the head with a rolled-up copy of *The Sun*, so Jono responds by pulling Gavin's hair.

'You sold that story. I know you did,' Gavin squawked.

'I certainly did not leak that story, you mincing queen,' Jono said. 'If anyone sold it to *The Sun*, it was you!'

'How dare you?' Gavin hits Jono again.

Campion sighs and butters her toast. These breakfast spats are quite common in the palace canteen – and usually have nothing whatsoever to do with the matter at hand. The much more probable cause is that, during the previous night's hijinks, Jono rebuffed Gavin's advances. Though it was equally possible that he welcomed somebody else into his bedroom, perhaps even a woman. Two-timing was commonplace in the palace.

'Only three of us knew that Bendicks bit Agatha – just me, you, and Agatha. Now, I know I didn't leak it, and Agatha would never have leaked it, so it must have been you.'

Campion can't resist. It would be easier just to let these two idiots continue to scrap it out, but at heart, Campion is a peacemaker.

'Guys,' she calls out. 'Not that I want to intrude, but there isn't a person in this room who doesn't know that Bendicks bit Agatha.'

'Quite,' Jono says. 'I heard you blabbing about it to one of the chauffeurs.'

'That's neither here nor there,' Gavin says. 'I overheard you on the payphones. You were selling the story.'

'That was in a phone call to my mother, you wally. And how dare you listen to my private conversations.'

'Listen in to your private conversations? You, with your foghorn voice, I'd have heard you from the Tower of London—'

Campion is distracted for a moment by a footman standing by her table. She looks up.

'Mind if I join you?'

She gestures to the other side of the table.

It is Lawrence, the new footman who joined a week ago, the new footman about whom there is something decidedly off. He carefully places his black tailcoat on a chair and sits opposite her. 'Sorry about last night,' he says. 'I do hope you're not in too much trouble.'

'Nothing at all,' Campion says.

'Well… I'm sorry all the same.' He pours milk onto his cornflakes as Gavin and Jono continue to bark at each other. 'What are they so upset about?'

'Gavin has accused Jono of leaking a story to *The Sun*,' Campion says. 'I pointed out that this story has been the talk of the palace for over a week now, but Gavin is still convinced that Jono was the mole.'

'How naughty.' He smiles as if at some secret joke. 'Would that be the story about Prince Andrew's Norfolk Terrier biting a maid on the leg?'

'Bendicks definitely takes after his master,' Campion says. 'Agatha was in a really bad way. Her tights were all ripped, and the dog had drawn blood. She had to have a tetanus jab. And you know what Andrew did when he heard the news? He just laughed!'

'What a creep. And because he's a creep, one day, he'll get his comeuppance. And the beautiful thing is, Campion, that you won't have to do anything about it. It will just happen. You know what Sun Tzu said?'

'The guy who wrote *The Art of War*?'

'If you sit by the riverbank long enough, you will see the bodies of your enemies float by. I don't know how long we'll have to wait. Might be twenty years, might be thirty, but one day you will see Prince Andrew's body floating by.'

'I wish.'

'And I'll tell you one more thing. His undoing will not be because of his entitled behaviour or foul-mouthed rants. It'll be something that's completely out of left field.' He takes a small spoonful of cornflakes. 'So, why's the dog called Bendicks?'

'Named after Fergie's favourite chocolate.'

'Could have been worse. Imagine if she loved a Flake.'

Campion snickers. 'Or a KitKat. Can you see Prince Andrew in Hyde Park yelling, "Come here, KitKat!"'

Lawrence leans over and looks at her magazine. '*Company* magazine?' he says with a wry smile. 'Haven't seen that in a while. They have an annual party for beautiful people.'

'How do you know that?'

'I've been,' Lawrence says before coughing. He wipes a cornflake from his scarlet waistcoat. 'By that, I mean I had a friend who went to last year's party.'

'What was it like?'

'Society bimbos, society meatheads, a lot of money, and a lot of very beautiful people. You'd love it.'

'I haven't been to a party in ages,' Campion says wistfully. Of course, there'd been the staff parties in the palace, stocked with stolen gin, but a party party? A party where she can dress up and rub shoulders with the dazzlingly beautiful? She hasn't been to a party like that since she started work at the palace. In fact, the last time she dressed to kill had probably been her twenty-first birthday. Her poor old grandparents had scrimped and saved – they didn't go on a holiday for three years – until they'd finally saved enough money for Campion to take nine friends to a private room in The Snooty Fox in nearby Tetbury. Now that was a night! And it's about time she had another one. Well, a girl can dream.

'I better go and sort out the teddies,' Campion says.

'Is it really true about the teddies?'

'I am afraid it is.'

Campion drops her tray off and picks up her basket of cleaning things. Then it is up to the nursery corridor with the principal royal suites. Prince Andrew had split from his wife the previous year, so his rooms are a monument to his ocean-going obsessive compulsive disorder. This OCD reaches its pinnacle in his bedroom, which contains seventy-two teddies. They are mainly the old-style Steiff teddies, and most are dressed in hats and military uniforms. Since it is morning and since the prince is usually up and about doing whatever he does to pass the day, the seventy-two teddies are dotted all around the room. The smaller teddies have all been neatly stacked in size order in an unused fireplace near the four-poster. More bears have been placed on the floor at the foot of the bed, while Andrew's two favourite bears, both in sailor suits, have been positioned on two wooden thrones on either side of the bed.

Campion heads off to clean the bathroom. Towels and a bathrobe are on the floor, and, as usual, the toilet looks like something out of a cheap nightclub. After the bathroom, she vacuums the carpets and makes the bed, but finally, there is no getting away from it. It is time for her least favourite job on earth, the teddies.

Frankly, the whole setup just gives Campion the creeps. What sort of guy has this number of teddies and is so insistent that every day, and every night, they all have to be positioned in exactly the right place? Fair enough, Campion thinks, if Andrew personally wants to place all his teddies so very precisely on the bed or in the fireplace – or indeed, if he is so minded, placing them in a worshipful circle around his toilet. But for this thirty-three-year-old prat to insist that every morning and evening, his maids have to waste their time putting these damn teddies in their exact designated position. It is bonkers!

She scoops up all the teddies in the fireplace and dumps them in the middle of the bed. The teddies on the floor are also tossed onto the bed, along with the king and queen. Might be quite nice to start drop-kicking the teddies onto the bed – and won't that just be a magical moment if Prince Andrew blunders into his bedroom just as King Ted is punted against the back wall?

Campion retrieves the necessary laminated sheet from the top drawer of the bureau, and then, after taking off her shoes, she kneels in the middle of the bed. Each teddy has to be checked off against the laminated sheet and then placed in its specific position on the bed. Six of the smallest teddies are in the front row, followed by another row of six slightly larger teddies, continuing for row after row until the final twelfth row with the six biggest teddies.

After thirty minutes on the bed, Campion admires her handiwork. If the teddies belonged to a six-year-old girl, and if that little girl spent all morning constructing these rows and rows of teddies, then it may almost be cute. A parent may be *slightly* perturbed to see all the teddies arranged line abreast, as if on parade, but kids deserve a little latitude. But for a prince – a prince who's fought in the Falklands! – to be so obsessed with his teddies is positively creepy. God, it gets on her wick that, for the prince's odious pleasure, she has to waste her time with these teddies, while in the evening, Anne, his other maid, has to take all the teddies off the bed and put them on the floor and in the fireplace and on the two thrones – and then, the queasy kicker, she has to hide a ghastly grey monkey in a cupboard, or a boot, or under the bed, so that Prince Andrew can round off his evening by playing his own weird version of hunt the thimble. How come no one has ever had the gumption to point out to the prince that it is a tad odd? Perhaps no other royal knows about Andrew's teddy obsession because if they did, he'd be a laughing stock. Certainly, if Campion had a brother who was even half as irritating as Prince Andrew, she'd bring up his teddy fetish every chance she got.

Campion clambers off the bed, pulls the bedspread straight, and returns the laminated sheet to its drawer. The bedroom is given a final once-over – seems fine enough. She tries to look at the bedroom objectively, as if she is a woman seeing it for the first time – as if, foul thought, she is a prospective girlfriend. Well, if Andrew had escorted her to this bedroom, and if she'd seen all the hideous pillows and all those teddies, then no matter *how* desperate she'd been to bag a royal, she'd have run an absolute mile.

Andrew comes into the bedroom wearing chinos and a simply hideous Argyle-pattern jumper with large pink and black diamonds.

'Morning, Campion,' he says. 'Never seen you in my bedroom before. Bed comfy enough for you?'

She ignores the question. 'Good morning, Your Royal Highness.'

He goes over to his dressing table and retrieves his golf putter.

'Wouldn't want you to start getting ideas.' He sniggers and walks out of the room.

The innuendo's obvious. What an utterly revolting thought – a revolting thought from a revolting man.

It is now gone 11 a.m. Still vexed and stewing, Campion moves into another suite of rooms. Perhaps Mrs Boyd really will give her the sack, in which case she can get a job at one of the posh hotels and at least double her miserable £600-a-month salary. She'd earn more as a street sweeper.

Campion tuts as she goes into the bedroom. The valet has left the curtains closed. She tugs them open, then pushes the sash windows to clear the fug of stale alcohol. That done, she takes a look around the bedroom for the first time. Somebody's in the bed. She goes over to have a look. The man is still asleep – and still wearing the same state livery that he was wearing the previous evening when he'd finally clambered out of the back of Campion's smashed wardrobe. She gives him a poke with her duster. The man grunts and turns over. So the next time, she whacks him over the year. He shot bolt upright.

'You've got a nerve,' she says, and hits him again round the other ear.

CHAPTER 4

There was high excitement in *The Sun* offices. I'd brought in the letter I'd just received from Buckingham Palace.

My mercurial deputy editor was absolutely pinging off the walls. 'You might even do it, you big ugly mutt!' he gloated, reading and re-reading the letter I'd tossed onto his desk. It was a formal note requesting me to present myself to the sergeant footman, a Mr Simon Brook, for an interview.

Spike, Robert, and I had spent far more time on my bogus CV than we'd ever spent on a splash. Spike had still been mumping about the CV and covering letter even after the third draft. 'It looks too polished,' he'd said. 'This lad has spent the last couple of years working for a firm of caterers in London. He doesn't know the first thing about writing a formal letter.' He then uttered four words that I'd never dreamed I'd hear from a *Sun* executive. 'Make it more clunky.' Then, like a pungent silverback gorilla watching over its firstborn, he stood behind my shoulder as I re-jigged the covering letter, positively crowing with approval as I added a spelling mistake. (It was 'accommodation' – always a tricky one.)

A week after I'd received the good news from Buckingham Palace, Spike went into full mother hen mode. The suits I wore at *The Sun* were deemed too flashy, so I was sent off to buy a grey single-breasted suit from Marks and Spencer's.

Fleet Street reporters tended to dress in inverse proportion to the status of their papers. Thus, *Times* and *Telegraph* reporters tended to wear tweedy jackets, while reporters from

The Sun and *The Mirror* invariably wore immaculate blue suits. Some *News of the World* reporters actually wore three-piece suits, as if that would somehow make you think that those exquisites would never, ever stoop to phone hacking. As for those too-cool-for-school reporters on the world's worst [*The Guardian*], they turned up for jobs wearing jeans and black leather jackets. I ask you!

On the eve of my big day at the palace, Spike even opened a bottle of champagne. I was wearing my new M&S suit, complete with blue cotton shirt and stripy tie, hair Brylcreemed to perfection and acidic tongue properly under control. I was the very model of a demure palace footman.

I sat primly on the edge of my chair while Spike lounged on the windowsill. Robert was monitoring proceedings from an armchair. It had been decided that only the three of us would be in on the secret – though, of course, my hyper-vigilant colleagues had not failed to notice that I had been having all this wonderful quality time with both the deputy editor and the news editor.

'What the hell have you been doing in there?' Grubby asked after buttonholing me in the lift.

'We're staging a coup,' I'd airily replied. 'I will become the new deputy editor. You shall be my valet.'

He continued to pester, but he got no change.

You might well wonder why *The Sun's* editor wasn't in on the loop. Perfectly simple answer. Though the editor was the titular boss of the paper and represented *The Sun* at various worthy functions, it was Spike, his deputy, who had the real power. Very similar, actually, to the relationship that the boneheaded US President George Bush Jr had with his vice-president Dick Cheney.

Spike topped up his glass; he did not offer any to me. 'Why do you want to work at the palace?'

'I've always been a great admirer of the royal family,' I said. 'And though I've enjoyed working in the catering trade, I think it's time to stretch my wings. I need a new challenge, and I can think of no greater honour than being allowed to serve at Buckingham Palace.'

'Too greasy?' Robert said.

'Maybe,' Spike said. 'But I think they like them pretty greasy at the Palace. Tell me about your day-to-day work.'

'Ah, yes,' I said. Now, this was the one part of the interview where I was on slightly dodgy ground. My godfather, Ronnie, owned a firm of London caterers and had been delighted to provide me with a bogus reference. Over the last three years, I had, apparently, been one of his most diligent staff members, hard-working, sober, and discreet – not overly endowed in the top level, but certainly more than capable of opening palace doors and polishing Her Majesty's silverware. That was all just fantastic, except that I hadn't bothered to find out what the day-to-day job entailed.

'Well, I tend to be one of the backroom staff, working in the office, dealing with the orders, that sort of thing—'

'You are a complete idiot!'

'What's wrong with that?'

'What's wrong with it is that you said on that damn CV that we spent so long concocting that you were the smiling, sycophantic face of the firm, the front of house, the meeter and greeter who signs the punters up.'

'As I was about to add,' I said. 'Along with my backroom duties, I am also very much front of house – I am the firm's interface between staff and clientele.'

'And don't forget it! So, I see you used to work in a hotel, the Knoll House in Studland. Why did you leave?'

'Very good question,' I said. Now, the reason why I'd in fact left the Knoll House was to become a journalist on that bastion of media rectitude, the *Wilts and Glos Standard*, but that obviously wasn't going to cut it with the sergeant footman. 'I left because there was a position available at my godfather's—'

'Your godfather's!' He hurled his champagne against the wall. The glass just missed the Beryl Cook, though a spattering of champagne did dribble onto one of the fat lady shoppers. I suddenly realised why there were so many dents in the wall. 'How many times? How many times do I have to tell you?'

'Yes,' I said smoothly. 'What I meant to say was that I had, in fact, seen an advert for this prestigious firm of London caterers and that, though I adored hotel work – and was truly a most accomplished waiter and can still wield my trusty waiter's friend like the best of them – I felt that my many talents were wasted in Studland. The bright lights of London beckoned.'

'What do you hope to be doing in five years' time?'

'Well, if all goes well, I can imagine nothing finer than becoming Her Majesty's personal boot licker—'

'Just for one moment, can you be serious?'

'You don't think they'll like a jolly footman?'

'You're going to screw it up. I know you will.'

With those winning words of endorsement still ringing in my ears the next morning, I caught the Tube to Green Park and made my way to Buckingham Palace. I had left my phone and pager at home because mobile phones and pagers were only really used by low-life bankers and that even scummier breed, the tabloid reporter.

It would have been nice to have breezed in through the main entrance gates like Her Majesty, but the staff entrance was over on the side by the Royal Mews (on the left as you look at the palace from The Mall). Like the good little flunky that I aspired to be, I presented myself at 11.55 a.m. prompt. They were expecting me.

I was exceptionally nervous, all sweaty palms and jittery legs, as I was left to cool my heels in a waiting room for a few minutes before a footman took me to see the great Mr Brook. The master's corridor had a plush red carpet that was as thick as a bearskin and walls lined with tasteful gilt-framed paintings. The royals never threw anything away, and pictures that had fallen out of favour were first relegated from a drawing room to an old passage before eventually winding up in one of the servants' corridors. It was so silent it was as if I had entered some secret sanctuary; not a squeak or car horn could be heard from the outside world. Like *The Sun* newsroom, there was a sign above the door. To all intents and purposes, it was the Buckingham Palace staff motto. It was a line from a poem by Milton, "They also serve who only stand and wait".

The sergeant footman was waiting in his snug parlour, sitting by the gas fire and sipping lapsang. The walls were thick with royal photos, a fair number of which had the sergeant footman himself lurking somewhere in the background. Behind his desk was a glass-fronted cupboard that brimmed with royal memorabilia – a whistle, a feather boa, a pork-pie hat, some rusty nail clippers that had been given to him during his thirty years of loyal service. And in pride of place on the mantelpiece was Mr Brook's collection of porcelain cups and saucers.

Each year at Christmas, the queen presented every one of her staff with a gift of their own choosing, and since his first Christmas, Mr Brook had always requested the same present, to wit, the latest cup and saucer to have been commissioned by the palace. He had cups for the marriages of Prince Charles, Prince Andrew, and Princess Anne, and also, from his very first year in royal service in 1964, there was a cup commemorating the birth of Prince Edward. These elegant cups were no mere dust-catchers because Mr Brook assiduously used them for his morning tea. That morning, for instance, his cup was from the queen's 1977 Silver Jubilee.

On his lap was one of the queen's dorgis, a great corgi-dachshund cross called Chipper. Chipper had a livid red scar on his stomach, and as for Mr Brook, his comfortable potbelly was swathed in a butcher's apron so that his waistcoat wouldn't get covered in dog hairs. In short order, I was sitting with him by the fireside and drinking tea out of one of his Christmas presents (it was the 1969 one marking the investiture of the Prince of Wales. In case you're interested). After all my rehearsals with Spike, it was all exceedingly pleasant – not a swear word uttered and not a thrown cup to be seen.

Now, it might come as a surprise to learn that, in one respect, Buckingham Palace had been at the very vanguard of Britain's equal-opportunity employers. Despite its fusty reputation, the palace had long been a haven for what was once one of the UK's most vilified minority groups. I am talking, of course, about gay men. Homosexuality only became legal in the UK in 1967, but long before that date, the palace had become a Mecca for gay staff. It was said that without gay servants, the royal family would quickly be reduced to self-service. Word soon got around London that if you were a gay man looking for a great time, then you couldn't find a cushier billet than Buckingham Palace. The royals themselves, of course, couldn't have given a hoot that a large proportion of their footmen and pages were gay, and, in fact, it suited them perfectly, gay men being unlikely to go off and start families. For these men, who tended to adore all the costumes and the pageantry, the palace became their family.

Amongst the gay staff at the palace, there was no one more affable and more welcoming than its sergeant footman, Simon Brook. Or more bizarre. He had a great beaming football of a face, with a slightly arch voice that reeked of naughtiness. He was diligently rubbing a white cream into the dog's belly. I didn't know it at the time, but the queen was a firm believer in homoeopathy and insisted that this type of alternative medicine was the default remedy for all her dogs' ills.

Mr Brook screwed the top onto the ointment tube and, after wiping his hands on a towel, addressed himself to me. 'I,' he said with a theatrical roll of his eyes, 'am a dog whisperer.'

I gave an encouraging nod. 'You can talk to dogs?' I said. This was not exactly how I'd envisaged the interview going.

'I can, Lawrence, I can.' He was using my middle name, Lawrence, because "Kim" would have been too risky. Although nobody in this world apart from journalists ever bothered to look at newspaper bylines, there was a slim chance that my name might have been recognised by a palace press officer. 'Would you like to see a demonstration?' Every syllable was beautifully enunciated, and as for that last word, it dripped off his tongue. Mr Brook was the very model of high camp.

'I can think of nothing I would enjoy more, sir.' Christ alive. Only five minutes in the palace and I'd already bagged a centre-page spread. 'The Queen's Real-Life Dr Dolittle!'

'Chipper, say hello to Master Lawrence,' Mr Brook said. 'He's going to come and work in the big house.'

I waited, agog, for what would happen next. Had he trained this fat corgi to bark on cue? Would it start waggling its ears? I'd have believed anything – anything at all – except for what actually happened.

The dog opened its hairy little mouth and spoke to me – in a very squeaky Yorkshire accent. ''Ullo, Master Lawrence, the name's Chipper. Chipper by name and Chipper by nature.'

I goggled. It was the most extraordinary piece of ventriloquism that I had ever seen. Mr Brook's lips hadn't moved once.

It seemed correct to lean over and scratch the dog behind the ear. 'Pleased to meet you, Chipper.' The dog sniffed at my fingers and gave them a lick.

'Oh, he likes you,' Mr Brook said. 'You like Master Lawrence, don't you, Chipper? You like him?' He leaned back in his armchair with a light smile playing on his lips. The dog was given another light tickle under its chin, and as soon as it opened its mouth, it started talking again. 'You can take me walkies any day you like, Master Lawrence.'

'You two should be on TV.'

'We are not a circus act.' Mr Brook sniffed. 'We only perform for our more choice friends.'

'Quite right too,' I said and was rewarded by having Chipper plonked on my lap.

'You don't mind the dog hairs, do you?'

'Not in the slightest,' I said – and though I was no

ventriloquist, I was certainly capable of putting on a squeaky voice. I bent down by Chipper's head, tickled his throat, and said in my broadest Yorkshire accent, 'Though I do mind human hairs!'

Mr Brook giggled and mopped at his mouth with a florid silk handkerchief. The dog had taken a fancy to my salty sweat and was licking my hands.

Mr Brook contentedly looked on. 'I can see you're going to be one of Her Majesty's dog walkers,' he said. 'Though, as you can see from the scar on Chipper's tummy, they do get into the most terrible fights—'

I scratched the dog's chin, and Chipper opened his mouth. 'You should have seen how the other dog looked.'

'I did indeed see how the other dog looked, Chipper. It was touch and go whether he would need to be put down,' Mr Brook said. 'The worst of the lot are the hellhounds owned by the Princess Royal. If I can give you one single tip, dear Lawrence, it is that if you insist on getting involved in a dogfight, you should avoid using your hands at all costs.' He held up his left hand. It was minus one index finger.

'A dog bit off your finger?'

'Gobbled it down like a sausage, didn't you, Chipper?' He eyed the corgi as it enthusiastically licked my wrists. 'Got quite a taste for human flesh, haven't you now?' He couldn't resist throwing me one last bone, as not a moment later, a squeaky Yorkshire voice piped up again.

'I'm a proper little cannibal me.'

CHAPTER 5

The footman, who's in bed and who's still wearing the full state livery, blinks at Campion. 'Excuse me?' he says.

Now, this is the absolute limit. It's been bad enough sorting out Prince Andrew's teddies, and now this!

'Excuse me?' she says. 'Excuse me?' She swipes at him again with the duster, missing his head but hitting his shoulder. 'What the hell do you think you're doing here?'

'What – what do you mean?'

Campion speaks very slowly, as if talking to an idiot toddler. 'What are you doing in this bed? And what are you doing in this bed wearing state livery?'

'Oh – this?' he says. For the first time, he seems to notice that he is indeed wearing state livery.

'And more to the point, what were you doing up on the staff corridor last night?' She brandishes the duster again. He retreats across the bed. 'You don't even work here! You nick the state livery. You spend the night in one of the suites – which I've now got to clean – and you smashed up my wardrobe. Know what you are? You're a pain in the arse.'

'I'm very sorry,' he says. 'And I'm particularly s-sorry about your wardrobe—'

'I'll bet you are.'

She sizzles with anger. Being a palace maid means generally having to suck it up. You have to suck it up from the senior staff, and you really have to suck it up from the royals. So, after a few months of all this sucking it up, Campion is just about ready to explode – and this guy, this dolt, seems just about the most perfect target on earth.

'I've had it with people like you,' she says. 'You know what I'm going to do. I'm not even going to bother with you. I'm just going to call up security. They can deal with you—'

'Please—'

Campion steamrollers on. 'As far as I'm concerned, they can send you off to jail. In fact, you probably will be going to jail, and that, my friend, will give me very great pleasure as every day I wake up, I will think of you in your cell, and I will rejoice! I will be happy because there will be one less low-life in this world to make my life a misery—'

Campion has more to say – quite considerably more – but for a knock at the door. She opens it. It was Mrs Boyd.

'What's going on here?'

'I'm sorry?' says Campion. 'What's going on where?'

'What is going on this suite?' Mrs Boyd says. 'I heard you shouting at someone.'

'Shouting?' says Campion. 'I was singing.'

'I've heard better tunes out of the queen's corgis,' Mrs Boyd says, shouldering her way past Campion and into the room. The bed is empty. 'Why has this bed not been stripped?'

'I've only just got here,' Campion replies. 'I've just spent the last half-hour sorting out Prince Andrew's infantile collection of teddies.'

'That is not an appropriate way to describe His Royal Highness's collection.'

Campion laughs out loud. 'You don't think it's infantile? What adjective would you prefer? Bizarre? Weird? Preposterous?'

Mrs Boyd draws herself up to her full height, though she is still a good half-head shorter than Campion. 'Your disrespect has been noted,' Mrs Boyd says. 'Though I am not here to talk about Prince Andrew's teddies. I am here to tell you that the week's holiday you requested for next week has most unfortunately had to be cancelled. We are short of staff.'

'Bang goes my holiday in Skegness.'

'Further to that, the staff rota has had to be adjusted. For the foreseeable future, you will be working evening shifts. I do so hope this will not inconvenience you.'

'Not in the slightest,' Campion says.

In the clear morning light, Campion notices for the first time that Mrs Boyd has a lustrously hairy mole in the middle of her forehead. She does not look Mrs Boyd in the eye. She looks at the mole.

'Since you will be doing the evening shifts, it will perhaps mean that you are forced to curtail your partying.'

Campion twitches her duster and takes a little swipe at a cobweb in the fireplace. 'I can see you've forgotten what those corridor parties are actually like, Mrs Boyd.' Campion inspects the candyfloss cobweb on her duster; rather pleasingly, she's taken the whole thing in one. 'They are vastly overrated.'

Mrs Boyd gives Campion a grey-toothed smile. 'You may continue with your duties.'

'Thank you, Mrs Boyd,' Campion says. 'And thank you very much for promoting me to the evening shift.'

After Mrs Boyd leaves, Campion goes over to the wardrobe where, naturally enough, the footman is hiding. She barely gives him a glance. 'Hiding in another wardrobe again?' she says. 'I'm going to clean the bathroom. Get your stuff and get the hell out.'

'You're called Campion?' He attempts what he obviously thinks is a winsome smile. 'What a beautiful name. We used to have them in our her-herbaceous border.'

'We grow them in our her-herbaceous border, do we?' For the briefest of moments, she feels bad about taking the piss out of his stutter, and because she feels bad, she slams the wardrobe door with added venom. 'Spare me.'

CHAPTER 6

While all this palaver is going on upstairs, the queen is doing something that she does not especially enjoy but which, after sixty years of practice, she does quite beautifully. She is making small talk.

Since it's a Saturday, she should be putting her feet up at Windsor Castle and having two days of delicious downtime, but events have conspired against her. Some terribly important reception just *has* to be attended, so instead of being toastie in Windsor Castle, she is stuck at the palace having luncheon (never lunch) in the Chinese Dining Room – and though the Chinese Dining Room is a glorious room, packed with treasures, the queen would much prefer to be cosy in front of the TV, drinking Malvern water and sipping Heinz Tomato Soup as she watches the racing.

The Duchess of Montagu is one of the queen's most long-standing acquaintances – they've known each other for nearly sixty years – but in those six decades, the woman has not evolved by so much as a jot. The queen sometimes jokes to Philip that she feels herself fortunate indeed to be the monarch because otherwise the duchess, a snob of the first water, would have nothing whatsoever to do with her; she especially despises the nouveau riche, that vulgar breed of people who have made their money from their own endeavours.

The duchess is at that moment complaining. She seems to spend a lot of her time complaining – complaining about the staff or the general uncouthness of the British public, as well, of course, as that hardy perennial, the nation's ill-mannered drivers.

'... I mean, it's all right for you, with your outriders and your police escort, but you don't have any idea what it's like on the roads today. The people are just insufferable, ma'am,' she says, pronouncing the word ma'am to rhyme with jam, not smarm. 'Why, when I was coming in this morning, we were just driving at a perfectly respectable pace down the Bayswater Road when this man, this jogger, just jumped out right in front of us!' The duchess waves her empty glass in the air. The ever-attentive Gavin immediately tops her up. 'And what do you think he did, ma'am? Do you think he apologised? No, he did not! He came right over to the window and stuck two fingers right up into my face. My father would have had him horsewhipped, but no, we can't do that now, and mark my words, ma'am, the way things are going, we won't even be allowed to spank our children.'

The queen, exceedingly good-natured by temperament, smirks at the thought. The duchess mistakes her smile for encouragement.

'... So, we went around Marble Arch – why did they ever move it from the palace? It was always so much better here than on that glorified roundabout – and Tobias had just started down Park Lane when this rubbish truck pulled clean out in front of us, and, of course, Tobias gave him a toot, and you'll never believe, ma'am, what the rubbish man did?'

Her Majesty looks down from her inspection of the flower-shaped chandelier, quite beautiful, one of the many things that her great-great-grandmother, Queen Victoria, retrieved from the Brighton Pavilion before it had been sold to the council. 'Did he also give you a two-fingered salute?'

'Yes, he did, ma'am,' the duchess replies. 'And then, when we drove past, he gave me a simply obscene hand gesture. I had no idea what it meant until Tobias explained it to me, and even to think of it makes me quite shudder.' She pauses a moment and, shark-like, inhales a vast piece of smoked salmon. As is often the way with the upper classes, her table manners are abysmal. The duchess does not tend to bother with such fripperies as knives or thank yous.

The queen has a very large portion of salmon, of which she intends to eat only a small mouthful. She cuts the salmon up into nine pieces, and then, as the duchess chunters on, she feeds the nine corgis that are nestled at her feet. She's been obsessed with corgis since she was seven years old, when she'd fallen in love with one that belonged to Viscount Weymouth. The queen had been given her first corgi, Susan, by her parents when she was eighteen years old, and the corgi had even joined her and Philip on the first part of their honeymoon. The queen never looked back and, over the next four decades, had dozens of corgis and dorgis. All of them descended from Susan, and they had all inherited one of Susan's naughtier habits – they were all biters. Though it could have been down to be the dogs being royal pets. It wasn't just her dogs that were biters, but also Anne's bull terriers and Andrew's Norfolk Terrier; as for the Queen Mother's three dorgis, most particularly Ranger, they were completely feral.

The queen recites her dogs' names in a silent mantra – Brush, Jolly, Shadow, Myth, Smokey, Piper, Fable, Sparky, and not forgetting the pack leader and the only male, Chipper. After each dog has its piece of salmon, it obediently lies at her feet. The corgis are the queen's unofficial tasters and, except for the state banquets, share almost all of her meals.

'Anyway, Your Majesty, that is more than enough of my travails getting here—'

'You could try the Tube. We're only a short walk from Green Park.'

'The Tube? You must be joking!' The duchess squints at the queen. 'Oh, ma'am!' She pauses a moment to recollect herself. 'Joke. Haha.' It's a most unnatural, pale imitation of a laugh, as if it has been learned by a person who had no trace of a sense of humour. 'No, I am proud of the fact that I have never once been on a Tube train, nor on a bus, and in actual fact, I do not even believe that I have been in a taxi. But then, being brought up at the park, we really had so little need for taxis…'

The queen moves from her inspection of the chandelier to the mantelpiece, and the Kylin clock, very ornate, with a pair of squatting lions in turquoise. If only Campion were here with her, because Campion would stand by the clock and tell her stories of what the lions were doing, why their tongues were lolling out of their open jaws. In fact, as soon as she can prise herself away from the duchess, she will seek Campion out and ask her to explain why one lion has a ball under its paw while the other has a cub.

'… And forgive me for prying into internal palace affairs, ma'am, but have you heard any news yet about your temporary equerry-in-waiting?'

'Mason's got the job.'

'Oh, ma'am! Thank you – thank you, thank you, thank you!' The Duchess of Montagu is so overcome that she drains her glass in one. 'I am sure it will be the making of the boy for, as you know, I have been so very concerned about the path he has chosen to tread. I am not at all sure that joining the Blues and Royals was the best move for Mason. It is, I know, the smartest of regiments – such a dashing uniform, ma'am – but now that he is based in London, he has become something of a dilettante. Last month, those impudent curs at *Tatler* magazine had the gall to run a piece about him in their gossip column. I have been worried about him, very worried, ma'am, and in particular that he has started mixing with drunken ne'er-do-wells. I feel that here, at the palace, with you taking him under your wing, so to speak, he will be so much happier, and that he will come to find someone of the correct station…'

Sitting with her hands in her lap, the queen puts on her most inscrutable sphinx-like face and does what she has long been trained to do when she is bored – she twiddles her thumbs, first in one direction and then in the other. She remembers Viola when she was a girl. Pretty as a teenager, and then, as a young woman, she turned into an absolute head-turner, with cheekbones, bee-stung lips, and limpid eyes, all things which Her Majesty did not possess and which she did not much care about. But the queen certainly witnessed the effect that Viola's beauty had on men. Even before Viola came out at the age of eighteen, she had always had a large retinue of besotted suitors.

Viola's father had been a belted earl, and it had been a cause of the most intense annoyance for Viola that, while she had to content herself with merely being a lady, the earldom had gone to her bovine younger brother. But eventually, after playing the field for a full two decades, Viola parlayed her looks into a marriage. The fact that her new husband was sixty – some twenty years older than Viola – was an irrelevance because the man was a duke. What sweet satisfaction it had been to become the Duchess of Montagu, in one fell swoop effortlessly outranking her younger brother. It had been most important, of course, to have a son – and quickly – because otherwise, the title and all its accoutrements would have gone to the Duke of Montagu's first cousin. The duchess had thrown herself at the task and, in time, been rewarded with a son – the blessed Mason. Then, the icing on the cake, after five years of marriage, the 8th Duke of Montagu was thrown from his horse. The duke was in a coma for just over two weeks, and though there had been a slim chance of a recovery, the duchess had decided that it would be best for all concerned if the duke's life-support machine was switched off – well, who wants to spend their days looking after a tetraplegic? – and with a heavy (-ish) heart, she herself had done the deed.

Viola had rather taken to widowhood. All her old suitors were back with a vengeance, carefully played off one against the other, but now there was none of that tiresome business of having to get married. Besides, not a single one of them had a title to touch a dukedom, though had there been a king amongst them, or possibly a prince, she might have been tempted.

After the duke's tragic and untimely death – she wore

black for a full year, how well it suited her – it had just been Viola and Mason against the world. What a joy it had been to guide and mould the young 9th Duke of Montagu without any of that most vexatious business of having to compromise on your principles just because your husband disagreed with you.

That, then, is the very same duchess who sits beside the queen at the round lacquered table in the Chinese Dining Room, and who still grimly retains some of her old icy beauty. The queen presumes Viola is using fillers. Viola's face is, at sixty-six, still relatively unlined, though more tellingly, Philip informed the queen once that when he kissed Viola on the cheek, it was like brushing his lips against a dead salmon – rock hard and clammy.

If the duchess has a fault, it is that she spends rather too much time with lackeys and luckless swains, with the result that she truly believes that every word to fall from her lips is utterly fascinating. Or, as Philip so charmingly puts it, at every meal and every function, everyone always ends up getting spattered by Viola's verbal diarrhoea.

Speaking of which…

'I see you have a new footman, ma'am,' Viola says. 'I found him discourteous.'

'Oh, yes?'

'Yes, ma'am. Now, not that I wish to get him into trouble, as I am sure he is still learning the ways of the palace, but he really was rather rude.'

'What did he do?' The queen is intrigued. It is of course possible that the new footman has been discourteous, but more likely, by far, that the prickly Viola has chosen to take offence.

'Well, ma'am, I came to the Privy Purse Door, just as I usually do, and your footman, Ollie, was waiting there for me, where he was being shadowed by your new footman. I believe his name is Lawrence. They both bowed and addressed me as Your Grace, which was correct, but when they escorted me up the stairs, your new footman suddenly cried, "Mind out!" and took me by the arm and tried to pull me towards him.'

'Really?'

'I would have missed the dog poo on the carpet altogether, ma'am, but by tugging me towards him, he made me actually step straight into it. It was simply ghastly.'

'I'm sure he was only trying to help.'

'Be that as it may, I had dog poo on my patent leather court shoes, ma'am. The other chap, Ollie, went off to clean up the mess on the carpet, and I was left with this young fellow Lawrence, and do you know what he said to me?'

'I really can't imagine.'

'He said, ma'am, "Lucky I caught you. Otherwise, you'd have hit it smack in the middle". So, I told him in no uncertain terms that I had hit it square in the middle. He looked at my shoe, and he just totally disagreed with me! He said it was more of a sideways squidge and then he offered to clean my shoe. And this time, he really was downright rude, as he said he could either do it in situ, like a farrier, or he could take the shoe off to the bathroom.'

The queen is having great difficulty hiding her amusement. 'And what did you decide?'

'I ordered the young man to find me a chair and go off and clean my shoe, which he did, though he took his time about it. All of which explains my slight tardiness. When he came back, sauntering up the stairs, he was whistling. As he bent down to put my shoe on, he said he felt like Prince Charming. Then he had the gall to tell me that my foot would never have smelled so sweet as he'd dosed my shoe in perfume!'

'That all sounds eminently sensible to me,' the queen says.

'I do not necessarily wish to see him sacked, ma'am, but I would certainly like to see him reprimanded. Severely.'

'I will see that this young man gets his just desserts,' the queen says, making a mental note to commend this Lawrence chap to the sergeant footman personally. 'Though I must say, I did notice the perfume, and I think he might be right – your feet have never smelled so sweet.'

After that most entertaining interlude, the conversation

reverts to type. Viola drones on about whatever comes into her head; she has no filter.

The queen mournfully stares at the four colossal Chinese towers – also retrieved from the Brighton Pavilion, and now festooned with golden bells. Why, amidst all this beauty, does she have to listen to this woman's burbling? She wonders how much longer she will have to wait before she can give Gavin the secret signal of placing her handbag on the table so that, within a matter of moments, Gavin can discreetly call her away to attend to other duties that just can't wait. Will it be too rude to leave before the main course, a cold cut of beef? Most probably, and besides, the dogs do so love cold beef. No, she will have to stay for four mouthfuls of beef – or one enormous mouthful if you have the Duchess of Montagu's table manners – but she'll be damned if she stays for pudding, let alone cheese.

CHAPTER 7

It was the biggest bollocking I had ever had in the newsroom – and I'd had a few. But, for the first and only time, I was actually rather enjoying myself. Spike, bless his cotton socks, was also getting into it.

After my exemplary interview with Mr Simon Brook, I was invited to become a footman at Buckingham Palace. (I still have the letter, framed, now in pride of place in my lavatory.)

"On behalf of the master of the household, I am pleased to offer you the position of Footman in the royal household, commencing on Monday, 6 September 1993. This offer is conditional on security clearance, your passing of a medical examination conducted by the royal household doctor, taking into account the requirements of the post and the royal household employment obligations under the Disability Discrimination Act, and on references satisfactory to the royal household being obtained."

It went on in more of the same vein, but the important point was that so long as my references held up, I was in.

I'd be working in the master of the household's department, the general household staff (G-branch as it's known), which comprised the valets, butlers, footmen, and drivers.

There were other branches too, C-branch for the craftsmen, F-branch for the food and drink, and H-branch for the housekeeping and cleaning, but G-branch was far and away the biggest department in the palace.

There were some four hundred of us, all told, including cleaners, plumbers, gardeners, electricians, and two people whose sole job was to look after the three hundred clocks. I'd be earning £11,881 a year, cut to £9,338 after living costs.

A couple of weeks earlier, I'd been back to the palace to be fitted with my various uniforms. For general day-to-day wear, I was to have a uniform of very distinctive black tails, scarlet waistcoat, and black tie, along with three white shirts. I was also kitted out with a summer uniform of white tropical livery with gold trim, plus another livery, all scarlet, capped off with a black topper banded with gold brocade. And, last of all, for the royal panto season (the state opening of parliament and coronations), the full state livery. The jacket alone weighed over twelve kilos. It was as gaudy as anything, all scarlet and gold. To go with it was a velvet riding cap in navy blue, a white starched ruff, embroidered waistcoat in black, velvet breeches that tied below the knee, pink stockings, black buckled shoes, and white cotton gloves. It was well over two hundred years old, passed down from one footman to the next and to the next, and the only thing that changed was the insignia stitched into the left sleeve – EIIR, surrounded by the rather obscure royal motto, *"Honi soit qui mal y pense"* (Honest sweat makes smelly pants).

After my references had come through, I'd been sent another letter containing my contract, a security and counter-terrorism form, an employee manual, and medical documents. There remained one last teeny tiny detail to be resolved. I had to sign a Non-Disclosure Agreement that stipulated that after I'd left the royal household, I couldn't go spilling my guts to the press or, indeed, write a book about my experiences. The very thought!

We had spent some time on a cover story to explain my absence from *The Sun*. At first, we'd thought that I might have contracted some terrible illness – cancer, brain haemorrhage, galloping syphilis, take your pick – but this might have caused unnecessary angst to my colleagues. In the end, we decided to go down route one. Spike and I would have a good old bust-up in the newsroom. He'd swear at me. I'd give him some sauce. He'd take a swing at me. Then – thank the Lord and all his angels! – I, Kim, was to be gifted the quite unimaginable pleasure of punching the deputy editor, and though I was only supposed to give him a light tap, I was fully intent on knocking Spike clean off his feet.

The fight was to be staged on Friday afternoon, three days before I was due to start at the palace. At 5 p.m. exactly, and with the newsroom pulsating with febrile energy, Spike stormed out of his office.

'Where is he? Where is that useless piece of shit?'

Subs stopped typing. News reporters abruptly ended their calls. Layout artists looked up from their easels. Feature writers laid off from manicuring their nails. News editors and picture editors swivelled from their screens, and over on the back bench, those grizzled grey heads sensed something historic was about to take place. The newsroom came to a complete standstill. I languidly turned another page of the *Evening Standard*. That day's crossword seemed particularly fascinating. The shouting got louder. I looked up, feigning slight interest in what all the ruckus was about. It looked like dear old Spike was coming over for a chat.

He stood by my desk. 'You're an absolute moron!' he yelled. 'What do you call this piece of shit?' He held up some dodgy copy that I'd manufactured a couple of hours earlier. He ripped it up and hurled it in my face.

I leaned back in my chair and took a leisurely bite out of the ruby-red apple that was sitting conveniently by my keyboard. I had a thoughtful chew and swallowed. 'Have you been on the sauce again, Spike?' I mimed a wino tippling at a bottle of booze. 'I think you need to calm down.' I gave him an impish wink. It seemed to do the trick very nicely.

'What did you say to me?' he said. 'You expect me to

calm down when you file the biggest pile of garbage that I have ever read in my entire life?'

It should perhaps be noted, by the way, that though this is an exact rendering of Spike's diatribe, it has been shorn of swearwords and has therefore been cut by about half. These days, since becoming an ex-*Sun* reporter, I am such a delicate flower that I can't abide four-letter words – both written and oral.

'Why are you always shouting?' I shot my cuffs and got to my feet. Spike shimmied in front of me like a boxer at the first bell. 'If you've got a problem with my copy, then just tell me in a reasonable manner. But, no, you can't do that. You shout at me. You swear at me. You swear at everyone. You know what, Spike, I've had enough of it.'

'You've had enough of it?' Spike shouted. He was standing on his tippy-toes, fingers clenching and unclenching. I knew we were only play-acting for the benefit of the newsroom, but he was giving a most realistic portrayal of an absolute madman. 'Are you threatening me?'

'I'm not threatening you, no.' I took a step closer to him. 'I am telling you to moderate your foul language. You're always screaming. And it's always about the most trivial things. I'm sick of it. The whole newsroom's sick of it. We are fed up with you.' I heard a collective gasp from the reporters. Robert, who was also in on the act, started to wander over.

'Say that again.' No longer shouting, voice icily under control.

'We're fed up with your toddler temper tantrums, Spike. In fact...' – I gave him three provocative little slaps on the cheek – 'we're fed up with you.'

At this stage, Spike was supposed to give me a light cuff on the cheek, upon which I would deck him with an uppercut to the chin.

Unfortunately, Spike had really been getting into char-acter. It was also possible that he was truly incensed. He leapt at me, hands lunging for my throat. We collapsed in a heap on the floor. I didn't know how he did it, but he managed to keep his hands around my throat all the way to the ground.

'Steady!' I tried to say, but it came out as a light hiss. This wouldn't do at all. For one thing, it was me who needed to hit Spike in order to get thrown out of the newsroom, and for another, he was genuinely throttling me.

I lurched sideways. A chair went flying. A glimpse of Grubby springing for his camera. For a brief moment, Spike loosened his grip. I head-butted him, and beautiful claret spilled from his nose. Then I was on top of the bastard, and since I'd been half strangled, my blood was well and truly up.

'I've been looking forward to this!' I said.

I had him completely pinned down, utterly at my mercy. I drew back my fist. With a bit of luck, I'd knock out so many teeth he'd need a full set of dentures.

Somebody cannoned into me. It was Robert – just a few seconds too early. He could at least have allowed me one good punch. The three of us started rolling around the floor. I saw Grubby firing off a couple of frames before stepping in and dragging me away, though I did manage to get in two sharp kicks, one to Spike's stomach and the next one, a great scything swipe that was intended for his groin, but which regrettably only glanced off his leg.

'Do you want some?' I yelled. 'Do you want some?'

Spike got to his feet. Blood was still geysering out of his nose. I honestly thought he was going to have another go at me, but with a great effort of will, he desisted.

'Call security,' he said to Robert. 'This reporter must never be allowed in the newsroom again.'

He mopped at his nose with a handkerchief before turning to me. 'It gives me very great pleasure to say this. You. Are. Fired.'

I adjusted my tie and put on my jacket. 'Well, Spike,

it gives me very great pleasure to tell you that if I ever see you again, you'll have a sight more to deal with than a nosebleed.'

'Get out of my newsroom!'

I sauntered out. 'You've had it coming a long time, Spike,' I called. 'My only regret is that I didn't do it years ago.' Grubby took another picture of me as I gave the newsroom a cheery salute. 'Sayonara suckers!'

And with that, our little comedy was over, though as I waited for the lift, I noticed with distaste that my shirt had been soiled with some of Spike's blood.

Three days later, at 9 a.m. on a Monday morning, as I presented myself at Buckingham Palace, all traces of my life as a *Sun* reporter had been expunged. I left my car in the News International car park, and my phone, pager, and *Sun* security pass were all locked away in my flat. Kim, the cocky *Sun* reporter, was dead, replaced by the smiling, loyal, and ever-so diligent toady, Lawrence. Farewell, backchat! Goodbye obnoxiousness! Cheerio, cheeky boy! In their stead, my rather more challenging character traits would be replaced by total fawning subservience. I was going to suck it up so avidly that I could have given my news editors an object lesson in how to be the perfect human sponge.

Well, that was the plan anyway. And for a short while, I managed to stick to it, but although you can mask your character, you can never quite change it – and so it was of course inevitable that one day, after perhaps imbibing a little too much palace gin, my slimy toad mantle would slip, and, like some hideous skeleton emerging from the grave, my old perky self would reassert itself.

A smiling Mr Brook greeted me at the door and even carried my suitcase as he and Chipper took me up the winding staircases to the footman's floor in the section known as London Bridge. My room was pretty basic, just a bed, wardrobe, desk and sink, with a window that looked down onto the Royal Picture Gallery.

'Welcome to your new home, Lawrence,' Mr Brook said with a courtly flourish. 'It's my old room, actually, before I moved up in the world. I hope you'll be as happy here as I was. You can still see the notches on the bedpost.' He elbowed me in the ribs. 'Only teasing, dear.' He guffawed. 'If I'd actually cut notches in the bedpost, it'd be nothing but kindling.'

I laughed. Why couldn't all my bosses be like him? 'Thank you, sir,' I said. 'I think I'm going to love it.' Amongst other things, in the past fortnight I had spent a little time practising a magic trick; now seemed as good a time as any to use it.

'Good heavens, Chipper,' I said. 'What's that in your ear?' Chipper looked up expectantly. I bent down and from his ear produced a small dog chew. Chipper gulped it down.

I looked in wonderment at Mr Brook before turning again to the dog. 'Chipper, there's something else in your other ear.' I palmed another dog chew and produced it from his other ear. The dog nearly bit my fingers off.

Mr Brook clapped his hands like an entranced schoolboy. 'I adore magic, Lawrence, I adore it,' he said. 'Can you do anything else?'

'I could have a look-see to find out if Chipper's squirrelled a dog chew up his bum?'

'Sauce!' Mr Brook gave a little tug on Chipper's red leather lead. 'I'll leave you to settle in and put on your uniform,' he said. 'Toilets and showers are at the end of the corridor. In an hour or so, I'll send Ollie up to give you the tour. Ollie is one of our most capable footmen. You'll be shadowing him for a month just to see how you fit in.' At that, and just like my granny used to do, he leaned over and gave me an affectionate pinch on the cheek. 'If you remember my motto, you'll be just fine.'

'And what is your motto, sir?'

'Everybody I meet, I vow only one thing, to be relentlessly agreeable to them.' He beamed at me. 'That's the way to thrive in the palace. Come now, Chipper, we be must away to your harem of bitches.'

I unpacked my bag. I hadn't brought very much at all, just toiletries and underwear, as well as jeans and a hoodie for my day off. To help with my general homework, I had a number of books about the palace and the royal family, and to win over the most important members of the royal household (the corgis), I had a large bag of dog treats. Meanwhile, tucked away at the bottom of my suitcase were a couple of pens, a pad of paper, and my trusty Olympus Twin camera. My mad masters at *The Sun* had decided that I should spend the first few days settling in, but that as soon as I'd found my feet, I should start taking pictures inside the palace. We didn't know yet what I'd be taking pictures of or which rooms I'd be allowed in, but the general idea was that, on the one hand, I should take pictures of anything and everything, the saucier the better, and that on the other, I should do nothing whatsoever to jeopardise my position at the palace. It had been deemed too risky to leave any used film in my room or in the camera, so Spike had decreed that the moment I had any pictures in the bag, they had to be sent to him at his home address. I had also been tasked with sending Spike regular write-ups about life at the palace, as well as every bit of royal tittle-tattle I could lay my hands on. Spike was to be my only point of contact.

I donned my new uniform. It was a perfect fit. The tailcoat was of a type I'd never worn before, cut away at the waist like evening tails. I washed my hands and looked at this stranger in the mirror, a pink-faced smoothie-chops in a black tie and black tails with a scarlet waistcoat piped with gold. I couldn't believe it. I was a Buckingham Palace footman! No one would have swallowed it – not my dad, not my granny, and certainly not the rest of the blunts on Fleet Street. I was astonished that no other reporter had tried this stunt years ago.

There was a knock at the door, and in bounced Ollie.

He was a little shorter than me, but from the way he pinged around, he seemed much bigger. He quite filled the room with his energy. Like me, he was clean-shaven; the queen did not like stubble, beards or moustaches on any of her staff. For some reason, he was carrying a large red hob kettle.

'Morning, morning,' he said as he shook my hand. 'We ready for our royal grand tour?'

'Looking forward to it.'

'Woaahh!' he said, taking a step back. 'You're not gay.'

'What gave me away?'

'Work here for a year and you can smell it. Straights are in a minority round here. You'll be catnip to the women.' He set off out the door. 'Beware, Lawrence, you are entering an old-fashioned establishment.'

He took me at breakneck speed through the labyrinthine corridors of the palace, keeping up a running commentary throughout as he pointed out anything of interest. 'There's three miles of corridors,' he said merrily. 'Only took me a year to learn my way round. They've got over two hundred bedrooms, fifty-two for the royals and their guests and a hundred and eighty-eight for us menials at the bottom of the heap. They've got ninety-two offices, ninety-eight bathrooms and lavatories – seven hundred and seventy-seven rooms in all. And before I leave, I hope to have had a kiss in every single one of them.'

'With the same woman?' I asked. We weren't quite going at a trot, but it was certainly a power walk.

'For preference, yes,' he said. 'But for now, I'm just doing the best I can until I find the right one.'

Ollie's dad owned a restaurant in Ely, in the Fens, and Ollie had spent most of his teens working there as a waiter. After school, he'd done a catering course, and though he'd been all set to return to his dad's restaurant, he'd happened upon an advert for a palace footman in one of the trade papers. He'd never looked back.

'After three years here, I'll have my NVQ with City and

Guilds, and then the world will be my lobster. Know what I'm going to do then, Lawrence? I am getting the hell out of this royal dodge. I want to be a butler for a multi-multi-millionaire. American, Russian, I couldn't care less.' He courteously opened another door for me. 'First things first, though, I'd like a girlfriend, preferably a very pretty one.'

'Maybe you'll marry the daughter of your multi-millionaire boss,' I said.

'Perfect,' Ollie chuckled. 'That's the way to make your fortune, Lawrence – marry a rich man's daughter. Just look at Commander Tim Laurence. Seven years ago, he was skivvying around in the navy. Now, he's only gone and married a princess.'

Just so: in the year that Prince Andrew split from Fergie, Princess Anne spliced herself to Tim, her mother's one-time temporary equerry-in-waiting. I've often wondered what Her Majesty made of her daughter dallying with one of the staff, but she has never said a word on that subject. As for Commander Tim, he never looked back and, at the last count, was a Vice Admiral with a knighthood to boot.

We were now below stairs, down right in the palace's underbelly, and the contrast with the state rooms was hilarious. It was a strange Dickensian world of lino and little cubicles with women repairing uniforms under 40-watt bulbs. Ollie knew every single one of them. 'Morning, Morag!' he called. 'Hello, Veronica!' Though we never paused for an answer.

We raced past pantry after pantry, each of them filled with glass-paned cupboards and each of those in turn filled with all the glass and china that was brought out for coronations and state banquets. Then it was back up to the state rooms again. They were piled high with all the garish French *bric-à-brac* that had been bought by George IV and Victoria – quite nice in moderation but wearying when you went through room after room of it.

'I wouldn't mind one or two of these pieces,' Ollie said

as we skipped past yet another priceless Sèvres vase. 'But they've got so much of it, it makes your eyes bleed. It's about as boring as going through the British Museum.'

The royals called it simply "The House", but inside The House was a thrumming township. We raced past the bank, the post office, the police station, the gym, the swimming pool, and all the staff social clubs.

Ollie checked his watch. It had just gone noon. 'Time for a drink, don't you think?'

We went up another flight of back stairs (even after two months at the palace, I never even came close to mastering all of its myriad secret passages) and emerged onto another red-carpeted corridor.

'Mind you don't walk in the middle,' Ollie said. 'Or at least don't get caught walking in the middle of the carpet. Lots of people get terribly uppity with us worker bees if we're not walking on the edge – though personally I don't think the queen could give a hoot. Prince Andrew's an absolute stickler for all that nonsense. Nothing he likes more than catching you out over some piffling piece of etiquette. Morning, Campion.' A maid looked up from polishing a gilt door frame and smiled. 'That's Campion,' Ollie continued. 'Tell you the amazing thing about Campion, she's not only pretty but she's lovely, and that's a pretty rare combination, the queen absolutely adores her, she tells her stories apparently – and here we are! The Bow Room – one of my favourites.'

We walked into one of the palace's more iconic rooms, dead centre on the ground floor, with columns and red carpet and, set into the walls, oval gilt portraits of the innumerable European royals who'd been related to Queen Victoria. The best part of the Bow Room is not actually inside it. It is the view of the garden from the great bow of windows. Most days, the Bow Room was used as a waiting room for the queen's private visitors, though it was also occasionally turned into a luncheon room for visiting heads of state – and, indeed, for the queen's Christmas luncheon.

'Victoria and Albert loved canoodling in here.' Ollie bustled over to the drinks trolley. 'What can I get you? I usually like to start with a sherry, but we've got whisky or gin. Or I could make you a martini if you fancy – probably not dirty though, as they haven't bothered to restock the olives.'

'I'd love a sherry.' I was a little perturbed. Not that I knew the first thing about palace life, but it seemed to me that, generally speaking, it would be frowned upon for a new footman to be found drinking sherry at noon in the Bow Room.

Ollie hummed to himself as he topped up two exquisite cut-glass schooners with Harvey's Bristol Cream. 'Bottoms up, as we palace footmen like to say,' he grinned.

We made our way over to the window to admire Her Majesty's garden. We could just make her out walking her dogs on the far side of the lake.

Ollie gave a sigh of the most sublime contentment. 'It's moments like this that make it all worthwhile – all the bowing, all the scraping, the door opening, the boot brushing, not to mention the boot licking. Yet, here we are, drinking the queen's sherry. Crowned heads of state couldn't hope for any better – and here we are, living it! The saddest thing I can imagine is getting used to luxury.'

Yes, just like all the other swells who had been there before us, we had sherry in our hands, and we had in front of us a view of the finest private garden in all of London. I closed my eyes and felt the sun beating down on my face. What bliss it was in that room to be alive – and to have a drink in hand was very heaven. Better still, thinking of my colleagues at *The Sun*, toiling away in the newsroom, scribing stories of soap stars on the wane, and all the while being relentlessly hectored and chivvied by news editors, sub-editors, and one particularly despotic deputy editor. And here I was, in my fancy uniform, literally drinking sherry at

Her Majesty's expense. Like stolen kisses, filched sherry always tastes like nectar.

'You haven't yet told me what the kettle's for.'

'The kettle?' he said. 'Glad you reminded me! No footman should be without one. First of all, the pages and equerries are forever prying and nosing into your affairs. They want to know where you're going, what you're about. But if you've got a kettle, then you can just tell them you're taking it to some nabob in the palace. And second... Well, let me show you.'

Ollie returned to the drinks trolley and picked up a huge glass decanter. The silver chain around its neck proclaimed it to be filled with gin. He unstoppered the decanter and then, using both hands, poured a good two pints of gin into the kettle.

'That's a man-sized portion,' I said.

'Should keep us going till teatime,' he said. 'Want another sherry?'

CHAPTER 8

Two days after the unfortunate party incident in the maids' lobby (or Finch's Lobby as it's known) and two days after her sparring session with Mrs Boyd, the housekeeper, Campion is on the last of her day shifts. For the rest of the week, perhaps even the rest of the month, Campion has been earmarked for the graveyard shift, which will give her a little more time for daytime shopping but will leave no time whatsoever for night-time partying.

Campion has been up since 6.30 a.m., sweeping the carpets with a heavily bristled brush before, at 9 a.m., switching to a vacuum cleaner. The cardinal rule of royal vacuuming – apart, obviously, from not disturbing the royals' beauty sleep – is that maids have to go backwards so that no unsightly tracks are left on the thick, red, pile carpets.

Vacuuming accomplished, Campion is allowed into one of her favourite rooms, the Green Drawing Room, just adjacent to the Throne Room. The room is vast, far bigger than her grandparents' entire house, and lined with green silk. Like all the other staterooms, it is stuffed with artworks, porcelain, and pictures; these also include two of her all-time favourites, a pair of metre-high candelabras. They are beguiling and magnificent and also just a little bizarre. Beneath the five candles stand three topless women on a base of black marble. The three women, made of patinated bronze, are very dark brown in colour. They all stand back-to-back with their heads in their hands; they are all weeping.

Not that the candelabras need it, but Campion gives them a perfunctory waft of her duster. She laughs to herself. Here she is with one of her favourite artworks, and deliciously she has the room to herself. She prefers – by far – to view great art alone. The more people with her, the more her experience is diminished.

She hears the sound of pattering feet, with yaps and a blur of hairy movement. The corgis have arrived, followed very soon after by their mistress.

'There you are, Campion,' the queen says. 'My dogs have finally tracked you down.'

Campion makes a full curtsy. 'Your Majesty.'

As the dogs sniff around, the queen joins Campion by the candelabra. She is obviously going out to some event or other as she is wearing a hat and gown. Perhaps, possibly, she is allowing herself a story before she gets down to the burdensome business of the day. Campion is struck, not for the first time, by the queen's famously youthful skin – sugar-pink cheeks with a radiance of pure porcelain.

'I've always wondered, Campion, just why are these women crying? Tell me the story of these sad ladies.'

'It would be an honour, Your Majesty.'

The queen waits with her hands loosely clasped in front of her and Campion, aware that she has a captive audience, takes a slow turn around one of the candelabra. She does not actually know how the story will end, but she does know that once she's started, it will all work out fine.

'These women are not actually weeping, Your Majesty.' Campion stands by the candelabra and mirrors the queen's attitude with hands clasped in front. 'They are playing a most unusual game of hide and seek. All three of the princesses have had the great fortune to fall in love, but it is their unhappy lot to have fallen in love with the same man.'

'Who have they fallen in love with?'

'You know this man very well, Your Majesty. You have looked at him many times over the years – and, personally speaking, I would say that he is far and away the most handsome man in the palace, but with a severe Byronic edge. When you see this man, you just know there's going to be trouble.'

'The rake!' The queen claps her hands. 'I'm so glad you've confirmed what I've always thought about him.'

'Yes, Your Majesty, the rake – truly mad, bad, and dangerous to know – and though I'm sure you don't need any reminding, the rake is stuck in the debtor's prison.'

'Just so.'

'The three princesses, Alice, Louise, and Helena, had gone to the debtors' prison to spend their morning looking at the inmates, but when they arrived, they discovered the most beautiful human being any of them had ever seen before. His name was Christian. He wore baggy trousers and a baggy cream shirt, a scarlet neckerchief tied loose about his neck, and a coat of gold brocade that had been given to him by a friend. There he sat, a glass of red wine in hand, wryly amused at how things had come to such a pretty pass. He'd inherited a vast fortune but had lost it all at cards, so there he was in a debtor's prison with nothing but his looks to trade upon.

'The three princesses immediately decided to spring Christian from the gaol. Knowing that their mother would have nothing whatsoever to do with such a venture, they immediately petitioned their father—'

'Prince Albert.'

'That's right, Your Majesty, and though Albert did not think so very much of his sons, he was completely wrapped around his daughters' fingers. Within short order, he had begged the money from his wife, the queen, and the girls set off back to the prison with a bag of golden guineas. Christian was quickly released, and the girls spirited him to the palace and into this very room. There was, however, one last question that had yet to be resolved. The three princesses were all in love with Christian, but it was not possible, in those days at least, to share him. So, how ever do you think they decided, Your Majesty, who would have him?'

'By playing topless hide and seek?'

'Yes, Your Majesty. The three princesses had all wanted to display themselves to best effect and so had allowed Christian to have a peek at their great bounties—'

'They did such things in the reign of my great-great-grandmother?'

'Love drives people to do the strangest things, Your Majesty – particularly when there is an edge of competition with your sisters. It was decided that whoever found the rake would have the perhaps dubious pleasure of becoming his *inamorata*. As for Christian, he also faced a dilemma. All three of the princesses were achingly beautiful, so how could he possibly limit himself to just the one?

'Christian tore out of the room, and the three princesses stood in this circle where we now see them, heads in their hands as they counted to one hundred. Christian did not know where to hide – nor even if he wanted to hide, but soon enough, the decision was made for him. Queen Victoria herself had entered the lobby. She was in conversation with one of the finest craftsmen of the age.

'Christian had no option but to go through the first door that came to hand and immediately entered—'

'The Silk Tapestry Room.'

'And as you know very well, Your Majesty, that room has not so many hiding places. No sooner had Christian entered the room than Queen Victoria followed him inside. With nowhere at all to hide, Christian had no option but to jump into the middle of a picture, where he remains to this today.'

'*The Mock Election*,' the queen says contentedly. 'By Haydon.'

'If Christian had held off from jumping into the picture even for a moment, he might have continued to lead his dissolute life. Queen Victoria had taken her master craftsman into the wrong room. She stepped smartly out of the Silk Tapestry Room and led the craftsman to the Green Drawing Room, where the three princesses had not even counted halfway to one hundred. The queen was scandalised. Her craftsman, Benjamin Vulliamy, was utterly entranced. The image of the three topless princesses was so utterly seared into his brain that even years later, when he came to make these candelabras, he could recall each princess down to the very last detail.'

The queen looks at her watch. As so often happens when Campion embarks on a story, she is running late. 'Thank you, Campion. I'll never see the princesses in the same way again.'

'Thank you, Your Majesty,' Campion says, and after another curtsy and after the queen has left the room, she continues with her dusting.

Campion goes to her room to freshen up before lunch. The wardrobe still irritates her. In place of the broken leg, it is now propped up with seven of her books. It is only when she is leaving the room that Campion notices the letter that has been pushed under the door. It says simply, "For Campion". She takes the envelope to her desk as the thick creamy vellum paper deserves a knife rather than her index finger.

It is an invitation to a party – and, of course, it has to be *that* party. Probably just a joke, but if it is a joke, then somebody has gone to a great deal of trouble. Alongside the invitation is a £300 Harrods voucher, worth more than a week's salary. Across the top is scrawled, "Treat yourself".

Campion goes to the staff payphone in the basement and calls up the RSVP number, which also appears to be genuine. *Company* magazine is not just expecting her at the Great Gathering of the Eligibles in three days – they are looking forward to it.

Campion makes a disbelieving sniff. This is either the most elaborate practical joke in history or... it is the inexplicable real deal.

She finds out the next day when she presents the voucher at Harrods. It turns out to be genuine.

Campion buys a dress, not in black, but in a much more sophisticated dark blue. She also picks some party shoes.

In all, the bill comes to quite a bit more than £300, though Campion so charms the Harrods staff that they take the voucher and nothing else.

There remains one last matter, and she knows straight where to go. He is in the canteen; tailcoat draped over a chair, waistcoat undone, and, as usual, his breath smells of sherry.

'It was you, wasn't it?'

'What was me?' He barely looks up and continues to cut a tomato into very precise quarters.

She takes a seat opposite him. 'You gave me the invite to the *Company* party. You gave me the voucher.'

'I don't know what you're talking about.' Lawrence gives her a cool look, just a trace of a smile.

'It couldn't have been anybody else.'

'I still don't know what you're talking about, Campion.' Lawrence eats a small piece of tomato and delicately pats his lips with a paper napkin. 'Why could what only have been me?'

'Let me tell you something, Lawrence. I know palace footmen. I don't know what on earth you're doing here, but you whiff to high hell.'

'Charming,' he says. He looks at her dead square, eyes flickering with amusement – no doubt about it. He is nothing like a footman. 'So, will you be going to this party?'

Until now, Campion hadn't made up her mind. 'I think I will.' She gets up from the table. 'And thanks.'

'I thought Mrs Boyd had put you on the evening shifts.'

'She has,' Campion says.

Two days later, when Campion should have been starting her evening shift, she skulks from the palace wearing trainers and a nondescript black coat. She's put on some lipstick and brushed her hair, but anything more would have been just gilt on the lily. It is only a half-mile to Old Burlington Street in Mayfair, so she walks and she wonders just what she's let herself in for. Why does she even want to go to this party when she doesn't know a soul there, and where, more likely than not, if she speaks to anyone at all, they'll be a complete prat – well, they'd have to be. Who else but a prat would even think of going along to Legends to join the so-called hundred most eligible people in Britain? As for herself, well, she's going out of general interest and amusement. And hadn't she only just admitted to Lawrence that she hadn't been to a party in years, and lo and behold, the invite had instantly appeared – and wouldn't she just love to know how Lawrence had fixed it – so it would have been churlish in the extreme not to have attended.

Dear old Anne is pulling a double shift to cover for Campion – though, most likely, nothing will happen. The evening shift is never overly taxing. There just has to be a maid or two on standby in case a royal needs a fresh cotton earbud, or perhaps a helping hand with the toothpaste, or another hot-water bottle. Not for the first time, Campion thinks about how the royals have become completely infantilised by their staff, utterly incapable of doing anything for themselves.

The previous evening, Prince Andrew had been loafing in his office doing, as always, precisely nothing when he decided that the curtains needed closing. But rather than getting up and closing the curtains himself – they were only three yards from his desk – His Royal Ridiculousness rang for Campion to do the job. She had to trot up four flights of stairs to the duke's apartment, and then, as Andrew perved at her figure, she heaved the heavy curtains together. The curtains were full length, floor to ceiling, and it had taken all her strength to shift them and all the while the duke just sat on his fat backside and watched her. Naturally, there had been no word of thanks. No, all the idle sod could do was bark out to Campion that she'd missed a spot at the top where the curtains hadn't quite come together. She actually laughed in his face.

'Yes, Your Royal Highness,' she said, with just a lovely hint of irony that nearly but did not quite overstep the mark. Well, if she didn't laugh, it would have driven her mad. As she left his office, she said, 'Will that be all, Your Royal Highness?'

He looked at her with what she could only presume he imagined was a devilish smile and said, 'That will be all. For the moment.' It had of course occurred to her that it might not have just been about the curtains…

Just before she arrives at Legends, she switches her trainers for party shoes. She's heard of the club, a relic of the 1980s that is still somehow just keeping its head above water; most of its clientele have ditched it for the giant raves that are being set up in fields on the edge of the M25.

A couple of burly bouncers are standing at the door, and behind them, just tucked inside, is a brisk, efficient woman who is obviously in charge. Next to her is a man with a clipboard.

'Good evening,' the woman says. She has severe black hair and lips that are bright scarlet. 'Here for the party?'

'I am. It's Campion.'

The woman and the man do a double take. 'You're Campion?' she says. 'I was wondering who you'd be. Kim told me to take extra special care of you. I'm Lyndsey.'

Lyndsey leads the way down a sweeping chrome staircase and into a basement that is a shrine to 1980s kitsch, all chrome and mirrors with black and silver Marilyn Monroe wallpaper. At least sixty people are already there, most of them chatting in clusters, some already paired off around the tables. The Pet Shop Boys pump out of the speakers as a few of the rich and the beautiful do minimal moves on the dance floor, a small step here, a hand twitch there.

'Who's Kim?' Campion says.

'Kim?' Lyndsey says. 'Kim from *The Sun*? I thought you knew him.'

'Kim from *The Sun*?' Campion says. 'What does Kim look like?'

'Let me take your coat,' Lyndsey says. The coat comes off, and out of it emerges a dark-blue butterfly. 'I guess he's a bit over six-foot tall, floppy hair, slightly receding. He's got a greasy snub nose, though he likes to call it *retroussé*. All in all, I'd give him about a four out of ten.'

Campion gives a grim nod. 'And he works for *The Sun*?'

'He's the cheekiest bastard on the whole damn paper,' Lyndsey says. 'So, how do you know Kim?'

'He's just a…' She draws breath. 'He's a friend. Though I know him by a different name.'

'He's a weasel!' Lyndsey laughs. 'But as weasels go, he's okay. I'll just take this to the cloakroom, and then I'll introduce you to some of our devilishly handsome bachelors.'

'Thank you.'

Campion sits on one of the bar stools as two barmen make cocktails. She knew it. She absolutely knew it. Of course, he works for *The Sun* – and has got himself a job as a footman, and in a few weeks' time, *The Sun* will be running wall-to-wall pictures of the palace, along with every piece of gossip that Lawrence can lay his grubby hands on.

A barman comes over. 'Like one of our specials, a tequila slammer?'

'Yes, please.' Campion stares sightlessly into the mirror behind the bar, looking without looking at the shelves and shelves of spirits. A *Sun* reporter in the palace? She's not sure how she feels. Is it so awful? Is it a bit of fun? Is it, in fact, an issue of national security?

The tequila slammer is placed on the bar. She thanks the barman. Looking at the twee paper doily on which the glass has been placed, her gaze drifts back to the mirror behind the bar. She becomes aware that somebody else is also looking in the mirror, is looking at her. For some time, they just look at each other in the mirror.

Campion picks up her tumbler, takes a sip – not bad, actually – then turns to face the man standing at the bar.

'I have to admit it,' she says. 'As gatecrashers go, you're pretty resourceful.'

'Ye… years of practice, Campion,' he says. 'I started

gatecrashing my mother's cocktail parties when I was six years and I… I never looked back.'

Campion absorbs little details about the guy; well-cut suit in dark grey, open neck cream shirt, mother-of-pearl cufflinks, and where there should be a fat gold signet ring, half his little finger is missing. Possibly a banker, but the Paisley-pattern handkerchief in his pocket doesn't really go with that. Crinkly cut blonde hair and a face that's not… unattractive, but neither was it attractive or beautiful. A perfectly amenable face. Then there's the stammer which, for some reason, she finds oddly endearing. Sometimes he seems to mask it with lengthy pauses, and sometimes he just stammers the word out.

'So, do you do anything else apart from gatecrashing parties?' she says.

He laughs at that; very white teeth, a lot of expensive dentistry going on there. 'Gatecrashing is a full… full-time job.' He rewards himself with a sip of tequila. 'Not bad, but I'd only want one,' he says. 'I've spent the last week tending your namesakes.'

'In your mother's herbaceous border, as I remember.'

'You remember it ex… exactly,' he says. 'I have been… tending my m… my m… my m-m-mother's campions as well as all the other flowers in her garden. In fact, I could tell you the name of every shrub, flower and tree in the garden.'

'Finally,' she says, 'we have something in common. I learned the plant names from my grandparents.'

'Did you learn the… the birds too?'

'More than that, I learned to identify them from their bird song.'

'May… I test you?'

'What – on bird songs? How are you going to do that? Got a bird caller in your pocket?'

'I have… not,' he says. 'But I do have these.'

He flutters his fingers in the air. Campion looks sceptical. 'What you going to do – a wolf whistle?'

'Watch me.' He cups his hands together to form a hollow

ball, and though Campion can't quite see the mechanics of what he is doing, he softly blows between his thumbs, a throaty coo, redolent of woods and ripe fields of wheat.

'A wood pigeon!' she says, perhaps a little more enthusiastically than she intended. 'How did you learn that?'

'Charley, the gardener, taught me.' He nods to himself. 'In fact, Charley probably taught me every useful thing I know.' His words hang in the air. Before he can steel himself to say any more, Lyndsey breezes over.

'Glad you've already met,' she says. 'You two ready to fall in love?'

Campion looks warily at the man. He responds with a look of utter confusion. 'Excuse me?' she says.

'You ready to fall in love?' Lyndsey repeats.

'Has my m... mother been on at you?' the man says.

'It's the very latest thing from America.' Lyndsey produces from her bag a plump white envelope. 'A series of questions that you both have to respond to. Devised by psychiatrists, just published in the *New York Times*. Now, for the very first time, exclusively brought to England – with just a few added tweaks courtesy of *Company* magazine.'

Campion takes the envelope, tapping it in the palm of her hand. 'So, we do this questionnaire—'

'And if you're both single and well, let's say, not averse to the idea of falling in love, then you'll fall in love.' She gives Campion a smile. 'So long, of course, as you're not physically repulsed by each other – but given enough time, even Beauty fell for her Beast.'

Campion appraises the guy again. Well, she isn't overly attracted to him. But then he isn't hideous either. For a moment, she even thinks about what it'd be like to fall in love with this guy – then smartly brings herself up short. What a fantastical load of bilge! Falling in love, or at least the little she knows of it, takes time and chemistry, and the very idea that she could fall in love with this stuttering, wardrobe-smashing gatecrasher is beyond farcical. Besides: So not her type. No chemistry. And without that, the whole thing is beyond pointless.

'I don't ever think I've been in… in… in love,' the guy says.

See! He can't even spit the word out. No. Chemistry. Whatever! 'I've been in love,' Campion says. 'It is grossly overrated. It's nice for a while, but sooner or later, you'll get your heart broken, and that heartbreak does not even come close to the fleeting pleasure of being in love.'

'That's a great attitude to have, Campion,' Lyndsey says. 'Being in love is a risky business, so if you're risk-averse, it's probably not for you.'

'All downside, v… very little upside,' the guy says.

'That's right,' Lyndsey says. 'The upside of love is pitiful! Negligible! Kissing all those frogs in the vain hope that you might find your prince, when, guess what, the only prince you're ever going to find is in fairy tales!'

'You… you sound like you know what you're talking about.'

'Year in, year out, we do this list of eligibles, we throw this party for the sexiest people alive, and how many weddings do you think we've had out of it? Not. One.' She beckons to the barman. 'Probably quite a lot of shags, but they're not quite the same. God, I need a drink.'

'All right, all right,' Campion says. Not that – even remotely – she wants to fall in love with this guy, or that she wants him to fall in love with her, but she is intrigued. 'Tell me about the questionnaire.'

'It's just thirty-six questions. Nothing too spicy.' Lyndsey necks the glass of champagne that has been brought for her. 'There is a surprisingly good kicker at the end.'

'Forgive my scepticism,' Campion says. 'Hey – Gatecrasher. What do you think?'

'I… I'd love to be in love,' he says.

'Well, isn't that just dandy?' she says. 'You sure you want to do this questionnaire thing with me? I gather some of Britain's most eligible spinsters are here – some of them must be just dying for a chat.'

'Are…' He gulps. 'Are you sure you want to do it with me?'

'Why not?' Campion shrugs. 'I'll give you one thing, Gatecrasher. You're not going to break my heart.'

'I've… I've never broken anyone's heart,' he says. 'I better order a bottle of champagne.'

CHAPTER 9

Seeing as it was my first day at Buckingham Palace, I decided to follow Ollie's lead. For lunch, our spaghetti bolognese was washed down with kettle gin and lime cordial, and we continued to tipple on the gin as Ollie showed me how to lay up in one of the staff dining rooms. I'd never seen such a palaver – but such was life at the palace, where staff measured their worth by how their meals were served and how much time had been spent on laying out their dining tables.

Buckingham Palace had several staff dining rooms, each of them just a little more luxurious. Along with the staff bedrooms, it was these dining rooms that reflected where a staff member stood in the palace pecking order.

Right at the bottom, obviously, were the footmen, the maids, the craftsmen, and the carpenters. We all had our meals in the self-service canteen on the ground floor, with its plastic seats and lino floor – raucous, loud with laughter, just like any other work canteen. The next rung up the staff ladder was the stewards' dining room, which was for the pages, yeomen, and anyone who'd served twenty or more years at the palace. It had carpets and comfy upholstered chairs, and its members were treated to a selection of breads, cheeses, and crackers. Next up was the officials' dining room for the personal secretaries, clerks, and press officers. Another dining room, Lady Barrington's Room, was where the master of the household would sip a pre-prandial with the chief housekeeper and the paymaster, and where fine wines and vintage brandies were served with the meals. Then right at the very top of the tree was the dining room next to the Bow Room, complete with Royal Collection portraits and Chippendale furniture. Here dined the ladies-in-waiting, the mistress of the robes, the queen's chaplain, the Lord Chamberlain, and the equerries-in-waiting. It was in this dining room that I would cut my teeth as a palace waiter. It was terribly stiff, as if all of them were terrified that their poor table manners would give the game away. The only genuine laughter I heard in the room was from Ollie as he showed me the ropes.

There was a long, rectangular table, and we'd already laid out a fresh white linen tablecloth. While I polished the silver cutlery to a high sheen, Ollie was doing some basic maths in a little booklet that had been set aside for the purpose. 'My C-grade GCSE finally comes into its own,' he said. 'We've got eighteen people dining here tonight, one at each end, so that'll be eight down each side. Now for the clever bit. The table is currently seven metres long, so we divide that by eight to give us the magic number, which is…' He fiddled around with his pencil. 'Eighty-seven point five.'

'Eureka!' I said, trying to get into the spirit of things.

'Then, using my magic butler's stick, which is nothing more than a glorified ruler, we can measure off each setting so that every guest gets their apportioned 87.5 centimetres and not a millimetre more.'

'Is it a big deal?' I said.

'It's a massive deal!' he laughed. 'They're absolute pedants. If you got one of the place settings out by as much as a centimetre, they'd not only notice, but they'd tear you off a strip.'

'Last time I had a bollocking, the guy tried to strangle me,' I said chattily. I gave a spitty breath onto the back of a spoon and worked on it with a cloth. It came up a treat – positively gleaming.

'They're unlikely to strangle you here.' Ollie was setting out the first placement at the end of the table. 'But they can get quite shouty. It all comes from the top. Prince Philip is constantly shouting and swearing over anything at all that's not entirely to his liking, so his underlings then take it out on their underlings, and so it cascades all the way down to the bottom of the heap, which is you.'

'Who do I get to shout at?'

'You can scream into a pillow – quite common in the palace, as you know, though they're mainly pillow-biters.'

We were snickering just as the door opened. Ollie's face dropped and he busied himself with some of the glasses.

'What's going on here?' I recognised the man from all my homework over the previous month. He looked like a jungle fighter who had somehow been shoehorned into a two-piece suit. His general air of menace was capped off with a savage scar above his nose, said to have been the result of a fight to the death with a leopard.

'Just laying up, sir,' Ollie said while I, in my very meekest manner, continued polishing the spoons.

'What were you laughing at?'

'Just a quip, sir, nothing more.'

'Who is this?'

'This is our newest recruit, sir. Lawrence. Just joined us today as a junior footman.'

The man took a stroll around the dining room. 'Do you know who I am?'

'I certainly do, sir,' I said. 'You're the master of the household, Major General Sir Richard Arnison-Newgass, KBE, DSO, MC Bar.'

He couldn't quite tell if I was taking the piss. 'Do you normally recite somebody's honorifics?'

'Only when they're as distinguished as yours, Sir Richard.' I don't know what had got into me. First day at school, and already I was cheeking one of the prefects.

'I presume you know what my role is within the royal household.'

'You're in charge of everything below stairs, Sir Richard,'

I said, and before I could stop myself, I blurted, 'Sort of like a hotel manager.'

Ollie gave a brief, desperate shake of the head.

Major General Sir Richard Arnison-Newgass recoiled. 'As it is your first day, I will ignore your impudence,' he said. 'But I will thank you to remember that the master of the household is a lot more than a hotel manager.'

'Yes, Sir Richard,' I said. 'Much more.'

He gave me another scowl. 'Furthermore, you address me as sir.'

'Yes, sir. Sorry, sir.'

'I don't know whether you are endeavouring to vex me, but you, young man, are most certainly succeeding. As you well know, you are here on a month's trial. I shall be keeping a very, very close eye on you. If I hear any more lip to either me or any other senior member of staff, then your trial period will be brought to a very abrupt conclusion. Am I clear?'

'Yes, sir,' I said, though I could see he was still irritated; I think it might have been the jaunty way that I was polishing the spoons. He let out a petulant tut, turned on his well-shod heel, and departed.

I was about to speak when Ollie shushed me, miming that the master of the household was, pathetically, still standing behind the door. Hadn't he got anything better to do? We continued to lay up in silence, me polishing while Ollie measured out his 87.5 centimetres. After five minutes, he thought it was safe to talk.

'Christ alive.' He laughed. 'You called Sir Richard a hotel manager. To his face!'

'I thought that was pretty much what he was.'

'It's exactly what he is.' Ollie shook his head. 'But you don't tell him he's a hotel manager. Why don't you go and tell Prince Andrew that he's a randy old lech?'

'Point taken,' I said. 'Got any more gin?'

Ollie gave me a laminated sheet so I could get the exact placements of the cutlery and the glasses – all utterly ludicrous, but that's how they liked things at the palace. Or, at least, that was how the staff liked things. Personally, I didn't think the queen could have given two hoots if she had fish fingers and beans for her supper off a tray, but every meal, every day, she had to have the complete works – and the staff, in their turn, insisted on the same privileges. They'd have spent the past twenty years measuring out place settings to the last millimetre, so when they finally made it to the top table, they wanted the same level of service that was afforded to Her Majesty – though more so.

Most people might imagine that the person at the top of the Buckingham Palace tree was the queen. This was not the case, for, in Buckingham Palace, there was one cantankerous resident to whom even the queen had to defer. She was immensely powerful and had such a network of spies that nothing could occur either below or above stairs without her knowing. Her name was Margaret MacDonald – though she was universally known as Bobo.

Bobo had been not just the queen's nursemaid, but also her dresser, stylist, and most intimate of confidante bar none. Why, she'd even slept in the same room as her charge until Princess Elizabeth was thirteen years old. Bobo had a level of closeness to the queen that the ladies-in-waiting could only have dreamed of.

Margaret MacDonald had been brought up in the Black Isle, north of Inverness, and had worked as a hotel chambermaid. When she was eighteen, she joined the Duke of York's household to look after the duke's baby daughter Elizabeth. The story goes that the young nursemaid would play hide and seek in the gardens with the toddler Elizabeth, crying out 'Boo!' to which Elizabeth would clap her hands and cry, 'Boo! Boo!' – and so she was christened Bobo.

The queen, in her turn, had her own childhood nickname. She was called Lilibet because she'd found the name Elizabeth such a tongue-twister. Bobo was one of the few people in the world who were allowed to call the queen by this affectionate nickname. (Prince Harry and his Meghan cheekily filched that name for their daughter. The queen, of course, sucked it up, just like she'd long been trained to do, but I'll bet she absolutely hated it.)

This then was the most powerful person in the whole of the palace, a woman who had survived sixty-seven years of palace infighting – thrived on it – and who, when it came to backstabbing and intrigue, could have tutored Niccolò Machiavelli. Bobo had even shoehorned her own sister into the royal household as Princess Margaret's dresser.

Though it was some time before I was allowed to meet the queen, I met Bobo on my first afternoon. Had I been aware of the honour that was about to be paid me, I would not have become, as my grandmother so liked to say, "fusionless with drink".

Ollie and I had been down in the kitchens preparing Bobo's tea tray. Like all the senior royals, her tray had to be laid out in a very specific pattern; every royal had their own little idiosyncrasies, which all had to be catered for. The layout of Bobo's tray had all been duly recorded in a thick file.

'So, what would happen,' I said to Ollie, 'if we put the teapot on the left and the milk on the right?'

'She'd probably hurl it in your face,' Ollie laughed. 'As you will soon discover, the senior staff are much bigger sticklers for their tray layouts than the actual royals – with the exception of Prince Grumpling.' (This had been Prince Andrew's childhood nickname – and like Bobo's nickname, it had also stuck.)

'Shall I take the kettle?' I asked.

'Leave that here. Bobo knows exactly what we use these kettles for.'

Like drunken sots the world over, I placed the kettle on the table with exaggerated care and somehow lost my balance, and Bobo's cucumber sandwiches ended up on the floor.

'You better go to bed,' Ollie said, cheerfully picking up the sandwiches and returning them to the plate.

'No, I'm good. I'm good,' I said. 'I'll be fine. I'm ready to meet her. I want to meet her.'

Ollie looked askance. 'Just keep your mouth shut and stand by the door.'

'Got it. Keep my mouth shut. Stand by the door,' I said. 'So, what's Bobo like?'

'Like a lighthouse,' he said.

'What's that mean?'

'You'll soon find out.'

The kitchens were deep down in the palace basement, so it took us some minutes to walk to Bobo's apartments. (As it is walking to any of the royals' suites in Buckingham Palace. I guess they just like eating their food stone cold.)

'Get to the edge of the carpet,' Ollie said.

'I know, I know,' I said. 'They'll go mental if they catch me!'

'I should have left you in the kitchen.'

'I'm fine!'

Ollie knocked on a huge door, and after a sufficient pause, we went into Bobo's parlour. (Though I never went into the queen's apartment, it was always said that Bobo's apartment was more luxurious than Her Majesty's.) It had all the usual palace trimmings, Sèvres china, Royal Collection pictures, polished French furniture, vast ceiling – surprising how quickly I had become immune to it all. As for the great Bobo, she was sitting at a table by the window, leafing through an old photo album. Since she'd accompanied the queen on every single one of her tours, she had a lot of photo albums.

You wouldn't have guessed that she'd spent the last sixty-seven years being waited on hand and foot because to look at, you'd have taken her for a dour hard-working Scottish crofter. Ferociously lined and with a sour, puckered mouth that looked like she was permanently eating a crab apple, she was wearing a grey dress with a Black Watch tartan shawl over her shoulders.

'What do ye want?' she said in a very thick Scottish brogue.

'I've brought your tea, Miss MacDonald,' Ollie said.

'Och, but it's no teatime. I havenae had my breakfast.'

Ollie gave me a slight raise of his eyebrows before placing the tray on the table. Despite Ollie's admonitions to stay by the door, I wandered into her room and took up station by a coffee table that had been quite overloaded with silver-framed pictures.

'Maybe you didn't have breakfast, Miss MacDonald, but we have a lovely tea for you. Cucumber sandwiches, your favourite, and some Battenburg cake.'

She looked at him suspiciously. 'Where are me crusts?'

'The chef cut the crusts off, Miss MacDonald.'

'I want crusts.'

'Very good, ma'am. I'll just see about getting you some crusts.' Ollie placed the tray on the table. 'First, let me pour you a cup of tea.'

Imagine a very pampered Scottie dog, old, hungry, and most ill-tempered. That was exactly what Bobo looked like as she watched Ollie pour the tea. She might not have had much of a handle on life, but she certainly knew the correct way to pour tea. Ollie took great pains to get it right. He poured the tea, then added milk and two lumps of sugar but refrained from stirring. Within the royal household, it was considered bad manners to stir your tea. The correct etiquette was to wait patiently for the sugar to dissolve. 'Your tea is ready, Miss MacDonald.'

'So it is, so it is.'

She sipped the tea, eyes wandering around the room before they finally latched on me. Fully focused.

'Who is this young man?'

'This is Lawrence, our new trainee footman, Miss MacDonald.'

'Another one.' She sniffed. 'I have seen them come, I have seen them go – and a lot of them I have seen under the sod.'

'A pleasure to meet you, Miss MacDonald.'

'I am sure it is.' She took another sip of sweet tea. 'Well, be off with you. Be back in thirty minutes with my Laphroaig, and make sure the water is tepid. Last time it was too cold, much, much too cold.'

'Yes, Miss MacDonald.'

Now that the ordeal was nearly over, my guard was down. Somehow, my foot became entangled in the coffee table. Instead of stepping smartly out of the door, I managed to kick the table halfway across the room. Every one of Bobo's silver-framed pictures cartwheeled across the floor, and at least a couple of them were smashed. I staggered into the wall but just managed to stay on my feet.

'Miss MacDonald, I must apologise,' I said.

'Ye're drunk.'

Ollie started shooing me out of the room. 'I'll get all this tidied up just as soon as I can, Miss MacDonald.'

'He has been drinking Her Majesty's gin. I can smell it from here. The master of the household will be informed. I will be much surprised if he is still here tomorrow.'

Ollie hoofed me out of the room.

'Wait here while I clean up.'

Ollie plonked me down onto one of the chairs in the corridor, where I spent the next five minutes contemplating my misdeeds. Spike would go mad, no doubt about it. I mean he was mad most of the time, but this time it was going to be Hiroshima. Even though I was soused, I was already wondering how best to dress it up. Maybe one of the palace press officers had recognised me.

I was just musing on whether there'd be time to nip up to my room to get my camera. Even with just a few pictures in the bag, I might still be able to salvage something from the whole fiasco. True, I wouldn't have all the salacious tittle-tattle Spike had been longing for. But, nevertheless, I, a *Sun* staff reporter, had been given a job as a Buckingham Palace footman: it was nothing short of The Most Deplorable Security Scandal! Why, given half a chance I could have slipped a dose of cyanide into Her Majesty's gin…

Ollie popped his head out of the door and jerked his thumb. 'Come in here,' he said with a big grin on his face.

I returned to Bobo's apartment. Bobo was studying her photo album. She gave us another of her suspicious looks. 'What de ye want?'

'Just come to pick up your tea things, Miss MacDonald.'

'My tea? But I havenae had my breakfast.'

'Very good, Miss MacDonald. I'll just see about getting you some.'

The coffee table had been righted, Bobo's pictures all once again crammed back-to-back. As for the three broken picture frames, they had been slipped onto the tea tray.

'I'll be back shortly with your whisky, Miss MacDonald,' Ollie said as we made to leave the room.

'Whisky?' she said. 'I dinnae touch the stuff, I dinnae touch it. Get oot me room. Get oot.'

Outside, Ollie leaned against the wall and started laughing. 'You got away with it, you goon!'

'She is a lighthouse,' I said. For most of the time, all was darkness. Then, for a brief period, the lighthouse beam was full upon you, quite shockingly bright, giving you a glimpse of this woman's once formidable power, and then, as quickly as it had come, it had gone again, and all had returned to a formless void.

CHAPTER 10

Mason, hit by a freight train and still punch-drunk, goes to the bar and orders one double Talisker and then a second. People occasionally come over to chat – it is, after all, a party for the most eligible people in Britain – but now that, just as Lyndsey predicted, he's fallen in love, small talk with strangers isn't going to cut it any more. Just one other thing, not much, but still vaguely pertinent. Are his feelings even remotely reciprocated? It all ended so very abruptly that he does not have the faintest idea.

Lyndsey breezes over, clipboard still in hand. 'So how did it go with Campion?' she says.

'P…pretty well,' Mason says. 'At least I think it did.'

'It always goes fine with the questions until one comes along to trip you up.'

'I had that.'

It more than tripped him up, though, more like kicked him to the ground. A worm of a memory that had been eating away at him for over a decade, and tonight, for the first time, it had reared up into full, bright consciousness.

At least the start had been amazing.

Mason thinks back to an hour before when he had led the way to a discreet table underneath the winding chrome staircase. He – the Gatecrasher – was about to spend time with Campion, and though it was probably just Lyndsey's ludicrous hokum, by the end of the evening, they might have… have…

He couldn't bring himself to think the word. Falling in

love with Campion was not only possible, it was probable. But Campion falling for him: debatable. He was more than aware of his limitations; his mother, Viola, trotted them out every chance she got. These included, in no particular order, his love of drink, which bordered (said Viola) on alcoholism; his feckless dilettante lifestyle; his wilful refusal to accept his destiny; and not forgetting, of course, his terrible st-st-st-stutter. That alone aggravated his mother to distraction.

He pulled out a chair for Campion.

'Thank you,' she said.

Mason took his seat, incredibly nervous; Campion's intense beauty did not help.

A bottle of Taittinger was brought over. He topped up two glasses – that, at least, he could do proficiently.

'Your good health,' he said.

'Cheers, Gatecrasher,' she said. 'Want to give this thing a shot?'

'I am… game.' He swallowed. The problem, as Mason well knew, was that his stuttering got worse when he was stressed and much, much worse when he was in the company of a beautiful woman. So his stuttering was about to go off the charts. He'd be lucky to manage more than ten words a minute. Should he mention it? Apologise in advance? No, be damned to that.

Campion broke the seal on the envelope and pulled out a slim wad of cards. She placed them in the middle of the table and took the top card. 'Gatecrasher,' she said, 'given the choice of anyone in the world, who would you want as a dinner guest?

He chewed on his lip. 'The… The Dalai Lama,' he said. 'Intelligent and… and funny.'

'Good choice, Campion said. 'It's not often you get to dine with a living god.'

'And you?'

'Me?' Campion said. 'I think the Queen Mum. I hear her lunches are hilarious.'

'They are. She likes to get everyone drunk on… on gin, and then when they've let their guards down, she gets all the gossip. She hears every… everything, but she never gossips herself.' He peeled the next card from the stack. 'Would you like to be famous? In what way?'

Campion laughed. 'I could not care less for fame,' she said. 'And I have no idea how I'd ever get to be famous. You?'

He shook his head. 'I would h… hate it. Though I could be infamous.'

'I could see you as a pariah,' Campion said. She stretched over to the ice bucket with her long, toned arm and topped up their glasses.

'I had an infamous ancestor,' Mason said. 'General M… M… General Monck. Forgive me.' He knocked back the champagne in one. 'I have, as you can see, the most t… terrible stutter.'

'Take your time,' Campion said. 'Take as long as you need.' She stretched over to take his hand and gave it a friendly squeeze. 'I'd like to apologise. When I found you that morning in the wardrobe, I mimicked you. It was mean. I wasn't having a great day. Anyway, I'm sorry.'

'Thought I got off lightly,' Mason said. 'You should hear what my m… m… mother says.' It was always the same with the M-word. For a while, he'd tried calling her Viola, but she'd disliked that even more than she'd hated his stutter.

'If your mum's like that, what are your enemies like?' Campion took the next card. 'Before making a telephone call, do you ever rehearse what you're going to say? Why?'

Mason laughed. 'I don't just r… rehearse my phone calls. In my head, I rehearse everything that I am going to say, and in my h… head, it comes out perfectly. But the reality is, as you can see, rather different.'

'I don't make many phone calls,' Campion said. 'Only to my grandparents, and when I'm talking to them, I just say the first thing that comes into my head.'

They worked their way through the pile of questions.

They were an intriguing mix, a lot of questions that he'd never even considered before – For what in his life did he feel most grateful? Answer, his health, and his long legs, which could carry him for miles and miles. And, awful, awful question – What was the greatest accomplishment of his life? Answer, he knew not what; as far as he could see, there was nothing whatsoever in his life that could be considered an accomplishment, let alone a great one.

Campion's answer was much more beguiling. While Mason stuttered his way through the very modest achievements of his life, Campion announced that her greatest accomplishment was becoming the queen's storyteller.

'Forgive me,' Mason said. 'You are the queen's storyteller?'

'Not an official position,' Campion said. 'I tell her stories. She hunts me down in the palace, and then, wherever I am, she asks me to tell her a story.'

'Is this a story?' Mason said. It did sound a little unlikely.

'It's true,' she said. 'I never lie.'

'Well, you must be a very... very good storyteller,' Mason said.

'I don't know about that,' Campion said. 'But the queen likes them.'

She asked him if there was something that he'd been dreaming of doing for a long time. 'Some things,' he said.

'So why haven't you done them?' Campion said.

'I'm biding my time,' he said. 'I am waiting for my thirty-second birthday. And when that happens, I... I will be free.' Mason corrected himself, 'More free.'

'Thirty-two?' Campion said. 'That's an unusual age to be given your freedom.'

'It is, b... but it's true.'

'That'll be one hell of a birthday party.'

The questions, as far as Mason saw, started off quite softly, but they gradually dug much deeper. Along with the questions and the confessions, there were also strokes for each other. 'Alternate sharing something you consider a positive characteristic of your partner,' Campion said. 'Share a total of five items.'

'Easy,' he said. 'Your hair. I love it.'

And he did. It was… he hesitated to use the word because it didn't nearly do her hair justice, but it was an afro, a glorious tawny brown afro. To Mason, it was nothing less than a halo.

'Thank you,' she said. 'Your bird calls.'

'Your ability to say sorry like you mean it.'

'Your tasteful but understated clothes.'

'Thank you, Campion. Your very beautiful dress.'

'You not minding being hit by my duster.'

'A duster! I've been thrashed since I was seven.' He gave a dismissive flick of his fingers. 'That you're named after one of my favourite flowers.'

'I like that you even know I'm named after a flower.'

'And for my fifth choice, I like that you are somehow able to… to overlook my stutter.'

'I find it oddly endearing,' she said. 'And for my fifth choice, I like… I like that you like walking because I am a walker too.'

'You are?' he said, beside himself with glee. 'I don't believe it.'

'It's true,' Campion said. 'I told you, I never lie.'

It had all been going so well – astonishingly well. It was light and breezy; it was the most enjoyable time he'd had with a woman in years. He'd asked for another bottle of Taittinger, and, as always, the champagne had weaved its wonderful magic, and his stutter had started to drop away, turning from a st-st-stutter into a ponderous pause that sort of added weight to his words.

And then… then the disaster.

Campion filled their glasses again. 'No need to chug it in one,' she said, turning the next card. 'What is your most terrible memory?'

'Terrible memories?' Mason said. 'How long have you got? I, Campion, have got terrible memories by the…

barrel-load. But my most terrible memory? The one that still makes me wince at the thought...' Up until then, he'd been larking. He'd had a few horrors; others had had it a deal sight worse. Then it came to him, as sharp and as savage as a shank into the base of his neck. Should he... Could he share it?

'Doesn't have to be the most terrible,' Campion said. 'Middling awful will be fine.'

'I might need a glass of whisky for this,' Mason said. 'I've never told anyone before. I haven't even thought about it in over a decade.'

'Don't tell me if you don't want to.'

'I'd like to,' Mason said. Two double shots of Talisker were brought over, ice for Campion, water for Mason.

Campion sipped the whisky and snuggled back into her chair. 'I'm ready.'

'The most terrible thing that ever happened to me?'

'You've given this story quite a build-up.'

'I hope it's worth it.' Mason added water to his whisky, and the story began.

'One of the greatest reliefs of my life was being sent to boarding school when I was seven years old,' he said. 'It meant that, in a small way, I could do my own thing. I was away from my... my mother. But for four months of the year, I was back at home, and when I was there, I used to spend as much time as I could with Charley, the gardener. He had a shed next to the greenhouse, and most days in the holidays, this was where I would go straight after breakfast.'

'I'm enjoying this,' Campion said.

'Good,' Mason said. 'I was not much use about the garden, but I'd follow Charley around and help as best I could – planting in the spring, gathering in the autumn – and along the way, Charley taught me the names of everything in the garden – every bird, every creature, and every plant. I learned of all the various types of grasses, mosses and lichens, and not just their names but their Latin names too. And, of course, I learned how to talk to wood pigeons, owls, and cuckoos.'

Mason closed his eyes and remembered the shed – its smell of peat and creosote, the cobwebs over the windows, the dust hanging in the spangled air.

'At teatime, or pretty much any other time that Charley fancied, he'd prime his stove, and as the water came to the boil, he'd grind a handful of coffee beans. There was never any milk, so the coffee was always black and sweetened with honey from the hives at the back of the garden. We'd drink it out of battered enamel cups, and Charley would tell stories from his childhood.

'His first job at the big house had been as a human bird-scarer, but his voice had been so extremely musical that it rather allured the birds than terrified them. After two days, Charley was told to stop singing and was given a pair of clappers.

'If it was wet, we would often indulge in our hobby, grafting. It was the one thing Charley loved more than anything else,' Mason told Campion. 'And pretty soon, I loved it too. In the winter, we'd graft branches onto trees. It was just a bit of fun, but the trees looked amazing. In the greenhouse, there was an orange tree that grew lemons – and a lemon tree that grew limes—'

'You can do that?'

'Yes,' Mason said. 'You do it in the winter when the orange tree is quite young, not much more than two years old. You cut off a branch from an orange tree and trim the end into a V-shape. Then you cut off a similar size branch from a lemon tree. Splice the two together, bind them up tight, and with a bit of luck, in three years' time, that tree will be growing both oranges and lemons.'

'I'd love to see it.'

'Charley's most amazing plants were his roses. Close by to the conservatory, he had this large patch of them. I can't really remember how big it was, but in my mind's eye, it was enormous – maybe even the size of a tennis court. Some of the older rose bushes had three or four other rose branches spliced onto them – which meant that one single bush could be growing red roses, yellow roses, white roses, and bright orange roses. In the summer, I would lie for hours on end in the middle of the rose garden, and the smell would suffuse my soul.'

'I'm dreading what's going to happen,' Campion said.

'One day, in the summer holidays, when I was about fourteen, I'd made up a little bouquet of flowers for my m… my mother. I was a bit late for lunch – my m… my mother always insisted that luncheon, as she called it, started at one on the dot. The maid had just brought in the soup, and though I'd brought in this nice bunch of roses, all my mother could talk about was that she'd been kept waiting and that her soup had gone cold.' Mason sighed and stroked the back of his hand. 'Even though I was only fourteen, I still had the wit to try to change the subject.'

Funny that he hadn't thought about it in a decade – because now he could remember every last detail.

He'd proffered the flowers to his mother. 'I am very sorry that I am late for luncheon,' Mason had said. 'But don't these roses smell heavenly – and they're all from the same rose bush.'

His mother had sniffed. She felt that Mason had not yet been properly dealt with. 'Don't be so ridiculous,' she'd said.

'It's true,' Mason had said.

'It is not possible,' she'd said, thereby bringing the matter to a close.

Mason could have let it ride. What was the point in arguing with an ignoramus? But then… where did you draw the line? If you had to deal with an ignoramus day in and day out, then at some stage, you had to call them out.

'You don't know what you're talking about,' Mason had said.

'Do not contradict me in front of the staff,' his mother had said. The maid, Alison, was still in the room, standing limply by the bread basket.

'You certainly d…don't… don't mind contradicting me in front of the staff,' he had said.

'Th… th… that is a different matter entirely,' she'd said.

'Why's it different?' Mason had said, blood rising after she'd mimicked him, realising he was in so deep he couldn't go back. 'Especially when you don't know what you're talking about.'

'Oh, don't I?' she'd said, the winter queen made real.

'You don't know the first thing about the garden,' Mason had said. 'Charley has spent years splicing different roses onto different bushes.' He picked up the bouquet of roses. 'See this pink rose? This is from the original bush. A Shropshire Lad. It's called Rosa Ausled. Then Charley added on a branch of these yellow Golden Celebrations, Rosa Ausgold, and then three years ago, he added on these white Icebergs, Floribunda Rose. I helped him splice the branch myself—'

'Go to your room.'

'If that's how you want to shut me up,' Mason had said as he got up from the table. 'But you're still wrong – and you still don't know what you're talking about. These roses are from the same bush.'

It was a small win, but even then, as he went up the stairs, he knew there would be a reckoning. And what a reckoning.

Mason looked at Campion. 'What happened?' she said softly.

'I'll tell you,' Mason said. 'The next day, I was down for breakfast at 8.30 on the dot. That was when breakfast was served. But my m… my mother was a little late; this was very unusual for her. She came into the breakfast room not from the house but through the doors that looked out onto the garden. She was wearing torn jeans and a thick shirt, and she was dirty and very sweaty. I'd never seen her like that before.'

'"Good morning, mother," I'd said. "What have you been doing?"

'"Oh, just a little gardening," she'd said. "At our last luncheon, you rather piqued my interest in roses." She went over to the sideboard to help herself to some kedgeree. "Gosh, I'm famished."

'"Have you been gardening?" I'd asked.

'"I've been up all night," she'd said brightly. "I do hope you like it."

'I already had an inkling of what she'd done. "I've had to let Charley go," she'd said as I went out into the garden. "I don't think there's enough work for him now."

'Out in the garden, I found Charley on his knees by what was left of the rose garden. Tears were pouring down his ash-stained cheeks. My m… my mother had spent the night hacking down every single one of the rose bushes and had capped off her work by setting light to the barrel of creosote in Charley's shed.'

Campion's mouth was a perfect circle of astonishment. 'What a monster.'

'I suppose she loves me in her own way,' Mason said.

'What happened?'

'I left the house that day and started the longest walk of my life. It took them nearly a month to find me – I'd made it up to the Borders. By the time I got back, the rose garden had been grassed over, and as for Charley, he was gone.' Mason nodded to himself.

'He was gone?' Campion said. 'Where?'

'I was never quite sure. After my m… my mother kicked him out, I think he went to live with his daughter. Pathetic that I never made the effort to track him down.'

'You should.'

'I should,' Mason said. 'I should and I will.'

'What a terrible, terrible story,' Campion said.

'Certainly taught me not to argue with my… my… mother.' Mason glumly signalled for more champagne. Lyndsey was hovering by the staircase. 'Can I help you?'

'Sorry to butt in on what looks like a highly engrossing story,' Lyndsey said. 'Call for Campion.'

Campion had stroked Mason's shoulder as she got up.

She'd walked up the stairs. What an amazing woman! What a connection! Maybe it was the love questionnaire – maybe it was Campion. Stunningly beautiful. And she probably liked him, at least a little bit. The way she'd touched his shoulder when she left, affectionate and kind, but it might have meant something more, might have. He loved her hair, and he loved her mouth. He wondered. No. Way too early for that, and he had no experience whatsoever. He wondered... Wouldn't it be great if she even found him the slightest bit attractive, if, even by the smallest degree, his feelings were just slightly reciprocated?

Campion bustled down the stairs, already pulling on her coat. 'I'm so sorry,' she'd said. 'I've got to go.'

Mason got to his feet. He couldn't understand what was happening. 'You're going?' he said.

'I'm sorry,' she said again. 'And thank you.' She put her hand lightly on his shoulder, kissed him on the cheek, and before he'd been able to say another word, had darted up the stairs.

Mason crumpled back into his chair. Then he went to the bar and did what he usually did when he was being tormented by memories of his mother and ordered two large whiskies.

CHAPTER 11

As soon as she is out of Legends, Campion swaps her high heels for trainers and sets off for the palace. Anne hadn't been very specific about what the problem was, but it was clear enough that, as usual, the problem was Mrs Boyd. Campion waves at the policeman at the entrance gate, and then there in the cloakroom, just where Anne had left it, a carrier bag is hanging from one of the hooks. Campion goes into the toilet, quickly changes into some shorts, a top, and a dressing gown and puts on her slippers. Best to leave her dress and shoes down here in the carrier bag; she can pick them up in the morning. A brief look in the mirror – Christ, she still has her lipstick on! She grins at herself as she wipes her lips with a paper towel, then simply trots upstairs to her room, taking as circuitous a route as is necessary in order to avoid the militant Mrs Boyd.

Campion takes to the backstairs and the back passages and, at length, arrives in the Finch's Lobby. She takes a peek around the corner. Mrs Boyd appears to be on sentry duty, pacing up and down the maids' corridor; Campion is going to need a change of tactics.

Campion doubles back to the bathroom and splashes water on her face. In the kitchenette, she heats up some milk in the microwave before thinking sickly thoughts and padding back to her room. She's been ill, so very ill, in and out of that bathroom like a yoyo. She is now trying to settle her stomach, has made herself some hot milk – is there a problem with that? Has dear Anne not been covering for her? Have Prince Andrew's teddies not been put into the fireplace and around the bed? And have the two big teds not been correctly seated on their thrones?

'Where have you been?'

Campion looks up – sick, sick, so very sick, feeling so queasy, not remotely thinking about the gatecrasher. Mrs Boyd comes bowling down the corridor towards her.

'Oh, hello, Mrs Boyd,' Campion says. Visions of throwing up in the lavatory, not at all well. She might need to take the next day off.

Mrs Boyd inspects Campion, eyeballs raking her from head to toe. 'Don't you "Hello, Mrs Boyd" me,' she says. 'Where have you been?'

'I don't know what you're talking about, Mrs Boyd.'

'I will tell you then,' she says, squaring her shoulders. 'Where have you been for the last hour?'

'I've been sick.' Campion does so love being nearly a foot taller than Mrs Boyd. She lets her gaze fix on the boil on Mrs Boyd's forehead. 'I couldn't get to sleep. I had a little walk, and now…' she let out a deep breath, 'I've made myself some warm milk. I hope it might help me get to sleep.'

'Poppycock.'

'Poppy-what?'

'Nonsense,' Mrs Boyd says. 'You've been out gallivanting.'

'Oh, Mrs Boyd – I love gallivanting as much as the next maid, possibly more so, but tonight, honestly, I couldn't have partied even if it had been at the personal invitation of Prince Andrew.' She takes a sip of the milk and lets a little trickle slip down her chin. 'I'm just not feeling very well.'

'Where have you been?'

'Just walking, Mrs Boyd, I like walking in the palace very much, especially at night-time, when it's dark—'

'God give me strength!' says Mrs Boyd. 'You are lying through your teeth, and one day, one day, you're going to slip up, Campion.'

'Thank you, Mrs Boyd. How very kind of you, Mrs Boyd. Can I go to my bed now, please?'

Mrs Boyd storms off down the corridor. 'And never mind that the queen listens to your fairy tales because when I am done with you, you will be through.'

And there, Campion realises, is the explanation. Senior palace staff are very particular about who has the ear of Her Majesty, and for a junior maid like Campion to be telling stories to the queen goes against the natural order of things. Campion should know that her station is to bow, scrape, dust, and vacuum. Dawdling with the queen – chit-chatting with Her Majesty – while the likes of Mrs Boyd only get to speak to her at Christmas time. It is just unconscionable!

'Night, night, Mrs Boyd,' Campion calls, but the housekeeper is already off down the corridor. Campion turns, and with a jaunty stride, goes to her bedroom. What a way to end the evening. In fact, she wouldn't have had it any other way.

* * *

It takes until lunchtime the next day before Campion locates her quarry. He is sitting by himself, eating a salad, tailcoat neatly folded on a chair next to him, and generally looking like butter wouldn't melt in his mouth.

'Hi Kim, how's it going?'

'I'm pretty damn cheery, thank you, Campion. How...' He tails off.

'Gotcha.'

'I don't know what you're talking about,' he says, primly patting his lips with a napkin and trying to busy himself with a bean sprout.

'So, what's it like working on *The Sun*?' Campion says.

'I'm sorry?'

'Would you like me to speak a little more loudly?' Campion says, now thoroughly enjoying herself. 'Okay, I will.' She dials the volume up a couple of notches. 'What's it like working on—'

'All right, all right,' he says. 'Keep your voice down.'

'So' – with the enemy thoroughly vanquished, Campion, now in full possession of the battlefield, slips into the chair opposite him – 'you admit it. You're a *Sun* reporter.'

He attempts his most winsome smile. 'For my sins.'

'What are you doing here?'

Lawrence – even though he is Kim, she still thinks of him as Lawrence – paws at his mouth. 'Well, umm …' He tries to buy more time by having another stab at the bean sprout. 'It's a, err, security story. I'm a staff reporter for *The Sun*. Yet, somehow, I've landed a job as a palace footman. Shocking lapse in security. Why, if I'd had a mind, I could have poisoned the queen.'

'And how long are you going to stay here?'

'Good question,' he says. 'Not quite sure.'

Campion helps herself to one of his cherry tomatoes, taking her time eating it, and then, what the hell, she just stretches over and has another one. 'Seems to me that you've had over a week here. You've already got the story you want. How's it going to get any better if you stay for another week or two? Surely the security scandal is that you weren't properly vetted in the first place. Doesn't make it any worse if you've spent one week here or three.'

'Campion, of course, in one sense, you're right, but – not that I'd expect you to understand – these are difficult editorial decisions to make—'

'What a load of twaddle,' she says. 'You're just staying here to pick up the gossip!'

'Gossip? Moi?' Lawrence gives a nervous laugh. 'So, how was the party last night?'

Campion holds her hand up to cut him short. 'We will get onto the party shortly,' she says. 'Let's stick with you for the moment. Just tell me why I shouldn't turn you in right now? That'd earn me a few brownie points.' Campion doesn't rightly know who in the palace would award her these brownie points; they probably won't even bother to thank her. Still, once you've got the boot on your victim's neck, it is usually best to keep it there.

'You'd turn me in?' Lawrence says. 'I'm just having a bit of fun minding my own business, not doing anyone any harm. And you want to turn me in? After all I've done for you!'

Campion chuckles. For once – for once! – she's got the whip hand. God, it feels good. And not just anyone. A slimy *Sun* reporter! And she'd got him absolutely bending! 'After all you've done for me?'

'Got you that party invite. How was the party, by the way?'

'You're all heart.'

'Well, I do the best I can,' he says. 'I didn't have to get you an invite to the party. If I'd done nothing, you'd be none the wiser.'

'I knew something was off,' Campion says. 'You're nothing like the other footmen.'

'But you won't blab? Please – pretty please?'

'I'll think about it,' Campion says. 'I do have one very large condition. When you write your story, no smut on the queen.'

'Is there any smut on the queen?'

'You heard me.'

'Campion, Campion,' he says. 'How little you think of me—'

'Says *The Sun* reporter who lied through his teeth to get a job as a footman—'

'Not lied. Dissembled – that's a nicer word.' The sweat is now freely dribbling down his forehead. 'No one wants to read smut about the queen. She's a sacred cow. Everyone loves her.' His eyes brighten a moment. 'Prince Andrew though... If you've got any dirt on him.'

'You seriously think I'm going to become one of your moles?'

'Hey! If you are going to blow the whistle, you'll give me some notice?'

Campion is not remotely ready to cede the total victory that she has just won for herself. 'Might do,' she says noncommittally.

'Well, that's just great,' he says. 'I get you an invite to the hottest party of the year... I get you a fat Harrods voucher... And you'd just throw me to the wolves?'

Campion starts laughing. This isn't simply funny – it is side-splitting. 'Says *The Sun* reporter who makes a living out of throwing people to the wolves.'

'On the contrary, Campion,' he says. 'You entirely misunderstand the role of a modern-day journalist. I give a voice to those who do not have a voice. I hold the great and the powerful to account.'

'Have you started moonlighting for *The Guardian*?'

'All right, all right.' He holds his hands up. 'I'll just have to appeal to your better nature. My future is entirely in your hands.'

'And that's just how I like it,' she says, leaning back in her chair, hands luxuriantly behind her head. 'Tell me about the gatecrasher.'

'The gatecrasher?' he says. 'You mean the guy who borrowed my state livery? The one who hid in your wardrobe?'

'The guy who also smashed the wardrobe.'

'Yeah,' Lawrence says, enthusiastically changing the subject. 'Dented my livery hat. I had to swap it with someone else's. Did you meet him last night?'

'I did, as it happens,' Campion says. 'Is he like a professional gatecrasher?'

'Suppose you could call him that.'

'What's his name?'

'His friends call him Mason. Would you like to see him?'

'What? Right now?'

Lawrence airily looks at his watch. 'Sure, we've got plenty of time.' He twiddles with a tomato, thinks better of it and puts the half-finished salad onto the trolley tray. 'Follow me.'

Campion is ablaze with questions, though she knows she'll never get any answers. Does this Mason guy work in the palace? And if so, what does he do? Part of the press office? Seems unlikely. Accounts? Even more unlikely. Or perhaps he is one of the new under-gardeners, there to attend to Her Majesty's lawns and borders?

Lawrence takes her up to one of the grander corridors in the palace, just bedrooms and suites; as far as Campion knows, there are no offices at all up here.

Campion can't stop herself – 'You're really taking me to see Mason?' – and instantly regrets it. Lawrence is just as smug as she knew he'd be.

'Patience, patience, sweet Campion,' he says. 'It'll be worth the wait.'

Campion bites back her tart reply. Maybe she will tell Major-General Sir Richard Arnison-Newgass that a rogue *Sun* reporter is working in the palace – just for the sweet hell of it.

She hears the corgis before she sees them. All nine of them trot around the corner and into the corridor, and wherever the corgis go, the queen soon follows – as she does. Campion gestures for Lawrence to get off the red carpet and move to the edge of the corridor. She gives a full curtsy, and Lawrence – thankfully – gives a deep bow. The queen, today in a dress of canary yellow, has been talking to a companion. She breaks off when she sees Campion.

'Campion!' she says. 'Good afternoon.'

'Good afternoon, Your Majesty.'

'I have been looking all over the palace for you. Where have you been hiding?'

'I've been on the late shift for the last few days, Your Majesty.'

'Late shifts?' the queen says. 'We can't have that. I want to see you in the daytime, not in the evenings.'

'I'll let Mrs Boyd know, Your Majesty.'

'No, don't do that, at least not if you want to remain in

her good books. I will attend to it...' The queen trails off. The corgis are snuffling around Lawrence's feet; Chipper is ecstatically rubbing his back against Lawrence's ankles. Lawrence remains as rigid as a statue.

The queen looks at Lawrence for the first time. 'I don't think I know you.'

'I am Lawrence, Your Majesty.'

'Chipper seems to like you.'

'Yes, ma'am. We've already been introduced by Mr Brook, the sergeant footman.'

'It's uncanny,' the queen says, peering down at the dogs. 'Chipper never does this with a footman.'

'He can use me as a scratching post any time he likes, ma'am.'

The queen inspects Lawrence over the top of her glasses. Campion gives Lawrence a sharp look. What sort of numpty starts bantering with the queen on a first meeting?

Campion's gaze drifts over to the man standing next to the queen; shiny black shoes, sleek army uniform, Blues and Royals from the look of it – and, of course, it has to be. Who else?

The queen looks up. 'Oh, forgive me,' she says. 'Campion, may I introduce Captain Mason Monck?'

'We've already met, thank you, Your Majesty,' Campion says.

'Have you now?' The queen raises an arched eyebrow. 'You don't hang around, do you, Mason?'

'N... Not with someone like Campion, ma'am.'

'Well, we mustn't dilly-dally.' The queen gives a nod and trails off down the corridor with the corgis. When the dogs are finally out of sight, Campion turns to Lawrence, who is smoothing his greasy hair off his forehead.

'Job done, Mr *Sun* reporter. You've met the queen,' she says.

'And you've been reacquainted with the queen's temporary equerry-in-waiting,' Lawrence says before adding, 'Not that I know much about guys, Campion, but I reckon His Grace is quite keen on you.'

'His Grace?'

'My new buddy, the 9th Duke of Montagu, don't you know?' Lawrence says. 'Affable chap from what I've seen, though the mother's a complete nightmare!'

'I've heard.'

CHAPTER 12

Six weeks after having had the most brilliant idea on the planet, it seems that my stellar career at the palace is on the very verge of being brought to the most abrupt of halts. Not that Campion is necessarily going to shop me to the master of the household – we were, after all, pals. Out of the kindness of my heart, I'd wangled her an invite to that wretched eligibles party, and much thanks I've had for it – i.e., not a damn word, and all she's done is threaten to expose me. I ask you! 'Tis a cruel, cruel world we live in.

So, not that by nature I am an untrusting individual, but it seems best to presume that my palace career is about to come to a speedy and abrupt end – and therefore, of primary importance, I need to get some pictures in the bag. Tabloid reporters can easily write the words, can spin out pages and pages of purple prose from just the measliest of storylines (Spike, the deputy editor, mimes playing a grand piano when he wants us to give a story some oomph), but pictures are much more difficult to fake.

After my drunken escapade with Bobo MacDonald, I spent the next ten days being the very model of a modern royal footman, servile, discreet, and certainly not prowling around the palace with my little Olympus Twin camera. But since my, ahh, pleasant luncheon with Campion, I have thrown caution to the winds. Of course, I could just go around the palace firing off my camera willy-nilly, but pictures of dull corridors and empty staterooms are no use to man or beast. What I need first are pictures of me inside the palace dressed up as a royal footman. Then, after the films have been safely delivered to Spike, I can start snooping through the royals' private quarters. What I want – what *The Sun's* army of readers demand! – are juicy pictures from Prince Andrew's bedroom, paying most particular attention to the seventy-two teddies in line abreast on his four-poster. Then a little frolic around Prince Edward's bathroom, complete with an avocado-coloured bath that apparently looks like something out of a 1960s bedsit. And, for the full trifecta, a picture of Her Majesty's breakfast table, laid – or so I've been told – with a white tablecloth, white china, a vase of flowers, and some incredibly depressing plastic Tupperware for the queen's Special K.

But we are getting ahead of ourselves. First, I need pictures of me in the palace in my fine footman's uniform.

'So, who are these pictures for?'

'They're for my buddy Spike,' I say cheerily as I loll against the bannisters at the Ambassadors' Entrance. 'He still doesn't believe I'm working at the palace.'

Ollie fires off a couple of frames. 'Where also do you want to go?'

'Just take a few pics of me attending to my every-day duties – you know the thing. Carrying a tray down a corridor. Polishing His Nibs' shoes. Picking the fleas off Chipper's ears—'

'That dog's taken quite a shine to you.'

'That's because I've always got a packet of doggie treats in my tailcoat,' I say. 'Chipper knows that every time he sees me, he's going to get fed.'

By now, we've moved up to the staterooms. One of the sheer beauties of our uniforms is that we can go anywhere we please in the palace, no questions asked. Our black tailcoats are the ultimate pass key. We breeze into the White Drawing Room – no alcohol there, unfortunately – and I lean against the mantelpiece, the gentleman at home. It is just another of the queen's huge vast staterooms, mainly white and gold, with an antique piano that is never played and a roll-top desk that nobody ever sits at. I admire myself in a full-size mirror in the corner.

'You'll like this even more,' Ollie says and presses a button on the wall. The whole mirror swings out, and behind it, the royal closet is revealed, a small drawing room where the royals have their pre-function drinks before they join the main party.

'Christ!' I say.

'They like to surprise people,' Ollie says. 'A month ago, this old girl was looking at herself in the mirror when I pressed the button, and she suddenly found she was looking at the entire royal family. She was so shocked she dropped her glass. Philip loved it.'

Ollie takes me through to the Throne Room. Before we go in, he pleads with me not to sit on the chairs.

'Of course not!' I say. 'That would be the most unpardonable *Lèse-Majesté*!'

'What's *Lèse-Majesté* when she's at home?'

'It's French,' I say. 'It is causing offence to the dignity of Her Majesty.'

'Would drinking the queen's gin qualify as *Lèse-Majesté*?'

'Certainly not,' I say. 'Her Majesty's gin is a small recompense for our derisory salary.'

We continue to wander around the palace, ostensibly attending to our duties as Ollie fires away with my Olympus Twin. When, two hours later, I walk out of the palace with three rolls of film in my pocket, I feel considerably more at ease. Even if the whole thing goes belly up this evening – even if Major General Sir Richard Arnison-Newgass takes my bedroom to pieces – I still have enough for a great story.

But it is the reporter's lot that, however much he delivers, his mad masters always want more.

It is my evening off, and a pub meeting has been arranged for 8 p.m. I could have picked any pub in Mayfair or Whitehall, but since I am a journalist, I set upon The Plumber's Arms in

Belgravia. Not many people know of its place in history – but us hacks, we know all about it.

In the 1990s, there was one white whale of a scoop that we all knew was out there but which no journalist had ever been able to land. Tens of millions of pounds have been spent on sending journalists to all ends of the earth in the vain hope that they might bring this monster in. We all know it's out there. We've even had occasional glimpses of the beast. But as yet, nobody has come even close to cracking it. And unlike the entirely fictional Loch Ness Monster (which was invented as a publicity stunt), this beast is real. Whoever eventually brings her in will get all the cash and all the plaudits, and they will have sealed their reputation for life. They will become a journalistic legend. I'm talking about the most infamous fugitive of the 20th century, a peer of the realm who disappeared off the face of Earth and who has never been seen or heard of since. I'm talking about Lucky Lord Lucan, the 7th Earl of Lucan.

Although no one can be truly certain about the facts, the most likely scenario is that on a dark night in November 1974, Lord Lucan tried to murder his estranged wife, Veronica – but instead of killing her, he mistakenly bludgeoned to death his children's nanny, Sandra Rivett.

Having murdered Sandra with a piece of lead piping, Lord Lucan then had a fight with Veronica in the family home in Belgravia. He hit her over the head with the lead piping, but she was made of tough stuff, and she kneed him in the groin. Shell-shocked and winded, the unhappy couple sat on the staircase and had a calm chat about what had happened to Sandra Rivett. Lord Lucan said he'd seen her being attacked by an intruder. The earl excused himself and went upstairs to wash his hands – and Veronica took her chance and fled the house, screaming and screaming as she tore down the pavement. As for Lord Lucan, he had perhaps five minutes to make himself scarce before the police arrived. One of his daughters came out onto the landing to ask what was happening; he told her to go to bed. And that, as far as we know, was the last time Lord Lucan ever saw his children. That night, he drove in his getaway car to a friend's house in Uckfield in Sussex, where he had a whisky and wrote some letters. Three days later, the car was found dumped in Newhaven in Kent – and as for Lucky Lord Lucan, who'd gambled away his entire fortune, he disappeared without a trace. His family, of course, put it about that he'd done the decent thing and killed himself, but Lucan had many very dodgy, very rich friends, and they could easily have spirited him out of the country to a safe haven in Africa. Who knows, who knows – the story is still out there, still waiting to be landed. It's more than possible that Lucan might yet be alive.

Forgive my little meander down memory lane – I find Lucan's story just as riveting now as when I first heard it. Let us return to Veronica, Countess of Lucan, just after she fled the family home in Lower Belgrave Street. She ran hard, screaming at the top of her voice. Blood was pouring from the scalp wound where Lucan had hit her. She didn't know where she was going. She'd even left her three children behind. All she knew was that she wanted to put as much distance as possible between her and her estranged husband. And there, at the end of the street, ablaze with light, alive with gossip and laughter, was her local pub. And thus – at least for us journalists – The Plumber's Arms secured its place in history.

It is all just as I remember it, a lovely old London pub, red lino floor, an array of hand pumps and some dusty wine bottles behind the bar. The Plumber's Arms is a little rough at the edges, and still just about providing pints for the local tradesmen. I get a pint of Theakston's and, rather than taking a table, I go to study the pictures on the wall. They are a small tip of the hat to the pub's place in history, framed front pages from 1974. There is one from the *Daily Mirror* asking the same question that we have continued to ask: 'Where did he go?'

I hear a familiar rasp at the bar. As normal, he is twenty

minutes late. I consider going over to him but decide it will be more satisfying to watch. He buys a pint of Stella, takes a long pull, and then – as I hoped – has a watery look around the bar. There aren't many people, just a few codgers and a couple of women nursing gin and tonics. It doesn't take long to spot me. He nearly drops his pint.

'Cheers,' I say.

'What in the blue blazes are you doing here?'

'I'm waiting for you. What do you think I'm doing?'

The penny drops and Grubby smiles. 'It's a secret squirrel.'

'Super secret.'

We go to one of the banquettes near the door – perhaps even the very banquette that the Countess of Lucan had collapsed on after running into the pub shouting, 'Murder! Murder!'

Grubby chuckles to himself as he happily polishes his glasses. 'I thought there was something fishy about that fight with Spike.'

'How is Spike's nose?'

'You didn't quite break it.'

'Shame.'

'But the pictures came out perfectly. I'll send you a couple.' He gulps down half the Stella and starts laughing again. 'Good to see you,' he says. 'Tell me about the secret squirrel.'

'What do you know?'

'I don't know the first thing,' Grubby says. As always, he looks like he's slept in his grey suit. His shirt collar is askew, with the number three shirt button anchored to the number two hole. 'I don't even think the picture editor knows. I was just told to be here at 8 p.m. and wait.'

'And what a pleasant surprise it must have been to find me here.'

'It was, actually,' Grubby says. 'What a kerfuffle after you left. They still haven't stopped talking about it. And no one could get hold of you. You'll have about a hundred messages on your mobile. Should have told me something was up.'

'True,' I say. 'Only two other people know about it, Spike and Robert.'

'And I'm going to be the fourth,' he says. 'Somewhere along the line, you need a cameraman.'

'Correct.' I produce the three rolls of film from my pocket. 'Could you develop these and give them to Spike?'

'Sure. But what's the story? What are you doing?'

'I've got a job at Buckingham Palace,' I say, eyeballing him as I sink the rest of my pint. 'I'm one of the queen's footmen.'

'Brilliant,' Grubby says simply. 'We're going to need more drinks.'

He returns with pints and whisky chasers and I tell him of my life at the palace. 'So, these are the pics of you in the palace,' he says, tossing one of the rolls of film into the air. 'Who took them?'

'I took a few, but most were taken by another footman, my mate Ollie.'

'A *Sun* reporter in the palace.' Grubby cackles. 'They're going to have absolute kittens.'

'I hope so.'

'What do you need me for?'

'The money shot,' I say.

Buckingham Palace has many famous rooms and vistas: the Throne Room, so beloved by royal family wedding photos; the steps down to the garden where so many royal fiancees have been introduced to the world; and, of course, the ballroom where the great and the good get their gongs and knighthoods.

But if you were to pick any one single place at the palace that spells out royalty, grandeur, and tradition, it has to be the balcony where every royal since Queen Victoria has stood, smiled, and waved to the masses – a few have kissed there too, including Prince Charles and Princess Diana, though the queen has never so demeaned herself.

'The balcony?' Grubby says. 'I'll need the Big Tom.' [The

biggest lens he's got, at least a metre long.] 'When are you going to be there?'

'Not sure,' I say. 'I'll try to be there between 11 a.m. and 1 p.m. tomorrow.'

'I'll be by the railings,' Grubby says. 'Just hope to God the coppers don't think I've got a bazooka in my holdall.'

CHAPTER 13

As Mason takes possession of his fabulous suite of rooms in Buckingham Palace, he ponders the wisdom of taking this post as the queen's temporary equerry-in-waiting. On the one hand, as he well knows, the queen's equerry-in-waiting is little more than a glorified bag handler. Equerries-in-waiting have a few more perks than the footmen. These include the most luxurious apartment he's ever lived in; a dining room, shared with other senior household members, that is second only to the queen's; and, joy of joys, his own personal valet. On the debit side, however, there is the fact that, for the next three years, he's just another palace flunky – though a flunky with social skills. Footmen (with the exception of the rather peculiar Lawrence) do not speak to the royals unless spoken to. Equerries-in-waiting are not just allowed to make the odd quip, they are positively encouraged to grease the social wheels. Equerries-in-waiting, along with the ladies-in-waiting, are generally seen as a safe pair of hands, with a gift for small talking to bigwigs' spouses. And although Mason has his t… t… terrible stutter, he is a congenial chap who can keep up a prolonged conversation about the weather and other newsy tidbits.

But three years of it? He could manage a day or two of flunkiedom, even a week of it, but three years seems like quite a stretch. Afternoon tea has not yet been served, but he pours himself his first slug of whisky of the day. He ponders how, yet again, he has been forced to bend to his mother's will; the severe boarding school; straight into the army – and now, he doesn't know how she'd done it, probably by dint of leaning on Her Majesty, he has become the queen's equerry-in-waiting. Not for a moment that he is going to wallow in self-pity. But what he wonders is this: if Viola was not in the picture, and if he had been left to his own devices, how would he now be spending his time? Answer: He does not know. But it would probably not involve being a flunky.

Notwithstanding all the almighty perks of being an equerry-in-waiting – the rooms, the valet, the silver-service dining experience – there is one reason and one reason only why being at the palace is the best thing ever. He gets to court Campion. Assiduously. Mason more than knows his limitations, but he is also essentially a generous, warm-hearted guy who is, above all, kind. Given enough time, Campion will come to see that, and, given an even longer run-up – say a year or three – she may even fall in love with him.

And what a flying start with those thirty-six questions to fall in love! Of all the people in all the world, and he just happened to be paired off with Campion, whom he was already entirely smitten with – and, well, you never know, if he plays his cards right, if he cures his stutter, if he doesn't allow his mother anywhere near Campion, then in time, he might... Naah, he'll blow it – and even if he doesn't, his mother will soon get wind of it, and she certainly will blow it.

As he lounges on the sofa, unbuttoned tunic on the back of a chair, his grasshopper mind moves on to what will eventually happen when/if Campion meets his mother (preferably when they are already married). Although his mother is, without doubt, an unstoppable force, it seems to Mason that Campion may just be the grounded yin to Viola's electric yang. Campion is the immovable object – and he has a hunch that when the two eventually collide, the unstoppable force might prove to be... just that little bit stoppable.

He chuckles to himself. He doesn't know if his feelings for Campion are even remotely reciprocated. Yet, here he is, already constructing the most outlandish fantasies where Campion turns out to be his knight in shining armour – talk about role reversals – who finally tells his mother where to get off when, if he had any gumption at all, he himself should be telling Viola to take a running jump, though, in his defence, even Her Majesty seemed to be in thrall to his mother.

Although he'd already spent a few nights at the palace – hence that epic night of nights when he'd first met Campion – this is the first time that Mason has actually been billeted with the royals. He sets about unpacking his bags. They'd been carried up to his suite of rooms that morning by his new valet, Ollie, and by the trainee footman, Lawrence – and there had then begun the painful business of sounding each other out. The palace has its own ideas about how a valet should attend to his master. Mason feels otherwise.

Ollie had been going through the whole rigmarole of what time Mason liked to be woken up at and how he liked his tea in the morning when Mason had held his hand up. 'Guys, Ollie, Lawrence, can I… I stop you right there?'

'Of course, sir,' Ollie said.

'I… I detest formality,' Mason said. 'I… I have had enough of it to last a lifetime. Just call me Mason. And I… I don't need to be looked after at… at all. I… I don't need a bath run for me in the morning. I… I don't want my shoes polished – I… I like polishing shoes. I… I even like unpacking my own bags. And in the mornings at 8 a.m., I… I guess a cup of tea might be nice – bring a pot and two cups, one for me, one for you.'

Ollie had looked like he'd just been told that Mason planned to open a whelk stall in the palace gardens. 'Very good, sir.'

'Mason.'

'Yes, Mason.'

'Happy with that, Lawrence?'

'Delighted, Mason,' Lawrence said.

'So just leave me be, and I'll be very happy,' Mason said.

'Very good... Mason,' Ollie said. 'And cleaning and pressing your uniform?'

'If you could get me an...an iron and ironing board, that would be most kind, Ollie.'

'Very good,' Ollie said, a little nonplussed. 'We don't get many equerries-in-waiting like you, Mason.'

'Possibly not.'

The valet and the trainee valet had eventually been ejected. Alone, Mason took full possession of his new rooms, opening the windows wide and throwing himself on the bed and fantasizing about the possibility of one day spiriting Campion into this apartment and perhaps sharing a pot of tea or even a gin and tonic.

Not that he wants to get ahead of himself, but if everything – absolutely everything – goes to plan, then he may yet become friends with Campion. It has occurred to him that the senior household members may frown on an equerry-in-waiting courting a palace maid – but, what the hell, only the previous year Tim Laurence had actually married the Princess Royal, so they are hardly in a position to get sniffy about an equerry-in-waiting falling for a palace maid. His mother is, of course, another matter entirely. Still, since his mother has spent her entire life complaining, she will find fault with any woman Mason falls in love with. Anyway, he is rather getting ahead of himself since he hasn't yet sounded out Campion on whether she wants to be his friend, let alone his girlfriend.

Funny how Campion was one of the first people he'd met at the palace. Is it a sign? Mason isn't much one for destiny. If it is a sign of anything at all, it is a sign that Mason has to take positive action.

After meeting Campion in the corridor, Mason had a rather stiff lunch with some of the other senior members of the royal household – three ladies-in-waiting and the royal chaplain. It was pleasant enough. The dining room, next to the Bow Room, is glorious, but his dining companions were perhaps just a little too aware of their grand station in life. It is difficult to move beyond small talk when you are aware that your conversation is being monitored not just by everyone else at the table, but also by the palace footmen. And not just any footmen. The two waiters were his two valets, Ollie and the trainee. The only moment of levity during the entire lunch had occurred when Lawrence, attempting to do silver service, had tripped over a lady-in-waiting's walking stick, sending an entire bowl of boiled potatoes spiralling across the carpet. The three ladies-in-waiting laughed like it was the funniest piece of slapstick they'd ever seen and continued to guffaw as Lawrence grovelled around on his knees as he picked up potatoes from underneath the table.

Back in his rooms, and with free time on his hands, Mason writes a short letter, and then gets out his box of brushes and cloths to polish his shoes. He used to do this with Charley in the shed. They would sometimes polish the shoes of everyone in the house. Years on, just the smell of the polish and the soft sigh of the cloth on the toecaps sends him to a state of transcendent tranquillity.

A knock at the door, and in comes Lawrence with a tray of tea and biscuits. The trainee footman seems much more at ease than the full-time staffer. Lawrence isn't even remotely deferential. In fact, he seems to conduct himself as if he is more than Mason's equal.

'How did you find lunch?' Lawrence places the tea tray on the desk. 'Like the episode with the boiled potatoes?'

'It was certainly the only thing that raised a sm… smile from the ladies-in-waiting.'

'I've noticed that,' Lawrence says, 'the royals and the senior household members just love it when something goes wrong. If I managed to upend a jug of custard over my head, they'd howl like banshees. Though I do wonder if they'd laugh so loud if I tipped the custard over them.'

'There's one famous story about the actress Beatrice Lillie at a royal banquet. A footman went and slopped some red wine over her haute couture dress. She didn't mind in the slightest. Yet, even forty years later, they still talk about her one-liner.'

'What did she say?'

'Never darken my Dior again!'

Lawrence laughs as he picks up the teapot. 'Shall I be mother?'

'Thank you, Lawrence. And if you could be… so kind, please never use that phrase again.'

'Oh, yes, right.' He glances over at Mason. 'You really do like polishing your own shoes.'

'Happy memories.' Mason smiles as he looks up,

'I've brought you a tasty selection of biscuits, Bourbon, Chocolate Digestives, and Hobnobs. Though, I should tell you that they're also my favourite biscuits. If you don't eat them, I will.'

'Do help yourself.'

'You don't mind?'

'No – and take a… seat. There's something I wanted to ask you about.'

Lawrence hitches up his trousers and sits. 'And would that something go by the name of Campion?'

Mason continues to polish, fixing his gaze on the toecap even as the blush spreads to his cheeks. 'It… would.'

'Lovely girl,' Lawrence says. 'Queen loves her. How can I help?'

'Now that… that I have become a member of Her Majesty's household, it may be more difficult for me to go to Campion's room—'

'Too right,' Lawrence says. 'Can't have equerries infesting the Finch's Lobby. Next thing, they'll be joining in the staff parties, hiding in the wardrobes, getting drunk on Her Majesty's gin—'

'Quite,' Mason says. 'I wondered if you c…could give her a letter.'

'Be a pleasure, Mason,' Lawrence says. 'If she gives me a reply, I'll be sure to bring it right down.'

'Thank you.'

Lawrence stands at the door, tapping the letter in the palm of his hand. 'Ever see that film *The Go-Between*?'

'Starring Julie Christie?' Mason says. 'I have.'

'And now that's me – the royal go-between, helping to bring two palace lovers together—'

'Doesn't Julie Christie's lover end... end up shooting himself?'

'Yes, he does, now that you come to mention it – so let's scrub the Go-Between analogy. Whatever Campion's reaction, whether it is the thumbs up or the thumbs down, I will insist she replies immediately – can't leave you swinging in the breeze now, can we?'

'Thank you.'

Twenty minutes later, boots now thoroughly polished, cases now perfectly unpacked, there is another gentle knock at the door. It is Lawrence again.

'Just come to pick up the tea things.'

'Oh, yes, very good, thank you, Lawrence,' Mason says breezily, though unable to mask the disappointment in his voice.

'You thought I was bringing you Campion's reply, didn't you?'

'Her reply?' Mason says before suddenly recalling the trivial mission that Lawrence had been tasked with. 'Oh yes. Did you manage to give Campion that letter?'

'Yes, I did.'

'Oh good, very, very good,' Mason says, trailing off with several burning questions left unasked – principally, has she read the damn letter and is there a reply? Will it seem too eager to ask? Well, he is eager! And Lawrence knows he is eager because he's just delivered Mason's letter. 'And?'

Lawrence has returned the cup and saucer to the tray and is casually munching on a Bourbon biscuit. 'And what, Mason?'

'And did she read my letter?'

'Oh yeah, she read the letter.'

'Did she seem happy when she read it? Did she smile? Did she say anything?'

'To tell you the truth, Mason, I couldn't really be sure if she was happy or unhappy.' He sniffs and picks up another biscuit, a Hobnob.

'Oh... Like that was it?'

'Yeah, bit of a cold fish if you ask me.'

'I've never sensed that,' Mason says. 'In fact, quite the contrary.'

'Though she did write a reply.'

'What?' Mason says. 'You've got a letter?'

'Where is it now?' Lawrence pats his breast pockets, then fishes through his waistcoat. 'I know I put it somewhere.' He finally flicks up the tail of his coat and retrieves the letter from the pocket. 'And here it is.' He gracefully hands the letter over.

'Thank you, Lawrence,' Mason says. 'You don't think you could have milked it any further?'

'I did my best,' Lawrence laughs. 'Would have been much too easy just to have handed it over.'

'I suppose it would.'

'Well, I better leave you to your letter,' Lawrence says. 'I'll be back in a short while to pick up your reply – if, that is, she's responded in the affirmative.'

'How do you even know I was asking her a question?'

'Had a look at the letter on the way up.' Lawrence cackles, waiting a second for Mason to look sufficiently scandalised before continuing, 'Just joking, just joking! What else were you going to be writing apart from asking her if she'd like to go out for a drink sometime—'

'A walk, actually.'

'A walk, eh, very classy,' Lawrence says. 'Well, if she's given you the go-ahead and if you want to firm up the details of your assignation, then I'll be more than happy to take another letter to her.'

'Good, thank you,' Mason says, now itching to read

the letter. 'By the way, are you like this with all the senior members of the royal household?'

'Only the ones I like, Mason,' he says, and with that, Lawrence is gone, and Mason has Campion's letter to himself.

He goes to his desk, flicks open his Swiss Army penknife, and slits the envelope open. It is on palace stationery, no less. The letter, a single page, has been folded into four and looks very brief. Is it good, is it bad – as he holds up the letter, he is still on that delicious cusp of hoping but not knowing.

He unfolds the note.

It is only one word, the shortest letter he's ever received in his life. Though, definitely the best. He'll get it framed.

Yes, she's written. But there is one more thing, and although it may have meant nothing, it means a lot to Mason. It means he is in with a chance. She's signed it not with her name or her initials but with an *X*.

CHAPTER 14

Campion and Mason walk four miles from Orpington Station to a National Trust property that she's not heard of before, Down House. After buying their tickets, they ignore the house completely and instead go straight to a scrubby wood that is five minutes from the house. It doesn't look like much of a wood, barely four acres.

Mason takes a handful of pebbles from his coat pocket.

'I thought we'd start with twenty.' He kneels on the ground and places the pebbles in four rows of five by the side of the path.

'This is the walk?' Campion says.

'Let's go.'

They follow the sandy path into the wood. It is a perfectly ordinary woodland walk – some oaks, some birch, some scrub, some trees that have been toppled and left to rot. They walk no more than two hundred yards through the wood before emerging back into the sunlight. On the left is a small hut with a bench, but they turn right and continue along a long, straight path next to the wood, with rolling views of the valley that falls at their feet. When they reach the end of the wood, they take another right and arrive back where they started ten minutes earlier.

Mason kicks away one of the twenty pebbles and they begin a second loop through the woods.

After all the build-up to this walk – "mind-blowing!" he'd called it – Campion is a little underwhelmed. The walk is nice enough, though she's certainly been in many more beautiful woods. The views out over the valley are pleasant, though not in any way mind-blowing. As they start off on their second turn through the wood, she realises that this is the walk in its entirety – they are just going to go round and round the wood, and since Mason has put down twenty pebbles, they'll probably be going through it twenty times.

Campion does not give Mason the satisfaction of asking any questions. She presumes that, in his own good time, he will eventually reveal why they are walking around and around this boring wood.

Another pebble is kicked away.

A rabbit darts across the field when they turn onto the long straight stretch. A father and son join them through the wood, walking just in front, but after a single loop, they leave.

At first, the walk irritated her. She felt swindled. When Mason promised to take her on one of the most historic walks of her life, she had been expecting, well, possibly a big hill, perhaps even a mountain; maybe a winding river; and, without question, views to take her breath away.

Her misgivings started when they took the train from Charing Cross to Orpington. Orpington! In Kent! And not that she's ever been to Orpington before, but since it is inside the M25 ring road, the views were unlikely to be breathtaking.

From Orpington station, they'd walked four miles before arriving at this National Trust house, Charles Darwin's home apparently, and very nice it looked too. There was no mention of walks, historic or otherwise.

But since the fifth loop, the sixth loop, she has changed her mind. It has become a meditation. She is in the moment. She enjoys entering the wood, looking at the same toadstools, the same fallen trees, then coming into the sun. She likes the views, and she likes it when Mason kicks away the next pebble. Life has been distilled down into nothing more than the next step and the next moment.

'You're warming to this walk,' Mason says. 'In the last

h… hour, I have felt you going through this whole range of emotions – first disappointment, then intense irritation, and through to acceptance, and n… now I think I can detect something approaching joy.'

'You've got me, Mason,' she says. 'I am enjoying myself.'

'And now you are in the right frame of mind to hear its history. And when you know its history, you… you'll come back here.'

'How often have you been here.'

'This is my tenth visit,' Mason says. 'You are the first person I've ever brought here.'

'I'm honoured.'

Mason kicks another pebble away, and for a while, they trudge through the wood in silence.

'It was in this wood, on this very path, that one of the world's gr… greatest scientific theories was born. This path – this path that we are walking – this is where Charles Darwin worked out his theory of evolution.'

'Is that so?'

'Darwin called it his thinking walk. He lived at Down House for four decades. And e… every day he was here, he would come to this wood and walk this path. At the start of each walk, he'd put down a number of pebbles, and after each circuit, just as we have done, he'd kick away a pebble. And when all the pebbles were gone, then he knew that he'd done his circuits for the day – though sometimes his children would sneak in more pebbles so that instead of doing ten loops, he might do twenty. But when he was doing his circuits, he had enough space to dream and to think. This walk changed history – and now we, together, are walking in Darwin's footsteps. Do you approve?'

'Very much.' And she does. She loves the story. She loves the walk. They both added to the magic. But what seals the deal is when he brings out the love questionnaire again. She gives a mock groan when he wags the thirty-six questions in her face – and tells her that she still owes him the story of her most terrible memory. But as she tells him the story, she realises that the memory has evolved. It had been her most terrible memory, but now, two years on, it is a feel-good memory, and it comes with a glow. It was the day she finally got shot of her philandering husband.

CHAPTER 15

Wearing the full regalia of state, His Serene Highness Prince Kim steps smartly through the doorway to find that the Balcony Room is pleasingly empty. Since the insanely handsome young prince is about to pose for a formal picture, a glass of whisky seems in order. No, on second thoughts, a glass of sherry – too early in the day to be drinking spirits.

Though the balcony doors have yet to be opened, he can already hear the ecstatic crowds out on the Mall. Many of them have been waiting all night to greet their new princeling. Another tot of sherry would have been most agreeable, but it is 11 a.m. on the dot, and since, as we know, punctuality is the politeness of kings, he chooses not to keep his faithful public waiting any longer.

I open the glass doors and am greeted by an ear-splitting roar – the extra-time equaliser in a World Cup Final. I walk out onto the balcony and give a confident, regal wave, arm still, hand turning, not too wristy. I scan over the sentries and look out past the railings.

The bastard isn't there.

Typical! Absolutely typical! I told him – twice – that I'd be on the Balcony between 11 a.m. and 1 p.m., so is it too unreasonable for me to expect Grubby to be here?

I am just a little disappointed. In fact, I am vexed. No, that doesn't quite do it justice, either. All right. I am absolutely livid. If Grubby were anywhere near me at this moment, I would happily have kicked him off the balcony.

I'd spent the last fortnight working my fingernails to the bone (metaphorically speaking, palace footmen, it seems to me, spend most of their time just hanging around waiting), and the least Grubby could have done was actually turn up on time for once. But no, Grubby couldn't turn up on time. Grubby is physically incapable of turning up on time for anything, ever, just on a point of principle because, I don't know, he has yet to finish his second cappuccino of the morning.

I scan the railings again. A couple of Japanese tourists are waving at me. I give them a wave back. What the hell is the fat idiot doing? Does he just expect me to hang around on the balcony – in full view of sentries, coppers, and probably even the queen herself as she rolls in through the entrance gates – until he deigns to show up?

I left Ollie on duty by the Ambassadors' Entrance, where he is busy opening doors for foreign diplomats. Not that there is any great urgency for me to return – it really doesn't need two footmen to open a palace door, I promise you – but if I am caught out on the balcony, it will be ticklish.

I check my watch. I've been on the balcony for three minutes. Still no sign of Grubby. I wonder whether to get down low and just pop my head up every so often to check if Grubby has arrived. One of the tourists has started taking pictures of me. I go back inside and have some more sherry.

It might be smarter to return to the Ambassadors' Entrance, wait for an hour with Ollie and then return to the balcony at noon; Grubby might even have turned up by then. But then I'll have to run the whole gauntlet of getting up to the state corridor again, where, strictly speaking, trainee footmen have no business whatsoever.

I go out onto the balcony and, ever hopeful, scan the railings again – still no sign of Grubby. Why, why, should I have ever expected Grubby to be there? It is only 11.10 a.m. The idea of him being just ten minutes late is ridiculous. I pad up and down the balcony as I wonder what to do next. I'll give him till... till 11.20, then I'll leave, and when I next see him face to face, I'll… I'll… I'll jolly well give him a piece of my mind!

'Good heavens! What are you doing here?'

I nearly jump out of my skin. Before I turn, I have the good sense to toss the sherry glass over the edge of the balcony.

'Oh, good morning, sir,' I say.

Major General Sir Richard Arnison-Newgass joins me on the balcony. 'What are you doing here?'

'Me, sir?' I say. 'I'm on the balcony.'

'I can see quite clearly that you are on the balcony, young man.' He stands like an army officer at ease, spring toed and hands easy behind his back. 'What I wish to know is why you are on the balcony and why you are not at your station with Ollie.'

'I just came to have a look, sir.'

'You just came to have a look, did you?' he says. 'Have a little wave? See what it's like to be a member of the royal family?'

'No, sir.'

'And are there any other rooms in the palace that you'd just like to have a look at?' he says. 'Her Majesty's bedroom? The Duke of Edinburgh's dressing room?'

'No, sir.'

'You seem to be under the impression that you can just wander around the staterooms as you please.'

'No, sir.'

'May I remind you that all the staterooms are out of bounds unless you have been specifically requested to enter them.'

'Yes, sir. Sorry, sir. I didn't know that, sir.'

'You didn't know that?' he says. 'You're either lying, or you're an even bigger idiot than I thought you were.'

'My mother always said I was thick, sir.'

'Get off this balcony immediately and go to your station!'

'Yes, sir.'

As I walk to the door, I have a brief look out at the railings

– Grubby, of course, is still not there – well, he is only twenty minutes late, so why on earth should he be there?

Sir Richard follows me through to the Balcony Room. 'Young man,' he says. 'In two weeks' time, we will decide whether to keep you on at the palace. I have to say that unless there is a marked improvement in your general demeanour, your employment will be terminated.'

'Yes, sir. Very good, sir.'

As bollockings go, I think it went very well indeed, registering about a two out of ten. He didn't hit me. He didn't even swear at me. Sir Richard, I feel, could do with a short stint at *The Sun* to learn how a proper bollocking is conducted.

I feel that I have earned a soothing cup of tea in the sergeant footman's parlour.

There were to be two consequences to my taking tea with the most delightful Simon Brook. These were, firstly, that one of the most senior footman would be summarily sacked, and, secondly, that not five hours later, the Royal Standard would be hauled to half-mast and the Royal Household would enter a sustained period of mourning.

CHAPTER 16

When the last of the twenty pebbles have been kicked away, Campion and Mason climb over the fence into the field and walk a little way down the valley. Mason pulls out a blanket from his rucksack. They drink Thermos coffee and eat cheese and tomato sandwiches.

'My most terrible memory.'

'D... don't feel pressured.'

'No, I'm ready.' She smiles. 'It's nothing like your story with the roses. Just a tale of everyday heartbreak.'

Campion composes herself.

'I've never told anyone this story before – certainly not anyone in the palace,' she says. 'My most terrible memory. It was the day my marriage ended.' She looks out over the valley, very pretty now in the afternoon sun. 'Odd thing is, it's now also one of my best memories.'

Mason nods.

'I know what you're thinking, Mason,' she says. 'You're thinking I'm much too young to have been married, let alone divorced.'

Mason is inscrutable. He never moves, sad eyes steadily looking at her.

'In my third year at university, I was sent on a placement to Christie's, the auctioneers. I spent two months there, and I absolutely loved it – I was handling masterpieces every day. I loved the job, and very, very quickly, I fell in love with Colin. He was an Irishman, one of the auctioneers. He was a real smoothie, and, like all the best auctioneers, he had the gift of the gab.

'He was older than me, quite a lot older. I found it quite sexy. All the Christie's girls used to swoon over him, but the one he went for was the new intern. He went for me. I was thrilled! I was flattered. I was in love.'

Campion plucks a dandelion and pulls off its petals one by one. 'He loves me,' she says. 'He loves me not.'

'As soon as I'd graduated, Colin asked me to marry him – and because I go with my gut, I said yes. I was all in. My grandparents didn't have any money, but Colin wanted a wedding with all the bells and all the whistles so that I could have, as he described it, "the wedding of my dreams". How little he knew me. I couldn't have cared less.'

At least she can laugh about it now. Colin, the delicious, the divine Colin, had even sold one of his mother's paintings, a Van Eyck, to pay for the wedding – and what a wedding it had been, costing a cool £500. A head. It was only on the honeymoon, a dismal skiing trip, that Campion realised that the amazing wedding hadn't even remotely been for her. It had been for Colin to show off his beautiful, obedient bride. And to think, she'd even gone along with the 'Obey' bit in the vows. He'd joked about it during his perfectly turned speech as Campion basked in her new husband's glory. After the dancing, there were fireworks. Colin had insisted on it. The display alone had cost over £10,000. It had lasted just over half an hour – as good an analogy as any for the entirety of her marriage. A brief fizz, a bang, a sparkle of fairy dust and then, with a sigh of the wind, it was gone.

Campion had joined her husband at Christie's, working as a lowly trainee, valuing pictures, occasionally being wheeled out to talk to clients. About once a week, Colin would take her out for lunch. Sometimes they wouldn't bother with lunch and would just go straight back to their bijou little flat in Kensington. But most of his lunches were devoted to wining and dining Christie's most valued customers – or so she thought. Until one day, when she'd gone out for a walk and a sandwich, she'd seen Colin having lunch with a very glamorous young woman. Except the woman wasn't a valued customer. She was Christie's newest intern.

There'd been something about the body language which had been... off. Campion asked Colin about it; of course, he denied it all. Maybe it was her. Maybe marriage had turned her into a shrew. They started rowing – arguing over the most trivial things, but all along, she knew exactly what they were arguing about. The bastard was cheating on her – with interns, with colleagues, with clients, with any beautiful woman who batted her eyelids at him. She knew it. And he knew she knew it.

Mason doesn't say a word as she sips some coffee. It has gone quite cold.

'We'd been married about a year. I remember it distinctly. It was a Friday, about noon. Colin had been leaving the office for some meeting when he caught my eye. He came over to ask how I was doing, and then he walked off. The moment he left the room, I knew he was going to see his lover.

'I followed him out. He caught a cab – and I immediately caught the next one. "Follow that car!" I said. The taxi driver loved it. However, he did not need to follow the cab because I quickly realised where he was going. He was going back to our flat.'

Campion had bought a coffee, wondering who it would be. And what a surprise, it was the intern. She gave them twenty minutes and then slipped silently into the flat.

'I went up the spiral staircase,' Campion says. 'I could hear them before I saw them. They were on the sofa. I was standing there for nearly a minute before the girl saw me. She screamed, and Colin turned round. His face! I lost it. I threw a fruit bowl at him; it hit him on the shoulder. I stormed out. As soon as I'd left, I burst into tears. And so that, Mason, is my most terrible memory – catching my husband having sex with another woman.'

'You trumped my rose garden story.'

'No, I haven't,' Campion says. 'Your story was unremittingly awful. Mine was just terrible at the time. Within three months, I'd realised it was the best thing that could have happened – I was shot of Colin. No matter how much he grovelled – and he certainly grovelled - it was over. Every day now, I give thanks – because every day, for the rest of my life, I'm not with Colin.'

'That's… that's one way to see it.'

'It was the only way it was ever going to end – and better by far that it ended quickly. We didn't even have kids. I got off scot-free.'

They return to Darwin's thinking walk for another twenty laps – it is that last walk that seals the deal for Campion. They continue with the thirty-six questions. It all has been so easy and genuine that she takes his hand after a while. So many intimate questions that she's never considered before – What does she value most in a friendship? What, if anything, is too serious to be joked about? – that they barely even realise they've completed the final loop.

Mason turns the final card. '*Congratulations,*' he reads. '*You've answered all the questions. Now for the hard part.*'

'It gets harder?'

'In order to solidify your… your love—'

'My love?'

'Th… that is what it says. *In order to solidify your love, you have to look into your partner's eyes for four minutes. In silence. It's hard, and you'll squirm, but you'll learn an incredible amount. Good luck…*'

They go to the hut by the side of the path and sit on the bench. Mason sets his watch alarm for four minutes, and without another word, they look into each other's eyes. At first, it is disturbing, then hypnotic, and then so difficult that it is all she can do not to flinch and break the spell. Mason starts to cry. First, one tear and then another and another, gliding down the side of his nose and onto his lips. His glistening eyes have turned from beautiful to a mesmerising window into his soul, which is, she can see, above all, a kind soul, and that is a quality that she values above all else. When the four minutes are up, she can't believe it, but she knows it to be true. The thirty-six questions have woven their magnificent magic, and she is, well, if not in love, then on the very cusp of love. She leans forward and kisses him, full, sweet, solid.

CHAPTER 17

Just as I have been trained, I stand tall in the sergeant footman's parlour, hands loose by my sides.

'And begin.'

'I told her that her stockings were wrinkled.' I say it beautifully, not so much as a tremor on my lips.

'Perfect.' Mr Brook is in heaven, snug in his armchair, a cup of tea on the side table and Chipper dozing by the gas fire.

My voice shoots up an octave, and for better effect, I put on a German accent. I've tried French and Kiwi, but for some reason, I always feel comfier with German. 'Then why wass she so angry?'

'Good!' Mr Brook says. 'Keep smiling – easy smile, pleasant smile, lips quarter of an inch apart.'

I flex my smile, slightly rigid, but I am still only a novice. I revert to my normal voice. 'She wasn't wearing any.'

Mr Brook has heard the joke a dozen times over, but he hoots with laughter. Chipper wags his tail. 'Brrrr-illiant!' Mr Brook says. 'You're getting better by the day.'

'Thank you, sir.' How very pleasant it is to be having ventriloquism lessons from the delightful Mr Brook, who is always fulsome with his praise, and rarely, if ever, raises his voice.

I've spent the previous two weeks assiduously practising in my room. I don't know why it has so taken my fancy, but in the evenings, after I've written up my notes for the day, and if there isn't much going on, I sit in front of the mirror in my room, take a deep breath and with an easy, relaxed smile, sing through my vowels. The vowels are the easy part – even the rawest novice can sing 'Aye-eee-eye-ohh-you' without moving their lips.

Within a couple of days, I was singing the first line of 'The Star-Spangled Banner' – "Oh, say, can you see…"

After the basics, I moved on to the trickier consonants. These are what us vents call the labial sounds – they need lips. The toughest consonants are 'P' and 'B', which come with an exhale, almost as if your lips pop. Most of the time, they switch the trickier labial consonants for easier sounds – so 'Vs' are turned into 'Ths' with the tip of your tongue against your top teeth, and 'Ms', which need your lips together, are replaced by 'Ns'.

Never in his life has Simon Brook had such an eager pupil. 'Tomato,' he'll say, and I dutifully reply, 'Tongue-ato.' We soon moved on to "Mary had a little lamb", (N-ary had a little la-ng), and to vent jokes that are over a century old. I have a vent dummy that I've made out of an old sock, but most of the time, I prefer to perform with Chipper. He is a most amenable partner, compliant and docile, and so long as there is a treat nearby, he opens his mouth when you tickle his throat.

I pick the dog up from the rug and put him on my lap. He doesn't seem much interested in either me or my treats. No matter – my audience awaits. Simon takes a sip of tea and sits there expectantly with his hands settled on his plump tummy.

I take a deep breath and smile. 'What time is it?' I ask Chipper.

'It iss very easy to tell,' Chipper says with a soft German lilt. 'How?'

'There isss a sundial in ze hall.'

'That's silly,' I say. 'It's dark in the hall.'

'So take a torch!'

Simon claps heartily. 'Bravo.' he says. 'I can't believe how you've come on.'

'Thank you, sir,' I say, returning Chipper to the floor.

'We have more work on your Bs. You've got to alternate the B sound with either a D or a G, particularly if you've got two Bs together like bread and butter or a bottle of beer.'

'Gottle of deer.' I try again. 'Dottle of geer. Dread and gutter.'

'The main thing is, Lawrence dear, that you've got to believe that you are saying the letter B. You have to commit. If you believe it, then your audience will.' He hums to himself as he takes another sip of tea. 'Sometimes a Th sound can work. Try saying hamburgers and a bottle of beer.'

'Han-dur-gers and a dottle of th-eer.'

'Excellente,' he says. 'When you're practising, try reading the newspaper out loud in front of the mirror.'

'I'll start tonight.'

'I so wish we had more footmen like you,' Mr Brook says.

'You could start a circus troupe.'

While all this merry chatter has been going on, Chipper has been out for the count. He makes to get to his feet, staggers, then collapses on the rug. I kneel down. 'How you feeling, Chipper?' When I waft a treat in front of his nose, there is no response. I bend my head, and the whiff is unmistakable. 'Oh,' I say. 'You can smell it.'

I pass Chipper over to Simon. He takes one sniff and then, for the first and only time, comes very close to losing his temper. 'It's that Freemantle,' he says. 'I knew it, I knew it – he's been spiking the dogs' meals for over a week now.' Chipper is placed on the floor to sleep off his hangover. From the smell of his breath, he's been dosed up with malt whisky.

Simon is pacing back and forth in front of the fire. 'What shall I do, Lawrence?' he says. 'Tell His Lordliness, Sir Richard Arnison-Newgass? If I do that, Master J. Freemantle Esquire will be out of the palace so fast his feet will barely touch the ground.'

I shrug. It is certainly no skin off my nose if Freemantle is given the boot. As with so many of the royal flunkies, he is most particularly aware of his position in the palace pecking order, fawning to his betters and all smug condescension to the minions.

'Do I want him sacked?' Mr Brook asks. 'No, I do not wish to see him sacked – not that I am overly fond of young Freemantle, but he is a part of our family, and we do not throw family members out on the street, even the ones who have been lacing Her Majesty's dog food with drink.' He stands by the fire, head bent as he looks down at Chipper, double chins nestling against his neck. 'No, I'm fond of the old fruit, despite his growing bumptiousness since he became one of Her Majesty's principal footmen. Would you be so kind, Lawrence, as to prise Mr Jono Freemantle out from wherever he is skulking in the palace and send him down to have a brief word with me?'

'Of course, sir,' I say.

I find Jono Freemantle up in his little cubbyhole just outside the queen's apartments. There are fourteen footmen working in the palace, of whom I am the lowest of the low, spending my days polishing shoes and delivering government boxes from the Privy Purse Door to the private secretaries' rooms. But the top two footmen, the queen's principal footmen, come into regular daily contact with the queen, often engaging in light chit-chat, principally about the weather or the queen's corgis. These two principal footmen work in shifts and tend to spend most of their days in their snug just outside the queen's apartments. When she wants anything, she'll ring the bell, and they'll scuttle through to her apartments where, like some palace genie, they will recite the magic mantra, "What is your wish, Oh master?" (At least that's what I presume they say, but seeing as I never spent that long in Her Majesty's service, I never got to find out.) The queen then sends them off for a gin and tonic or whatever else takes her fancy, though most of the time, she is pretty self-sufficient. As far as I can see, her two principal footmen spend their days with their feet up in their too-hot office, reading the papers and bitching about the equerries.

Since I am on legitimate palace business, I have a good

snoop around as I wander up to the queen's apartments. My abiding memory of the palace in those days was the miles and miles of red carpet and the complete silence. Not a sound from the Mall and all you could hear was the tick of the occasional clock.

I give a meek knock on the door to the page's lobby; just a wee mild-mannered mousie going about his business, not doing anyone any harm, just looking to get on with the mousie duties of the day.

'Come.' (That is very grand indeed – the only other person I know who'd ever talk like that is my old headmaster, and normally, when he said it, he had a big knobbly cane in his hand and was expecting to beat you.)

Discreet and mousie-like, I enter the page's lobby and give him my most affable smile. 'Ah, there you are,' I say.

Mr Freemantle has his feet up on the desk and is giving his glasses a leisurely polish. He is a handsome brute and he knows it, all chiselled cheekbones and a thick thatch of slicked back hair.

'What do you mean, there I am?' I am not sure, but I think he has a bit of a South African accent.

'I've found you,' I say. 'I was wondering where you'd be.'

'Where the hell else would I be?' He puts on his gold-rimmed glasses.

'That's a very good point – where else were you going to be? You might have been attending to Her Majesty. You might even have been attending to a call of nature.' I look around the room. Very cosy, he has it, a few shelves of books, some magazines, a TV, and of course, right by the desk, Her Majesty's summoning bell. There is also a comfortable-looking sofa. 'Mind if I take a seat?' I plonk myself down, and as there is a convenient footstool, I put my feet up. 'I must say, you've done this little room up very nicely indeed. Snug – that's the word.'

I don't think that young Master Freemantle is used to being

so treated by junior footmen. 'Make yourself at home, why don't you?' he says.

'I will. Got any tea? Or perhaps coffee?'

'What do you want?'

'Just come for a little chat,' I say. 'Always nice to get to know my colleagues.'

'Now you've had your chat get out.' He jerks his thumb towards the door.

'Charming,' I say. 'And I was hoping we'd be such good pals.'

'Sod off. Get out of here.'

'Oh, before I go, just one thing – the sergeant footman would like a word.'

'That fat nonce?' he says. 'What does he want with me?'

'I really can't say.' I shimmer to the door. 'Though it might be best to pack your things. I don't believe you'll be spending much more time in this delightful room.'

For the first time, he looks rattled. 'What are you talking about?'

'I wouldn't dream of ruining Mr Brook's surprise,' I say, opening the door. 'But may I be the first person to welcome you back to the ranks of the junior footmen.'

I finally go off to attend to my duties at the Ambassadors' Entrance, loafing along the corridor, hands in pockets and whistling 'Lilliburlero'. (One of Britain's great martial tunes, but you may know it better as the music that's played on the hour by the *World Service*.)

I hear a terrible shout from behind me – 'Shut that bloody whistle up!' It is almost certainly Prince Philip, but I scuttle off down a staircase before he can reprimand me in person.

Back at the Ambassadors' Entrance, it is all exactly as I'd left it: Ollie standing around waiting to open the doors for the top-hatted diplomats. Of all the queen's many mind-numbing duties, this must be one of the most boring. She must have performed the ceremony thousands of times over. When a new ambassador is appointed by a sovereign state, they are obliged to present their credentials to the queen at Buckingham Palace – though, for some arcane reason, they always call it the Court of St James. A horse and carriage, complete with driver, co-driver, and two liveried footmen, are sent to the relevant embassy, and then the ambassador, plus spouse, is driven in high state to the palace. They usually wear a top hat and tails, and most of them adore the pageantry and will wave at the gawking tourists. The queen, meanwhile, does what she has always done so beautifully, and that is to put on her most serene smile and not utter a single word of complaint.

Ollie cackles with delight when he hears the good news that Freemantle is out of a job, and as we continue to bow and scrape, I wonder when to phone the story through. 'Flunky Got the Corgis Drunky!' – Palace footman sacked for spiking corgis' food! On a slow news day, it is a splash.

But as it happens...

As it happens, *The Sun* has bigger stories by far than piffling palace gossip about drunk dogs. And rather bizarrely, I don't just report the story. I am the cause of it.

Just after lunch, there is a sudden flurry of activity amongst the minions. Freemantle is out, and my good friend Ollie replaces him as the queen's principal footman. I am to continue shadowing Ollie around the palace, though occasionally attending to his former chores.

Down in the palace kitchens at 4.45 p.m., I have the laminated sheets out and am carefully laying up Bobo's tea tray. She likes her pot of Twinings tea in the middle, cup and saucer at three o'clock, sugar bowl at six o'clock, the jug of milk – fresh from the Windsor dairy – at nine o'clock, and her sandwiches and other dainties at twelve. I lay the tray meticulously, already forewarned that if any of the items are out of place by even so much as an inch, Bobo will upend the tray on the floor and demand a new one.

Since my first disastrous outing with Bobo, I've seen her

most days, usually when Ollie is either delivering or taking away one of her meals. She has always studiously ignored me.

I find her in her bedroom, lying in state on her four-poster, with Chipper lolling next to her. The dog seems quite recovered. He must have accompanied the queen on her daily visit to Bobo and decided to stay.

'Good afternoon, Miss MacDonald.' I set up the bedtable over Bobo's legs. She is wearing a white nightgown and an embroidered pink nightcap.

'Where is the other footman?' she says in her Scottish brogue.

'Ollie is attending to Her Majesty,' I say.

'Is he now?'

'Yes, he is, ma'am,' I say. 'Shall I pour your tea?'

'Leave that to me, you English pig.' She pours the tea and adds milk. (The royals are absolute sticklers for the milk going in after the tea – not that it makes a blind bit of difference to the taste, but pouring the tea first marks you out as a toff, while milk-firsters are riffraff. It's purportedly to do with the quality of the porcelain teacups, but believe me, it's all so much snobbish nonsense.)

'You are Lawrence.' She takes two jam pennies, little round jam sandwiches about the size of an old penny, and puts them into her hairy maw. Her false teeth wander around her mouth as she chews. 'You are the one who was drunk on his first day.'

'I'm afraid I don't know what you're talking about, ma'am.'

'I telt the queen all about you.'

'That was kind of you, ma'am. Thank you.'

'I'd have had ye sacked.'

'Will there be anything else, ma'am?'

She snatches up a piece of Battenberg cake. As she brings the cake to her mouth, Chipper slobbers beside her. Her face softens, she smiles, and for a moment, the queen's hatchet-faced dresser has disappeared to be replaced by a sweet little girl.

She starts singing to herself. I don't know where she's gone now, but probably back to her childhood home in the Black Isle. I've not heard it before, but it sounds like an old Scottish nursery rhyme.

'Skinnymalinky Longlegs,
Big banana feet,
Went tae the pictures,
And couldnae find a seat,
So he couldnae pay his fare,
So the rotten old conductor,
Went an' threw him doon the stair.'

She smiles and cuddles the dog. Chipper leans over and tries to take a biscuit off the tray.

I can't resist.

'That was a nice rhyme, Mistress Bobo.'

Bobo stares at the dog, watery eyes blinking in amazement.

'Chipper?' she says. 'Is that you?'

'Yes, Mistress Bobo,' the dog says with a slight trace of a German accent. I look on, hands at ease, a pleasant smile on my face.

'Good doggy,' she says.

'Give me a bickie.'

'Aye, Chipper, you may have a bickie.' She gives the dog a chocolate Bourbon.

'Good, Bobo,' the dog says.

'Do ye want another bickie?'

'Give me a bickie.'

The dog wolfs down another biscuit. Bobo has a little smile on her lips as she stares at the dog.

'You can talk,' she says. 'Good doggie.'

'I love you, Bobo.'

She gives the dog an affectionate stroke. 'I love you too,' she says. 'I've never talked to a dog before.'

'I only talk to friends.'

'Does you talk to the queen?'

'I do.'

'Good doggie.'

'Good Bobo.' The dog rolls around on its stomach and lets off a most noxious fart.

'Do you mind?' Chipper says.

'Ye farted, not me.'

I have no idea how this whole ridiculous scenario is going to pan out, but I am enjoying myself.

'Me?' Chipper says. 'You've been farting like a lodging house cat.'

A wheezy sound bubbles from Bobo's throat, like a series of short, nervous hiccups before gradually evolving into a laugh. The laugh grows and grows in both noise and stature until Bobo's mouth is agape, and tears are pouring down her cheek. She has almost recovered herself when the dog farts again. Another paroxysm of laughter, now punctuated with little machine-gun yips. It culminates in a final shriek – and just like that, she's gone. With her fast-fading eyes still staring adoringly at the dog, her head lolls to the side.

I quickly pick up the bedtable and set it on the floor. 'Miss MacDonald?' I check her pulse, but I know it is a no-go. Her hand is still on the dog's back and her face is wreathed with the most beatific smile.

I could try mouth-to-mouth, but it is over. As deaths go, you can't hope for a better one.

I am in two minds as to who to tell. I could go straight to Simon Brook, but it seems to me that the person who'll most want to know is the master of the household, Sir Richard Arnison-Newgass.

I close the door to Bobo's apartment and set off at a sprint for Sir Richard's offices. His door is open, but I knock anyway, still panting a little. He is taking tea with the mistress of the robes. Like all the other senior members of the royal household, they have the obligatory cakes and sandwiches.

'Yes?' he says. He slowly places his cup on the saucer. 'You look like you've been running.'

'I have, sir,' I say. 'Could I have a brief word – in private?'

He is about to tell me to spit it out, but there must be something about the way I look because he gets straight up from his armchair. 'Do please excuse me one moment,' he says to the mistress of the robes.

He leads the way out and closes the door behind him. 'What's happened?' he says.

'I am afraid Bobo MacDonald is dead, sir,' I say.

He only needs a moment to digest the news. 'Are you sure?'

'Quite sure, sir. I've just been taking her tea.'

'Does anyone else know?'

'No, sir.'

'Good, lad.' He even stretches over and grasps my shoulder.

He makes a quick phone call to the palace doctor before turning back to me. 'Let's go.'

We go back up to Bobo's apartment. It's not seemly for the master of the household to be seen running, so we go at a brisk walk. 'How did you find her?' he says.

I have already decided to keep my story as simple as possible. 'I'd just taken up her tea, sir,' I say. 'She was dead on the bed.'

'You didn't see her die?'

'No, sir.'

We go straight through to Bobo's bedroom. Chipper is still lying beside her. Just for formality's sake, Sir Richard takes her pulse, but her skin has already taken on a waxy grey pallor, and her pupils are dilated wide.

The doctor bustles into the room and has a quiet conflab with Sir Richard. I stand by the window, awaiting my orders.

'Thank you, Lawrence, that will be all,' Sir Richard says.

'Yes, sir.'

'And by the way, Lawrence, don't mention this to anyone else.'

'I wouldn't dream of it, sir.' Indeed, I would not – leastways not to any of the palace staff.

'You've done well.'

'Thank you, sir.'

I bolt up to my room, throw my coat and waistcoat onto the bed, put on a jumper and dart down backstairs. It has just gone 5.30. Might be able to make it – at a pinch.

It is much too risky to use the staff payphones down in the basement, so I quit the palace and run to the nearest public payphone at Green Park. It is as I am calling up the News International free-phone number that I realise my error. I should have Spike's mobile number – because in order to get through to the deputy editor, I'll have to go through at least two gatekeepers.

I ask for the editor's office, but the switchboard unhelpfully puts me through to the news desk. The phone is picked up by one of the more gossipy news editors, Tophe.

'*Sun* news desk,' he says, curt as can be.

'I vish to speak to Spike, the deputy editor,' I say, putting on my trusty German accent.

'Who is it, and what's it about?'

'My name is Gustav, and I am his close personal friend.'

'Close personal friend, my arse,' he says. 'If you were his close personal friend, you wouldn't be coming through the news desk.'

'No, I am – I am. He vill vish to speak to me.'

'What's it about then?'

'I haff a story for him.'

'You tell me the story, and I'll decide.'

'I must speak to Spike.'

'Hang on,' he says, tone suddenly changing. 'Is that Kim?'

'Who?'

'Is that you, Kim?'

The game is well and truly up. There is no point in denying it. 'Yes.'

'And why do you want to speak to Spike?'

'Just put me through, will you?'

'Last time I saw the pair of you together, you were pummelling each other on the newsroom floor.'

'Could you put me through?'

'What's it about?'

'Put me through.'

'Tell.'

If I were in the same room as the prattling oaf, I'd have happily shoved the phone straight down his fat throat. 'I'm saying nothing,' I say. 'Put me through.'

'You're on a secret squirrel.'

'Why don't you go and ask Spike? Put me through.'

He puts me on hold, and I am left to muse on the fact that within ten minutes, this phone call will be the talk of the newsroom. Even someone as thick as Tophe may be able to work out that my phone call is somehow related to the flurry of activity that will soon be kicking off in the newsroom.

The next person to pick up is the chief sub on the back bench. She, at least, is a little more accommodating.

'May I speak to Spike, please?' I say.

'Who's speaking?'

'Kim.'

A long pause. 'I thought you'd been fired.'

I am overcome with weariness. 'Can you just put me through?'

'Sure.'

I am put on hold again. Eventually – eventually – Spike picks up. He cuts straight to the chase. 'Have you been rumbled?' he asks.

'Not yet,' I say.

'What's happened?'

'I've got tomorrow's splash.'

'Anything could replace this claptrap we're running tomorrow,' he says. 'What you got?'

'The queen's nanny is dead,' I say.

'What do you mean?'

'What I mean,' I say with infinite patience, 'is that Bobo MacDonald, who looked after the queen when she was a baby, and who then went on to become the queen's dresser, has kicked the bucket. Bobo is dead.'

'The queen's nanny is dead?' Spike says.

'Yes. The queen's nanny, Bobo MacDonald, is dead.'

'How did she die?'

'She had a heart attack this afternoon. As of now, the queen has entered a period of very deep mourning.'

'Good story,' he says, which is high praise indeed from Spike. 'Hang on.' He does not put me on hold, so I am able to listen in on the merry shouting match as Spike summons his troops and orders a reverse ferret [wholesale change] on the next day's splash. I admire the cards that are plastered all over the inside of the phone box. I can't be sure, but it seems to me that the Green Park escort girls are just a little classier than the ones over in Wapping; they certainly charge more.

After two minutes of hollering, Spike is back on the phone again. 'Okay, Kim,' he says. 'Now, not that I want to piss on the chips, but is this story actually true?'

'What?' I say, mildly outraged. 'You think I just made it up?'

'No, no, nothing like that,' he says. 'But you do have a bit of a reputation for stretching stories.'

'Oh yeah, you're right.' I am now thoroughly hacked off. 'I'm sorry. I should have clarified this earlier. Bobo's not really dead. She's just a little bit stunned.'

'But she is dead?'

'She is dead.'

'Swear on it?'

'Look, I've seen her with my own eyes! She's dead! There is no doubt, whatsoever, about it. She's dead as a doornail! As dead as Jacob Marley—'

'Who's Jacob Marley?'

'Scrooge's partner. Oh, forget it. What more do you want me to tell you? She's dead!'

'Calm down,' Spike says. 'I just wanted to check.' He pauses. I can hear someone shouting in the newsroom. I study the escort girls in more detail... 'What about if we call the palace?' he muses.

'Call the palace?' I say. 'You must be joking! If you call the palace, the whole thing will be on the wires in five minutes flat, and your whole world exclusive will have gone up in smoke.'

'All right, all right.' Spike sighs. 'Guess we're just going to have to trust you on this one.'

'I guess you are.'

'I'm going out on quite a limb with this. We're clearing nine pages. But just to check...'

'What?'

'She really is dead?'

'For God's sake!'

CHAPTER 18

Campion is alone when she boards the return train to London. The carriage is fairly full, mainly day trippers returning from Hastings. She perches on an end seat next to a family of four; tipsy father, shattered mother, and two teenagers, a boy and a girl.

She has much to digest.

It was her first kiss since her divorce. And quite a good kiss too. It has been… wholly discombobulating. That morning, when she'd dressed for this long walk, she had not considered the possibility of kissing. But then there had been the walk, and Darwin, and evolution, and four minutes of staring through the windows into each other's souls, and Mason's tears dripping down his cheeks. The thought of kissing him had seemed not just appropriate, but wholly desirable.

The first kiss had been quite soft, and then, because one kiss can never be enough, there'd been another, and another, and after quite a lot of kisses, she'd started to get quite into it, one hand on Mason's cheek, and another snaking around his chest. He'd cupped her waist with his hand, skin to skin. She hadn't been held like that in a long, long time. There had been more kissing, and yet again, Campion had been taken by surprise because, after a short while, she found herself quite consumed with desire for this, well, guy. 'Excuse me,' she'd said, and stood up, and then – well, there is no polite way to describe it – had brazenly straddled him, knees resting easy on the bench in the hut, and though they had both been wearing jeans, there had been… She smirks at the memory… Well, let's just say there had been some friction. She'd broken off to undo a couple of buttons on her blouse, his fingers roaming delicately from waist to breast. Dammit to hell, they might have started making love then and there on the bench, but they'd been interrupted by one of the National Trust staff, who had made a soft cough before telling them that the house was closing in ten minutes. Buttons were speedily buttoned – how had his fly-buttons become undone? He'd had his hands on her since that first kiss… How shamelessly wanton!

They'd caught a cab to the station and then… and then she'd boarded the train alone.

There is a guy sitting opposite her. He is sitting next to the teenage girl, but obviously isn't part of the family. He is staring up at the ceiling. She quietly appraises him. Not a bad-looking guy, jeans, a North Face coat, well-worn walking boots; he keeps himself in good shape. He is missing half the little finger on his left hand. What is that all about?

'Do you come here often?' she asks. Seemed as good a way as any to break the ice.

The guy's eyes trickle down from the ceiling to look at her. 'How d… did you know I was a trainspotter?'

Campion likes that he has a trace of a stutter. It is so deliciously different from her ex-husband, who had wooed so many women with his words, and who used his silvery tongue to batter down a girl's defences.

'My grandad was a trainspotter,' Campion says. 'Once you know what you're looking for, you can't miss 'em.' She glances over at the mother sitting by the window. They are all listening, the two teenagers staring curiously while the father looks out of the window with a faint smile on his face.

'But you d… didn't take to trainspotting?' the guy says.

'No,' Campion says. 'I just like going on random journeys. Each Sunday morning, I join the ticket queue, and I ask for a ticket to anywhere – and the ticket seller decides where I'll be going that day.'

'And today, the ticket seller sent you to Orpington?'

'Apparently, Charles Darwin used to live nearby,' Campion says, smiling pleasantly at the teenage daughter. The girl is staring with a beguiling mix of disgust and incredulity. 'Tell me how you lost most of your little finger.'

The man laughs and holds up his left hand – a pleasingly toned hand. 'That's a very dir… direct question,' he says. 'There might be a terribly embarrassing story behind it.'

'I insist,' Campion says.

She is getting to like this new authoritative persona. Just say what you like. No matter how rude or intrusive a question, just blurt it straight out. Maybe this is what it feels like to be a *Sun* reporter.

The man – more than just "not-bad looking", he is passably handsome – smiles as he plays with the stump of his little finger. 'I am afraid that this missing finger is down to the most middle-class injury that you can p… possibly imagine.'

'Never thought about middle-class injuries before,' Campion says. 'You're saying there are injuries that only happen to middle-class people?'

'Lots of injuries only happen to middle-class people,' he says. 'In the winter, in Waitrose, you will see lots of shoppers hobbling around on crutches with grey plastic orthopaedic boots. Injured while skiing – a th… thoroughly middle-class sport.'

'Fair enough,' Campion says. She looks over at the two elderly couples sitting on the other side of the aisle. They are also openly listening in to the conversation.

'Avocado thumb,' the handsome man says. 'Another classic. Is there any more middle-class food than an avo… avocado? You cut the avocado in half. You chop into the stone with your heavy-duty knife—'

'And you miss the stone altogether and take a chunk out of your thumb,' Campion says.

'Avocado thumb. But there is no more middle-c… class an injury than losing half of the little finger on your left hand. It is definitive.' He holds up his hand and, in slow, stately fashion, eyeballs his audience. First the girl, then the boy, then the mother and father and four pensioners, before his eyes finally come to rest on Campion.

'I used to wear a signet ring on the little finger of my left hand. It was, unfortunately, a most substantial signet ring made of solid gold. The family crest was on it, a chevron between three lion heads. I wore it all the time. I didn't even take it off when I went to bed.'

He acknowledges the conductor. The conductor has paused from checking tickets to listen to the story. 'Two years ago, we were on a night-time ex... exercise. My troop was being driven to some spot on Salisbury Plain. I was the first off the back of the truck. I put my hand on the tail of the lorry and jumped down.

'The pain was... intense. At... at first, I thought someone had trodden on my hand, but when I looked, I saw what you see now – most of my little finger was gone. My signet ring had caught on a spigot on the tail of the truck – the ring turned out to be much... much stronger than my little finger.'

The teenage girl's eyes widen.

'Go on,' Campion says.

The man milks the moment, nodding as he holds Campion's gaze. 'By the time I realised what had happened, the rest of the troop was pouring off the back of the truck. After five minutes, both my ring and my little finger were found in the mud. For some r... reason, the squaddies found it much funnier than I did.'

'What a way to lose your finger,' Campion says. 'What happened then?'

'The finger was left at the hospital after the doctors failed to re... reattach it,' he says. 'As for the ring, it is a little bit twisted. It sits in a box somewhere at home. My... my mother would like me to wear it, but on this, if nothing else, I have de... decided to take a stand. I do not wear rings.'

'I approve your story,' Campion says, and then, impish,

devil-may-care-ish, she takes the man's hand and kisses the tip of his missing finger.

'No one's ever kissed my lit… little stump before—'

'That what you call it now?' Campion says.

Mason blushes.

Campion enjoys having such complete mastery over her audience. She throws them another bone. 'Would you like to be my boyfriend?'

The man looks at the girl, looks at the boy. 'Very much.'

'I'm just going to try something,' she says. 'I hope it doesn't go badly.' She leans in towards him, and they kiss – every bit as good as the kiss on the thinking walk. She wants more, but this is perhaps neither the time nor the place.

The train pulls into Charing Cross. Campion stands up and gives her onlookers a full curtsy. 'And that,' she says, directly addressing the teenage girl, 'is how it's done.'

She takes Mason's hand, and to general slack-jawed amazement, she leads him down the aisle and off the train. They kiss each other again when they are on the platform, then simultaneously burst into laughter.

'My boyfriend,' she says as they stroll out onto the street.

'My girlfriend.'

'And where does my boyfriend stand on the matter of lovemaking?'

'I th… think I'm all for it.'

'I should hope so too,' Campion says. 'But how many dates? One? Two? Are you a three-date kinda guy?'

'I… I don't have that much experience, Campion,' he says. 'I'll follow your lead.'

Campion stops. She is in need of more kisses. They nestle into an empty doorway; Campion is nicely squeezed against the door, enveloped by Mason's coat. 'On due consideration,' she says. 'I think now would be as good a time as any.'

'I quite agree.'

'I think your bed will be bigger than mine.'

'Not for now at the palace,' he says. 'I'll book a room.'

'Where?'

'Claridge's.'

'When?'

'This minute,' he says, and he kisses her and in this moment, Campion knows for a certainty that going on that walk, that morning, has been just about the best decision of her life – because this guy, he is interested, interesting, and funny, and above all else, he is a keeper.

They are in a hurry. It takes them twenty minutes to walk to Claridge's, three minutes to check in, and another three minutes to get into their room and slam the door behind them. But now that the entirety of the evening stretches ahead of them, they kiss and then Mason orders up a bottle of champagne before joining Campion in the shower, where he assiduously helps her wash away the day's dust. By this point, the bath is abrim with bubbles, filled with every gel that Mason could lay his hands on. He takes her hand and leads her from the shower to the bath, each openly admiring their lover's beautiful nakedness. He joins her in the bath, and they lean together and kiss; beneath the bubbles, fingers languidly tease. Campion has just eased on top of him when there is a knock at the door. Mason slips on a bathrobe and accepts the champagne, but he does not return to the bath because Campion is now quite dry and is beckoning him from the bedsheets. He opens the champagne and pours two glasses. They have a sip and a toast to health and happiness. Then, for the first time, they gradually and ever so sweetly become a couple.

And here, perhaps, might be the perfect place to end our story, with love triumphant and with Kim, for once, having covered himself in glory. But the story does not end here as there remains one very large elephant in the room – the mother, that vile snob, the Duchess of Montagu, who will be unlikely to take kindly to her son dating a maid at the palace.

CHAPTER 19

The queen has dealt with a lot of death in her life, so after Bobo's death, she does what she did when her father George VI died. She seeks solace with her horses in the stables, grooming them with heavy brushes until their coats gleam, nothing but her and the horse, one hand on its flank and one hand on the brush. She occasionally rests her head against the horse's side, cocooned by the warm wall of solid muscle.

She first started grooming horses on the death of her grandfather, George V – but those had just been her little toy ponies. She'd brushed the manes and the tails so often that the horsehair had started to fall out, and the wooden toys had to be sent away for repair. Then, seventeen years later, when her father died, she'd sought the same solace in the palace mews. As she'd once told her daughter, Anne, you can't feel properly sad when you are grooming a horse. Very sad when you are grooming yourself, but it is impossible to be sad when you are grooming a horse. Inside, you may be in knots, but you still have to wield the brush. You still have to have one reassuring hand on the horse's flank.

The death of her father, when she'd been staying with Philip at Treetops in Kenya, had been a hammer blow. She'd allowed herself just two hours to process her father's sudden death, and then, well, it had been back to business – though upgraded to being The Queen's business. The same day that she'd heard the news, she'd been back at her desk, perusing all those top-secret documents that had been for the monarch's eyes only. Her sister, Margaret, went to pieces when their father Bertie died, spending days and days in a darkened room where she did little more than polish her collection of seashells. They were a very nice collection of seashells, lots of shells that Margaret had collected from her trips to the world's finest beaches, but polishing them did seem like rather a banal occupation.

In 1947, when the queen made her first speech to the Commonwealth, she had set out her life's purpose – and every day after, she remembered that pledge. She recalled it when her father died, and now, as she grooms the horses, she repeats her promise. 'It is very simple,' she says – and in this moment, it is very simple because you brush the horse's flank, mane and tail, and you keep on brushing until its hair gleams like burnished copper. With long smooth strokes down the horse's foreleg, she continues her chant, 'I declare before you all that my whole life, whether it be long or short, shall be devoted to your service and the service of our great imperial family to which we all belong.'

The queen laughs at herself; she is fully aware that in matters of grooming, she is a trifle OCD. The job is not finished until there is not a hair out of place – not on the horse's flanks, or its mane, and most especially not its tail.

Crawfie, the queen's governess – who'd been dropped like a hot rivet after publishing her royal memoirs – always teased the queen about the way all her toy horses had to be lined up before she went to bed. Marion Crawford had also unhelpfully revealed that the young Princess Elizabeth would jump out of bed in order to check that her shoes had been lined up perfectly parallel to each other. Just a small detail of her life, but how the public latched on to it when Crawfie's damnable memoirs had been serialised in the gutter press.

Crawfie had died five years ago, in 1988, and not a single royal had turned out for her funeral. The sheer shamelessness of what Crawfie had done still makes the queen seethe. Is she entitled to no privacy whatsoever? Why, why, why do people feel this extraordinary need to know the everyday details of life in the royal family? Don't they have anything better to do?

Bobo, on the other hand, had been entirely dependable. Not for her, the temptation to go into print with all the little details of her dealings with Elizabeth. To the very end, Bobo had been steady, discreet, devoted, and utterly loyal. The queen well knows that Bobo had accrued a lot of power during her time at the palace – and had not been shy of using it! – but the queen could deny her nothing.

It was true that Bobo was not the woman she'd once been, just occasional flashes of lucidity followed by minutes of darkness. Winston Churchill, dear old Winston, had been the same. In the late 1950s, when they'd had luncheon together, he spent most of the meal staring around the room or mumbling into his soup, but every so often, he'd be back – back on full power, as bright and as brilliant as the colossus she'd first met when he led Britain through the Second World War.

The queen had been up to see Bobo just a few hours before she'd died. In years past, Bobo would have filled her in on all the palace gossip. The queen would laugh, long and loud, as she heard about the many below stairs' escapades, so much more interesting and exciting than the staid lives of the royals above the stairs. Tales of the footmen falling in love – usually with each other, though sometimes with a maid or a cook – were invariably followed by the next week's bust-up, often capped off with a fight, which would mean that for the next week, the queen would be forced to ignore her staff's purpling eyes and black bruised cheekbones.

Over the years, Bobo's stories had dwindled. Bobo's palace moles were not as efficient as they'd been when Bobo had been in her prime. When the queen visited Bobo towards the end, she mostly reminisced, and Bobo was mostly away with the fairies. Though she had dropped one titbit. Bobo had been singing to herself. The queen had been about to leave the room. The singing had stopped, and just like that, the real Bobo – the pin-sharp Scotswoman – was back.

'Your new equerry-in-waiting,' she'd said. 'He's fallen in love.'

'How ever did you know that?' the queen had said. 'I wish I had your sources.'

'He's fallen for your storyteller,' Bobo said.

'Campion?' the queen said. 'But that's lovely! I've never even seen her look at a man.'

'She's certainly making cow-eyes at him.'

'The best news I've heard in ages,' the queen said.

She leant down to give her old nanny a kiss on the cheek. Bobo was the only member of staff who the queen ever kissed on the cheek. She'd started kissing Bobo on the cheek when she was just a little girl.

'Good night, Bobo,' she'd say as Bobo tucked her into her bed, and there she was, nearly sixty-five years later, still kissing her on the cheek in exactly the same way.

'Not everyone's as nice as you are, dear,' Bobo had said.

The queen didn't quite know what she'd meant at the time, but two weeks later, two weeks after Bobo's death, the queen now realises exactly what Bobo had been driving at. Not everyone is nice as her. Some people are positively awful.

The queen has all but finished grooming the horse. There are still a fair number of liveried helpers in the stables, though with none of the usual chatter and whistling, just this deep, respectful silence, with the stroke of the brushes and the occasional snicker from the horses. No one will speak to her unless she speaks to them, and that, while she mourns Bobo, is just how she likes it.

'Where is she?' A loud screech comes from the stables' entrance. Wearily familiar, it is a reminder that wherever she is in the world, the call of duty is never more than a minute away.

'Can't tell you, ma'am.' It is Jerry, a chauffeur and one of the senior grooms, stout fellow.

'You very well know that you address me as Your Grace,' comes the screechy voice again. 'I was distinctly told that Her Majesty was in the mews.'

'That is as may be, Duchess—' The queen, entirely hidden by her horse, has a sudden fit of the giggles. The way Jerry addresses her as "Duchess" makes it sound like the Duchess of Montagu is a pearly queen. 'I haven't seen hide nor hair of Her Majesty.'

The queen, still sniggering, had no idea that Jerry was such an accomplished liar. He had personally welcomed her to the stables an hour earlier and then, quite unsolicited, had brought her a mug of tea; what a genuinely nice man.

'Well, dammit, man, find her for me!'

'There is seriously nothing I would enjoy more, Duchess, than looking for Her Majesty, seriously,' Jerry says. The queen can imagine him contentedly chewing on a piece of straw as he eyeballs the Duchess. 'But I've got other matters to attend to. See, Duchess? Horses to feed. Carriages to be polished. Cars to be cleaned. So, though I love, love, looking for the queen, I really can't help you.'

'Well, you're a fat lot of use, aren't you?'

'That's exactly what the missus tells me, Duchess, when she wants me to go shopping with her, and she needs me to hold her bags, and I tell her that I've got to see a man about a dog—'

'Is this insolence studied?'

'Studied, Duchess? Don't know what you're talking about. I talk to you just like I talk to the queen—'

The queen has been mightily enjoying herself, but as ever, duty calls, and it is time to bring Jerry's tomfoolery to an end.

'Ah, good morning, Jerry,' she says as she glides out from behind her horse. 'Good morning, Viola.'

'Good morning, Your Majesty,' he says, giving her a bow.

'Your Majesty,' the Duchess says with a curtsy.

'I'm afraid, Jerry, that I sneaked in here when you were otherwise engaged – I do hope that's all right.'

'Sneak in any time you like, ma'am,' he says. 'Always a pleasure to see you here with the horses. The lads love it.'

'Well, thank you for accommodating me,' the queen says,

and then and there decides to reward Jerry with a Royal Victorian Order, Commander at the very minimum, one of the small things that are within her boon, and she knows that it will mean a lot to him.

The queen leads the way into the palace, Viola by her side. With all the turmoil of Bobo's death, she's forgotten that they were supposed to be walking the dogs that morning. Viola is, predictably, dressed for a cocktail party rather than a walk, wearing a cream dress and black high-heeled court shoes.

The queen takes the scenic route to the dogs' room, snaking through the staterooms; there is somebody she rather hopes to see. As the queen guessed, she is in the Picture Gallery. Viola is the first to spot her.

'Good heavens, ma'am,' Viola says. 'You have a half-caste maid. You do keep up with the times.'

'I'm sorry?' The queen's mind had been on Campion rather than her companion.

'You are very with it, ma'am,' the duchess says. 'You are employing a maid who is a half-caste.'

'You sound like an old racist,' the queen says. 'I could not care less about the colour of Campion's skin. But what I will tell you is that I like her. Very much indeed.'

'Oh, ma'am, I didn't mean it like that,' the duchess says. 'I have a number of coloured friends.'

The queen winces again. Viola isn't the only one of her acquaintances to be a bigot, but the very thought of evolving, or indeed of moderating her language, is obviously anathema to her.

'Excuse me one moment,' the queen says, and ignoring Viola, she joins Campion, who is ostensibly dusting Rembrandt's *Shipbuilder and his Wife*.

'Your Majesty,' Campion says with a curtsy.

'Campion dear,' the queen says affectionately.

'I am very sorry for your loss, Your Majesty,' Campion says. 'Bobo was a great woman.'

'She was that.' They both turn to look at the Rembrandt,

an old shipbuilder sitting at his desk, turning to his wife as she passes him a note. 'They look like they have fun together,' the queen says. 'I bet there's a good story behind it.'

'There is a wonderful story behind the picture, Your Majesty.'

'I very much look forward to hearing it,' the queen says. 'But now, as you can see, I am otherwise engaged.' She is about to join Viola when she mischievously turns to Campion and adds. 'Would you care to meet Mason's mother?'

'Is it wise, Your Majesty?'

'You'll have to meet the Duchess of Snob sooner or later,' the queen says. 'If anyone's going to introduce you, best that it's me.'

'Mason would probably come out in hives, Your Majesty.'

'Quite.'

Viola is standing awkwardly in front of a Canaletto. Since Viola has never knowingly admired a painting, the queen presumes that she is making such a detailed study of the Canaletto in order to avoid the horrific ordeal of having to talk to a maid.

'Ah, Viola, lovely Canaletto, isn't it?' the queen says. 'Always makes me want to go back to Venice. Campion, may I introduce the Duchess of Montagu? Viola, this is Campion, my storyteller.' Both the queen and the duchess – and indeed Campion – are very aware of the niceties of this introduction, the queen having overturned all the most basic protocols. In an introduction, the "lesser ranking" person (socially, by age, or by profession) is introduced to the "higher-ranking" person. This, at least in more formal times, gives the higher-ranking person the chance to turn on their heel smartly and duck the introduction. But in the Royal Picture Gallery, of course, Viola has just been introduced as if it is she, the Duchess of Montagu, who is Campion's inferior.

Campion gives the Duchess a curtsy. 'Your Grace,' she says.

'Campion? Is that your name?' The Duchess is not used to

being introduced to the palace maids, nor does she generally enjoy chit-chatting with the servants.

'Yes, ma'am. Campion, after the flower.'

'After the flower?' the duchess says. 'I didn't know there was such a thing.'

Campion smiles pleasantly; the queen is silently but fervently rooting for her. 'Apparently you grow them in your herbaceous border, ma'am.'

'In my herbaceous border indeed? Wherever did you hear that from?'

'I met a journalist once, and I asked him the same question – and I will give you the same reply that he gave to me: I couldn't possibly reveal my sources.'

The queen turns to wipe the smile from her face. If only she could master this easy puckish banter. 'I think we've got some campions in our herbaceous border,' the queen says. 'I specially requested them in honour of a service that my storyteller paid me last year when I was not feeling my best. If you care to come out to the garden, Viola, I'll show them to you.'

The Duchess, realising she is outnumbered, tries to get the conversation back onto a more formal footing. 'So, do you like being a royal maid?'

'I adore it, ma'am,' Campion says.

'I'm sure you do,' the duchess says. 'A bit of cleaning here, some dusting there, not overly taxing.'

'Certainly not as taxing as living the life of a Duchess, ma'am,' Campion says smoothly. 'I really don't know how you manage it.' She smiles as she speaks, just so effortlessly beautiful; alongside the face-fillered, sagging botoxed beauty of the Duchess, it is like comparing a live lily with a dusty plastic carnation.

The queen studies Campion more closely. Campion looks more girlishly happy than she's ever seen her. It could be down to a lot of things, but it is almost certainly down to just one thing; she's got a boyfriend. And, unless the queen is very much mistaken, a Duke to boot. Won't that just be the most wonderful wedding on earth to attend – God willing! – the bashful groom and his most beautiful bride, whilst there, simmering in the corner, is the duchess, rolling her eyes and gnashing her teeth at the sheer ignominy of it all (A duke marrying a common maidservant!). Well, it may yet happen – only the previous year, the Princess Royal had only gone and married a common-or-garden equerry, and if the queen can suck it up, then Viola can most certainly learn to do the same.

'I'll see you tomorrow, Campion,' the queen says.

'I look forward to it, Your Majesty.' Campion makes a graceful curtsy and rewards Viola with one of her astonishingly brilliant smiles. 'Enjoy finding me in your herbaceous borders, Your Grace.'

The duchess gives a regal sniff – of course – and they go off to find the dogs.

After the despicable Jono Freemantle had been caught spiking the dogs' food with whisky, he had been relieved of his position as the queen's number one footman. His replacement is Ollie, and it is Ollie who should be preparing the dogs' food in the little pantry next to the dogs' sleeping quarters. Though it doesn't sound like Ollie.

Before the queen opens the door to the pantry, she can hear a number of rather peculiar voices, including, she realises, a very squeaky voice with a German accent. Viola is behind her, still in a pet at having been forced to talk to a lowly maidservant. The queen puts her finger to her lips and silently eases the door open. The new footman, Lawrence, she remembers, is standing in the middle of the room, and all nine of the corgis are sitting around him in an obedient semi-circle.

'And what do you want for your tea, Chipper?' he says.

Chipper's mouth seems to drool open. 'You know what I want,' Chipper says in this extraordinary Yorkshire accent. 'I want what I always want. I want steak.'

'Good boy.' Lawrence bends down and gives the dog a treat. 'And how would Chipper like his steak?'

'I like it so undercooked it can eat the salad.'

'Good boy!' Chipper is rewarded with another treat. Lawrence turns to Myrtle. 'Myrtle.' The dog wags her tail. 'Tell me a joke.'

Myrtle's mouth drops open, and – seemingly – starts talking with a saucy French accent. 'I bet my butcher he couldn't reach the meat on ze top shelf,' she says. 'He wouldn't take ze bet. He said ze steaks were too high.'

The queen giggles as she closes the door – what a simply ridiculous thing to have trained the dogs to do. Ridiculous but also rather remarkable. How does he do it? As far as she knows, Lawrence and Ollie have only been bringing up the dog food for about a fortnight – actually, since Bobo died.

Now that she thinks of Bobo's death, the queen recollects that, by odd coincidence, it had been Lawrence who'd found Bobo's body. Not that the queen had mentioned it to anyone, but there had always been one part of the story that never quite fitted. She'd been told that this footman, Lawrence, had taken up the tea and had walked into her bedroom to find Bobo dead in bed. And yet... when the queen had gone to make her last farewells to Bobo, she'd noticed that the tea things were still there. More than that, she'd noticed that a cup of tea had been poured and that some of the biscuits and sandwiches had been eaten. Now, either the doctor or this Lawrence chap had become a little peckish and had decided to help themselves to Bobo's tea... or Lawrence was lying through his teeth. And from the way he was cavorting around with the dogs – he had them all barking on cue now, like some little corgi choir – the queen guesses that it is most probably the latter.

CHAPTER 20

Oh, what a cheery worker bee you would have found in the palace those last two weeks of September. A humble footman who was happy with his lot, content to open doors and close doors, to deliver letters and serve tea, and in every way act like the unctuous little toad that I had always been born to be.

There had been one mildly irksome conversation with Grubby when I saw him in The Plumber's Arms a few days after the balcony debacle. As usual, I arrived on time, and as usual, he was late; only ten minutes late, which was good for him.

Before I'd managed to spit out so much as a word, he launched into a blistering tirade. None of the normal courtesies for hard-working, mild-mannered Kimmy, such as, perhaps, "How are you, Kim?" or "You're looking very well, Kim," or even, "Kim, you bastard, come and give Grubby a hug!" No, there was none of that. Instead, all I got was Grubby shambling over to the bar in his stained grey suit and just going straight for the throat.

'Where the hell were you?' he said. 'I was out on the Mall for four hours waiting for you – waiting for you in the rain – and His Nibs never showed up! Thanks a bunch!'

I finished my cool pint of Guinness, and, just as Granny had told me, I counted to ten. It still didn't work. I'd have had to have counted to a hundred if I was in any way going to refrain from giving Grubby the broadside that was coming to him.

'*You* waited for *me*?' I said. '*You* waited for *me*?' I gave him a sharp poke in the stomach.

'Do you want a fight or something?' He jabbed me in the chest. 'I'm not nearly as much of a push-over as Spike.'

'Listen to me, you fat idiot. It was me who was waiting for you, and if you ever bothered to turn up on time, you'd have seen me on the balcony, but as it was, you were late, just like you normally are, and I was damn nearly sacked.'

Did he suck it up? Did he have the good grace to admit that, yes, he was a tardy bastard, and that, yes, he'd been wrong to have a go at the diligent, mild-mannered Kim? Not one bit of it. He doubled down!

'Late?' he said. 'Who are you calling late? I was there bang on noon, just like you told me. I wasn't—'

'Hang on. Hang on!' I held up my hand to try to stem the flow of bollocks. 'I told you I'd be there between eleven and one. I never said noon.'

'You certainly did, you toe-rag,' he said, and even had the gall to pull out his pocket diary where he had indeed written the words, *Kim, Buckingham Palace, Noon.*

'I couldn't care less what you've written in your diary, you moron,' I said. 'I told you I'd be there at eleven.'

'No, you didn't.'

'Yes, I did.'

'No, you didn't.'

I leant over and cupped my arm around his neck, half hug and half throttle. Actually, let's make that eighty per cent throttle. 'We'll just have to agree to disagree,' I said magnanimously. 'Can I buy you a pint of Stella?'

'Please.'

We waited in silence for our pints to be poured, and when we had gone to the back of the pub, we settled into an uneasy truce.

'Cheers,' I said.

'Cheers.'

'Can I ask you one question, though?'

'What?'

'You never turned up at noon, did you? I grant that you thought I was supposed to be on the balcony at noon rather than eleven, but you still turned up late.'

He began to polish his glasses. 'Maybe just a little,' he said, a slow smile spreading over his stupid face.

'I knew it,' I said. 'So it wouldn't have made any difference if you'd thought I was on the balcony at eleven because you'd still have turned up late, and I'd still have been kicked off by the time you deigned to show up.'

We arranged another time for me to go out on the balcony – between noon and two the next day – and rather unbelievably, not only did I manage to skulk out onto the balcony without being caught, but Grubby was actually there waiting by the railings. After strutting around on the balcony for a couple of minutes, I gave him a cross between a wave and a Sieg Heil, then stepped back into the Balcony Room, where, thankfully, there was no hyper-vigilant master of the household waiting to tear me off another strip.

Now that we had the main picture in the bag, everything else was going to be just gravy – or so I had imagined. But Spike, of course, always wanted more. After my astonishingly brilliant World Exclusive about Bobo's death (not my byline, though. Spike had bagged that for himself), we had a particularly cosy chat on the phone.

'What we really need,' he said. 'Is a bit of the stuff from Windsor Castle. Don't get me wrong, I like all the palace stuff you've sent over. Great read. But if you could get into Windsor Castle, that'd be great.'

'You want me to get myself posted to Windsor Castle for the weekend?'

'Yeah, and while you're at it—'

'While I'm at it?' I said. 'You make it sound like I'm popping down to the supermarket.'

'Well, how hard is it? So, while you're at it, see if you can get in one of those coaches, the ones that they cart the ambassadors around in. You know they've got all the fancy red gear.'

'Yes, I do know, as it happens. I've got some in my wardrobe.'

'Fantastic! Just get yourself on the back of one of those carriages, give Grubby a wave—'

'So, is there anything else you're after?' I said, before adding, with heavy (heavy) sarcasm, 'Want me to sniff around the royals' apartments? Have a look-see into the queen's breakfast room? Have a wander into Prince Andrew's bedroom?'

'You can do that?' Spike said. 'That's brilliant! We'd love pictures of Randy Andy's bedroom. The queen's bedroom too – but only if it's safe. Wouldn't want you being shot or anything like that.'

'That would be terrible.'

'Terrible,' he said without the slightest trace of concern. 'So, number one, get into Windsor Castle—'

'Number two, get onto one of the royal carriages, and number three, start digging around the royals' private quarters—'

'Without getting shot.'

'Yes, without getting shot.'

And there, in a nutshell, we have what it is to be happy. Not that I want to get all philosophical, but to be happy is to be in pursuit of a fruitless dream. As they used to say in that touchy-feely mantra from the 1990s, "Success is a journey – not a destination." The end of the quest – whether it's the Holy Grail you're after, or even just a World Exclusive – is irrelevant because when you finally achieve your goal, you will have a fleeting moment of joy that lasts for all of ten minutes before you're up and about, looking for the next diversion.

So my Palace quest had been extended, just a little, by Spike, and I was more than happy to continue pottering around Buckingham Palace, sniffing through Prince Andrew's undies and the like; besides, anything that kept me out of The Sun newsroom had to be a good thing.

A palace footman's job is, of course, as banal as can be. It'd drive you crazy in the long run, but for a month or two, it's positively restful. Polishing shoes or glassware or silverware; standing around waiting to open doors; hotfooting it up the stairs with breakfast trays and tea trays and luncheon trays, and all the while hoovering up all the gossip just as diligently as Bobo MacDonald when she'd been at her absolute prime.

There was love, also, in the palace – and I myself had played a modest part in it. The first time I had caught wind of it was when I'd gone up to Mason's room at 7 a.m. with his morning tea. Normally in the morning, I'd have found him up and about, happily polishing his shoes – given half a chance, he'd polish my shoes too – but that particular morning, Mason was still in bed.

'Morning, Mason,' I said as I breezed into his room. 'It's another fine September day, hardly a cloud in the sky.'

I put the tray down on a side table and yanked open the curtains. 'Bit of a fug in here, I'll open the windows,' I said. 'Smells like a tart's boudoir, if you don't mind my saying so.'

I heaved up two of the window sashes, and a deliciously salt zephyr of wind fluttered into the room. It was only then that I turned towards the bed. Mason had company – and, from the mop of dark tawny hair that was poking out from the top of the duvet, I was pretty sure who she was.

'Is that you, Campion?' I said. 'Morning.'

Campion squinted at me in the bright sunlight, not a trace of shame on her face, in fact rather brazen. 'Morning Lawrence,' she said. 'You've brought tea, how lovely.'

'I'll pour you both a cup,' I said.

'You've got two cups?' she said. 'Did you know I was going to be here?'

'It's the talk of the palace,' I said.

Mason rolled over and kissed Campion on the cheek. 'He's talking utter rub... rubbish, Campion darling,' he said. 'He always brings two cups, one for him and one for me.'

I took them their cups of tea – large cups, they were; it's

another weird palace tradition that gentlemen are served their morning tea in large cups while the ladies have their tea in much more refined smaller ones.

It might have been nice to have stayed to chat, but I could see they were itching for me to leave the bedroom.

'Well, I'll be off then,' I said in my meek, docile manner, and mooched off to the canteen for breakfast.

So, you see, everything in the garden is rosy. There remains only the delicate interview that I am due to have with Sir Richard Arnison-Newgass, where he will decide whether my job will be made permanent. Just as a matter of personal pride, I am very keen for this to be the case. Through diligence and hard brown-nosing, I will have earned the right to call myself a full-time palace footman, and ever after, I will always be able to style myself as a one-time member of the royal household.

There is one other reason why I hope to stay on as a palace footman – notwithstanding all the tasks that Spike has given me. I have decided that, at least for the latter part of my palace career, I will become (drumroll please) a force for good. Maybe it is because I like Campion; perhaps it is because I am also a Mason fan (which other equerry on earth shares his morning tea with his flunky and then, to boot, polishes his minion;s shoes?); and maybe, just maybe, it is because at heart I'm a lumbering great softie. So, for whatever footling reason, I have set my heart on turning Campion into a Duchess. As far as I am aware, there isn't a person in the palace who would not heartily approve of the match. Although – such sweet ecstasy – outside the confines of the palace, there is going to be one person who'll be spitting tacks: Mason's mother.

CHAPTER 21

In the palace, certain senior members of the household have begun to realise that dirty work is afoot.

The master of the household, for instance, has seen how in the last month, the trickle of tittle-tattle that constantly leaks from the palace has turned into a spate. And though Sir Richard has long been aware that palace staff occasionally ameliorate their meagre wages by selling stories to the tabloids, what has occurred since the beginning of September has been utterly unprecedented. Every single piece of palace gossip to come his way – and, indeed, some palace gossip that he had not been privy to – has ended up not just in the tabloids but in that most disreputable piece of filth, *The Sun*. (Amongst the senior royals, *The Sun* is considered so vile that its presence is not allowed to sully the queen's apartments. Every morning over breakfast, Her Majesty peruses a full selection of the British press, starting with *The Racing Post*, then moving on to the broadsheets and the tabloids like *The Daily Mirror*. For some reason, however, Her Majesty never touches Britain's biggest-selling daily, *The Sun*.)

That there is a mole in the palace, there is no doubt. But of more concern to Sir Richard is the mole's efficiency. The very day after Bobo MacDonald died, *The Sun* devoted nine pages of purple prose to her death, indicating to Sir Richard that *The Sun's* editors must have learned of Bobo's death just as quickly as he had. There is one person in particular who he is keen to interview about the matter: the young footman who found Bobo's body.

The queen also has questions of her own about Bobo's death. Thankfully, she is alone; Viola has taken her leave, thence to bore somebody else to tears. She is standing outside the door to the corgis' room. Lawrence is singing. It takes the queen a few seconds to place the song. It is being sung very badly, but it is nevertheless unmistakable. He is singing, attempting to sing, Fred Astaire's 'Dancing Cheek to Cheek'. She opens the door a crack and peeks inside.

Now, to give the queen her due, she has witnessed many eccentricities amongst her staff over the years and often quite enjoyed them; of an evening, these little quirks are great fodder for entertaining her family. But few of her staff, not even Simon Brook, can top this fellow Lawrence. As the other corgis obediently watch, Lawrence has Chipper in his arms and is actually dancing cheek to cheek with the dog, swirling Chipper around the room with his hind legs spiralling outwards like a windmill. Simply unbelievable! She would tell them tonight, but no-one would ever believe her.

The queen knocks on the door, waiting a few seconds for the footman to re-adjust himself. When she walks in, she finds Lawrence soberly fiddling around with the dogs' chicken breasts.

'Your Majesty,' he says, giving her a neck bow.

'Good afternoon, Lawrence,' she says. 'Did I hear you singing?'

'Many apologies, ma'am, it won't happen again.'

'One of my favourite songs,' she says. 'I watched *Top Hat* when I was a little girl. My parents would dance to it when we were on holiday in Scotland.'

'That's a very beautiful memory, ma'am,' he says. 'Thank you for sharing it.' He makes to leave the room, but the queen stays him.

'Just one second, Lawrence, before you go,' the queen says. The footman is looking particularly furtive. 'I understand that it was you who found Bobo.'

'That is correct, ma'am,' he says.

'You were taking up her afternoon tea, I believe,' she says. 'How did you find her?'

'She was quite dead, ma'am.'

'Is that so?'

'Yes, ma'am.'

'Is that really so?'

He starts to crack. 'I'm not quite sure what you mean, Your Majesty.'

'Perhaps you could help me out with one small detail, Lawrence,' the queen says. 'After you found Bobo, did you help yourself to a cup of tea or perhaps eat a couple of sandwiches?'

'I don't quite follow, ma'am.'

'Let me explain, then, Lawrence. When I was taken to Bobo's room, I found a half-drunk cup of tea. Some of the sandwiches had been eaten.'

'Did you, ma'am?'

'So did the doctor eat them? Did the master of the household eat them?'

'Bobo had eaten them, Your Majesty.'

'Not quite so dead after all then, Lawrence,' she says. 'Would you care to tell me what actually happened?'

'Of course, ma'am,' he says. 'It was all just a little embarrassing, that's all.'

'I shall be the judge of that.'

'Yes, ma'am.'

He starts tugging at his lower lip in the most unseemly fashion. The queen busies herself with the dog bowls. She is aware that some staff begin to squirm if she looks at them for too long.

'And?' She picks up a still-warm chicken breast with some silver tongs, puts it into the Chipper's bowl and tops it off with some dog biscuits.

'Umm,' he says.

'Come now, Lawrence, it can't have been that bad!'

She scoops up the next chicken breast and pours on the

biscuits. In the past, Philip used to cajole her about the way she served the dogs their food – telling her that it would be much more efficient to dole out all the chicken breasts at the same time and only then to pour out the dog biscuits. But efficiency be damned. Preparing the dogs' dinners is one of the highlights of her day – if it takes a little longer to individually make up each dog's bowl, then so much the better.

'It was like this, ma'am,' Lawrence says. 'You know how Bobo was sometimes, err, with it, and sometimes she wasn't quite there.'

'I did know that.'

'I'd taken in her tea and sandwiches, ma'am, and – as you correctly surmised – she poured herself some tea and had some sandwiches. And then, just like that, she was gone. She was singing some old Scottish nursery rhyme.'

'Slinkymalinky?'

'That's the one, ma'am,' he says.

'She used to sing it to me when I was a child,' the queen says. 'It was our favourite.' She is so distracted that she drops a chicken breast on the floor. Chipper beats the other dogs to it and wolfs it down in two swift bites. 'Chipper, you greedy brute!' she says. 'So, what happened next?'

'Well, ma'am…' Lawrence starts tugging at his lip again, shifting uneasily on his feet.

'I understand that you are still on probation here, Lawrence. If you wish to continue working at the palace, you better tell me what happened.'

'Of course, ma'am,' he says. 'Chipper was lying next to Bobo on the bed, and, umm…' He starts to gabble. 'Over the last few weeks, I've been learning to throw my voice, so, umm, Chipper started talking to her—'

'Good heavens!' the queen says. 'And Bobo, who was away with the fairies, genuinely thought that Chipper was talking to her.'

'Yes, ma'am,' Lawrence says. 'It was a very nice chat. She

told Chipper that she loved him, and Chipper told her right back that he loved her.'

'Yes,' the queen says. The queen delicately slices one of the chicken breasts. The smaller dogs like Myrtle preferred their meat in dainty bite-sized chunks. 'But you still haven't got to the nub of it, have you?'

'No, ma'am,' the footman says. 'Chipper, ahh, passed wind on the bed, and he then blamed Bobo, who promptly retorted that Chipper was responsible for the foul stench.'

The queen smirks at the thought of dear old Bobo having an animated conversation with Chipper about who'd farted.

'So, you took it into your head for the dog to blame Bobo?'

'That is correct, ma'am,' he says. 'So, they were both amiably bickering away when Chipper went and passed wind again—'

'Please just say, he farted.'

'Quite, ma'am. Chipper farted again, and Bobo blamed the dog, and Chipper told her that she'd been farting like a lodging house cat—'

'What an extraordinary expression,' the queen says. 'Are lodging house cats famed for their farting?'

'I believe so, ma'am. Anyway, the long and the short of it was that Bobo started laughing, really, really laughing, side-splitting laughter, and… and that's how she died.'

The queen digests this thought as she prepares the last of the dog food. She places the bowls in a line on the ground and gives the royal command, 'Din dins!' – watching with satisfaction as the dogs dart to their bowls. 'So, Bobo died laughing?' the queen says.

'Literally, ma'am.'

'What a lovely way to go,' the queen says.

'I'd take it any day, ma'am,' he says.

'Thank you for telling me,' the queen says. 'Though, I will not tell the master of the household. He would not approve.'

'My thoughts exactly, ma'am.'

'You're a very strange young man, Lawrence,' the queen

says. 'I will inform Sir Richard that your probation has been a success.'

'You are very kind, ma'am. Thank you.'

'So, you talk to my dogs, you sing to my dogs, you even dance with my dogs,' the queen says. 'Do you do anything else with them?'

A smile flickers over his lips.

'Yes?'

'I do, as it happens, ma'am,' he says. 'We like to play hide and seek.'

'Hide and seek?' The queen thought she'd heard it all. And now this.

'Yes, ma'am,' the bizarre footman says. 'And if I may say so, they're very good at it.'

* * *

Viola, the Duchess of Montagu, has always resented the fact that the queen is the queen when it is patently obvious to anyone but a congenital halfwit that she, Viola, the Duchess of Montagu, would do a much better job of being Queen of Great Britain and Northern Ireland and her other realms and territories. Whenever Viola consorts with the queen, she can't help but be struck by the fact that Her Majesty is letting the side down. Of course, it is all the most brilliant act, but Queen Elizabeth II genuinely appears to not care a jot for her position or title. When the queen talks to she, herself, the Duchess of Montagu, she seems to converse in the exact same way that she talks to the grooms or, indeed, that coloured maid. In point of actual fact, Viola, the Duchess of Montagu, has noticed that when the queen *does* talk to her half-caste maid, she seems to make herself markedly more agreeable than when she is talking to members of the nobility. And she, Viola (the Duchess of Montagu), is thrice a noblewoman – that is, by birth, by breeding, and by marriage. Frankly, the way that the queen deals with her servants as if they are in some way her equal is more than unseemly. It is spectacularly revolting (especially so for ladies of genteel tastes.) And not that Viola wants to belabour the point, but just to go back to that half-caste maid, the queen even had the nerve to treat her as an equal. It still rankled, even some days afterwards. The way she had been introduced to that, that coloured woman – half black, half white, God knows what else in between – when out of spite or malice, the queen had the gall to introduce her to that chit of a girl with that ridiculous name, Campion, as if it was she, Viola, the Duchess of Montagu, who was a cap-clutching vassal being presented to an empress.

Sweet Jesus, it rankled.

And now – now! – Her Majesty the queen has the nerve to beg a favour.

She wants Viola to throw… a party.

But not any old party. Oh no. She, Viola, Duchess of Montagu, has thrown scores, hundreds of parties over the years – cocktail parties, birthday parties, hunting parties, shooting parties. She is quite at home throwing a party, thank you very much indeed, Your Majesty. But never – never, never! – a party quite like this.

They'd been walking with the dogs in the Buckingham Palace gardens – and, irritatingly, the Queen had insisted on walking on the grass when any sensible person would have kept to the gravelled paths.

The queen is wearing tweed and tasteless rubber galoshes with some silk scarf, probably another Hermes, around her head (looking, frankly, like some suburban housewife on her way to Waitrose to pick up a pint of milk). She has been striding towards the lake with no thought whatsoever for Viola, who is having to teeter along on tiptoes so that her stilettoed heels don't sink into the grass. The dogs are scampering around, charging off in one direction or another, with that damned Chipper leading the pack. If ever there was an animal in need of castration, it was Chipper (followed, in short order, by most male members of the human race).

The queen has been talking, though Viola has not really been able to catch a word of what the woman has been saying. Something about the terrible, terrible woes of being a queen.

Viola then watches the queen perform one of the more revolting spectacles of the day – if not *the* most revolting spectacle of the day. It is bad enough having to watch the queen feed her dogs titbits from the luncheon table, but this – this! – is the limit. There is no polite way to describe what she is doing. She is shit-flicking.

When the dogs defecate on the grass, the queen flicks away their shit with this simply disgusting turd-encrusted stick, swishing the shit either into the pond or into any convenient herbaceous border. Why does she so demean herself? Why doesn't she do what any sane monarch would do, which is to have an underling deal with the disgusting business? But no, no, the queen does not do that – can't do that – and instead takes it upon herself to personally deal with all her dogs' defecations. Viola, the Duchess of Montagu, is hard pushed to think of anything that is so utterly repulsive as the sight of the queen flicking dog shit.

The queen flicks two golf ball-sized pieces of muck into the pond. Chipper is rewarded with a smile.

'One of the many joys of dog walking,' the queen says. 'There is no joy whatsoever to be had out of picking up dog poo in a little plastic bag, but as soon as I discovered the art of the poo-flick, I became a complete convert. Better for the environment, better for me – and I am quite sure it's better for the dogs. It can't be doing them any good at all to see me, their mistress, stooping down to retrieve their ablutions.'

'I'm sure, ma'am.' Now standing next to the queen, Viola has to awkwardly hover on her toes; it is all most undignified.

'Sometimes, I wish that some of my loyal subjects could see me like this – it might stop them from getting so very tongue-tied.'

'How do you mean, ma'am?'

The queen continues to saunter around the pond, gaily

swinging her shit-stick. 'It's simple, Viola,' she says. 'Once you've seen a woman flicking dog poo, it is difficult to be in awe of her. As it is, whenever I go into a room, everyone's so nervous there is this immediate silence – as if all the conversations have been cut with a knife. When I walk through the room, I watch as people peel away, like water parting before the bow of a thrusting warship.'

'What an image, ma'am. Very poetic.'

The queen peers at her, not quite sure if Viola is being sarcastic; this gives Viola deep satisfaction. She is certainly not being sarcastic; she is being ironic, teetering along that sweet knife edge of sarcasm.

The queen bends down by one of the borders to pull out a couple of weeds.

'Don't you have gardeners for that, ma'am?' Viola says.

'I like to lead by example,' the queen says. 'When they see me bending down like this, they know that even the queen is happy to do a little weeding. Besides, Viola, I like it. It gives me joy.'

'What do you do, ma'am, when you come across a weed that has been spattered with your dogs' faeces?' Viola says.

'I do what anyone else does when they get dog poo on their hands – I wipe it off on the grass.'

'Quite, ma'am.'

'So, I wondered, Viola, if I could beg of you a favour.'

'Whatever pleases Your Majesty.'

'Thank you, Viola – and the thought of this pleases me very much indeed,' the queen says. 'Do you know what has taken my fancy? I would love to be able to slip into a party and wander around incognito – talk to whomever I please, and for once drop the whole horrid formality of being queen.'

'You want me to organise a party, ma'am?'

The queen gazes at her dogs gambolling by the rushes. 'Please,' she says. 'It would be so very kind, and it would mean so very much to me. The most important thing is that we all wear masks.'

'You would like me to throw a party where everyone wears a mask, ma'am?' Viola says. 'But then no one will know who their friends are.' The idea does not even remotely appeal. No one will recognise their friends; they may not even recognise their hostess. Besides, what is the point of having the queen as a party guest if no one knows she is there?

'Nothing big, nothing formal,' the queen says. 'Just drinks and nibbles, I don't really care. All I want is for once to be a complete nobody.'

'How very refreshing, ma'am,' Viola says. 'All everyone else wants is to be a somebody.'

'Yes, Viola. Well, we all of us desire what we can't have, and for me, that means one evening when I can get to see people as they really are.'

'It is not very edifying, I can tell you, ma'am.'

'All the same, I'd be much obliged to you if you could arrange it,' the queen says.

Viola is, in fact, throwing a party later in the month – and, hitherto, would not have dreamed of asking the queen. But then... why not?

'I am actually throwing a small party on October the 31st,' Viola says. 'Would that suit?'

'Hallowe'en!' the queen says. 'What could be more appropriate for a masked party?' The queen sounds positively girlish, like some debutante invited to her first ball.

'And would Philip like to come, ma'am?'

'I don't think it's quite his cup of tea,' the queen says.

'Very well, ma'am. I will let everyone know that masks are going to be the order of the day.'

'Thank you, Viola. You are too kind.'

They continue to meander through the gardens, the queen still weeding and shit-flicking, and then, thankfully, Viola sees Mason step through the bow windows and come out to the lawn, which can only mean that the walk is about to be curtailed.

Viola watches him stride towards them. He carries himself

very well indeed – he carries himself like a Duke, shoulders back, head high. His suit, Prince of Wales check, is a perfect fit, and so it should be since it has been made to Viola's own specifications by Johns and Pegg, the tailors of her late husband, the Duke (who, in his finite wisdom had introduced Prince Philip to the firm – and much thanks he'd had for it.)

'Good afternoon, Your Majesty,' Mason says, ambling over, giving a nod to Viola. 'How are you, m... mother?'

And there it is, the entire problem in a nutshell. It doesn't matter how Mason dresses or how he carries himself because who will ever take him seriously while he still maintains this simply hopeless stutter. The boy would bungle even a five-word sentence. She's spent a fortune on trying to remedy it, has even suggested corrective surgery, but short of the complete removal of his vocal cords (now there is a thought), it has all been just so much money down the drain. Why, his stutter is still as bad as when he was a teenage bed-wetter.

'Good afternoon, Mason,' the queen says. 'Come to inform me of some great matter of moment that just can't wait?'

'Afraid so, ma'am,' he says. 'The Ambassador to Thailand has arrived early. I left him and his wife cooling their heels in the Picture Gallery.'

'Very sensible, Mason – I can't think of anywhere nicer to cool my heels.'

'They each have a glass of champagne, ma'am.'

'Splendid,' the queen says. 'Your son is the perfect host, Viola.'

'At least he's good for one thing,' Viola says.

'Now, now, Viola,' the queen says. 'Try to control yourself.'

But that is just it. When Viola is with her son, she spends her entire time trying to control herself, trying to bite back insults, but it is simply impossible. The boy grates. Do all mothers feel like this about their sons? Presumably this is exactly how the queen feels about Prince Charles. Sons always get on their mother's nerves; it is their nature.

'Anyway, Mason,' the queen continues. 'Your mother is soon to be hosting a Hallowe'en party.'

'I know all about it, ma'am.'

The queen laughs. 'But your mother has most graciously acceded to my whim. It's going to be a masked party. Can you guess why?'

'So that, for a little while, ma'am, you can slum it with us mere mortals.'

'How very perceptive you are, Mason,' the queen says. 'I do so hope you'll be joining us.'

'I will, of course, be there, ma'am,' he says. He happens to catch his mother's eye, and the easy *bon mot* dies still on his lips. 'I'll... I'll do my b... best not to give the game away.'

CHAPTER 22

'Where are you taking me?' Campion asks. She is feeling quite excessively happy, but she is one of those people who finds it difficult to revel in these moments of sun-dappled joy. Instead, she teases and frets at her happiness, wondering how much longer it will last before frantic normality is resumed.

'I've told you,' he says. 'It's a surprise.'

It is now some three weeks since Campion had officially become Mason's girlfriend, still very much in the honeymoon period, still on best behaviour. One of the nicer things about the relationship is that when they are alone together – and only when they are alone together – Mason's stutter disappears. He sometimes lingers between his words, pauses a little longer, but the stutter has gone. It pleases Mason and so pleases her, also.

'Give us a clue then.'

It is a Saturday afternoon, the queen has been whisked away to Windsor Castle, and the palace staff savour the freedom of the upstairs corridors and freely tipple on Her Majesty's gin.

Though they have been in love for three weeks, news of their relationship is still not common knowledge in the palace, and it suits them better to go further afield for their twilight trystings. And on this lazy October afternoon, they are walking hand in hand through one of London's hidden gems, the Victoria Embankment Gardens, a thin strip of delicious greenery by the Thames, hardly known, never visited.

'I'll tell you then,' he says. 'We are going to visit Arthur Sullivan's memorial statue.'

Campion laughs and brings his hand to her mouth, kissing his wrist. 'I never took you for a fan of the Savoy opera,' she says.

'It's got nothing to do with comic opera, though it is close by to the Savoy.' In his turn, he kisses her wrist. 'There's a remarkable statue there.'

'Remarkable?'

'Utterly remarkable, Campion,' he says. 'Present company excepted, she is far and away the most beautiful woman in London.'

'Next to a memorial to Arthur Sullivan?'

'She is also an object lesson in keening,' Mason says. 'I only hope that the pretty girls will all be howling in the same way when I die.'

'I'll see if I can squeeze out a few tears, if that helps.'

'That'll be fine.'

They arrive at Sir Arthur Sullivan's statue, the composer's bewhiskered bust glaring down from a monumental stone plinth. A woman, life-size in blackened bronze, howls beneath him. Mason stands back while Campion inspects her.

'She is pretty,' Campion says admiringly. 'Very pretty.'

'She's Britain's most erotic statue.'

'How do you think she lost her top?'

'She's so racked with grief that she ripped down the top of her dress,' Mason says.

'Well, when it comes to you, Mason darling, I'll have no clothes on at all,' Campion strokes the statue's long black hair. The woman leans towards the granite pedestal, long, toned arms despairingly above her head. 'She's got very erect nipples.'

'Apparently, erect nipples are easier to sculpt. Would you like to hear what they said about her ninety years ago?'

'Please.'

'Why, O nymph, O why display

'Your beauty in such disarray?

'Is it decent, is it just,

'To so conventional a bust?'

Campion looks up at Sir Arthur's bust. 'He does look a bit peppery,' she says. 'I'm not sure he'd approve of being upstaged by a half-naked woman.'

'I don't know,' Mason says. 'If it weren't for the woman, we wouldn't be here.' He checks his watch. 'We must be moving.'

'Where are we off to now?'

'Campion, my love, why do you always ask these questions when you know you'll never get a straight reply?'

'Well, one day you might relent,' she says, sweeping her arms around Mason before backing him into a tree and giving him a lascivious kiss.

'If Sir Arthur Sullivan's grieving muse could kiss, that is exactly how she would do it,' Mason says.

'I do my best,' she says. 'You know, Mason, one evening, we'll be going out, and you'll tell me exactly where we're going and what time we're due there.'

'How horrifically middle-aged, if you don't mind my saying so.'

'So where are we going?'

'What I can tell you, Campion, is that this is, apparently, Prince Charles's favourite form of evening entertainment.'

'That covers a lot of misdeeds,' she says. 'Is it a night at the Royal Opera House? Prince Charles loves that.'

'No, it's not. Besides, they might look down their noses at us if we turn up looking like this.' They are both dressed for a walk, much as they'd been on Charles Darwin's thinking walk.

They amble steadily northwards, up past London Zoo before arriving at the bottom of Primrose Hill. A few couples are strolling over the grass, and a family has set up a barbeque; the air drizzles with the smell of sausages and steaks. Flickering at the top of the hill is what looks like candles in glass lanterns, though they are so far off it is difficult to tell. Still holding hands, they walk towards the light.

'So, this is what Prince Charles likes doing of an evening?' Campion says. 'Walking up hills at sundown?'

'That is exactly what he likes doing,' Mason says. Then he tells her the story that he learned from his mother.

When Prince Charles was in his prime, and when he was staying at Balmoral or at his grandmother's nearby house, Birkhall, he would often take his friends for a teatime walk. The prince would lead his friends over the hills and along the riverside banks. When the sun was past the yardarm, they might stop off for a quick nip from a hipflask, but they would never linger long, and though it might be getting quite late, and time, indeed, to begin getting back for dinner, Charles would continue to lead his party deeper and deeper into the Highland hills. Eventually, at well past seven o'clock, he would begin to wend his way up a hill, or perhaps even a modest mountain, and not knowing what was ahead of them but not much liking it either, his little band would follow in his footsteps. The summer sun, setting so much later in Scotland than in England, would still have a few hours yet till dusk, but by the time the prince's party reached the top of the hill, or the modest mountain, they would all of them be fairly tuckered in, and quite desperate for a drink. When they arrived at the peak, a most amazing sight awaited them.

'I don't believe it.' Campion slows and stutters to a stop.

In front of her, right on the crest, and with probably the best view in all London, is a handsome square table with a crisp white tablecloth, formally set with white china plates, white napkins, silver cutlery, and glittering cut-crystal glasses. Down the middle of the table are six white candles, each one snug in a glass vase to shield it from the wind, while nearby are a series of high posts from which have been strung a long line of Chinese lanterns. Two footmen, in full palace livery, stand to attention at a nearby serving table.

'Good evening, Mason. Good evening, Campion.'

It is Lawrence. He has a white towel over his forearm as he strolls towards them. 'Tempt you to a glass of champagne?'

'That…' Campion stalls. It is all too much – the setting, the company, the whole effort that must have gone into creating this idyllic scene. No one has ever done anything like this for her before – ever. She turns towards London to wipe away a tear.

'Thank you, Lawrence,' Mason says. 'That would be most kind.'

As Lawrence pours the champagne into two vintage coupe glasses, Ollie helps Campion into the canvas fold-out chair.

'How was the walk?' Lawrence asks.

Campion laughs as she continues to wipe away tears. 'I've never had anything like it,' she says. 'I've just seen the world's most erotic woman – and now this.'

'Nice view, isn't it?' Lawrence says chattily. 'Mason brings all his girlfriends up here.'

'Do you have to?' Mason says.

'All right. Joke. Joke!'

The footmen retire to a discreet distance where, from the look of things, they are lolling on a rug and working their way through a case of beer.

Campion and Mason drink in the view, teetering on the cusp of the moment, not a word said. As Mason pours more champagne, the footmen bring over smoked salmon with a little light salad. The sun is gone, the first stars are out, and Mason carves a cold chicken. Far off to the west, a line of storm clouds trickle across the horizon.

'I've been thinking about something you told me during our thirty-six questions,' Campion says.

'Best thirty-six questions of my life,' Mason says.

'I asked you if there was anything that you wanted to do that you hadn't yet done – and you told me that you were biding your time.'

'That's right – waiting for my thirty-second birthday.'

'Isn't that quite a long way off?'

'About seven years away.'

'So, what happens when you're thirty-two?'

'I come into my own,' Mason says. 'For some reason,

perhaps down to my father, but more likely down to my mother, a trust was set up when my father died. It gives me a very modest income.'

'You only get hold of the loot on your thirty-second birthday?'

'I daresay they were terrified that I might fritter away my inheritance,' Mason says. 'Though there is the other possibility that my mother wanted to keep control of things, and in particular, to keep control of me.'

'Let me ask you one more question, then. If you were thirty-two, and if you had your inheritance, would you still be in the army?'

'No.'

'Glad I don't have a trust fund,' she says. 'Seven years seems like quite a long time to be diddling around until you allow yourself to do what you want to do.'

Lawrence comes over to clear the plates before bringing two bowls of strawberries, a silver jug of cream, and a silver bowl of sugar. 'That's very kind of you, Lawrence, thank you,' Mason says. 'You've looked after us handsomely. We'll clear up. You get yourself off to the fleshpots.'

'Thanks,' Lawrence says. 'We'll do just that. Here are the Land Rover keys. It's in the usual place.'

'Now, now!' Mason says.

'Is sir objecting to a little light teasing?' Lawrence says.

'There is a time and a place, Lawrence,' Mason says. 'Here I am having a wonderfully romantic dinner with my… my wonderfully beautiful girlfriend, and all you can do is bate me about the other women I've brought here.'

'I'm sorry, sir,' Lawrence says. 'I really shouldn't have brought it up.'

Mason throws his napkin at the recalcitrant footman. 'Be off with you.'

With a wave, Ollie and Lawrence are away, tearing down Primrose Hill, their tailcoats flying behind them, looking for all the world like Struwwelpeter's long-tailed scissorman.

Mason tops up their glasses with the last of the champagne. 'Where were we?'

'We were talking about you diddling away the next seven years till you allow yourself to crawl out of your mother's shadow.'

'Perhaps I've become institutionalised,' Mason says. 'I'm doing the best I can.'

'I want to give you something,' Campion says. Her grandfather had given it to her when she was thirteen years old – when she was a teenager with aeons and aeons of life still ahead of her. And when he'd given it to her, her grandad, Paul, had told her a story, and the story had struck such a chord that ever since, Campion had kept the present close to hand. And now, in her turn, she was giving it to Mason. Besides: she'd already got the message. It was so imbued, it was part of her hard-wiring. Mason, on the other hand: now it was his turn.

She produces from her pocket a little tissued triangle of paper, fairly flat and just over an inch across. Mason unwraps it.

'A shark's tooth?' he says. He peers at the little black triangle in the candlelight. 'A fossilised shark's tooth?'

'That's right,' Campion says. 'What I love about it is that even though it's fossilised and turned to stone, it's just as sharp now as it was when it first grew in a Hybodus shark's mouth two hundred and ten million years ago. You can still see its grooves and ridges. It's still sharp enough to draw blood.'

Mason strokes the edge with his fingertip. 'It is sharp.'

'It is,' Campion says. 'My grandfather used to be a bit of a fossil collector in his day. He picked it up from the Jurassic Coast – though it's actually from the Triassic era.' She pours cream onto a plate, spoons out some sugar, and then, just as the queen taught her, she takes a strawberry by its stem, dunks it into the cream, then the sugar, and pops it into her mouth, peeling the pith away with her teeth.

'I like it,' Mason says.

Campion helps herself to another strawberry. 'What I also

like about this tooth is that it is two hundred and ten million years old – two hundred and ten million years, right there in the palm of your hand. Do you know how long that is – in that amount of time, even the statue of London's most erotic lady will have been worn away to just a small nugget of bronze.

Mason tosses the little black tooth in his palm. 'Quite rare to hold something that's a million years old, let alone two hundred and ten million.'

'So, Mason, darling, if you have a good run, you'll have about fifty years before you retire into your doddering dotage – and this tooth is four million times that. All in the palm of your hand.'

'Rather sobering.'

'That's what it's meant to be.' She has another strawberry but decides against the sugar. 'It's a reminder that soon enough, we'll all be dead. And one day, in a relatively short time, we'll be two hundred and ten million years dead, and it might be our fossilised teeth that are being used as lovers' gifts. So, when my grandfather told me all this twelve years ago, I remember asking him, "What's the point, Pauly? If we're all going to be dead pretty soon, and if soon enough we're going to be a long time dead, then what difference does it make what we do?" You know what he told me?'

'Tell me.'

'He said that this shark's tooth, all two hundred and ten million years of it, was a great clarion call to those of us who are lucky enough to exist – who are here, now, alive and kicking. We shouldn't waste a moment because in not very long, we're going to be as dead as this poor old Triassic shark. My dad, he was a salesman, but he always dreamed of being a doctor. He put it off, and he put it off, and then one day, he and my mum were hit by a lorry, and whether he'd followed his dreams or whether he hadn't, it didn't make any difference anymore because he was dead and she was dead, and all their dreams were dead with them.'

'That's awful,' Mason says.

'It was awful,' Campion says. 'Certainly made me realise that I had to seize life by the throat.'

'And are you?'

'I'm not diddling around for the next seven years waiting for my thirty-second birthday.'

'Ouch,' he says.

'The truth can hurt.'

'Doesn't this sort of conversation normally happen when you've been dating somebody for over a year?'

'I thought you needed to hear it.'

The storm has crept up on them so stealthily that the first they know of it is when the first fat splashes of rain hit the tablecloth. In a matter of moments, they are in the middle of a deluge; the candles are snuffed, the Chinese lanterns sputter in the gusting gale, and the cream and the sugar have turned to watery soup.

Mason zips the shark's tooth into his fleece pocket. 'Follow me,' he says.

They dart off to the Land Rover, tucked away just past the prow of the hill, and though Mason asks Campion to stay in the car out of the rain, she insists on helping clear their dinner. Plates and cutlery and cut-crystal glasses are carefully strapped into a wicker hamper, and as Campion folds up the chairs and the tables, Mason hauls down the poles and the Chinese lanterns, and by the time everything has been packed into the back of the Land Rover, both Campion and Mason arewet through, socks, shirts and sweaters quite saturated with the rain, but both of them very much living in that special wet moment, and that is where the story of the fossilized shark's tooth might have ended, as they drive back to Buckingham Palace in companionable silence, gently steaming in the heat of the hot heater, but as the policeman waves them in through Buckingham Palace's side entrance, they can see somebody silhouetted in the large Palace-sized porchway, and though this person might have been doing anything at all in the porchway, as Mason eases towards her in the rain, they can see who it is, and they can see that she is waiting for them..

'Wh… at… what's sh… she doing here?' Mason says, almost to himself.

He wants to drive past, but with a heavy sigh, he pulls up alongside the porchway and switches off the engine.

He gets out of the car. Campion gets out of the car.

Viola, wearing a thick tweed coat, looks at her watch and then turns to Mason. 'Looks like you were caught in the rain,' she says. 'You might catch a chill.'

'Good evening, m… mother,' Mason says.

'Good evening, Your Grace,' Campion says.

Viola looks Campion up and down. 'For God's sake, Mason,' she says. 'Cavorting with a half-caste maid? What next – rolling around with a nanny? Getting your end away with a checkout girl?'

'M… Mother!' Mason says. 'Please d… don't talk about Campion like that!'

'I shall refer to this coloured girl however I please,' Viola says. 'I am only sorry that nobody else has had the guts to tell you. Well, I do – you, Mason, are a Duke, the Duke of Montagu, and this, this woman, is nothing but a gold-digger and not even a very good one at that.'

'God, you're a rude woman,' Campion says.

'Do you mind?' Viola says. 'I'm talking to my son.'

'Do you mind?' Campion says. 'You know, Viola, I'd heard you were foul. I'd heard you were a bore; and a snob; and a control freak; and a lady who lunches with all the table manners of a chimpanzee. I'd heard all of that, but I'd decided to ignore what everyone had told me. I decided to make up my own mind about you. And now that I've met you, I have decided what I think of you. And you know what I think, Viola? I think you're the rudest bloody woman I've ever met—'

Viola steps forward and, leaning in, gives Campion a

crisp slap on the cheek so hard that Campion staggers a pace backwards.

Campion slowly exhales as she strokes her throbbing cheek. There are a lot of things she could say, a lot of things she perhaps should say.

She looks from Mason to Viola and back to Mason again. He is stunned to the spot. So yes, now, calmer, there is much Campion could say, but then who is she to come between a mother and her son? Mason's mummy issues must have been rumbling on for twenty years now, and it is Mason and Mason alone who is the only person who is ever going to be able to resolve them. Campion isn't going to get involved.

Without looking at either Mason or his mother, she slips in through the porchway and into the palace. And though a small part of her hopes that Mason will follow, she knows it is never going to happen – and nor does it happen, and when, later, she is locked in her bedroom and hears him knocking at the door, she does what any self-respecting girl would do and tells him to go to hell.

CHAPTER 23

As a reward for outstanding services to journalism, not to mention diligence, loyalty, and sheer rat-like cunning, I am being treated to a meal courtesy of *The Sun* newspaper. 'Take your girlfriend out for dinner,' Spike had said, and since I didn't have a girlfriend, Ollie has been pressed into service.

Still fizzing from our Primrose Hill picnic, and from helping smooth the path of young love, we catch the Tube down to Green Park. We are ambling along the pavement. Ollie doesn't look quite as thrilled as he might be.

'You're taking me to The Ritz?' he says.

'My treat,' I say. 'Fine wines. Vintage brandies. Steak. Lobster. Have whatever you like.'

'Oh,' Ollie says, hands shiftily stuffed into his pockets. 'Now don't take this the wrong way, Lawrence. You're a really good guy, but I'm... I'm not like that.'

'Not like what?'

'I'm sorry,' he says, now actively backing away from the warm, wide, welcoming entrance to The Ritz. 'I didn't... I didn't know you were a... were...'

'Oh – gay?' I say. 'Is that what you thought this was all about?'

'Why else are you taking me to The Ritz?'

'Good point and well made,' I say, taking Ollie easily by the arm. 'Maybe I just want the pleasure of your company—'

'It's just I prefer girls—'

'Relax, Ollie,' I say. 'I've come into some money. I want to spend it.'

'Taking me to The Ritz?'

'I'm buying you dinner for the sheer hell of it,' I say. 'Besides, Ollie, you're so not my type.' I watch with great delight as his face falls before adding, 'Only pulling your leg, mate. I'm as straight as a die. Straight as Prince Edward. Straight as the sergeant footman, Simon Brook—'

'I knew it,' he says.

'I'm straight,' I say. 'Ollie, I'm shocked, shocked at how you, a Buckingham Palace footman, have become quite so homophobic.'

So, after just a little more teasing and a few more assurances that I am (almost) entirely straight, I lure Ollie through the Palm Court and into the great den of depravity, The Ritz restaurant. We slip out of our tailcoats and into a couple of sports jackets that I'd tucked into my rucksack (The Ritz can still get terribly uppity about a gentleman's wardrobe. The very thought of a gentleman dining in just tie and waistcoat gives them conniptions).

'Leave the ordering to me, Ollie,' I say, and then, to his utter amazement, ask for two dozen oysters, two medium rare ribeye steaks, a magnum of Bollinger, and a magnum of one of the great Lebanese wines, Chateau Musar.

Ollie catches a glimpse of the price tag. 'What are you doing at the palace?' he says.

'Me?' I say. 'I am merely a humble palace footman, diligently going about his duties.'

'You'll be dropping a month's salary on this meal.'

'I do hope not, Ollie,' I say. 'Two months at the very minimum.'

'It's just…' The dear lad tails off, for once a little unmanned. 'No one, no one has ever… I've never done anything like this before, and normally, well… you know what they say. No such thing as a free lunch.'

'Let this be a first for you, Ollie, then,' I say. 'It's my treat, and I'm treating you purely for the pleasure of your company this evening.'

'Really?' He still looks doubtful. Who in their right mind would take somebody for dinner at The Ritz without wanting some kind of payback?

'Let me tell you an old Hindu proverb – Lick up the honey, stranger, and ask no questions.'

'Okay,' he says, only slightly mollified. 'Just that my mum always told me to ask questions.'

We daringly chink our glasses (chinking is *très* riff-raffy, according to a Ritz diktat), and as I swirl the champagne in my glass, I savour our luxurious surroundings. The room is of a size with some of the larger rooms in the palace. It also has the same gaudy French vibe as the staterooms; Louis XVI decorations, swag chandeliers that glitter double in the floor-to-ceiling mirrors, a hothouse of flowers, and row upon row of middle-aged toffs making merry, with Ollie and me at least half their age and only just a little out of place. There is much more noise, though, than you ever hear at the palace, as much more alcohol is being consumed, and none of us is on best behaviour.

We chat about Campion and Mason ("Good guys!"), and the queen ("Playing a blinder after her *Annus Horribilis!*") and have just moved on to Prince Andrew ("Treacle-faced toad!"), when I happen to spy a dear old friend. He is dining with some other gent and has one of the best tables in the house, next to the windows and with a commanding view of the whole dining room. He does not appear to have noticed me, so I beckon over the prettiest waitress. Her name tag reveals that she is called Grace.

'Yes, sir?' she says. She is about our age and gorgeous.

'Oh, good evening, Grace,' I say. 'Do please call me Lawrence – only my dad likes to be called sir. Could you help me out? You see that chap over there by the far window?'

Grace follows the line of my finger. 'The brawny guy?'

'Exactly, Grace,' I say. 'The one who looks like a jungle

fighter. Could you take him over a glass of champagne with my compliments?'

'Certainly, Lawrence. I'll just get a fresh glass.'

I pour the glass myself, and another random act of kindness completed, we continue working our way through the magnum.

Grace returns to our table with the untouched glass of champagne still on the silver salver.

'What's up, Grace?' I say.

'He refused your champagne,' she says. 'He sent it straight back.'

'How very snotty of him.' I admit it. I am hurt. Who spurns a glass of champagne from a fellow traveller? 'Would you like the champagne then, Grace? I'd love it if you could join us, though that would probably be frowned upon at The Ritz. But if you'd like the champagne, then it's yours.'

'Thank you, Lawrence, I will,' she says, about to leave, then turning back. 'I hope you don't mind my asking, but are you footmen?'

'As it happens, Grace, we are,' I say.

'I recognised the waistcoats,' she says. 'What's it like working at the palace?'

'Glorious,' I say. 'You'd love it there. Much more fun than working at The Ritz. The clientele is classier and we have the best parties in town.'

'You do?'

'We'll take you tonight if you like,' I say. 'This, by the way, is my good friend Ollie.'

Ollie, who's been staring glassily at Grace, suddenly snaps to attention. 'Lovely to meet you, Grace.'

'Nice to meet you, Ollie,' she says. Then because it seems like the right thing to do, she shakes his hand – and just like that, another couple has been set off on the path to true love, which for us matchmakers is generally reward enough.

'She's terrific!' Ollie says.

'You think so?' I say primly.

'I think she likes me!'

We continue our merry analysis of the senior members of the household and then, you won't believe it, the Champagne has been finished off, but we aren't quite ready for the Musar, so I just up and order another bottle. The oysters and the second bottle all arrive at the same time, and since Ollie has never eaten oysters before, I show him the drill.

'Some people like to add shallots or Tabasco,' I say. 'But you can't beat a simple squeeze of lemon.'

Ollie pours the oyster into his mouth, chews, swallows.

'What do you reckon?'

'Delicious.'

'You'll probably need a few more if you're seeing Grace...' I trail off.

It seems that a certain pinstriped diner has come to pay us a visit.

'Good evening, Sir Richard,' I say magnanimously. 'How are you enjoying your dinner?'

'What are you two doing here?'

'We're having dinner, Sir Richard,' I say.

'I've told you before, Lawrence, that you address me as sir.'

'I'm so sorry, sir.'

I pick up my glass of champagne and take a leisurely sniff; heavenly, just heavenly – ripe fruit and spices, with notes of peaches and, and... I can't quite place it, but then it comes to me, roasted apple. 'I thought that was only while we were on duty.' I look over at Ollie who is willing the ground to swallow him up.

'Why are you two wearing livery waistcoats?'

'We've just come straight from work, sir,' I say. 'But as you can see, we have exchanged our tailcoats for sports jackets.'

'I couldn't care less about your jackets,' Sir Richard says. 'You know perfectly well that livery is only to be worn in the confines of the palace.'

'Very sorry, sir,' I say. 'Won't happen again.'

Sir Richard inspects the magnificent spread of oysters and the magnum of Bollinger in the ice bucket. 'How are you paying for all this?'

'I've come into a little money, sir,' I say. 'My grandmother, she died, so sad, but the dear lady left me a modest bequest, and though I know some people are all for jam tomorrow, I prefer jam today. In fact, I like my jam right now – for who knows what the morrow will bring?'

'I do not think it appropriate for Buckingham Palace footmen to be dining at The Ritz.'

Finishing my champagne, I toy with topping up my glass, but, in my docile way, I realise that such an act might be perceived as antagonistic. 'I'm sorry you feel that way, sir,' I say.

He gives me a foul scowl and stalks back to his table. Despite all the alcohol, his unsavoury intervention puts a pall over the evening, so it is with great relief that we see him quit the dining room half an hour later, assassin eyes dead ahead, not so much as a glance in our direction.

I need a brandy.

'Excuse me, Grace,' I say as she clears away the remains of our steaks. 'You couldn't bring us a couple of brandies, big ones. None of that house muck. We want the good stuff.'

'The good stuff?'

'The best you've got! Please!'

She brings us two football-sized brandy balloons. The brandy, the good stuff, is excellent. I ask for two more doubles. What the hell, we may as well have the whole bottle.

The bill comes. It is a big one, far and away the biggest bill I've ever claimed on my *Sun* expenses, though considering the number of exclusives I've already served up to my mad masters, let alone the world exclusive that's been teed up for when I finally leave the palace, then it's cheap at half the price.

Still clutching onto my brandy bottle, I weave back to the palace. Ollie stays behind to pick up Grace, and not an hour later, the pair of them arrive in the footmen's corridor, hand in hand, and well on the way to falling in love.

The next morning, early doors, and with only the mildest of hangovers (the key is to take the aspirin before you go to bed), I make tea and go off to see how my two other lovebirds are getting on.

I find Mason up and alone, moodily spit-polishing his shoes.

'Morning, Chief.' I put the tea tray on the table. 'Where's Campion?'

'She's... she's not here,' he says.

'Up and about, is she?' I say. 'The early bird catches the worm and all that.'

'No,' he says, giving me a speculative look. 'Our picnic did not end well.'

'Oh, what happened?' I busy myself with the cups and the saucers. In my confusion, I slop the milk onto the tray.

'My mother was waiting for us when we got back to the palace,' he says. 'She slapped Campion.'

'How unpleasant.'

'It was,' he says. 'But how did my mother know we were going to be there?' His nose wrinkles. 'I think somebody tipped her off.'

'Leaky place, the palace,' I say.

'Isn't it?' he says, and for one horrid moment, I think he is inferring that it was me, myself, mild-mannered Kimmy who has been the errant leaker.

CHAPTER 24

Like anyone else who's been burned by a divorce, Campion is not one for second chances. Is there anything so utterly pointless in this world as giving somebody a second bite of the cherry? When you give somebody a second chance, you are just giving them a free pass to turn you over again. If Campion has learned anything at all in her young life, it is that compromise is a complete waste of time; expecting someone to change – another complete waste of time. Trying to alter or in any way change a guy's relationship with his mother? Waste. Of. Time! Expecting a relationship to last for anything more than a few weeks without it all coming crashing back to earth? Naïve to the point of idiocy!

That doesn't mean Campion can't put up with a guy's quirks and idiosyncrasies. Having a few niggles is just part of the whole business of being a human being. But this thing Mason has going with his mother Viola is way beyond a quirk. It is a dealbreaker! That slap in the palace porchway had been nothing much in itself, and Viola's boorish behaviour hadn't been so very much either. Still, they were nevertheless the most revolting tip of an iceberg – and the thing about icebergs is that if the tip is revolting, then you can bet your bottom dollar that the rest of the iceberg is going to be equally revolting, if not more so, on account of the fact that it has spent its entire life submerged in freezing cold seawater.

As Campion vacuums the red-carpeted corridors of the palace, she is in no mood whatsoever to have any truck with idling footmen. As for her ex-boyfriend, the human stutterer, it would be greatly to the benefit of not just herself but the whole of mankind if he could take a long hike out of the palace and keep on walking.

So far, he has popped two notes under her door – both shredded without being read – and has accosted her once on the Ambassadors' staircase. 'Campion, c… can we talk?' he said, unable even to spit out four words without making a muck of them, at which Campion smartly turned on her heel and walked down the stairs. When a relationship is over, you have to have a clean break. Words and chit-chat and talking things through only prolong the agony and, worse, sometimes make you doubt yourself so that for two pins, you are suddenly back together again, lessons so not learned, because the only certainty of getting back with a guy after you've dumped him is that he'll let you down again. Not that she is remotely blaming Mason because his mother is a complete tyrant, but actually… when she thinks about it, and when she stabs the vacuum cleaner into the base of a hideous Ormolu clock, she realises that Mason is entirely to blame for his mother. If he had any spine whatsoever, he'd have told the wretched woman where to get off. But oh, no, he can't do that, else he might jeopardise his rinky-dink trust fund and his tidy annual income, and then, guess what, he'll be out there all alone in the big wide world, having to earn his keep just like everyone else did. And that's another thing that irritates her – all this gaudy gold furniture that George IV had shipped over from France, which, as far as Campion can see, was never used, never touched, and which just sat in the Palace as if preserved in aspic, and they weren't even beautiful, in fact they were nothing but the most repugnant dust-catchers, whose sole purpose on this earth was so that Campion would have to waste her time cleaning them.

Lawrence, the deviant *Sun* reporter masquerading as a footman, walks past her in the corridor. 'Morning, Campion,' he says with that stupid goofy grin on his face.

'What do you want?'

'Err... nothing,' he says. 'Just saying hello, nothing more.'

'What are you still doing here?' She switches off the vacuum cleaner, and, you know what, it feels right to have her hands on her hips, so she stands square in front of *The Sun* reporter; her attitude, her whole demeanour, shouts, "Bring it on."

'How do you mean?' he says.

'You've got what you want for that filthy rag you work for,' she says. 'What are you still doing here? Nosing through the queen's dirty laundry, picking up the palace gossip – it's pathetic. You're pathetic.' She sees that he has a kettle in his hand – and she knows exactly what's in it. 'And every day you just go and pinch another litre of the queen's gin. You're just a drunken sot.'

And you know what he does? He has the nerve to smile at her! 'This wouldn't be anything to do with Mason, would it?'

'Mason?' she says. 'What's Mason got to do with you being a serial boozer who lies for a living?'

'It's just that ever since that picnic on Primrose Hill, you've been in a bit of a bad mood—'

'I am *not* in a bad mood,' Campion says. 'But just having to look at you is pissing me off in the extreme.'

'I have that effect on a lot of people,' he says. 'But, if I may say so, you don't seem quite as tight with Mason as you once were. I was just wondering if there was anything, anything at all, that I could do to, ahh, make things better—'

That is it! If she has to spend even another moment with this insufferable git, she would not be held responsible for the consequences. 'If you don't get out of my sight this minute, I will go straight to the master of the household, and I will tell him exactly what you are and what you are doing here.'

'Fine,' he says, holding up his hands. 'Fine, fine, fine. Just trying to help—'

At this moment, she really could hit him, and it must show because Lawrence backs off down the corridor.

'Think I'll just be on my way,' he says. And with that, he flees.

Campion has the corridor to herself again, just her and the vacuum cleaner. Even the vacuum cleaner is pretty irritating, the way she always has to walk backwards with the thing, just so that the royals won't be confronted by the horrific sight of wheel tracks on the carpets. In fact, the vacuum cleaner is not just a symbol of her servitude, but is the complete epitome of all the prissy rules and regulations that are inflicted upon the palace staff.

The queen's piper has struck up, droning away beneath the queen's bedroom window, just as he always does – every damn day – at 9 a.m. exactly. Knowing that the racket will continue for another ten minutes, Campion abandons her vacuum cleaner in the corridor and goes to the Picture Gallery. She randomly wanders through the collection until she ends up in front of the picture that best suits her mood. Cristofano Allori's painting of his onetime lover Maria de Giovanni Mazzafirri, a great beauty of her time, who was known as *La Mazzafirra*. What a merry dance she had led Allori! *La Mazzafirra* spent all his money, caused him unending jealousy, and generally made Allori's life the most complete misery. What a woman!

The subject that Allori had chosen to immortalise *La Mazzafirra* was the 'Old Testament' story of the Jewish widow Judith. The Assyrians, led by Holofernes, had been on the verge of sacking Judith's city when she slipped into the general's tent at night. She got Holofernes drunk, seduced him, and chopped his head off, thus saving her city.

In the 1613 picture, *La Mazzafirra* is, of course, cast in the role of Judith; fair skin, dark hair, heavy-lidded eyes, so very calm after having hacked off the general's head, not a drop of blood to be seen on her gorgeous golden gown; *La Mazzafirra's* interfering mother plays the role of Judith's maid. As for Allori, the Florentine artist had cast himself in the melancholy role of Holofernes. In one hand, *La Mazzafirra* holds a sword, and in the other, clasped tight, she holds onto the long hair of Allori's severed head. Why couldn't more women be like *La Mazzafirra*? What a queen, truly a mistress of all she surveyed—

'Ah! There you are, Campion.'

Campion turns and curtsies. 'Your Majesty.'

'You've been in hiding,' the queen says. 'I've been searching all over for you.' The queen stands beside Campion in front of *La Mazzafirra*. 'Pretty girl, isn't she?' the queen says. 'Doesn't look like she'd have the pluck to chop off a general's head.'

'Looks can be deceptive, Your Majesty.'

'Quite so. I believe you owe me a story, Campion. In fact, I insist on it. Tell me about *The Shipbuilder and his Wife.*'

They walk to the far end of the gallery to Rembrandt's famous 1633 picture. The shipbuilder and his wife are each dressed in severe Roman Catholic black with white ruffs. The old woman has just rushed into his office; she is handing her husband a note.

Campion and the queen stand for a minute in front of the Rembrandt. She's seen the picture many times before, but so far, the story has eluded her. The key, obviously, is what is in the note.

'They are not actually a shipbuilder and his wife, Your Majesty,' Campion says.

'They're not?'

'No, Your Majesty. They are a shipbuilder and his sister. Their father was a shipbuilder, and from a very young age, they both learned the craft of shipbuilding. But it will not surprise you to know, Your Majesty, that the woman, Elvira, was a much more skilled shipwright than her brother Alfonse. It will also not surprise you that since this was the 17th century, Alfonse was the firm's frontman who got all the glory, while Elvira, who did most of the actual graft, was tucked away in one of the back rooms.

'But the brother and sister got along well enough. Elvira

got to do what she loved more than anything else, which was design ships, while Alfonse was the smooth front-of-house man, wining and dining the noblemen and politicians who were in need of ships.'

'Typical,' the queen says. 'She gets none of the credit.'

'Alfonse looked after her in his own modest way, Your Majesty, giving Elvira a third share of the profits, keeping a mere two-thirds for himself. This idyllic life could have continued until they both slid into graceful retirement, except that at the age of thirty-three when Elvira was in an advanced state of spinsterhood, she fell in love with a ship's captain – a terribly handsome man, a ladies' man, who had decided to bestow the benevolence of his charms on Elvira. This might have been down to her skills as a shipwright or because she was a thoroughly engaging woman, but most likely, the captain, Ernesto, decided to fall in love with Elvira because she was an exceptionally wealthy woman.'

'Just wanted her money, didn't he?' the queen says, now thoroughly hooked.

'He was what you would call, Your Majesty, a bounder,' Campion says. 'And since Elvira had never been in love before, had not even been kissed in action, she fell heels over head for the captain. Despite Alfonse's misgivings, the couple were speedily married, and as soon as the honeymoon was over, Ernesto took control of her fortune. It did not take long for his true awfulness to be revealed. That he was a profligate womaniser was an absolute given. That he had at least one woman in every port was also a thing that Elvira just learned to live with. But the one thing that did stick in Elvira's craw was that she had to personally fund Ernesto's mistress, who was kept in palatial splendour on one of the finest canals in Amsterdam.'

'Where is this story going, Campion?' the queen asks plaintively. It isn't remotely like Campion's usual stories.

'Elvira could have borne it all, Your Majesty, except that Ernesto attacked her one true gift. He didn't like her wasting her days on shipbuilding. He said it wasn't a woman's work and forbade her from doing the one thing she loved above all else. Her brother, Alfonse, tried as best he could to keep the business afloat, but without his sister at the helm, he had no one to design the ships. He tried to slip her some papers so she could continue with her designs when she was locked inside the house, but her husband soon found out. The plans were burned, and Ernesto said that if it ever happened again, he'd cut off her fingers with a blunt hacksaw.'

'Oh, Campion!' the queen says. 'I'm not liking the sound of this at all!'

'Patience, Your Majesty,' Campion says, though realising the story has to be wrapped up. 'This state of affairs lasted for twenty years, during which time Elvira turned into an old woman, Alfonso, her brother, became an old man, the business just about surviving on outdated designs, but by no means thriving, and as for Ernesto, he continued to plough through the ports of the Mediterranean. He also still kept a mistress in palatial style in Amsterdam, though she had received an upgrade.

'This was the position just before this picture was painted, Your Majesty. Then, out of nowhere, the most magical news came through. Elvira takes the note, pays good money for the note, and then, as happy as she can ever remember, she races through to her brother's office to tell him the good news – her husband is dead, drowned in an accident off the Scillies. She is free, her brother is thrilled, and life, for the moment, doesn't get any better.'

'What a jolly story,' the queen says. 'Quite a rib-tickler.'

Campion makes a small curtsy.

'Campion dear, may I tell you something?'

'Of course, Your Majesty.'

'My father had a stutter, you know. He was the kindest man I've ever met. For some curious reason, I've always liked men who have stutters.' The queen smiles. 'Now I realise, Campion, that I speak as someone who was lucky enough to marry the first person I fell in love with, but nevertheless, over the years, I have learned a thing or two about men and about love. Gentlemen, true gentlemen are not that common, particularly the ones who are solvent. Rarest of all are solvent gentlemen who are kind. I think that if a man is genuinely kind and wants the best for you, then that can outweigh quite a number of faults.'

'What kind of faults, Your Majesty?'

'Well, just for the sake of example, imagine that this kind man has a very domineering mother. I think that that may be overlooked. It's hardly his fault that his mother happens to be the bossiest woman I've ever met – I can't do anything about her, and I'm the queen, so what chance does Mason have—'

'So, we are talking about Mason, Your Majesty?'

'Oh, if you insist, Campion.'

Campion sighs because the queen, as always, has gone straight for the jugular. 'Thank you for that, Your Majesty. I like Mason well enough,' she says. 'I just don't have the stomach for his mother.'

'You'll find a way around her. I know you will,' the queen says, then she does something that Campion's never seen before. She reaches up and gently squeezes Campion's earlobe between her thumb and forefinger. 'Napoleon used to do that,' she says. 'His imperial guard loved it.'

CHAPTER 25

The queen is feeling unbelievably excited – as excited as she felt nearly fifty years ago when she slipped out of the palace to celebrate the end of the war in Europe. She caroused and danced till dawn and was never once recognised.

And tonight, at Viola's townhouse, she will be trying it for a second time. As she sits at her dressing table and applies her make-up, she wonders what it will be like not to hear the instant hush as she walks into Viola's drawing room. Instead, just to be able to walk over to the bar, get a drink and chat to anyone she likes the look of, about… anything at all! So long as they are jolly and interesting, she'll be happy to talk about anything and everything. She'll talk about TV shows (preferably *The Bill* or *EastEnders*, two of her guilty pleasures), or horses, or the weather. She fancies that she could have a moderate stab at talking about current affairs… Though how will she feel if the conversation turns to the monarchy and they start insulting her family members? Well… it's a free country! Doubtless, a lot of her subjects have to put up with listening to people run down their families, so in the unlikely event that it does occur, well, she will suck it up with good grace. She laughs again; contrary to popular opinion which held that she, the Queen, didn't have to do anything she didn't want to do, she seemed to spend her entire life sucking it up. In fact, to coin a pleasing phrase, she was the queen of sucking things up!

The queen applies the last of the eye shadow, pale blue to match her eyes, and moves on to the mascara. Since her mask

217

is to be almost full length, covering everything but her eyes and her mouth, she wants to accentuate these two features: blue eye shadow, black mascara, and blisteringly red lipstick. Angela, her dresser, has bought her a wig, a black-haired bob that falls to her shoulders. As for her dress, they spent some time discussing this important matter before the queen plumped for a tight-fitting knee-length dress, light grey-blue and in raw silk, obviously expensive, perhaps couture, perhaps not. Her mask is made of black lace with gold trim and is to be held in place with a blue ribbon. As for her shoes, the queen has opted for black six-inch stilettoes, classy and exactly three-and-three-quarter inches higher than her regular two-and-a-quarter inch heels. She's never have been so tall!

The queen gives herself a cheery wink in the mirror and starts to take off her jewels. It will be the first time in… in decades!… that she's ever been out of the palace without her jewellery. The pearl and diamond earrings come off first, followed next by her wedding ring, made of Welsh gold, and last of all comes her engagement ring, a three-carat solitaire diamond flanked on each side by four smaller diamonds. She tosses the ring in her hand and thinks of all the scenes, all the conversations that this little ring has been a party to. The diamond had been part of a tiara that Tsar Nicholas II of Russia had given to his niece, Princess Alice of Battenberg, when she'd married Prince Andrew of Greece. Years later, Princess Alice gave the tiara to her only son, Philip, with the stricture that he uses it to create an engagement ring for his royal fiancée. The queen has never once left the palace without it. Until now.

Angela knocks on the door and comes in with the wig. 'We ready, ma'am?'

'Willing and able, Angela.'

'Very good, ma'am.'

'Care for a drink, Angela?'

'Thank you, ma'am. I'll have what you're having, gin and Dubonnet.'

'I'll call for one,' the queen says. 'And you know what? I'm going to have another!'

She finishes her drink, sinks back into her chair and lets Angela get on with the blissful business of turning her into a normal human being. Fitting the wig takes only a few minutes, a few rogue grey hairs tucked out of sight, and then, most important of all, the mask, which Angela ties with a double bow.

'How's that, ma'am?' she asks. 'Not too tight?'

'Just perfect,' the queen says. She takes a sashay around the dressing room, studying herself in the full-length triptych mirror. She is unrecognisable! Not even Philip would recognise her! If he'd been coming to Viola's party, he'd probably make a pass at her!

Another knock at the door. 'Enter,' the queen says.

In comes Gavin with the drinks. The queen watches his delicious double take.

'Er,' he says, at a loss as to what to say next. 'Good evening. Two gin and Dubonnets?'

The queen, an accomplished mimic, thinks about giving him her full Yorkshire, but that would be unkind, so she speaks with her normal voice. 'Thank you, Gavin,' she says. 'That will be all.'

The footman goggles. 'Is that you, Your Majesty?'

'It is.'

'Wouldn't have recognised you in a month of Sundays, ma'am.'

'That is the correct answer, Gavin,' she says. 'Though,do please be sure not to blab to any of your colleagues – at least not tonight.'

'Of course not, ma'am.' The poor man departs.

'Well, here's to luck,' the queen says, raising her glass to Angela.

'Hope you have the time of your life, ma'am.'

The queen sips her gin and Dubonnet and checks the time. Her handbag. She's forgotten about her handbag! She can't possibly go out without a handbag, but if she goes with one of her usual Launers, it will give the whole show away. 'Angela,' she says. 'Would you care to trade your handbag for mine?'

'Your handbag for mine?' Angela says before the penny drops. 'Yes, please.'

Angela empties her bag onto the table. It is a very jolly bag, sky blue with daisies, a little smaller than the queen's Launer. The queen begins transferring the contents from her own handbag – such a lot of things, the good luck charms that she's been given by her children of horses and saddles and whips and tiny dogs; the clutch of photos, including her favourite of Andrew when he'd been a helicopter pilot in the Falklands War; a tube of mints in case she has a cough; a couple of crosswords snipped from the day's papers; a fountain pen (she loathes ballpoints); a small metal make-up case, one of her most prized possessions, that Philip had given her as a wedding present; a small camera, just in case; a mirror; and, last of all, a penknife.

There are a few other things that she'll be unlikely to need at a Hallowe'en party – diary, address book, sunglasses, reading glasses – so she leaves them on the dressing table. Oh, and she probably won't need the S-shaped meat hook either. This essential item was used to hang her handbag from the edge of the dining table, but as far as she knew, Viola was not having a sit-down meal.

She snaps the handbag shut. Still another five minutes till she is due to leave. She has decided that the correct time to arrive at Viola's is forty-five minutes after the start of the party.

'Did you know, Angela, that when my grandmother, Queen Mary, was on her deathbed, she had one regret?'

'And what was that, ma'am?' Angela is still admiring her new Launer handbag.

'She regretted that, in her entire life, she'd never once jumped over a fence.'

'Odd thing to regret, ma'am,' Angela says. 'I'm sure I'll

have plenty of regrets when I die, but not jumping over a fence will not be one of them!'

'That's probably because you've jumped over lots of fences,' the queen says. 'But for me, it would be a cause of very deep regret if, on my death bed, I realise'd that I'd never once been incognito at a party.'

'Maybe it'll become a regular fixture, ma'am.'

'I do hope so, Angela.'

Angela helps her into a nondescript beige coat, and then she walks along the corridor and down the staircase to the Ambassadors' Entrance, where there is not a footman to be seen and where she has the quite unparalleled pleasure of opening the door for herself.

Jerry, the groom, is waiting outside with Philip's black taxi cab – gas-powered, eco-friendly, just the most perfect vehicle on earth for a queen to travel in when she does not wish to be recognised. She'd toyed with travelling with one of her personal protection officers and decided against it. Jerry was more than capabe lof handling any situation that might arise. As requested, Jerry is just wearing a jacket and tie, none of the hats and suits that were usually required of royal chauffeurs.

'Good evening, Your Majesty.' He opens the cab door.

'Evening, Jerry. How are we?'

'Thrilled to be included in your adventure, ma'am,' he says. 'You could fool your own mum in that outfit.'

'Thank you, Jerry.'

They set off in the rain, scudding out of the gates, out of the palace, and out of this fusty, dusty world of the aristocracy. Jerry drives sedately to Hyde Park Corner but then, rather than going up to Marble Arch, he heads towards Knightsbridge. Knightsbridge!

'We're not going up Park Lane?' she asks.

'Quicker by Knightsbridge, ma'am.'

'You sure about that, Jerry?' the queen says. 'I'd have thought the Bayswater Road was best.'

'Now I've heard it all!' he says. 'Being backseat driven by the Purple One, who is now telling me the quickest way to get to Holland Park.'

'It's the way we normally go,' the queen says.

'That's because you've got twenty police outriders stopping off all the traffic on the way,' Jerry says. 'In the real world, if you're just in a black cab, it's quicker by Knightsbridge.'

'Oh, right,' the queen says. 'Hadn't thought about that. Sorry, Jerry.'

'No problem at all, Your Majesty.' He laughs as he looks at the queen in the mirror. 'We'll pop into a McDonald's on the way back if you fancy.'

'Let's just see how we get on at Viola's.'

They arrive a few minutes early, so the queen asks Jerry to make a short detour around Holland Park, but eventually, the witching hour is upon them. Jerry parks up a little way down from Viola's house.

'Good luck, Your Majesty,' he says, offering her an umbrella. 'Walk you to the door?'

'I'll go by myself. No need for the umbrella, either.'

'I'll be right here for you, ma'am. And… enjoy yourself!'

'Thank you, Jerry.'

Just like that, and just as she's always imagined it, she is on her own, no staff, no relations, nothing at all to identify her, just a perfectly respectable middle-aged woman out to enjoy herself at a Hallowe'en party.

Viola has fairly ramped up the Hallowe'en part of the party. The upstairs windows are ablaze with candles and the grand staircase up to the front door has been lined with black cats, grinning skulls and huge jack-o'-lanterns. She goes up to the front door and does a thing she certainly can't ever remember doing before – she rings the bell.

The door is opened by a red devil – at least she thinks he is a devil from the red horns on his head and the red mask, though nevertheless, quite a classy red devil as he is wearing a red tailcoat and red trews. 'Come in, come in, come in!' he says. 'Let's get you out of the rain. What a beastly night it is, beastly, beastly! Have you come far?'

'Er, no,' the queen says. She's decides that her accent for the evening will be a clipped Scottish brogue, such as was spoken by Miss Jean Brodie and the good ladies of Morningside in Edinburgh. 'Not very far at all.'

'Let's get you out of your coat, madam,' he says. Then, on this night of nights, another fresh experience. He, a man, touches her, the queen, standing behind her as he helps her off with her coat.

'Thank you.'

'Don't you just look as pretty as a picture, madam.' He carefully folds the coat over his arm. 'And if I may say so, you'd give Cinderella a run for her money.'

'I've never been compared to Cinderella before,' the queen says, and what the hell, she may as well start getting into the spirit of things. 'And if I may say so, you look like the jolliest devil I've ever seen.'

'You can come to my hell any time you like, madam.' He laughs. 'You know how that Frenchie Jean-Paul Sartre said hell was other people – but personally speaking, that's my very idea of heaven.'

She looks at him more closely… What is there about him? 'I don't know you?' she says.

'And I don't know you,' he says. 'But I do like you.' He makes an elegant gesture towards the double staircase in the hall. 'The party awaits you.'

She goes up the stairs to the first floor drawing room; the noise is immense. A jazz band is playing – Duke Ellington, no less. How very thoughtful of Viola. The queen is mildly surprised that the Duchess of Montagu knows of her fondness for jazz, let alone that she loves Duke Ellington.

At the doorway, she squares her shoulders, bracing herself, then she walks into the room, and the most incredible thing happens. Nothing happens. No shocked pause, no awestruck sigh, the noise, the mirth and Duke Ellington continue without a blip. For the first time in her life, the queen has become just another party guest.

She slips into the room. There must be at least a hundred people here already, devils and she-devils, ghouls, ghosts, wizards and witches. She presumes that she must have met at least half of them before, but because they are all in disguise, she doesn't have the faintest idea who anyone is.

The chandeliers have been turned off; instead the room is low-lit with hundreds of candles, all doubled in number by the vast gold-framed mirror. There are vases of spooky flowers, broomsticks on the walls, heaped coal blazing in the fireplace, and dozens of pumpkins.

What she needs, she realises, is a drink. On cue, one of the devil waiters sidles up to her. 'Eyy oop, love, fancy some fizz?'

What? Never in her life – never, never! – has she been addressed as "love" before, and certainly not by a waiter. Granted, she is now a nobody, but still! Is it really normal for devil waiters to address their guests as "love"?

The waiter is carrying a salver of champagne glasses. She squints at him. It suddenly comes to her when she remembers just where, exactly, she'd heard that Yorkshire accent before. 'Oh, it's you, Lawrence,' she says.

'Sorry, ma'am, couldn't resist,' he says. 'May I get you a gin and Dubonnet?'

'Thank you,' she says. 'Does anybody else know I'm here?'

'Only me, ma'am,' he says. 'And Viola and Mason, of course. And Ollie and Campion, and a few other palace staff who were recruited for the evening. But apart from that, no one's got the first clue who you are, ma'am. We've all been expressly ordered not to blab.'

'Let's keep it like that then, Lawrence,' she says. 'And get me my gin.'

Like a bumblebee browsing through a field of flowers, the queen glides into the drawing room, picking up snatches of conversation, listening to introductions, delighting in the simple pleasure of being ignored. If she liked, she could spend her entire time just trawling around the room listening to something she'd never ever heard before – a genuine conversation. But after Lawrence brings her gin and Dubonnet, she realises that sooner or later she will have to immerse herself in the hostile element. She will have to enter into a conversation. And of course she could wait for somebody else to start a conversation with her, but that wasn't very proactive – she might wait all evening for that to happen.

She takes stock of all her fellow party guests. She is looking for a man or a woman who looks affable and approachable (above all, she is looking out for Viola, who is to be avoided at all costs). After a few minutes of quartering the room, she starts to zero in on a man in a hand-me-down green suit. What she likes about him is that, firstly, he is inhaling the scent from a large vase of hot-house flowers; secondly, he is wearing a mask of the Green Man, that age-old symbol of spring and fertility; and thirdly, he has a fabulous rose in his buttonhole.

The queen goes straight over and with no messing comes straight out with it. 'You must love gardens,' she says.

The Green Man looks up, pleasantly surprised that someone is talking to him. 'I love gardens,' he says. He is obviously a little shy because there is a pause before he adds, just a little clunkily, 'Do you like gardens?'

'I adore them,' the queen says. 'But first, tell me about your extraordinary buttonhole.'

'Give it a smell first,' he says. 'Smells even better than it looks.'

And, for the first time in her life, the queen leans in towards a man's chest and smells his buttonhole. Just as he'd said, the smell is heavenly. Then, just as she's always imagined it, they are away, talking and even joking about gardens and flowers and trees and birds and all of the other beauties of nature. Lord knows how long they might have continued talking to each other, except someone is making a scene, and the queen does not even need to look up to know who it is. It is her hostess Viola and, *quelle surprise*, she is extremely unhappy..

CHAPTER 26

'Hi, Campion. Brief word?'

'Spit it out.'

Ollie makes to take a seat on the other side of the table.

'I didn't say you could join me.'

'I shouldn't have presumed,' Ollie says. 'Just putting together a team of waiters and waitresses for a party at the end of the month. Wondered if you'd like to join us.'

Campion tries to mash some peas onto the back of her fork. The peas just roll away. Who the hell decided that the correct way to eat peas was on the back of a fork? Was there any more ridiculous way to eat them? In any normal workplace canteen, it'd be fine to turn the fork over and scoop the peas up, but when fish and chips were served at the palace on a Friday, then everyone, even the maids and the under-cooks, was supposed to eat their peas as if they were actually dining with Her Majesty. One more irritation in a month of irritations.

And now, here was another. She was being asked to give up an evening to pour drinks and hand out canapés. If these snoots were so desperate for waiters and waitresses, why couldn't they just go to one of the agencies? But oh, no, the super snoots liked to show just how snooty they were by hiring out Her Majesty's staff from the palace.

'What's in it for me?' Campion says. She tries pronging the peas, but they are so hard she can't stab them. You know what? Why does she even bother with a fork? She tips the peas into an empty teacup and pours them into her mouth. A highly satisfactory way of eating peas; frankly, she is surprised that no one has thought of it before.

'The money's not bad,' Ollie says. 'They're offering £20 an hour, plus a dinner at some nearby restaurant—'

'A restaurant dinner for all of us?'

'And a bottle of red and a bottle of white when we're done.'

'Each?'

'The uniform's quite nice.'

That makes sense. Although palace staff were free to moonlight elsewhere, they were not allowed to wear royal livery. Instead they have to be kitted out in whatever uniform was provided by the hostess.

'What kind of uniform?'

'Red tails, red trousers, red mask, cute little devil horns.'

'It sounds like some foul fancy dress party.'

'Are you in?'

'I'll think about it.'

Well she had thought about it, and along the way she'd ripped up a few more of Mason's (unread) notes – even his cramped writing irritated her – and then, a couple of nights before the gig, she'd just thought, "Stuff it", and she'd told Ollie that she'd do it. He'd taken her measurements – height, waist, shoe-size, neck-size, all of that – and for the rest all she had to do was ship up to the servant's entrance at the Palace at 5 p.m. They are to be taken by minibus to the party venue, where they'll all change into their "red devil" uniforms, and that would all be just fine, except the last person who clambers on board the bus is Lawrence. He makes to sit next to Campion.

'This seat's occupied.'

'By whom?'

'By anyone but you. Go and leech off somebody else.'

'Now, now,' he says. 'Anyone else would think you'd been dumped by Mason rather than the other way round.'

The man… the man is unendurable. Campion knows that if she responds in any way at all, she'll end up planting a fist on the end of his greasy, snub nose, so instead she turns to look out of the window. Why doesn't she shop Lawrence right now? She'll be doing the queen a service, plus there'll be one less human irritant in the palace to deal with.

A butler, already dressed as a red devil, welcomes them into some mansion house in Holland Park. He is ticking off their names when he catches sight of Campion. 'And here we finally are,' he says. 'Campion, Campion – welcome to our humble party. Thank you so much for being a part of it.'

Seems a little strong. At her previous waitressing gigs, the butlers had barely spoken to her. 'Thanks very much,' she says.

'I am Eric, your master of ceremonies,' he says. 'Your splendid uniform is down in the basement, Campion. And I can assure you,' he says, with an arch eyeball roll, 'that you will love, love, *love* it. Please do make yourself at home.'

The maids are in one room, footmen in another. The uniforms hanging on a rail are from the fanciest of fancy dress outfitters, Angels and Bermans. Two bottles of chilled champagne have been left on one of the dressing tables, along with caviar, sour cream and blinis. Odd. Most hosts didn't give a fig for the staff.

Campion tries on the red devil uniform and decides that, all in, it is a good look, quite the woman of mystery. The tails are a perfect fit, almost contoured to her curves. She opens the champagne and pours seven glasses.

'I'm Campion.' She gives a glass to a very pretty girl. 'I don't think I know you.'

'I'm Grace,' the girl says. 'Ollie's girlfriend. I work at The Ritz.'

'Much better pay than at the palace – and you get tips,' Campion says. 'How did you meet?'

'He came to The Ritz for dinner with Lawrence,' she says. 'They asked me to a party in the palace.'

'Sounds about right.'

'They rang up one of the biggest bills I've ever seen.

Certainly the biggest bill for just two people. It was astronomical. I'd no idea the palace paid so well.'

'It doesn't,' Campion says drily. 'I'll bet Lawrence paid.'

'He did,' Grace says. 'Isn't he also a footman?'

'He...' She pauses. How to describe Lawrence? 'He's different from the rest of us.'

Grace helps fix Campion's half-mask and her red horns and they go up to the sumptuous party room. The footmen are already there. The jazz band strikes up and they all start drinking. Eric saunters into the room, a glass of champagne languidly in hand, and as the band eases, he takes centre stage. 'You, my friends, are in the presence of one of the greatest jazz bands of all time.' He tips his glass towards the band and is rewarded with a tally-ho from the trumpeter. 'You, meanwhile, are the best waitresses, the best waiters, in the entirety of the universe. You certainly don't need me to tell you what to do. But if you could remember just one thing...' and here, Eric appears to be looking straight at Campion. 'forget about the guests. You are primarily here to enjoy yourselves. If you are enjoying yourselves, then, my dears, it will ineluctably follow that our guests, those poor simpering sots, will enjoy themselves also.'

It could be the drink, it could be her uniform, which provides her with such sweet camouflage, but to Campion's surprise, she is enjoying herself. She has been put on sauntering duty, her preferred role at these sort of parties, mingling amongst the guests with a magnum of Moët, checking out their costumes, ear-wigging their conversations, and of course observing their manners. Some of the guests don't even look at her as she tops up their champagne, merely swaying their glasses in front of Campion as they continue to bray. The more genteel guests always thank her, and it is they, naturally, who receive first dibs on the canapés. The rude sods desperate for sustenance would sometimes seek her out, only to discover that the only thing left on her silver salver was a half-eaten sausage.

Campion is just leaving the room to replenish her canapé

tray when she catches herself in the vast mirror on one of the walls – she barely recognises herself. When she first espies this vision in red, she thinks, "Who is that?", then pleasingly realises that "that" is she, herself, and that though she may only be a waitress, she is still the sexiest damn woman in the room. Suck it up, ya rich fuddy-duddies! She blows herself a kiss in the mirror.

Downstairs, in the kitchen, Eric is helping himself to a mound of caviar on a tiny blini.

'Campion, darling,' he says in his arch voice, all mischievous camp.

She can't quite place it, but then it comes to her – the bald head, the plumpish figure, the theatrical tendencies…

'You don't happen to have a brother who works at the palace?' Campion asks.

'That would be my identical twin, Simon, the sergeant footman,' Eric says. 'At least we used to be identical, but as you can see, time has not been nearly so kind to dear Simon as it has to me.' He pops the blini and the mound of caviar into his mouth, chews, and gives a majestic swallow. 'Ecstasy,' he says. 'It is time you had some more Krug, my dear. The way you've been trotting up and down those stairs, you must be parched, quite parched.'

'I just might.' Campion places the tray on the oak table.

Eric hands her a glass of champagne. 'Vintage Krug for us, common or garden Moët for the guests – they've got no taste anyway.'

'Cheers. Who's throwing this party?'

'Have a guess.'

'Are they even upstairs?'

'In a manner of speaking,' Eric says. He pops a tasty looking sausage into his mouth. 'This party is actually more than just a Hallowe'en party – it is also somebody's birthday. But you know the fairy tale of Beauty and the Beast?'

'Of course.'

'Our beast is just as shy as the hero of the story.'

'How sad,' Campion says. She might have said more, but one of the guests walks into the kitchen. She is wearing a purple gown with a high Elizabethan collar, though the general effect of the dress is ruined by all the bits of crisps that are dotted down the front. Loose at her side is an antique mask attached to a mottled cane. The wicked stepmother live and in the flesh.

Viola doesn't bother to look at Campion. 'What's she doing here?'

'Your Grace,' he says, gently putting down his glass of Krug. 'Campion is one of the staff who we hired from the palace.'

'I can see that, you fat idiot. Well, get her out.'

'You want Campion to leave?'

'Immediately.'

Campion, who's been leaning against the marble island in the middle of the kitchen, puts her glass down and, sleek as a lioness, she glides over to the Duchess. For the first time, Viola looks at her.

'Could I just say something, Your Grace?' she says. 'You're a bit of a brute, if you don't mind my saying so—'

'I do mind you saying so—'

'You're not only a brute, but you have entirely brutalised your son. You're a grotesque, pampered monster. You're rude, you're ill-mannered, you're boring. You know what you are, Your Grace? You're a boor. A thick charmless Philistine—'

'Out with her, Eric.' The Duchess sniffs, then loftily disappears from the kitchen.

Campion retrieves her glass and finishes off the Krug.

Eric is giggling. 'We thought this would happen,' he says. 'And now it actually has happened.'

'It has?'

'Follow me.'

'Am I being escorted off the premises?'

Instead of taking her down to the basement to change, he leads Campion back up to the first floor, taking her into an anteroom next to the drawing room. He bustles over to a large bookcase and tilts a leather-bound book. With a solid click, a secret door swings open. 'Have a look-see before we go upstairs,' he says.

Campion walks up three steps and into a little leather-lined cell. A two-way mirror allows them to look out onto the riotous party in the drawing room. In front of the mirror are set two armchairs and a side table. The room stinks of old cigarettes, and the shag pile carpet is littered with crisps and peanuts.

'Rather than join her guests, the Duchess prefers to sit here bitching about them with one of her cronies,' Eric says.

'It's a pit for peeping Toms,' Campion says. 'I unwittingly blew her a kiss.'

'That explains it,' Eric says. 'We hadn't expected her for at least half an hour.' He takes a sniff of the stale air. 'That's quite enough of this foetid hole,' he says. 'Follow me.'

They leave Viola's horrid pit and Eric takes Campion upstairs to a handsome bedroom. A woman is waiting for them. 'Hello, Campion,' she says, getting out of a chair in front of a well-lit dressing table. 'I'm Noreen.'

'I'll leave you two to it,' Eric says.

With that, the door is shut, and Campion is upstairs in Viola's house with a woman she's never met, and in front of her is the most beautiful dress she's ever seen.

It all happens so fast. Noreen takes her mask and horns and helps her out of the tailcoat and the trousers, then somehow, the next moment, Campion is being zipped into the dress – Jean Paul Gaultier no less – emerald green, with a high neck and ruched zip-up bodice. The real showstopper is the enormous, ruffled skirt that cascades down into a train that is a full four metres long; matching green platform sandals; earrings in titanium and diamonds.

Campion sips Krug as Noreen finishes her hair and gives her the lightest trace of make-up. Noreen has pulled out the pins that hemmed in her hair. 'How would you like your hair, Campion?' she asks. '*Au naturel?*'

Campion studies herself in the mirror. With this dress, these earrings... no time for half measures. 'I would like the hair that I was born with.'

She gets the full afro.

Noreen produces a diamond tiara from a smart leather burgundy box, toying with it for a moment. 'You don't need this,' she says, and the tiara is returned to its box.

A dainty lace mask in emerald green is tied to Campion's face, covering her eyes and nothing more, and then, as she remembered it, she is ready, and Noreen is giving her a hug and she is walking down the stairs, and at the bottom of the stairs there is a man waiting for her.

He is wearing tails and a white tie, with a half mask going vertically down his face; quite dashing, actually, even for him. As she sashays down the stairs, her magnificent train sweeping behind her, she considers, for a second, whether to remain on her high horse. If this evening has shown her anything at all, it is that her boyfriend (yes, boyfriend) is not just a sweetheart and a romantic, but that, by the look of things, he is about to do something he'd never done before.

'You look like a p... princess,' he says as she glides down the last steps towards him.

'Never took you for a *Phantom of the Opera* fan,' she says.

'I was taken to see it on m... my eighteenth birthday.'

'Seven years ago, to the day.' She is standing next to him now. He has a new cologne, quite pleasant. 'Are we going in?'

He offers his arm and she takes it. 'We are.'

'There's going to be quite a fight.'

'With you here, I am f... finally up for it.'

Mason opens the door and they step into the drawing room, and it is just as if the queen in all her state has walked into the room. The conversations and the laughter falter and halt until there is no sound at all. Then after a nod from Eric, the jazz band strikes up, and everyone sings "Happy Birthday" as Ollie and Grace wheel in the most enormous birthday cake. Backs are being slapped, hands are being wrung, and the waiters and the waitresses mob-handed just join the party. The volume level, already high, dials up another notch.

Campion is in the dead centre of the room, standing next to Mason, when a frisson ripples through the guests, and the party eases into an edgy silence. Campion takes a sip of her Krug. She wonders if Krug really is any better than all the other champagnes; certainly more expensive, but any more delicious? Only one thing for it: she and Mason will have to have a blind tasting.

She counts to ten, and as she reaches the end of her count, she sees that Viola has arrived. Viola has disposed of her mask and carries herself like a stiff-necked guards officer; Campion still towers above her.

'I thought I asked you to leave,' she says to Campion.

Campion smiles at Viola before glancing at Mason.

'It was I who invited her,' he says. 'And it was I who asked her to stay.'

Viola smiles and nods to herself. 'How very gall… gallant of you, Mason – and not even a trace of a stutter. Well done.'

'I do my best.'

'As far as I can recollect, however, this is still my house, and it is still me, I believe, who decides who is welcome here and who is not.' She turns to Campion, dead eyes and a hyena smile. 'So please leave us now and, if it's not too much trouble, do not come back here again. Though, if you do come back again, it will be my pleasure to have you up for criminal trespass.'

'Your Grace.' Campion gives the Duchess of Montagu a very deep curtsy, as deep as the curtsy she gives to the queen. 'Shall we?' she says to Mason.

'We shall.'

She holds her hand up, and after kissing her wrist, Mason takes it.

'You're leaving your guests, Mason?' Viola says.

'I'm leaving with my most important guest.'

'You'll regret this,' Viola said.

Campion and Mason have their backs to Viola and are already halfway to the door when he stops and turns to her. 'My only regret, dear mother, is that I didn't do this years ago.'

Close by the door is a pedestal with a large vase of flowers. Next to the flowers is the Green Man, and alongside the Green Man is a woman in a blue-grey dress, and though she has a black bob and seems a little taller than the queen, she holds herself with the inimitable carriage of a sovereign.

The Green Man in the green suit starts clapping and soon enough everyone is clapping. Mason steps over to hug the grizzled old man with the thick gardener's fingers.

As for the woman who carries herself like a queen, she holds up her hand and Campion, who carries herself like a princess, completes the high-five, and is rewarded with one single ringing word of endorsement, 'Bravo!'

Eric gives them a double hug as he sees them out. In the spitting rain, they stand on the doorstep surrounded by jack-o'-lanterns, black cats and grinning grey skulls.

'Where to now?' Campion asks.

'Got a room at Claridge's,' he says. 'But Eric will soon be taking the team out for supper.'

'Claridge's can wait,' Campion says. 'Though before we go, I'm just going to try something.'

'I do hope it doesn't turn out too badly,' Mason says and with that, and still drizzled by a light rain, they turn in easily towards each other and meld into a kiss.

CHAPTER 27

While Her Majesty never suffers from a hangover, it would be fair to say that she is feeling a little rough at the edges. If she'd stuck to the gin and Dubonnet, she'd have been fine, but halfway through the party, the wretched Lawrence deserted her, and she ended up drinking champagne, which she didn't much enjoy, but it was better than no alcohol at all.

What a party – what a night! – especially after darling Viola had had her comeuppance, and what a charming man Charley the gardener turned out to be; he even asked for her address so that he could send her a cutting! What a sweetheart.

The wretched Lawrence is already waiting for her in the Bow Room with the corgis. She would not have believed it, but he looks disgustingly well.

'Good morning, Your Majesty,' he says. She sees that he has a small bag in his hands and a piece of rope. The dogs are obediently sitting at his feet.

'Good morning, Lawrence,' the queen says. 'Did you enjoy the party last night?'

'Very much so, ma'am. May I ask if you enjoyed joining the hoi polloi?'

'You may, Lawrence,' she says. 'I enjoyed it very much indeed, and I am planning to do it again – though perhaps not with the Duchess of Montagu—'

The sergeant footman, Simon Brook, enters the Bow Room. 'Good morning, Your Majesty,' he says. 'Morning, Lawrence.'

'Morning, Simon,' the queen says. 'I am ready for some hide and seek. What do we do, Lawrence?'

'You and I will go out in the garden, ma'am, while Mr Brook stays in here with the dogs. I'll lay the scent and Mr Brook will open the doors and the dogs will all charge out into the garden where they will go absolutely mad.'

'Very good,' the queen says. 'What do you have in your bag?'

'Mainly aniseed, ma'am,' Lawrence says. 'The dogs love it.'

'I am most interested to see how this turns out,' the queen says. 'My husband said it was perfectly preposterous.'

'We'll show him, ma'am,' Lawrence says. 'Could you give us five minutes, please, Mr Brook?'

The queen slips outside with Lawrence, and though the corgis are desperate to follow, Mr Brook has them all carefully corralled.

'Right, ma'am, may I suggest that while I lay the scent, you go over to the lake and I'll meet you by that spinney of trees?'

'Very well,' the queen says. She does wonder whether this is decorous behaviour for a reigning monarch – would Victoria have ever behaved like this, hunted down by a pack of corgis in a lunatic game of hide and seek? Or Edward VII? Or indeed her grandfather, George V? – almost certainly not. But as she walks towards the lake, the queen consoles herself with the fact that her father, George VI, would not only have played hide and seek with the corgis, but would have absolutely adored it.

She looks over at Lawrence, who is now haring down the King's Border with the aniseed bag bumping behind him. What a peculiar fellow, quite unlike any other footman she's ever met. He is fun. She hesitates to use the word about a member of staff, but she does concede that the adjective is apposite. Who else would have conceived of turning the dogs into a hunting pack? Well, possibly Simon Brook. In fact, more than likely, the pair of them cooked the whole thing up between them.

Lawrence, she sees, is now weaving in and out of the trees on the far side of the lake, sometimes even going full circle around a tree – with his tails flying, and that ridiculous little bag trailing along behind him, he looks completely demented. He is up now by Hyde Park Corner.

The queen wonders if the old story is true. It was said that the Shah of Persia was staying at the palace in 1873 when he murdered one of his more indolent servants. The servant had been buried in the dead of night at the far end of the garden – well, it is certainly one way to get rid of unpleasant staff.

Lawrence runs over the bridge and takes a turn around the perimeter of the island before cantering back over the second bridge to the garden proper, zigzagging along the side of the lake. Panting hard, he pulls up next to the queen underneath a plane tree.

'That looked like a good workout, Lawrence,' she says.

'Wait till you see the dogs, ma'am.' He mops at the sweat on his cheek with a florid silk handkerchief.

The Bow Room doors open and the corgis charge out, Chipper in the lead as they bark with excitement – the queen can't remember the last time she's seen them like this. She watches, enchanted, as the dogs fly after the scent, laughing out loud as they start circling the trees.

'Excuse me, ma'am.'

'Yes, Lawrence?' She continues to watch her dogs.

'Not that I wish to be presumptuous, ma'am, but these dogs can get pretty fruity when they catch you. It, err, it might be wise for you to hop over this fence and hide behind the pine.'

Hop over a fence? Was that proper and becoming behaviour for a monarch? Well, perhaps not for her dear grandmama, Queen Mary, but she'd be damned if she went to her grave regretting that she'd never jumped over a fence.

'Good idea, Lawrence.'

'Splendid, ma'am.' He looks over at the dogs. They are already on the island. 'Do you want a hand?'

'I'll manage,' the queen says, throwing her leg over the white picket fence, but it seems that fence-jumping is more awkward than she imagined it to be, and now she is stuck straddling the thing with one of the fence posts nudging up her backside. Now that she is confronted with the practicalities of fence-jumping, she realises that her grandmama would have been absolutely hopeless.

'Lawrence, come here,' she says. 'I need some help.'

'Would you like to use my shoulder, ma'am?'

'Too late for that,' she says. The dogs now have sight of their quarry and are baying for blood. 'Give me a heave.'

'Certainly, ma'am.'

She feels two strong hands around her waist. He simply lifts her up. She swings her leg over, and then she is clear.

'Thank you, Lawrence,' she says. 'Not many footmen get to do that.'

'I'll treasure the memory till my dying day, Your Majesty,' he says, giving her a bow. 'I'll distract 'em. One of us has to get out of here alive – I guess it ought to be you.' He gives her a wink – a wink! – and as the queen ducks behind the pine tree, Lawrence races back towards the palace, running fast but not nearly fast enough. The sight of him running over the main lawn with the dogs all charging behind him is one of the funniest things she's ever seen. At first, she has her knuckles in her mouth – unbelievable, simply unbelievable! – but when he slips on the bank and goes down, immediately to be engulfed by a solid wave of corgis, she is quite doubled over with laughter and can't stop herself from stamping on the ground.

Using a branch to climb back over the fence, the queen ambles towards Lawrence, whose trousers, tailcoat and waistcoat are now entirely covered in mud and dog hairs. He is sitting on the grass, singing to the corgis as Chipper nuzzles into his chest.

'Thank you, Lawrence,' she says.

'Thank you, Your Majesty, for allowing me to play with your dogs,' he says, and then he adds something which at the time she does not understand, but which soon enough she would understand all too well. 'I'd just like to say, ma'am, that whatever happens in the future, I think you are doing an outstanding job, and I will always admire you.'

'Yes, well...' The queen falters, unsure of what he is driving at. 'You are most kind.'

CHAPTER 28

All good things come to those who wait, and after two months of diligence, patience, and unquenchable sycophancy, I am about to reap my due reward. [In the past month, I have not appeared to have chalked off a single one of the various errands that Spike has tasked me with. These included, just to refresh your memory: nosing around the senior royals' apartments, getting snaps of said senior royals' apartments, being a coachman for one of the new ambassadors and lastly, getting myself posted to Windsor Castle.]

Despite all of my pleadings – "Please, sir, I want to go to Windsor Castle. Please, sir, I want to be a coachman." – I had been stuck in boring old Buckingham Palace doing nothing more than opening and closing doors and occasionally – when I could be bothered – polishing boots, silver, and glass. (Not so often with the glass, actually, after I'd smashed a couple of Queen Victoria's most prized wine glasses. Ollie and I had been up in the music room having a glass of sherry before lunch, and I'd been a little too lusty when we'd chinked our glasses. I contrived to smash not just one but both of the glasses. The cut crystal and sherry made an appropriately musical tinkle as they fell to the parquet floor.)

Not that the last four weeks at the palace had been a total waste of time. Why, who else could have rekindled Mason's stalled romance with Campion? Could have ensured that Viola was so royally hoisted by her own petard? Who, I ask you, could have trained royal corgis to such a perfect pitch of obedience that they could now tunefully howl on demand? And who, who in the entire history of Buckingham Palace, had managed to put his meaty hands around the queen's trim waist and then lift her clean over a white picket fence? Who else but I, Kim, royal bootlicker-in-chief!

Anyway, not that I want to get too big-headed about my many achievements at the palace, but now, at the beginning of November, I was finally put in a position to do something that might be of use to Her Majesty's *Sun* newspaper. To wit, His Royal Grumpling, Prince Andrew, was back in his palace apartments after a month-long stint on his boat, *HMS Cottesmore*. After a chaste month at sea, Andrew was obviously looking for what's known in the senior service as "Lady Action". So, rather than spending his first night back home with his mother, he was having a little supper party for two.

I was to be his nimble-footed waiter.

The good Simon Brook has Chipper on his lap and is inspecting the dog's teeth. Chipper had that morning taken a chunk out of one of Princess Anne's mad bull terriers, and Simon was concerned that Chipper might have chipped one of his canines; happily, the dog's teeth were as sharp as ever.

'You go and bite that bad doggy, won't you, Mr Chipper? You go bite him!' Simon says. He rewards Chipper with a wet kiss on the nose before turning to me. 'Sorry about this job, dear heart, but you are the most junior footman, so it is you who has to look after Prince Andrew.'

'Be a pleasure, Mr Brook, sir,' I say. 'I have been greatly looking forward to attending to the Duke of York's needs.' My voice is, I hope, tinged with the perfect amount of irony.

'You are a naughty, naughty boy, Lawrence.' He gives the dog another kiss on the nose.

'E'll be perfick, perfick,' Chipper replies. Simon glassily smiles at me as he tickles the dog's throat.

Simon runs me through my duties. They are not overly taxing. Once I've laid up a table for two in Prince Grumpling's morning room, I have to go downstairs to wait for his date to arrive. Then, making easy chit-chat along the way, I have to escort the woman up to Prince Andrew's apartment. He will welcome her in with a kiss on the cheek, and I will skulk away to my hidey-hole, popping into the apartments every so often throughout the evening to ensure that His Grumpling is happy. The evening could end in one of two ways – either His Grumpling will strike lucky, and his date will spend the night, or, more likely, the woman will come to her senses and insist on leaving immediately, at which stage I'll be summoned to escort her off the premises.

With my head held high and my trolley piled up with cutlery, crockery and cut crystal, I walk the walk of the righteous footman; a footman who has been tasked with a job and who will carry it out to the best of his abilities. On the chamber floor, I go over to an antique mahogany chest. In the top drawer on the left, tucked away in a small blue box, is the key to Andrew's apartment.

His Grumpling has been estranged from his wife, Sarah, for over a year, but the nametag on his door still reads, "The Duke and Duchess of York". I unlock the door and go inside. First thoughts on entering one of Buckingham Palace's principal state apartments? Tack-ola!

A more dutiful footman might have immediately laid up the table, but as I didn't know when His Grumpling would be back, I crack on. I take out my trusty Olympus Twin camera and start firing away.

His Grumpling is only thirty-three, but his sitting room could have been furnished for a pensioner. There is a table awash with family photos, particularly of his estranged Duchess and a mildew-green sofa with one white pillow cross-stitched with the words, "Eat, Sleep, and Remarry" and a second which read, "Before you meet your real prince, you have to kiss a lot of frogs"; opposite the sofa, there is a huge TV, stereo and satellite system; two ashtrays, which have been moulded out of shell casings, sit on a side table; a few gloomy oil paintings hang on the walls, nothing you'd ever want to look at, and a large picture of Andrew in his royal naval uniform (also something you would not choose to look at). This room is finished with an array of knick-knacks and dust-catchers, just some of the flotsam and jetsam that have touched His Grumpling's heart.

The bedroom is equally yuk, with a massive bed in gold and pale yellow and the walls covered in hideous stripy orange wallpaper. The room looks like it was decorated in the 1960s and hasn't been touched since. The teddy bears, all seventy-two of them, are in their daytime positions on the double bed – row after row of them, small ones at the bottom, bigger at the top. In strange contrast to the bears, there is a white pillow on the bed that has been embroidered with the word "Daddy". Dominating the entire room is just the sort of picture that every young man-about-town ought to have by his bedside – a huge photo of the child Grumpling and his mum.

I have a peek in the wardrobe. He's still got his estranged wife's wedding dress. Hanging from the top of it is the fabled grey monkey that Campion has to hide every evening now that she's back on night shifts.

At the end of the bed is an uncomfortable-looking sofa, also in pale yellow, with a fluorescent yellow hippo in the middle. One thing I can't fathom are the two wood kneelers underneath the sofa – does His Grumpling really pray on them? More likely, he uses them for something… rather unsavoury?

I take myself into the bathroom. Ever mindful of Her Majesty's dictum that when you have a toilet in front of you, you should use it, I have a happy pee. I am just scoping the room out in my usual sneery way – vile bath in avocado green with matching wallpaper – when there is such a terrific slam of the apartment door that I nearly do myself a mischief; a small amount of pee-pee may have ended up on the floor.

I've only just adjusted my *toilette* when Andrew storms into the bathroom.

'What are you doing in here?' he says. He is still in his naval uniform.

'Your Royal Highness,' I say and reward him with a full bow from the waist.

'What are you doing here?'

'Checking that all is in order, sir,' I say.

'That is for the maid to sort out,' he says. 'Why hasn't the table been laid up?'

'I was attending to it, sir.'

'Well, get on with it.'

'Yes, Your Royal Highness.'

I scuttle out of the bathroom like the mild-mannered cockroach I have become and am busying myself with the white linen tablecloth when Prince Andrew charges out of his bedroom and starts yelling at me again. Are there lots of people out there who like screaming? Or do I just happen to attract a lot of screamers? Perhaps I am a lightning rod for screamy people.

'You!' he shouts. 'You five-star turd! You have been using my personal lavatory!'

'Me, Your Royal Highness?'

'You didn't even flush!'

It seems that my fledgling relationship with the prince has not got off to the best of starts.

'Must have been your maid, sir,' I say. 'She's notorious for never flushing the lav.'

'Don't talk such utter bilge!' he says. 'Did the maid also piss on the floor?'

'I really couldn't say, sir,' I say, before helpfully adding, 'Though Campion has always been very messy.'

'Shut up!' he says.

'Me, Your Royal Highness?'

'Just lay the table and get out!'

Before I am able to say something servile, he shuts himself in his bedroom again, there to doubtless call Mummy up and complain about declining staff standards.

I throw the tablecloth over the square fold-out card table, only to be faced with one of the more daunting problems I've ever faced at the palace – where to put the placings. Should I go formal, with the place settings opposite each other, candles in between, or cosy, with side-by-side *placements*? I ponder this most perplexing of problems for some time – side by side just looks, well, better – but eventually plump for sitting the pair opposite each other. If Captain Grumpling is intent on wearing his uniform for dinner, then he is bound to prefer formal.

Duty done, another royal satisfied, I leave His Grumpling's apartments and go up to my room. I put the camera on the table, have a large shot of brandy, and go down to the Privy Purse Door to wait for Andrew's date. I sit down on one of the armchairs (tasteful lime green silk, just in case you're interested) and have a browse through the day's papers.

Two things irritate me in this waiting room. Firstly, there is a lovely fireplace, but no fire – we are already in November! The palace has over three hundred fireplaces, but thanks to some cheapskate bean-counter, the only fire that is ever lit is in Her Majesty's sitting room. Secondly, despite there being two writing tables, there are no pens and no palace paper – the guests apparently kept pinching them as souvenirs.

Andrew's date is twenty minutes late.

Though I presumed she would be beautiful, I didn't expect her to be *this* beautiful. She is a twenty-something supermodel. Her name is Caprice Bourret, though she is one of those stars who is so famous that she is known just by her first name – Caprice.

I decide not to recognise her. As far as I am concerned, she is just another American hillbilly.

'Evening, Miss,' I say. 'Had a good trip over?'

'Just the best trip,' she gushes. 'I caught a cab, but I asked him to take me the scenic route, and was it scenic. We went over two rivers, and we went to Battersea Power Station, and he showed me Westminster Abbey and Clapham Common, and then he took me to the Houses of Parliament, and over Tower Bridge and up to the zoo—'

'The grand tour,' I say.

'I had no idea London was so big!''

'Sure is,' I say before getting to the meat of the matter, 'Known Prince Andrew long?'

'Oh, we met at a dinner party,' she says. 'And then he just asked me over for supper. Anyone else coming?'

'Just you,' I say as we trot up another staircase.

'Oh, ma, God,' she says. 'He's not going to get handsy, is he?'

I look at Caprice; long blonde hair coiled around her neck, perfect teeth, perfect skin. As for her red dress, it is as tight as a second skin.

'He just might,' I say. 'If you want to get out quick, just ring the bell. I'll be right in.'

'Like the good ol' Seventh Cavalry,' she says.

'That's me.'

We arrive at Prince Andrew's apartment. Caprice gives me a shy smile and, like the sacrificial lamb, knocks on the door.

Andrew, who's obviously been prowling close by, opens the door. 'Ah, you snuck in,' he says. 'How are you?'

I leave them to it, retiring to my wee cubby hole. Five minutes later, Prince Andrew calls for some drinks. The two of them are sitting next to each other on the sofa, Andrew slouched back while Caprice is perched awkwardly on the edge.

I give him a courtly bow. 'You rang, Your Royal Highnessness?'

He gives me a sharp look. 'We'd like some drinks. A glass of freshly squeezed orange juice for me, vodka and tonic for the lady.'

'Yes, your Royal Highnessness.'

'What did you just call me?'

'Your Royal Highnessness?'

'Stop calling me Your Highnessness.'

'What would Your Highnessn... What would you prefer to be called?'

'You refer to me either as Your Royal Highness or sir.'

'And would Sir Andrew like some nibbles? Some Hula Hoops? Monster Munch – I hear they have a delicious new pickled onion flavour.'

Caprice smirks while Prince Andrew goggles.

'Get the drinks,' he says.

'Yes, Sir Andrew.'

'Call me, sir!'

'Yes, Sir Andrew.' I back out of the room, feverishly tugging my forelock.

Off to the kitchens I scurry, where one of the junior cooks squeezes a jug of orange juice. I make up the vodka and tonic, titify it with a lemon garnish, and dig up a bowl of nuts and a bowl of Monster Munch. After delivering the drinks, I go off to make a phone call. There isn't time to get to Green Park, so I have to use one of the staff payphones in the basement.

Eventually, he picks up. 'Yes?'

'Grubby, it's me, Kim!'

'What do you want?'

'I want you to get your camera out and drag your fat carcase over to Buckingham Palace.'

'When?'

'Now. Caprice is having supper with Prince Andrew!'

'Caprice? The American supermodel?'

'How many other Caprices are there?'

'He's a sly dog,' Grubby says. 'I'm pissed. I'll have to get a cab.'

'She'll be leaving in an hour or so.'

I slam the phone down. Another *Sun* splash sorted, and that might have been that, except that Jono Freemantle happens to emerge from one of the side rooms. Freemantle, you may remember, was that fop of a footman who lost his top spot after spiking the corgis' food with whisky. For some reason, he'd taken against me.

'Interesting,' he says as he walks past.

'Interesting?' I say.

He polishes his glasses with a white handkerchief and smiles. 'Very interesting.' He goes his way, and thinking nothing more of it, I go mine.

Half an hour later, my little bell rings again. They are ready for their first course, an avocado and prawn cocktail. I wheel the trolley into the lift and help myself to one of the jumbo prawns; it is just as tasty as the ones you buy in Marks and Spencer.

When I push the trolley into the room, Prince Andrew and Caprice are already seated at the dining table. He's unbent enough to light the candles and take off his jacket. 'Prawns and avocado, Miss,' I say, placing the plate in front of Caprice.

'Thank you.'

'Prawns and avocado, Your Majesty.'

'Only my mother is Your Majesty!' he spits. 'I am Your Royal Highness!'

'Yes, Your 'Iness.'

I pour Caprice a glass of Chablis. Andrew, who is teetotal, sticks with the orange juice.

Next to Andrew's side plate is the dreaded notebook that all members of the royal family use when they're dining at the palace. They occasionally note down something they've enjoyed, but most of the time they only put pencil to paper when they're peeved. The queen rarely writes in her notebook, but ominously, Prince Andrew has picked up his pencil and is scribbling hard.

There isn't much else to report about the dinner. I dutifully bring up some stone-cold fish and chips, followed by Prince Andrew's favourite pudding, crème brûlée with Sandringham oranges. Caprice says her thank yous as Prince Grumpling silently simmers. It appears that my antics have thrown a pall over the evening. The last I see of them, Caprice is recoiling as Andrew stretches across the table to hold her hand.

Ten minutes later, I am summoned to escort Caprice off the premises. I take her the long route back to the Privy Purse Door, showing her a few of the staterooms. She has a wave on the balcony and coos with delight when we go into the Throne Room. 'Can I sit on the throne?' she says.

'Course you can,' I say.

So, she sits on the same throne that the queen sat on during her coronation, and Caprice loves that, but what she loves best of all is her souvenir.

'Like a plate or a cup?' I ask.

'I'd love a plate,' she says. 'I'll send it to ma mom.'

I dig up a plate from the kitchens. When her cab arrives, I escort her out of the Privy Purse Door, down the five steps with their threadbare red carpet, and open the car door.

'You're so sweet,' she says. She leans over and gives me a lingering kiss on the cheek. 'My name is Caprice.'

'Lovely to meet you, Caprice,' I say.

'I'm staying at the Dorchester.'

'A short walk away.'

I close the door. She opens the window. 'You know how to walk, dontcha?'

She waves, then I wave, and as Grubby fires off frame after frame, the cab pulls away.

I go upstairs to clear the table.

It is all kicking off.

CHAPTER 29

It isn't specifically that she objects to cleaning Prince Andrew's apartment. Andrew's rooms are just some of the many rooms that Campion has to clean as part of her everyday duties as a maid.

What Campion objects to very much is, morning and night, having to rearrange Andrew's teddies – putting them on the bed in the morning and then returning them all to the fireplace in the evening. Another thing she objects to is that she never knows when in the evening Andrew wants his teddies moved. Sometimes it is 8 p.m., and other times, like tonight, she may get the call at 11 p.m., so there she's been, on tenterhooks, for the past three hours, not able to leave the palace, not able, say, to go and see her boyfriend. Instead she's got to hang around, waiting for the moment Prince Andrew decides that it's finally time for his seventy-two teddies to be moved and, indeed, for his grey monkey to be hidden somewhere in his bedroom.

So as she goes up the four flights of stairs to Prince Andrew's apartment, it isn't that she is angry or unhappy, but Campion certainly is not happy either. She is in that sort of prickling mood where she isn't looking for a fight, but if she senses hostile fire, then let us just say that she will not hesitate to return it.

Campion knocks on the door and finds Prince Andrew lolling on the sofa. She glances at what he is watching. She has not seen the film, but she recognises the scene – it is one of the most notorious scenes in movie history – Marlon Brando with a girl and a pack of butter in *Last Tango in Paris*.

'Good evening, Your Royal Highness,' she says.

'You've gone all afro,' he says. 'I preferred it straight.'

'I'll bear that in mind, sir.'

She is just going over to the bedroom when Andrew pipes up again. 'Hey, Campion,' he says. 'Can I ask you a question?'

There is something in his wheedling tone that isn't right. She stops and turns.

'Ever tried anal sex?' He smirks.

'I beg your pardon?'

'Here I am, finally watching *Last Tango in Paris*, and I was just wondering – what's anal sex like?'

'You'd know better than me,' Campion says. 'You're the one in the navy.' She goes through to the bedroom, slamming the door behind her.

Is there no end to his revoltingness? She's never met such a creep. He is thick. He is arrogant. He is entitled. He does not have a single redeeming feature; the only thing he has going for him is that his mother is the queen, and perhaps that is the problem. There is a chance, she thinks, that he might not have become quite so repellent if he hadn't been brought up in Buckingham Palace – but no, it wouldn't have made any difference. His brand of clod-hopping oafishness runs so deep that he'd have been just as repugnant if he'd been brought up on a council estate.

Campion climbs onto the bed and flings handful after handful of teddies onto the floor. She starts arranging them all in their positions in the fireplace – is there any more pointless an exercise on earth than moving these teddies from the bed to the fireplace and then back to the bed again? And what about that disgusting film he is watching? It is no coincidence that the creep has been watching the most infamous scene in the entire damn film just as she walks into his sitting room. And all so that the jerk can bring the conversation around to his all-time obsession – anal sex. It is beyond disgusting.

Andrew comes into the bedroom, standing over her as she kneels in the fireplace with the teddies. 'Your hair looks like a sponge,' he says. 'Can I touch it?'

'You certainly cannot,' she says.

'Somebody's a little tart tonight.' He goes through to the lavatory.

God, she is angry. Everything he does, every word he utters, is just awful. She throws the last of the teddies onto the pile in the fireplace, hurriedly places the two largest two teddies on their little wooden thrones and quits the room. The jerk has paused the film at the most disgusting moment in the whole movie.

Lawrence hasn't cleared the supper table yet, so she helps him out by putting the crockery and cutlery onto the trolley. The flowers and candles follow, along with the napkins and tablecloth. Just one last thing to do, plump up the pillows, and then she's gone, and first thing in the morning, she'll put in a request to be transferred to anywhere at all in the palace that is away from this spoiled brat.

Andrew returns to the sitting room. He is holding the grey monkey that has been hanging from the wardrobe.

'You didn't hide my monkey,' he says. He swings the monkey by its tail.

Seriously? Seriously! A grown man wanting her to hide his toy monkey?

But rather than just thinking it, Campion says it.

'What did you say?' Prince Andrew says.

'You heard me,' Campion says. 'You're a grown man. It's pathetic.' Out of the corner of her eye, she sees the door open and has a glimpse of Lawrence. He takes one look and backs away, shutting the door behind him.

'When you address me, you address me as sir.'

'What?' she says.

'You address me as sir.'

'Are you out of your tiny mind?' Campion says. 'You've just been asking me if I've had anal sex, and now you're telling me that you want to be called sir!' Campion draws herself up to her full height. 'You know what you are? You might be the queen's son, and you might be a royal highness, but what you actually are is a complete dickhead, and since you're so keen to talk about anal sex, let me tell you, never in my entire life have I met anyone who's quite so up his own arsehole—'

'You—'

'No, you shut up, and you listen, you royal arsehole. I've got a few home truths to tell you. I only wish someone had told you them years ago because if they had, you might not have turned out to be quite the insufferable prat that you have become. And it's not just me, by the way, so let's see if we can get this into your royal pea-brain – we all hate you. There's not a single member of the palace staff who likes you, who admires you, who thinks you're anything other than a thick, filthy-minded perv. Hey, and while I'm about it, let's talk about your teddies. Those seventy-two teddies that have to be lined up on your bed, then lined up in your fireplace, day in, day out. And they all have to be lined up just perfectly because otherwise, little Prince Grumpling will get into a pet, call up his mummy, and say that his teddies haven't been lined up properly. Well, you know what, I've had it with your teddies, we've had it with your teddies, and if in future you want your teddies all lined up in a row, then damn well do it yourself!'

Prince Andrew was so shocked when Campion started her diatribe that he'd taken an actual step backwards. Now she's finished, he looks like he is lost for words, mouth gaping like a guppy fish. But he does not have to think for too long as his instincts quickly kick in.

'You're an insolent slut!' He takes four smart steps over towards Campion and, hard as he can, slaps across the cheek.

Campion's head spins sideways. She is knocked to the floor.

She is on her knees when the door opens. It is Mason, still in his uniform. He is white-faced, bristling with anger.

'Get out,' Andrew says.

Mason goes straight to Campion, leans down, touches her on the shoulder. 'You okay?'

'I've been worse.' She tries to smile.

'Good,' he says. 'Excuse me one second.'

He seems to uncoil in slow-motion, pivoting on his left toe as his arm comes up like a pile driver. Andrew doesn't see it coming – wouldn't conceive that something like this is coming hard and driven by rage. Mason gives it everything he's got, fist driving upwards and catching Andrew full, sweet on the chin. His head snaps back and he is knocked clean off his feet. He keels into the trolley and in a rending crash of cut crystal and china, the prince is out cold on the floor, a trickle of blood oozing from his mouth.

After the stunning explosion of noise, all is suddenly silent. Lawrence comes into the room, quickly taking it all in.

'He had that coming a long time,' he says. 'You two go.'

'R-really?' Mason says.

'You're the last people he'll want to see when he comes around.'

'Shall I c-call the doctor?'

'Leave this to me.'

Mason offers his hand to Campion, helping her up. 'Let's get you out of here and get a drink.'

'Thank you,' she says. 'I'd like that.'

They hold hands and walk to the door. Campion surveys the scene one last time. It is an extraordinary tableau, the trolley upended, Lawrence swigging Chablis straight from the bottle, and, right at the centre of it all, Prince Andrew lying out for the count in a ring of smashed china.

'I wish I had a camera,' Campion says. 'I'd like a picture for when I'm old and grey and in need of cheering up.'

'You'll have one better than a picture,' Mason says.

'What's that?'

'You'll h-have me,' he says. 'And I... I won't forget a single detail.'

They go up to Campion's room because she has some arnica for her cheek. As soon as the door shuts behind them, the arnica is forgotten, the slap is forgotten. They celebrate their love in the only way worth a damn – by making love. Somewhere along the way, some books are kicked, and the wardrobe teeters towards them. They lunge onto the bed, and for the second time in as many months, Campion's wardrobe topples over onto the floor with a boom of noise that may not be quite loud enough to wake the dead but which is certainly loud enough to wake up the palace housekeeper, Mrs Boyd.

* * *

Mrs Boyd puts on her dressing gown and slippers and goes to investigate. That horrid boom has, she knows, come from the Finch's Lobby. She pads down the corridor in silence, listening intently for sounds of anything untoward – and hears it long before she even reaches the room, the simply shameful sound of a man and woman laughing. It gives Mrs Boyd considerable satisfaction to see that the source of this disgraceful cross-corridor fraternisation is emanating from Campion's room.

She smiles, but realising that a smile is inappropriate, her features resume their usual sour cragginess.

She gives the door a brisk rat-a-tat, which cuts straight through the laughter, and she opens the door. There, joy of joys, Campion is in bed with the queen's temporary equerry-in-waiting, both of them naked, with just a blanket to cover their modesty. She's got her! This time she's got her! Campion can wriggle all she likes, can grovel all she likes, can even plead her cause as "The Queen's Storyteller", but it won't make a blind bit of difference, not this time, because this time, Mrs Boyd has got her, got her good and proper, and it feels sweet.

Mrs Boyd has been focusing so intently on Campion and her lover that it has hardly even registered that the black wardrobe, its back broken, is flat on the floor in the middle of the room – another splendid reason (as if any more were needed) for Campion's summary dismissal.

Mrs Boyd rubs her hands together and savours the delicious moment. 'A-ha!' she says.

'Evening, Mrs Boyd,' Campion says. She pulls a pillow up to the headboard and, bold as brass, rests her head against it, elbows out, hands behind her head. 'What can I do you for?'

'What can you do me for?' Mrs Boyd says before repeating herself in mounting rage. 'What can you do me for? I'll tell you exactly what I can do you for, you little madam! Having sex with a man in your staff bedroom, how's that? As you well know, male members of staff are expressly forbidden from entering maids' rooms during the night-time. Further to that, we've also got the wanton destruction of palace property—' She gestures towards the wardrobe. 'And what I am wondering to myself, young madam, is how you're going to weasel out of this one.'

And you know what the girl is doing? Not only is she lolling like a slattern on her pillow, but she is openly smiling!

'Weasel out of this one?' Campion says. 'How do you mean?'

'I know perfectly well how you can bend and twist my words – why, you'll probably claim that this, this man, came round to deliver a letter, and the next thing, he'd fallen out of his clothes.' Mrs Boyd purses her prim lips as she takes another look around the room. The clothes, she sees, have been dumped willy-nilly – on the floor, on the chair, even in the basin.

'On the contrary, Mrs Boyd, I deny nothing,' Campion says. 'We've been having sex – or making love, as I prefer to call it – and if you'd arrived just two minutes sooner, you would have caught us, ahh—'

'*In flagrante delicto*?' says the man, Mason, whose insolent head is resting next to Campion's on the pillow.

'Exactly the phrase I was looking for. Thank you, Mason darling,' Campion gives him a kiss on the forehead. 'You would have caught us while the crime was blazing.' She turns to Mason. 'That is the literal translation?'

'It is.'

'You admit it!' Mrs Boyd says triumphantly. 'You admit it! You admit that here, tonight, in this room, you had sex with a man!'

'I do, Mrs Boyd, I do!' Campion says. 'I've just had sex! Here, tonight, in this room! And with a man!'

'I hope you find it just as funny tomorrow morning,' Mrs Boyd says.

Campion seems to lift her leg so that it is now lying over the equerry-in-waiting's knee. 'Now, I can see how much pleasure this has all given you, Mrs Boyd, but if I may, I have a word of warning.'

'How so?'

'I'm afraid you're going to be disappointed.'

'I doubt that, young woman! I doubt that very much indeed!'

'It's just that, when you go to make your report to the master of the household first thing tomorrow morning, you may have to join the back of the queue, so to speak – and that when you do finally reach the front of the queue, you may well find that Sir Richard has fatter fish to fry.'

Mrs Boyd can't make head nor tail of what this chit of a girl is driving at. 'I won't be the first person objecting to your monstrous behaviour?'

'Prince Andrew may have a prior claim,' Campion says. 'If, that is, he's made it back from the dentist in time.'

Mrs Boyd does not know what is going on, but she will most certainly make it her business to find out. There seems absolutely no point whatsoever in prolonging the conversation.

'I am going,' Mrs Boyd says. 'Enjoy your last night at the palace.'

'We'll try to make the most of it, won't we, Mason darling?'

As Mrs Boyd closes the door, she has to listen to the stomach-churning sound of the pair of them kissing.

CHAPTER 30

It is a very tired palace flunky who eventually makes it back up to his bedroom the next morning – tired and also a little bit tardy, actually, but I figured that Mason won't be complaining too loudly if he doesn't get his morning tea.

I have a shower and some breakfast and discover that my duties for the morning entail me hanging around the Ambassador's Entrance. Another morning of opening doors for dignitaries while bowing and making small talk.

I've been at the Ambassadors' Entrance for about three hours, and in that time, I have opened the door seventeen times – ten people have come in, seven have left. I've chatted about the weather and the London traffic, and when I've not been making small talk, I have been mulling over the extraordinary events of the previous evening – Campion and Prince Andrew; Prince Andrew and Mason; and, of course, Caprice…

Ollie finds me on one of the chairs by the door, feet outstretched, hands dug deep in my pockets, and eyes momentarily shut as I have forty winks. He shakes me awake.

I scratch my hair and wipe the sleep out of my eyes. 'What's up?'

'Sir Richard Arnison-Newgass wants to see you,' he says.

'I'll bet he does,' I say. 'Despite my best advice, Prince Andrew has been squealing.'

'Campion and Mason are in with him now.'

I heave myself out of the chair. 'See you later.'

I mooch off to Sir Richard's office and arrive just as Campion and Mason are leaving. They look very happy.

'We're off,' Mason says. 'It seems it is no longer t-t-tenable for me to remain as an equerry-in-waiting.'

'Guess punching a prince's lights out would put a dampener on things,' I say. 'How is he?'

'Still at the dentist,' Mason says.

'Are you off as well, Campion?' I say.

'I'm done.'

'Know what you're going to do?'

'We've got some plans.' She smiles. 'I'm certainly not going to share them with you.'

'Now, now, Campion – after all I've done for you.'

They wave and go on their way – what an attractive couple, and nice with it. I am mightily pleased that I had a small but pivotal role in bringing them together.

I knock on Sir Richard's door and go in. He is sitting behind his desk.

'Morning, sir,' I say. 'Bad do about last night.'

Sir Richard, in his usual blue pinstripe suit, is reading some newspapers – copies of *The Sun*, no less. He takes off his glasses, places them very precisely on his desk, and looks at me.

'How long have you been selling stories to *The Sun*?'

'Beg pardon, sir?'

'You've been selling stories to *The Sun*,' he says. 'And here, in front of me, I have the proof.'

'I'm afraid I don't know what you're talking about, sir.'

'Let me explain then, Lawrence.' He taps the papers in front of him. They appear to be all the same, four copies of *The Sun's* World Exclusive about Bobo MacDonald's death, a black-bordered front page with the headline "QUEEN MOURNS". 'These four papers are the various editions of *The Sun* the day after Bobo MacDonald died.' He picks up the top paper. 'It even made the first edition.'

'Not quite following, sir.'

'I, Lawrence, have been doing my research, and apparently, for this story to have made the first edition, *The Sun's* editors must have heard the news at just about the same time that I did. That's because you phoned it through to them.'

'Not me, sir.'

'Furthermore, I find you dining at The Ritz with one of the other footmen, racking up a bill that must have been a good four figures—'

'As I told you at the time, sir,' I say. 'I'd come into some money, a bequest from my dear—'

Sir Richard holds his hand up. 'Then last night, I hear, you were arranging for a photographer to take a picture of Prince Andrew's dining companion.'

Now that – that does momentarily take the wind out of my sails. I've been shopped! Shopped by that smug bastard, Jono Freemantle, who lost his own job, and now, for no reason whatsoever, is taking me down with him. Is there no honour – at all – amongst the palace footmen? Honestly! You can't trust anyone!

'Absolutely not, sir,' I say. 'I wouldn't dream of calling up a photographer. I wouldn't even know who to call.'

'How very typical,' Sir Richard says. He stretches over to a buff brown envelope on the side of his desk. 'Fortunately, I have these. I'll be interested to hear how you talk your way out of them.' He passes the envelope over. 'Very.'

I don't like this at all. I open the envelope and pull out a sheaf of photos. They look a little familiar – as well they might, since they are the pictures I'd just taken the previous evening of Prince Andrew's rooms.

'You went into my room,' I say incredulously. 'You searched my room without permission?'

'Never mind the rights and wrongs of searching your room, Lawrence, or developing your roll of film, you've been caught bang to rights—'

'It's a bit hot, sir,' I say.

'Sometimes, Lawrence, a little hot behaviour is necessary

in order to catch out reptiles like yourself,' he says. He picks up the newspapers and squares them off. 'You have been selling stories to *The Sun*,' he says. 'Your contract with the palace is terminated with immediate effect.'

'On my mother's grave,' I say. 'I swear I've never sold a story to *The Sun*.'

He looks up at me from his desk, giving a rueful laugh. 'I find it amazing, Lawrence, how, even after you've been caught red-handed, you continue to tell the most bare-faced lies.'

There doesn't seem much more to say. 'Thank you for the opportunity, Sir Richard—'

'On your way, young man.'

A security guard, one of the coppers, is waiting for me outside. He's not overly chatty as he escorts me back up to my bedroom. Honestly! Do they think I'm going to start pilfering the china? As the plod waits outside, I change into my suit and leave my livery on the bed. Five minutes to pack my bag, and I'm done.

I am still in a bit of a daze as I go down to the payphones in the basement. I gesture for my taciturn escort to back off a little. Spike is in a conference, but his secretary eventually puts me through.

'What's up?' he says.

'The balloon's gone up,' I say. 'They've kicked me out.'

'We'll start clearing the paper,' he says. 'You better come into the office.'

I am allowed to say goodbye to the sergeant footman, Simon Brook, who has already heard news of my departure. 'I'll be sorry to see you go, dear boy,' Simon says as he strokes the dog on his lap.

Not a moment later, Chipper pipes up, mouth yawning open as he says in his grotesque Yorkshire accent, 'But he's a naughty boy! A naughty, naughty boy!'

Simon cuddles the dog. 'Everyone at the palace is a little bit naughty, aren't they, Lawrence?'

I am about to be kicked out of the palace for the last time

when I decide there is just one more thing I ought to do: return my security pass. 'Won't be a minute,' I tell the policeman. I leave my bag in the corridor and lead the way back up to Sir Richard's office. I knock on the door again.

'Come!' He does not look best pleased to see me. 'What do you want now?'

'Thought I'd return my security pass, Sir Richard,' I say.

'Leave it by the door.'

'Just one more thing, Sir Richard,' I say. 'You were mostly right, but you were wrong about one thing.'

'Enlighten me.' He leans towards me, elbows on his desk, hands clasped in front of him.

'I have never sold a story to *The Sun*,' I say. 'And nor would I ever sell a story to *The Sun*.'

'Are you done?'

'I have no need to sell stories to *The Sun*,' I continue. 'And that, Sir Richard, is because I...I am a *Sun* staff reporter.' His mouth drops at the enormity of what I've just told him. 'Careful now, Sir Richard. You might start catching flies.'

I give him a courtly nod, and with one hand jauntily on my hip, I take my leave of the master of the household. 'I wish you joy of the day, Sir Richard,' I say, gently closing the door behind me.

With mixed emotions, I walk out of the palace for the last time, a little sad to be leaving this cosy, easy cage life; I'd have liked to have said goodbye to my friends, but I also feel the most unmitigated relief – the whole ridiculous charade is over! No more bowing and scraping, no more endless waiting to open a damn door, no more fawning over such preposterous sleazeballs as Prince Andrew. True, *The Sun* isn't the most egalitarian place on earth to work, and you are likely to be sworn at most days of the week, but it is a deal sight more fun than being a royal lackey.

Without so much as a backward glance, I stroll up the Mall to Trafalgar Square and catch the Tube back home. I put on my very best suit, pick up my phone, my pager and my security pass and take the underground to Tower Hill. A ten-minute walk to Fortress Wapping, and then, not ninety minutes after quitting Buckingham Palace, I am getting the lift up to the sixth floor. It feels more than just good. It feels great to be out of that ludicrous ivory tower and once again deal with real human beings. True, they are a load of low-lifers, boozed-up whiners, and self-aggrandising bitchers, and maybe a few of them are demented, if not clean off their rockers, but they are my low-lifers, my whiners and my bitchers, and I am a part of them.

Here, in front of me, is *The Sun's* magnificent call to arms – "Walk tall. You're entering *Sun* country!". When I walk through the double security doors, I am most certainly walking tall.

The newsroom is fairly full, but since it is only 2 p.m., not much is happening. Tophe, one of the news editors, glances over at me.

'Oh, hi Kim,' he says before continuing to tap away at his keyboard.

It isn't exactly the all-singing, all-dancing fanfare that I've been hoping for. I, Kim, a *Sun* staff reporter, have just successfully pulled off one of the most spectacular stunts in tabloid history. And all I get when I make my glorious return to the newsroom is a goonish news editor giving me a watery look and saying, "Oh, hi, Kim"?

I look over at the three secretaries in the corner. Stella, pretty as ever, hair in two blonde pigtails, is chewing gum and reading the *Evening Standard*. She looks up from her newspaper, blows the most enormous pink bubble, and gives me the finger. Having given me the finger, she idly returns to her paper.

Spike strides out of the managing editor's office. He is reading some papers and blunders straight into me. 'Mind out!' he says before realising who it is. 'Oh, it's you.'

'What do you mean, "Oh, it's you"?' I say.

'Well, you're back,' he says in the most inconsequential fashion, as if I've just come back from getting the teas in.

'Is that it?' I say. 'Is that it? I've spent the last two months working my guts out in Buckingham Palace to give you the scoop of the century, and all I get when I come back into the office is, "Oh, it's you"!'

'Sucker!' He laughs, engulfing me in a huge bear hug.

There is an old journalistic tradition called "Banging out", where retiring hacks are raucously banged out as they leave the newsroom for the last time.

I am being banged in.

The newsroom erupts. As far as the eye can see, everyone in the room is hammering at their desks – reporters pounding their keyboards, back bench, subs and secretaries drumming their desks with their fists, photographers bumping their chairs on the floor, and even the precious feature writers unbend enough to flap their glossy magazines onto the tabletops.

The news editors are out of their chairs and shaking me by the hand, executives and reporters are slapping me on the back, and the three secretaries all in turn kiss me. I'm sure the editor himself would have shaken my hand that day, except he is off in the country for a spot of shooting.

'Welcome back, Kim!' Spike says. He holds my arm aloft like a champion boxer. 'He's only been and gone and done it!'

When the hubbub dies down, and the backslapping has finished, Spike and Robert escort me through the newsroom to the editor's office. On the wall is a new addition to *The Sun's* series of blown-up front pages. It is about six feet by three feet with the single-word headline "SPIKED!" Underneath is one of the pictures that Grubby took of me the last time I was in the newsroom – Spike sitting astride me on the floor, looking like some Stone Age caveman who was about to batter my brains out.

I pause in front of the picture. 'That's not quite how I remember our fight,' I say.

'Luckily, I got to choose the picture,' Spike says.

'How's the nose, by the way?'

The three of us go into the editor's office and after coffees have been brought in, I am debriefed.

'Haven't heard from you for a while,' Spike says. He is sitting in the editor's chair while Robert and I are stuck on the sofa about two feet below him. 'You manage to do all that stuff I wanted?'

'It was difficult,' I say.

'Of course, of course,' he says. 'But you got to Windsor Castle? You got onto one of the coaches?'

'No,' I say. 'I couldn't swing it.'

'Fine, fine, fine,' Spike says, though from his tone I can tell that things are so absolutely not fine. 'But you've got pics of the royals' apartments?'

'It was precisely because I was caught with pictures of Prince Andrew's apartment that I was kicked out this morning,' I say before adding brightly, 'I've got a really good description of the queen's private dining room. She keeps her cereal in a Tupperware box. In the morning, she has a bowl of fresh fruit on the table, and there's a little Roberts radio that is permanently tuned to *Radio 2*...' I trail off. These succulent details of the queen's breakfast table aren't cutting it.

Spike eases at his collar and when that isn't enough, he undoes his top button. 'Forgive me for pointing out the bleeding obvious, Kim, but what have you been doing for the last month? All these pictures and all this copy – you sent it over four weeks ago.'

'It's been tricky,' I say. I have the distinct feeling that despite being served up the scoop of the century, Spike still isn't happy. As ever and is the wont of mad masters the world over, he still wants more. 'I tried to get to Windsor Castle,' I say. 'It was a no-go.'

'Okay,' Spike says glumly. 'I'm just a bit disappointed.'

Robert, the news editor, comes to my rescue. 'Still,' he says brightly. 'We've got tons of good stuff! It'll run for three days at the very least! It's a shame that we don't have pictures of the royals' apartments, but Kim can give us detailed descriptions, and that'll be just great.'

'Yeah,' Spike says. He sounds like he's just been told his pet dog has been run over. 'It'll be just great.'

There is a knock at the door. It is Adam Findlay, News International's ebullient legal manager. A meaty guy with white crew-cut hair, he is wearing a short-sleeved shirt, the better to show off his tattoos; he looks more like a bouncer than a lawyer.

'Hi, Kim.' He comes over to shake my hand. 'Just been looking at this Non-Disclosure Agreement you signed before you started at the palace. Things are going to get squeaky.'

'We knew all that when we started,' Robert says. 'So long as we keep on hammering the security line, we're in the clear. It's the biggest royal security scandal in history.'

'I know that,' Findlay says. 'But I've read all Kim's copy, and there's a hell of a lot of palace gossip that has got nothing to do with the security scandal.'

'It's a grey area, Adam,' Spike says, leaning back comfortably in his chair.

'We'll just have to argue it out in court,' Findlay says before turning back to me. 'Take me through what happened this morning.'

'Prince Andrew had Caprice over for dinner last night,' I say. 'I called Grubby up to come and get her picture, but unfortunately I was overheard by another footman. He shopped me to the boss. They searched my room this morning and found my camera with all the pictures I'd taken of Prince Andrew's apartment.'

Findlay tugs at his lip. 'So, what happened?'

'The master of the household, Major General Sir Richard Arnison-Newgass, called me in, accused me of selling stories to *The Sun*, and sacked me on the spot.'

'He thought you'd been selling stories to *The Sun*?'

'Yeah,' I say. 'He'd worked out I was the only possible source for the Bobo MacDonald story.'

'Good story!' Robert chimes in. 'What a scoop!'

'Just to clarify,' Findlay says. 'He just thinks you were selling stories to *The Sun*. He doesn't know you're on the staff?'

'Err,' I say. The blinding realisation that *The Sun's* star reporter may have blundered...

'What?' Spike immediately senses something is up. He bounces out of his chair and stalks over to the sofa. 'What did you do?'

'Err, nothing,' I say.

'Yes, you did. I know it,' he says. 'What did you do?'

'Nothing, nothing at all,' I say, and with those four words, I could not have made it more obvious that I had indeed done something.

'What did you do?'

'It was nothing much at all,' I say. 'Gosh, it's hot in here. Could we open a window?'

'What happened?'

'Well, umm, the master of the household had sacked me, and I'd packed my bag and said my goodbyes, and then I thought it would be a good idea to give him back my security pass.'

'And?'

'And?' I say.

'And?'

'I, err, well... I told him that I'd never sold a story to *The Sun* in my life because I was, in fact, a, err, a *Sun* staff reporter.'

The most stunned silence imaginable.

'Let me get this right,' Findlay says. 'You told him you were a *Sun* reporter?'

'I did,' I say. 'What difference does it make? It's going to be all over the front page tomorrow anyway.'

'What difference does it make?' Spike yells, giving me a savage poke in the chest. 'What difference does it make? The difference is that you've given them a twelve-hour head-start, you cretin! The palace lawyers are going to be all over this like a rash!' He goes over to the Beryl Cook picture and starts pounding his head against the wall. 'They'll have served us an injunction before we've even got the first edition out!'

'Oh,' I say. 'Sorry.'

CHAPTER 31

In December, just before Christmas, the queen receives a handwritten invitation. It is one of those maybe invitations that vaguely appeal but will involve a certain amount of hassle.

The queen is still mulling it over at Sandringham on Christmas Eve when Ollie, her first footman, brings up a box of Christmas cards. Each year, the queen sends out around seven hundred and fifty Christmas cards, each of them personally signed *Elizabeth R*, and in return, she receives cards by the thousand. Of these cards, the queen sees only a small, hand-picked selection.

The Christmas cards in the box are mainly from friends and family. They are all dutifully read, along with their bits of news and gossip. Towards the end of the pile, she comes across a lavish card of a partridge in a pear tree embossed with a gold crest. The queen not only recognises the crest but knows of only one person on earth who would adorn their Christmas card with one. It is from Viola, and the message inside is particularly stinging. It is this card and this card alone that decides the queen to accept the invitation.

She could go through the whole rigmarole of turning it into an official trip, but after *that* Hallowe'en party, she relishes the prospect of another incognito trip in Philip's black Metrocab. It is fun, she realises, just to pootle along without the escort and outriders, to view the world as an ordinary citizen.

It is quite a long trip from Sandringham to the Cotswolds, and since she needs to be there at 11 a.m., she has an early breakfast, just some toast, marmalade and an apple. How nice it is to be up and away before even a soul has stirred. It is Twelfth Night, 1994, and while most households will be taking down the Christmas decorations, at Sandringham, the decorations stay up until the 6th of February, the anniversary of her father's death.

Jerry is waiting out the front with the taxi and, as was now his custom on these trips, wearing a tweed suit. 'Good morning, Your Majesty.' He opens the rear door for her.

'Morning, Jerry,' she says. 'Is my outfit appropriate?'

'You look like a majestic canary, ma'am,' he says. 'Pretty as a picture.'

'Thank you, Jerry,' she says. It tickles her to be called a majestic canary. 'Or perhaps even a majestic banana?'

'Not sure bananas do majestic, ma'am.'

What a joy to be out on the roads on this crisp, clear January morning – the queen realises why people sometimes just like to go out for a drive, no place to go, just the journey alone is the prize. When they stop at traffic lights, she likes to look at the other drivers and passengers. She does not often see people in repose. At one set of lights, a teenage girl crosses the road with her mum. She happens to catch the queen's eye. The girl looks, looks again and then nudges her mother, but the mother misses the moment. As Jerry pulls away, the girl gives a wave and the queen waves back.

It had not been easy letting Campion and Mason go. They had quit of their own volition – well, having knocked Andrew off his feet, it would have been awkward for Mason to have stayed at the palace.

The queen did not condone Mason knocking Prince Andrew out (and, in the process, quite ruining his smile), but she did appreciate that her younger son had had it coming. Her boy had… tendencies. The business with all those teddies was slightly toe-curling. If the punch brings him to heel, that might not be such a bad hing.

They've just passed Peterborough when the queen has her first difference of opinion with her chauffeur.

'You're not taking the A1?' she queries.

'How many times, ma'am?' he says. 'How many times?'

'Jerry,' the queen says, 'I agree that taking the A605 is the more direct route, but I think you'll find we'll get there faster if we use the A1.'

'So, you know all about it, do you, ma'am?'

'On this occasion, I think I do, Jerry.'

'Well, do you want to come here and drive the car then, ma'am?'

The queen barely pauses a second before replying. 'Yes, Jerry, I do,' she says. 'As a special treat, you may sit next to me.'

'Thank you, ma'am.' He pulls over into a driveway. 'Always wondered what your driving's like – you certainly seem to know enough about it.'

'I drove trucks in the war.' The queen slips in behind the wheel.

'Did you really, ma'am?' He hops into the passenger seat next to her. 'I'd love to hear all about it.'

'Sarcasm does not become you, Jerry.' She adjusts the seat and mirrors, and after a quick flick over her shoulder, they are away – gosh, these electric cars have a bit of a poke!

'What is that beeping sound, Jerry?'

'It's because you haven't got your seatbelt on, ma'am.'

'But I hate wearing seatbelts,' she says.

'The beeping's just going to get louder then, ma'am.'

The queen dutifully straps herself in. They speed soundlessly through the countryside.

'Take it easy, ma'am,' Jerry says. 'Wouldn't want you done for speeding.'

'Who's the backseat driver now, Jerry?' she says.

After a while, she gets used to the car and is so happy that she starts singing, and Jerry, the dear, does not have much option but to join her. They rattle through a few World War II numbers before moving on to Elvis.

'Now I've heard it all, ma'am,' Jerry says. 'The queen is singing the King's songs.'

'Very good, Jerry,' she says. 'I will tell that to my children this evening.'

It is tight, much tighter than she thought it would be, getting to Fairford church on time, and she pulls up outside the church just as Campion is getting out of a taxi. Campion, wearing a simple white dress and white jacket, is being helped out of the car by an elderly man, presumably her grandfather.

'You park up, Jerry,' the queen says, leaning over to the back seat to retrieve her yellow hat. She is just in time to beat Campion to the lychgate.

Campion, clutching onto her grandfather's arm, sees the queen and curtsies. 'Your Majesty,' she says. 'I am truly honoured to have you here. Thank you.'

'Campion dear,' the queen says. 'Wouldn't have missed it – especially when I heard that your future mother-in-law would not be attending.'

'You are too kind, Your Majesty.'

'We do what we can to raise the tone, dear,' the queen says before turning to Campion's grandfather. 'Hello, Paul,' she says. 'I believe we met in Ballater.'

'That's right, Your Majesty,' he says and gives her a bow.

They shake hands, and the queen promises that they will talk later at the wedding breakfast, but they oughtn't to keep the groom waiting any longer. She leaves them by the lychgate and goes up the path and into the church.

She's never been into St Mary's before, but the previous evening she had done her homework, and Pevsner's guide to Gloucestershire had told her exactly what to look out for. The magnificent stained glass, probably the finest in Britain, was saved from the Puritans and then, three hundred years later, saved from the Nazis. She takes a quick peek when she goes into the church. It is The Last Judgement, and in the right-hand corner is a little red devil who is the dead spit of the genial butler at the Hallowe'en party. But this is no time for dawdling – Campion will soon be in the church. The queen would be mortified to have stolen the show.

There aren't many people in the church. Mason is standing at the front, talking to the vicar. She decides to take a discreet pew at the back.

Campion, blooming and beautiful, comes in with her grandfather. The two dozen guests crane their heads to admire the bride; none of them even notice the queen – how delightful it is to be unobserved and sitting quietly at the back.

The vicar is saying something, his words washing over the queen, when she hears the latch on the church door. In comes an elderly gent in a green suit with a red rose in his buttonhole – elderly but quite spry, and he has no need of a walking stick. He slinks into the same pew as the queen.

'Made it just in time,' he says.

The queen looks at him thoughtfully – who else could it be?

'Is that you, Charley?' she says.

'It is,' he says, at the same moment realising that he is sitting next to the queen. 'Your Majesty?'

'We met at a Hallowe'en party.'

'That... that was you, Your Majesty?' he says. 'I'm so sorry. I... I had no idea!'

'I liked that you didn't know who I was,' she says. 'And you've got another buttonhole, I see – I'm sure it will smell amazing.'

'It does, Your Majesty.'

And because she is the queen, and because she can, she bends her head towards the red rose and inhales; the scent is just as heady as she knew it would be.

The wedding ceremony goes without a hitch as Mason kisses his bride. Not a person in the church would have known that the queen was there, except that before they go off to sign the wedding documents, the bride and groom take a detour to the back of the church.

'May I be the first to congratulate you both,' the queen says.

'Thank you, Your Majesty,' Campion says.

'I miss your stories.'

'I'll write them down for you, Your Majesty.'

By now, the rest of the guests have worked out just who, exactly, is sitting at the back of the church.

'I was wondering, Your Majesty, if you might do us the great honour of being one of our witnesses,' Campion says.

The queen gets to her feet. 'It would be a pleasure to stand in for Viola.'

She follows the Duke and Duchess of Montagu down the aisle, though now it is all back to business as usual – the hush followed by everyone stumbling to their feet.

There is only one unsavoury moment.

Campion and Mason leave the church and the queen follows them out. When the queen poses with them for some pictures, she becomes aware of another photographer lurking by the lychgate. She does not know the man, but from his demeanour and shambolic grey suit, he can only be a Fleet Street photographer. Nothing wrong with photographers – her one-time brother-in-law, the Earl of Snowdon, was a photographer.

Standing next to the photographer is another man. A man in a blue suit – and this man she most certainly does recognise.

On what should be a bright, magical morning, the queen feels a wave of the most intense anger.

How could he? How could he? Just seeing him standing there on the pavement makes her so angry she could slap him.

The queen had been let down so many times in the past – by Crawfie and by all the other tittle-tattling maids and butlers and ladies-in-waiting – but nothing has stung quite so much as the realisation that Lawrence, the dog-whisperer, was working for *The Sun*. Why – she trusted him; she liked him. It has been more than a betrayal. It is personal.

The queen follows Campion and Mason out of the

churchyard. Does she discern a trace of embarrassment? Her expression becomes quite glacial. She gives him her hard stare, a very blank glare, the corners of her mouth turning down, looking at him but also right through him. Queens and kings have been using this devastating stare for centuries; without a word, it says that a person has become a non-person. He bows his head.

Jerry holds the door open. 'Your Majesty,' he says with a nod, keeping it very formal.

'I could do with a very large drink.'

CHAPTER 32

Sun reporters have limited attention spans. When our day begins, we sip our coffees as we sift through the papers, and we perhaps deign to make a phone call or two. Come lunchtime, we waft from the office to see a contact. By 3 p.m., we may even have a story which, with any luck, will be filed by 4 p.m. We spend the next two hours fending off queries from the sub-editors, and then at 6 p.m., we are free to leave the office and to continue our drinking – and as for our lovingly confected story, why, that's over. That's history. In the tiny mind of a *Sun* reporter, as soon as a story has been filed, subbed and laid out on a page, then the slate has been wiped clean. The next day, if the story has had a good show, there can be a fleeting fillip of joy to see your byline and your purple prose in print, there to be read by over ten million people. But, unless there's a follow-up to their story, most *Sun* reporters don't give it another thought. It's over! Done! Give me my next story!

We are in the dog days of January, misty, rainy, holidays over, not much happening, not much ever going to happen, but still, in *The Sun* newsroom, there is this unquenchable hunger for news. It doesn't matter how irrelevant, how utterly piffling it is; the next day's paper still has to be filled.

I am in the office with a couple of other reporters, trying to find a follow-up to the day's tedious splash – a B-list sports star, a snooker player, has been caught having an affair. These stories of stars' affairs are so commonplace they run on railroad tracks – just change the names of the star and the aggrieved nanny/close family friend and you're good to go.

Whether there's a follow-up to a "Star infidelity" story largely depends on the spouse (usually a woman). Will they take him back, or will the erring philanderer be dumped? Well, either way, it's a story. What is so not a story is if the spouse keeps her mouth shut and just says, "no comment." How's a hard-working *Sun* hack supposed to get a story out of that? It's not impossible – but it's tougher. You're now going to have to rely on incandescent in-laws saying something like, "Ditch the bastard. I always knew he was a low life!"

But ultimately, who cares? It's all just twaddle, another celebrity marriage on the rocks. Whether the story runs for one day or a whole week doesn't make it any the less drivelsome.

It is 11 a.m., and the mad masters are in conference, discussing the news list for the next day's paper. With all the senior executives couped up together in the same room, it is a pleasant forty minutes for the groundlings.

My phone rings. I always get a little kick when the phone rings because there is always a slim, slim chance that a plum story is about to fall right into my lap.

'*Sun* newsroom.'

It's Stella, the news desk secretary. 'Guy wants to speak to you,' she says. 'Wouldn't give a name.'

'Thank you.'

The phone clicks, and then I hear a voice that I have not heard in a little while, though he doesn't sound so good; he sounds like he's crying.

'Is that you, Lawrence?' he says.

'Is that Simon?'

'Himself,' he says.

'How… how very nice to hear from you,' I say. 'How are you?'

'You've been a bad boy, Lawrence,' he says. 'A very bad boy.'

'Queen still not happy?' I say.

'That's an understatement.'

I had every sympathy for her. I'd liked her – so effortlessly classy. She's been given a tough hand and she's been playing a blinder. Then, out of the blue, a new footman, who she'd not only liked, but trusted, had turned her over.

Royally turned her over.

Despite the head's up I had given him, Sir Richard Arnison-Newgass had not been quite quick enough out of the blocks. That first night, when the story ran, the palace lawyers just missed serving up their injunction. *The Sun* ran its full print run over all its editions. On the front page, the single word "INTRUDER" was slapped over Grubby's picture of me on the Buckingham Palace balcony. There then followed thousands of words of my most deathless prose – "The biggest royal security scandal ever is exposed today by a *Sun* reporter working secretly as a footman in Buckingham Palace."

Even when I had one of the first editions hot off the press, I still didn't have the stomach to read it.

Page after page of the palace gossip I'd picked up over the previous two months – fifteen pages in all.

Since the palace lawyers would certainly close us down the next day – if they didn't succeed in shutting us down that night – we went with every single word and picture that we'd got.

Most of it was froth – paltry details of Andrew's sitting room, Edward's bedroom, the queen's breakfast room – but naturally dressed up as "A Very Serious Security Scandal".

A small taster from Page Two: "For the past eight weeks, I have enjoyed unfettered access throughout Buckingham Palace as one of the royal family's key aides. Had I been a terrorist intent on assassinating the queen, I could have done so with absolute ease…"

Details of the dogs, details of my daily life and most of it so totally meaningless. It was a modicum of entertainment for the masses, but by the afternoon, my brilliant World Exclusive had reached the same fate as every other newspaper – old news that was fit for nothing more than the cat-litter.

The palace hit us with everything they'd got. On the very morning of my "Intruder" story, a dozen palace lawyers turned up in court to formally serve their injunction. They claimed I had reneged on the confidentiality agreement I'd signed as a footman. *The Sun's* lawyers argued, of course, that the thrust of the story was the security scandal, but – as was pointed out – that did not remotely justify the pages of palace tittle-tattle that had been published that morning.

The queen was prepared to drop her claim for breach of confidence in return for a £25,000 contribution to her legal costs, plus an undertaking not to publish any more about my role as a footman; all of our unpublished pictures were surrendered.

The next day's paper had been a follow-up of sorts, but by day three, we were spent. We eventually ran the story about Caprice having dinner with Prince Andrew; it was an okay splash, helped fill the paper on another low news day.

But within the week, my great scoop had become an irrelevance. The palace and *The Sun* were like two giant liners that had passed in the night and had spoken to each other in passing – and in the still morning the next day, they both continued on their courses with not a trace of their journeys left in the ocean behind them.

As for Campion becoming the new Duchess of Montagu, well, I was obviously pleased to have been the matchmaker-in-chief. I hadn't expected an invite to the wedding, nor did I get one. The story of the palace maid who became a Duchess might have been the splash, but it was blown off the front page by a footling footballer story – that's what the public wants to read these days, stories about footballers.

By the middle of January, my two months as a footman had become nothing but the most distant of memories.

I had not expected to hear another word from my erstwhile

colleagues at the palace – so I was astonished when the good Simon Brook called me up.

'How have you been keeping, Simon?' I say. 'How's Chipper?'

'That's just it.' He bursts into tears.

'What's happened?'

Sniffing and crying, he tells me the story. That morning, the Queen Mother had brought her three dorgis round to the palace, which included a vicious brute called Ranger. When they'd been out walking in the palace gardens, Ranger had suddenly turned on Chipper, and the rest of the pack had joined in the maul.

'He was ripped to shreds!' Simon wails. 'There was blood everywhere!'

'I'm so sorry,' I say. 'What an awful story.'

Simon gulps. 'Is it worth printing?'

'It's a great story,' I say. 'Probably a front page.'

'That's nice,' he says. 'I knew the story was bound to get out, and I thought that if it should go to anybody, it should go to you.'

'Thank you!' I say. 'I'll take you out for dinner when I give you your money.'

'Oh, goody!' He cheers up immensely. 'I hear The Ritz is nice.'

I tell the news desk the good news and tap out the story. We'll probably have to call up the palace for a comment – for which there will be a resounding "No comment" – but we'll save that call till after tea-time, which will give the palace press officers less time to leak the story to the rest of the press.

By now, it is coming up to lunchtime. Having provided my mad masters with a possible splash, I think I have earned a couple of pints in *The Sun's* local, The Rose.

The thrill of the phone ringing again – that slim, slim chance of another plum falling into my lap. This time it is Maria, the editor's secretary. 'Spike would like to see you in the editor's office.'

'I'll be right over.'

Now, jacket on or jacket off? Spike is undoubtedly a complete madman, but he is also the boss; probably best to keep things formal and put it on. I mooch past the back bench and the subs. Now that I've brought in yet another splash, I presume I am about to be rewarded with a long overdue pay rise.

I knock on Maria's door. 'Hi, Maria, how we doing?'

'Fine,' she says. 'Spike will see you now.'

Not quite as chatty as the last time I saw her, certainly no offer of coffee.

Spike is furiously hacking away at some of the next day's pages, flourishing his red pen like a machete. He doesn't look up. He doesn't look up for quite a long time.

'Afternoon, Spike,' I say.

He looks up, then returns to his angry red pen. It looks like I am being given the old silent treatment again.

'Seen that story I just filed about Chipper?' I say chattily.

'Yeah,' he says, rather non-committal. It isn't actually clear to me whether Spike has or has not seen the story.

'Great story,' I say.

Silence reigns. Spike isn't even making a token effort to keep up his end of the conversation. I think I'll take another look at the Beryl Cook picture. But just as I am turning towards it, Spike decides he is ready to chat.

'What's this?' he says. He is holding an A4-sized piece of green paper between his thumb and forefinger.

'I don't know, Spike,' I say. 'You tell me.'

'It's your expense claim,' he says, voice gruff but silky – imagine the wolf in *Little Red Riding Hood*. 'Your expense claim from when you were working at the palace.'

'Yes?' I say.

'Your dinner at The Ritz, to be precise,' he says.

'I remember it well,' I say.

'Now Kim, when I told you to go out and treat yourself to dinner, I wanted you to go out and have a pleasant dinner with a friend.'

'Just so.'

'What I did not expect was you to treat yourself to dinner at The Ritz—'

'Hang on,' I say. 'Aren't you forgetting all the exclusives I brought in?'

'You're taking the piss,' he says. Finally, he drops all pretence of being the calm, soothing voice of reason and reverts to type: he was shouting, 'Two magnums of vintage Bollinger! A magnum of this Lebanese muck—'

'The Chateau Musar?' I say. 'That's a great wine.'

'Shut up!' he says, hammering his fist onto the desk. 'And the final piss-take, you buy an entire bottle of the most expensive brandy I've ever heard of!'

'Sometimes, Spike, to get these quality splashes, you've got to throw a little chum on the water.'

'The final bill, you oaf, is for £5,582!' he says. 'That's more than my entire expenses for the month! The brandy alone was £3,500! You're just an idiot!'

'Listen, Spike. You don't just take palace bigwigs to the dog racing in Walthamstow!' I say. 'But pour two magnums of Bolli down their throats in The Ritz and they'll sing like canaries!'

'We'll pay for the steaks and one bottle of Bollinger, and that's it.'

'What?' I say. 'You have got to be joking!'

Right in front of my eyes, Spike tears up my receipt and my expense claim. 'If you keep on whining, we won't even pay for the champagne.'

'But...but—'

'Anyone you'd like to complain to?' He lets the scraps of paper trickle into the bin. 'The editor? The managing editor? You know what, Kim, why don't you try calling up Rupert Murdoch? I'm sure he'll have no problem at all in stumping up £3,500 for a bottle of brandy – frankly, after your amazing scoop, he'll think he's got off lightly.'

'You're a sod,' I say.

'And that's just cost you your magnum of Bollinger,' he says. 'Anything else you'd like to say? I see the steaks were £150 each.'

Before I blurt out another outraged word, I savagely bite on my tongue and make to leave. I reach the door when I decide on a change of tack. 'Spike, let's just talk about this,' I say, ultra-placatory, hands in open surrender. 'That bill is about two months' salary!'

'Nearly a year if you were still at the palace.'

'Come on, Spike,' I wheedle. 'I've brought in a ton of scoops. I've even given you tomorrow's splash. Can we just be reasonable?'

'I don't do reasonable.' He returns to his red pen and his feature pages. 'Get out!' – and out I slink.

CHAPTER 33

Seven years on, seven of the happiest years Campion has ever known – and now she is gearing up for another substantial change in her life. Mason has come of age.

When they first married and when Mason resigned his commission, they lived in a little cottage just outside Fairford in Gloucestershire. She started working at an auctioneers in Cirencester, valuing paintings and schmoozing customers. It had been a great help with some of the snootier clientele that she was a Duchess, albeit an impecunious one. By night, she did what she'd always done. She wrote stories. Short stories at first, but she eventually moved on to a full-blown novel. She sent the manuscript to her most avid reader, and when this avid reader not only gave the manuscript the thumbs up but offered to write a brief foreword, the book's global success was assured – not so very many books have the personal endorsement of Her Majesty the Queen.

As for Mason, finally unfettered from his mother, he went on to do what he had always been born to do. He started growing flowers, most particularly campions and roses. For a year or so, Mason and his old gardener, Charley, had rented a small market garden just outside Cirencester – Campion would sometimes bike over with sandwiches for lunch. Then in 1995, Viola, Duchess of Montagu (as opposed to Campion, Duchess of Montagu) relented enough to permit Mason, Campion, and their growing brood of children to move into the gatehouse of the Montagu family seat.

Campion never found out why Viola had had such a change of heart. After they married, Viola sent Mason a terse note telling him not to expect another penny from her. But someone very influential – possibly even someone who happened to own a large corgi pack – had leaned on Viola, informing her that if she wished to continue being welcomed into Buckingham Palace, then she would have to ease up on her daughter-in-law.

Naturally, Viola had kept the mansion house for herself – she needed it for the occasional weekend – but she unbent enough to allow Mason and Campion to move into the gatehouse at the end of the drive. Further to that, Mason was permitted to start growing his flowers, his campions and his antique roses, on the estate. On the edge of the rose field was a shed, and it was there, most days, that the family would convene for lunch. Campion would walk over from the gatehouse with a light picnic, and if it was fine, they would sit outside on the grass as the free-range kids roamed through the roses. When the shed had been up for two years, Mason made a small addition to the décor – it was in gold leaf, just above the doorway, a royal warrant. It signified that Mason had become Her Majesty's official flower supplier.

It is a dreich lunchtime at the end of October when Campion potters out of the gatehouse. Flora, her daughter, is strapped to her chest in a papoose. Since it is a Saturday, the three other girls are probably in the shed, where Charley will be showing them how to splice roses.

She has two bags, one with the food and one with the drink. She can see Mason from quite a distance away, stooped over a rosebush as he digs in some mulch. He spears his fork into the ground and comes over.

'All well?' he says, giving her and the baby a kiss before taking the two bags.

'All is particularly well,' she says. 'Enjoying it?'

'Very much,' he says. 'I've got you; I've got the kids – I've even got Charley back. Doesn't get any better.'

Since they married, all trace of Mason's stutter has

disappeared; Campion does not know whether it is down to the marriage or down to not seeing any more of Viola.

They go into the hut, where their three other daughters – Lavender, Hazel, and Rosie – are sitting by the stove with Charley. The two oldest are wielding wickedly sharp knives. They are being taught to whittle sticks.

The girls cluster around and dive into the game pie that Campion bought from the Cirencester deli. The adults have a glass of white wine each, though not too much, as there is still much to be done. The birthday cake is produced – and this, Campion has baked herself, a chocolate with cream filling. There are thirty-two candles on the cake, and though they have never discussed it, not even once, both he knows and she knows this is a big deal.

With the help of the three older girls, Mason blows out the candles, eyes closed to have his wish.

They leave the children with their whittling and walk out to their private garden. It is just over four acres, a hundred yards by two hundred yards. Mason planted it up five years ago and presented it to Campion on her birthday.

'How many stones?' he says.

'Why not thirty-two?' she says. 'That would be about eight miles.'

'Take us through till teatime.' He places four neat rows of eight white pebbles onto the sand.

Easy as anything, his hand slips into hers, and they start out on this Campion Walk that they have walked so many times in the last five years. It is similar to Darwin's great thinking walk at Down House – though, as Mason likes to see it, the Campion Walk is a little more highly evolved. It is not a circle, but a figure of eight, crossing in the middle – a figure of infinity for an infinite thinking walk.

They walk a few circuits, each alone with their memories, passing hundreds and hundreds of rose bushes, some with spliced branches, some that have yet to be spliced. There are plenty of campions.

'Thirty-two years old,' Campion says as she kicks away the fourth pebble. 'You've come into your majority.'

'I came into my majority when I married you,' Mason says. 'Now that it's here, I don't really know what to do.'

'Going to kick your mum out of the big house?' Campion says.

'Want to move into the big house?'

'I'm happy in the gatehouse,' she says.

'I'll think about it,' he says. 'Heard from her today – she called up to wish me a happy birthday.'

'How did she sound?'

'Quite nice – for her. She's even got me a present. The truck's delivering it tomorrow. A lot of rose bushes and also, she said, a lot of campions.'

'A lot of campions?' Campion says. 'She really does want to stay in the big house!'

'She wants to see more of the children,' he says.

'That'd probably mean we'll have to see more of her.'

'How do you feel about that?'

They've come up to the middle intersection – sometimes they go one way, sometimes the other, and sometimes they just stop. Beside the intersection, there is a statue of a woman in white marble. She is wearing a simple shift dress, similar to a palace maid's uniform. She is leaning over with a jug in her hands, and out of the jug, a perpetual stream of water pours into a white marble bowl. The woman is so beautiful that she might even give Arthur Sullivan's grieving muse a run for her money. The woman is Campion in all her bounteous glory.

Campion wonders how she feels about Viola, about Mason reaching his majority. It isn't as if there is any pressing urgency. She is happy just as she is.

'How do I feel?' Campion repeats. 'You've got the whip-hand. She might even behave herself.'

'Be a first!' Mason laughs.

He brings her wrist to his lips and kisses it and just as always happens when he does this sort of thing, they have their arms around each other. Soon enough, the kissing has moved up a gear, and he knows, and she knows, just exactly what is going to happen next, possibly even right there, at the very midpoint of the Campion Walk.

And who would have thought that so much love and so much happiness could have been sparked by a rogue footman amongst the servants at Buckingham Palace?

But that, my dears, is just the way it happened.

HISTORICAL NOTE

Most of this story happened – though I have been particularly fast and loose with the facts.

By that, I mean that in true journalistic tradition, I never let the facts get in the way of the story.

For instance, although *Palace Rogue* is based on the true story of the journalist Ryan Parry, Ryan was a reporter not for *The Sun* but for its deadly rival *The Daily Mirror*. He also pulled off his astonishing coup not in 1993 but in 2003. For various reasons to do with sequels and the like, not to mention that I was a staff reporter on *The Sun* rather than *The Mirror*, I decided to set the action in what was then the world's biggest-selling English-language daily. There was an added piquancy in knowing that the queen really couldn't stand *The Sun,* and that for many years she refused to have it in amongst her breakfast reading material.

I have done Ryan another disservice by turning my palace rogue into a feckless, reckless sot. Unlike Kim, Ryan was a consummate pro who ticked off all the jobs that he'd been tasked with. Ryan served in Windsor Castle and was a coachman on the back of an ambassador's carriage. He also delivered up a series of eye-popping pictures of Windsor Castle, the queen's breakfast room and the palace apartments of both Princes Andrew and Edward.

Ryan was never unmasked as a tabloid reporter, instead quitting the palace on the very day that President George Bush Junior moved into the palace's Belgian Suite.

Ryan's story ran in *The Mirror* for two days. The first day was devoted to all the gossip from Buckingham Palace, and the second to all the juicy stuff he'd gleaned from Windsor Castle. But on the third day, the palace lawyers did indeed succeed in shutting the story down after fielding – as described – an amazing twelve lawyers in court.

Ryan went on to win the coveted Scoop of the Year.

My *Sun* reporter, however, could not end up with anything other than egg on his face.

Other details have been blended and massaged. Most of the stories about the queen's corgis and dorgis are true but occurred over a much longer period of time than the two months that Kim was working as a footman. The 'Flunky Got The Corgis Drunky' story happened in 1999, while the queen's favourite dog, Chipper, was mauled to death by Ranger in 1989.

Most of the details of life below the stairs in the palace are accurate, from the various staff dining rooms to the corridor parties. The footmen and maids do have pretty boring jobs, but the camaraderie is terrific.

Queen Mary always wished she'd jumped over a fence, and the queen used to dream of going to a party where she would not be recognised; I do hope she managed it.

The queen's omnipotent nanny, Bobo MacDonald, died in her bed in September 1993 at the age of 89. I don't believe she died laughing with her devoted dog in her arms, but I can't think of a nicer way to go.

The descriptions of *The Sun* newsroom in the 1990s are spot on. I know because I was there. There was certainly a lot of swearing and shouting in the newsroom. I do remember one fight, though I don't recall any blood being spilt.

Company magazine did use to throw a party for Britain's hottest eligibles; I was one of them. I made *The Sun's* centrefold – stark naked apart from a copy of *The Sun* newspaper.

The thirty-six questions to fall in love are genuine. They were devised in 1997 by the American psychologist

Arthur Aron – and if a couple are single and even remotely compatible, then they will assuredly fall for each other just as Mason fell for his Campion.

Charles Darwin's sandy thinking walk is still being walked to this day – it's a glorious day out. I have walked it with my mum, Sarah, and my younger son, Geordie. At first, it may seem a little dull, but if you lean in, then it becomes quite wonderful. I don't know whether an infinite thinking walk in the shape of a lazy eight has yet been built, but one day, when my ship comes in, I will create one.

The Dukedom of Montagu no longer exists, but as for loyal, feisty girls like Campion, they are everywhere. With a following wind, these girls can do just about anything they set their hearts to.

One last detail that should be addressed, and that is the most toxic member of the royal family since Wallis Simpson – Prince Andrew.

When I started writing this novel at the beginning of 2022, Prince Andrew was embroiled in the Jeffrey Epstein scandal. Despite a mountain of evidence against him, he was still loudly touting his innocence. In March 2022, he struck a multi-million-pound deal with his chief tormentor, Virginia Giuffre. Legally, he was in the clear – but in a moment of beautiful clarity, I realised that as regards his reputation, Prince Andrew was sunk.

Prince Andrew probably doesn't go around slapping women and knocking them to the floor, but when I penned Andrew's climactic fight with Campion, I figured that no one would much care. Short of saying that Andrew is a serial sex killer, it is now impossible to defame the man.

Apart from that fictional slap, all the other peculiar details about Andrew are well documented – his rows of teddies, his monkey that had to be hidden every evening, his obsession with anal sex. The description of his palace apartment is exactly as detailed by Ryan Parry.

I only wish that an underling had actually punched

Andrew's lights out when he was younger. Things might have turned out very differently for Prince Grumpling; they certainly couldn't have turned out much worse.

There was one other detail of Prince Andrew's life that I wanted to include in the story – his palace dinners with the American model Caprice Bourret. Caprice went to Buckingham Palace at least twice to have supper with Prince Andrew, though the year was 2000, not 1993. I remember the story well because it made *The Sun's* front page. I was *The Sun's* royal reporter at the time – and I wrote the story.

Caprice front page, February 2000

Ryan Parry's original palace scoop, November 2003

ACKNOWLEDGEMENTS

Such a host of people who I have to thank! Because although I wrote this story in a matter of months, it has been many years in the making – both from my days on *The Sun* and then, latterly, from my days at the writer's pit-face, when I have had a whole coterie of friends standing ringside.

Huge apologies to anyone who's been missed out and who feels like they deserve a mention. If you're even remotely affronted then do please let me know; if the lapse is big enough, I might even name a character after you in the next novel.

From Fleet Street, I would like to thank Bill Akass, Bree Allegretti, Peter Allen, Oliver August, Richard Bath, Alison Boshoff, Fran Bowden, Robin Bowman, Alex Burton, Andrea Busfield, Andrew Butcher, Amanda Cable, Ingo Capraro, Makhosi Chiwashira, Simon Cobby, Lesley Cowling, Graham Dudman, Matt Dickinson, John Edwards, Mark Fleming, John-Paul Flintoff, Brian Flynn, Wayne Francis, Tom Fremantle, Paul Gilfeather, Glenn Goodey, Caroline Graham, Gerard Greaves, Allan Hall, Julia Hartley-Brewer, Mike Harvey, Anne Hayes, Adam Helliker, Aaron Hicklin, Stuart Higgins, Marina Hyde, Katie Jarvis, Matt Jowitt, Trevor Kavanagh, Fergus Kelly, Antonella Lazzeri, Adam Lee-Potter, Ken Lennox, Quentin Letts, Andy Lines, Barbara McMahon, Brandon Malinsky, Donald Martin, Richard Martin, Martel Maxwell, Henry Meller, Piers Morgan, Dawn Neesom, Tom Newton Dunn, Nick Hopkins, Victoria Newton, Mark Palmer, Nick Parker, Simon Parry, George Pascoe-Watson, Charlie

Rae, Louise Robinson, Ally Ross, David Sapsted, Sarah Schaefer, Phil Sherwell, Geoff Stead, Jules Stenson, Shannon Sweeney, Sue Thompson, Rupert Thorpe, David Usborne, Tunku Varadarajan, Mike Wade, Neil Wallis, Nick Watt, Peter Wells, Annette Witheridge, David Wooding, David Yelland – and not forgetting, of course, the original Palace Rogue, Ryan Parry.

I would also like to thank my cheerleaders. Gore Vidal, being an old sod, said that every time one of his friends succeeded, a little piece of him died. I guess I do have a few friends like that. But my true friends are the stalwarts who are actually rooting for me: Vicky Allan, Anthony Alderson, Candida Alderson, David Alterman, Malgosia Alterman, Simon Alterman, Bob Baker, Juliet Baker, Jonathan Barne, Miranda Bennett, Frances Borden, Harry Borden, Lavender Borden, Nick Borden, Archie Bouverie, Cass Bouverie, Jenny Brown, Finn Bruce, Cameron Buchanan, Emma Buchanan, Beatrice Dundonald, Shaun Bythell, Dom Chambers, Seb Chambers, Anna Christopherson, Mike Christopherson, Sandy Cross, Beth Coates, Geraldine Coates, Alf Coles, Bella Coles, Hector Coles, Joe Coles, Matt Coles, Prophecy Coles, Sam Coles, Thomas Coles, Toby Coles, Walter Coles, Eugene Costello, Angela Cottam, Gerv Cottam, David Crawley, Tor Crawley, James Cripps, John-Henry Cugley, Roy Davis, Ben Divall, Scott Douglas, Sue Douglas, Fiona Duff, James Evans, Alex Field, Henry Field, Adam Findlay, Charlie Fletcher, Domenica Fletcher, Francis Galashan, Shane Gleghorn, Isaac Goodwin, Rosemary Goring, Ali Grant, George Grant, Barry Gross, Ishbel Grosvenor, Jessica Fox, Alex Hall, Cassian Hall, Mike Hamill, Anwen Hamill, Seb Hamilton, Steve Hannay, Kate Hannay, Michael Hanson, Alistair Harkness, Bob Harris, Jeremy Hitchen, Sue Hitchen, Sir James Hutchison, Johnny Irish, Pete Irvine, Ann Jarman, Lucy Jarman, Lucy Juckes, Ali Kefford, Rob Lagneau, Sam Lagneau, Jane Laidlaw, Doug Lawson, Clinton Leeks, Alex Lewczuk, Richard

Lloyd Parry, Will Loram, Rehana Loram, Sandy McCall Smith, Finn McCreath, Robert McDowell, Angus McLean, Ailsa McLean, Calum MacLeod, Missy MacLeod, Charlie McMicking, Diana McMicking, Alistair MacRae, Maggie MacRae, Tim Maguire, Charley Mallalieu, Conor Matchett, Susan Mathieson, Simon Maxwell, Alex Meddowes, Jan Meddowes, William Micklethwait, Sir Jonathan Mills, Giles Moffatt, Nicki Moffatt, Lupi Moll, Sanya Moll, Jon Mountjoy, Andy Murray, Becky Murray, Annette Mussen, James Mussen, Liz Mussen, Miles Mussen, Rosie Mussen, Rupert Mussen, Zoe Mussen, Miles Nelson, Julie Newing, Jimmy Ogilvie, John Ogilvie, Kate Ogilvie, Charlie Ottley, Tim Parker, Rosemary Parker, Andrew Paynter, Nick Perry, Alice Pickles, Giles Pilbrow, Julienne Pilbrow, Kerrynne Pilbrow, Lucinda Pilbrow, Mark Pilbrow, Eve Poole, Lady Poole, Alex Renton, Wendy Robertson, Tom Rounds, Ali Russell, Andrew St Clair, David St Clair, Emma St Clair, John St Clair, John Sargent, Philly Sargent, Euan Scott, Catriona Scott, Philip Shaw, Ruth Shaw, Hannah Smart, Mitch Smith, Merryn Somerset Webb, Cameron Stewart, Richard Sweet, Anthony Tait, Claire Tait, Alan Taylor, Mark Taylor, Ben Thomson, Cornelia Topping, Hugh Topping, Maggie Todd, Adrian Turpin, Robert Twigger, Baron Sir Eric von Ibler, James Walter, Jen Walter, Andrew Wallace, Nick Webber, Victoria Webber, Euan Weir, Xanthe Weir, Jeremy Welch, Paddy Whitby, Sara Whitby, Alan Whyte, Anne Wilson, Fiona Wilson, James Wilson, Moi Wilson, Pat Wilson, Caspian Woods and Toby Young.

I'd like to pay especial thanks to the stellar team at Legend Press. Unbelievably, it's the same team that I had in 2007 with my first book, *The Eton Affair* – Tom Chalmers, Lauren Parsons and Lucy Chamberlain, though now with the addition of my superlative new editor Rachael Hedges.

And then there are the people who've really put in the hard yards – they've had to live with me! That'd be my parents, Bob and Sarah, still going strong, still yet to be consigned into an old people's home, my boys, Dexter and Geordie, and Margot, my wife. Frankly she deserves a medal! I thank you!

I have a penchant, I'm afraid, for naming characters after friends. The general rule of thumb is that the more odious the character, the greater the esteem in which I hold them. These include Richard Arnison-Newgass (merely a Captain in real life, though he certainly ought to have been a Major General), Charlie Bain, Simon Brook, Jono Freemantle and that great Fleet Street photographer Phil Hannaford – whose nickname really is "Grubby".

The next book in the Rogue series is *Eton Rogue* – soon to be published by Legend Press – when the world's most famous school will lock horns with *The Sun*'s most infamous reporter.

It's 1995 and Prince William has just started at Eton College.

Fleet Street is desperate for any sort of tittle-tattle from the school. One Etonian, Agent Orange, is delighted to spill the beans.

He's being paid – handsomely – by the cheekiest reporter on *The Sun*.

And he's spending the loot on the love of his life, a housemaster's daughter.

Eton Rogue is entirely based on a true story. Agent Orange was a genuine Etonian who left the school in 1996; William Coles was the *Sun* staff reporter who spun his stories into front-page news.

Follow Legend Press on Twitter
@legend_times_

Follow Legend Press on Instagram
@legend_times